DEAD MEN PLAY THE GAME

A NOVEL

I0565406

by

Jacqui Jacoby

Musical Work of References

The Beatles – *In My Life*

DEDICATION

For all those people who realized imaginary friends
were not only in your head, but also sitting across from you
smiling, talking and leading you through the rabbit hole.

And for Brittany, Bryce and Bridgette who knew all
along their mom seemed a lot like Alice.

And, as always, for Larry…my Prince Charming,
Mad Hatter and Seven Dwarves, all wrapped into one.

ACKNOWLEDMENTS

A Thank You to Joanne Firby, who not only served as a partner in crime, but who always seemed to get me anyway.

A thank you to Bridgette Wilson who sat on that couch with me for three days, told me I could, then helped me figure out how.

Editing by Nas Dean

nas_dean@ymail.com

Cover Design

Jen Connelly at JAJ Designs

justanotherjen@comcast.net

PART ONE

Vampire Laws

As written by Minos, Tisias, and Peneus, the First Vampires

Translated from Greek, Handed Down in Oral Tradition since 10 B.C.E.

First Law of the Vampires: The Law of Blood

Blood, the sustenance of life, will be required to move forward through time. Taking human life, feasting on their essence, is required of all vampires. No mercy given, no humanity shown. To disobey is to call for your own death by your own kind.

Third Law of the Vampires: The Law of Slaying

Humans, their lives sacrificed serve as food. Vampires, their lives preserved, serve as brothers. No vampire will hold the right to take another vampire's life, with exception of self-defense, prosecution or defense of another. To disobey is to call for your own death by your own kind.

Sixth Law of the Vampires: The Law of First Blood

Woman extraordinary, treated with respect, protected from harm. Vampires will stand before them, offering themselves in the woman's stead. If one vampire desires a woman another covets, he who drinks of first blood shall forever keep her protected. To disobey is to call for torture and expulsion

PROLOGUE: NIGHT SHIFT

"The difference between a moral man and a man of honor is that the latter regrets a discreditable act, even when it has worked and he has not been caught.

~H. L. Mencken

New Orleans, April 25, 1958

Dragon's Bridge Public House

At the bar from where he watched, Travis Ricci felt in his jacket pocket, pulled out the pill bottle and grabbed four more aspirin, tossing them back and drinking them with the bourbon neat just left by the blond bartender.

Smoke hung on the ceiling reaching downward into the room. In the far corner, a live band played New Orleans jazz and the headache he was fighting reminded him he never had liked New Orleans jazz.

Vampire and being drunk was not an easy accomplishment. To take it to the level of hangover like he did last night with that Stuart guy, was nuts. Travis's head pounded, his hands shook, his stomach sank and swam when he tried to move around the room. He stood very still leaning against the bar, both his elbows on the polished wood surface, the alcohol in front of him to chase away the six bottles of tequila from the night before.

Last night, the two of them were alone in that corner booth right over there, one waitress to themselves who brought the bottles and listened to their bad jokes and left them alone when they wanted to whisper. No one else had been here. All the others had been out, searching the city for the meek and mild, looking for a meal.

Travis's gaze went to the mirror above the bar and watched Walter Bennett in the corner booth, his masses adoring him. Travis hated the son-of-a-bitch more now than he had when Bennett had first walked in three weeks ago trailing that entourage like he was something special. The man was full of self-importance, making the others around him feel as if he was in charge. Well, Travis had new information now and knew the leader bit was nothing more than psychopathic tendencies leading him to use vampires and humans alike.

If Bennett got a victim last night, they had died a slow and painful death and Walter had probably loved every minute of it. Travis didn't like suffering and he hated those who caused it. A weird concept for his kind, he knew, but one he held dear.

Ian Stuart, dressed neat in slacks and a jacket, his dark hair longer than style allowed, leaned against the edge of the booth on one elbow, watching them all talk. Since he walked in the door an hour ago, he hadn't so much as looked at Travis and Travis wondered about everything they said last night.

Ian Stuart was the man Travis should hate the most. It was this particular bastard who knocked on Travis's door in 1928, waking Travis after a long day on the docks and an even longer night at the bars.

Travis hated Stuart for the existence he condemned him to, this whole fucking never-ending life of darkness and blood. And people like Walter Bennett who would kill you while laughing and call it a good night on the town.

For thirty years since their introduction, Ian Stuart was nothing but a bad memory. Then Stuart walked in three weeks ago with Bennett and his groupies, taking up space in this French Quarter bar.

Travis had never forgotten him.

Stuart had remembered Travis.

The beating Travis gave Stuart in the back alley that very night because he was pissed at the turning thirty years ago, was probably going to stick around a while in Stuart's mind. Though by tonight, the bruises had faded and the black eye was gone.

Travis stared at Stuart in the mirror, watching him in profile. The bastard hadn't even tried to fight back. He took the thrashing like he knew he deserved it and that infuriated Travis even more.

Last night when the bar was empty and it was only the two of them, Stuart ordered the first bottle, offered a drink to Travis and Travis reluctantly agreed. There was regret in Stuart's eyes and that was something you never saw in a vampire, the sadness even more surprising. They were nowhere near drunk when Travis had gotten Stuart to tell him his story, stories of long ago families in Scotland that vampires never shared.

"Steamers either leave in the daylight or they arrive in the daylight and there is no way to get around it, even if you stayed below deck the whole journey. Besides, it's 1958, they're all dead by now."

He took two full glasses and tossed them back one after the other.

Stuart stared at the table, holding his glass tight, his voice dropping even if there was no one else here.

"Do you ever stand in the middle of the room, all of them talking at once until it sounds like screams and you know you are the loneliest man in the world?"

His gaze came up and Travis was astonished by the revelation that mirrored his own thoughts. He reached out with the bottle and Stuart met him half way. Travis poured. He poured again, but they were still miles from drunk.

"I'm sorry," Stuart said, his voice full of sincere remorse, his blue gaze coming up. "For what I did to you."

Without a word because he didn't know what to say, Travis topped off the glasses again. He had never heard of a vampire apologizing. If anyone found out, Stuart would die for it.

In the mirror, tonight, Travis watched Stuart sigh, his chest rising and falling then he turned away from the table to move across the room.

Stuart admitted to Travis he hated what he was himself enough to miss meals.

Victims were left unharmed and alive. He showed mercy. He showed humanity. He broke their kind's most sacred law and he didn't care about the risk.

Travis watched the calm exterior in the mirror while remembering the words from last night: *"I have an idea but I can't do it alone."*

Either one of them could turn the other in, calling for their execution with the knowledge they now had.

Both of them had enough faith last night to trust the other. Not knowing why that feeling would settle over him like a comfort, Travis welcomed it. In a life where there were no friends, Travis looked at his most hated enemy and saw hope.

Stuart took the spot directly next to Travis and motioned to the bartender. He pointed at Travis's drink. "What he's having but a double."

The man turned to fill the order.

Stuart stared straight ahead and managed to avoid looking at the mirror. He reached up to rub his eyes with his thumb and forefinger.

Travis reached in his pocket again and pulled out the bottle. He shook out four more tablets and slapped them down on the bar beside Stuart. Stuart took a deep breath, let it out slowly then reached for the pills, throwing them back. His drink wasn't here yet so he picked up Travis's and used it to swallow.

He spoke low. "Have you heard about the kind of stuff they are doing out in Hollywood these days?"

"Hear it's pretty sunny out there," Travis said.

Stuart's drink arrived and he drank it down to half. "Lots of time to sleep. Little time for a night life."

"Night life requires some sort of work to survive, I've heard. Bills to pay, rent on time. A lot of responsibilities that are totally alien to us."

"I worked in a slaughter house for three years in New York. I could do that again and they have night shifts."

"Dock worker," Travis said. "If I ever wanted to do something else, I would have to look around."

Stuart picked up his glass and motioned with it to Travis's. Travis took the toast, the glasses clicked and he said *"Cheers."*

Stuart smiled. *"Air do shlàinte."*

Travis looked at him. "What the hell does that mean?"

"To your health."

Travis smiled and they emptied their drinks, slamming their glasses down upside down on the bar.

A hand came down on Stuart's shoulder, a body stepping between Travis and him. Walter Bennett smiled up at Travis.

"You're Ricci," he said.

"Yeah," Travis said. Now that he saw him up close, he hated him even more.

"We haven't actually been introduced."

"I guess now we have," Travis said, shifting his gaze from Stuart to Bennett. Stuart kept his gaze on the glass, his anger escalating while Travis watched.

"Why don't you go sit your ass down at the table," Stuart said, his accent only a little thicker. "I'll be over in a minute."

"I'm more interested in what you are talking about here. We have our family. We don't need to get friendly with the locals."

Stuart reached up to pull the hand off his shoulder, laying it on the bar. "Maybe I would prefer two minutes of conversation with a local over anything you might have to offer."

Bennett looked at Travis, his gaze hot.

He looked back at Stuart. "I'm going to the table. You will be back in two minutes. Do we understand each other?"

"Walter," Stuart sighed. "Go fuck yourself. I don't take orders from you or anyone else and unless you want to get hurt in front of all these people, I would suggest you move fast."

Walter paused and Travis could see the debate on his face. He looked at Travis, his gaze having shot from 'who the hell are you?' to 'you're going to die slow.'

Walter walked away and Travis looked at Stuart, no expression.

"It appears you have a problem."

"Aye, I know. You would think the asshole would get 'no' into his head at some point in five years, but every time I say it he thinks I'm playing hard to get."

"I think he hates me," Travis said.

Stuart laughed a little, bringing his gaze up to Travis's. "I should have your problems."

From the table, Travis saw Bennett kept a close eye on his boy with the new competition.

"Have you tried telling him you prefer a feminine touch?"

"I have tried for years in every way you can imagine. He seems to suffer from a type of deafness that makes him think next time the answer will be different."

"Persistent bastard," Travis said. "I think he's going to kill me."

"I think he's going to try," Stuart said. "Which brings me to my point. Hollywood," Stuart brought up again. "Glamorous. The Hollywood Sign. Sunset Blvd. Maybe see Marilyn Monroe hanging out at a corner diner."

Travis watched him talk in the mirror. There was a small smile on Stuart's lips.

"You know I had a girlfriend once. In 1928," Travis said.

Stuart looked at him. "No, I didn't know that."

"Her name was Jeanne. Twenty-six and built like Rita Hayworth." He looked at Stuart. "She was an actress at the Galaxy Star. Her in your bed was a thing to write home about," he smiled. "I was supposed to be at her apartment that night, but I got too drunk at the bar and she hated that."

"I am sorry," Stuart said. "There's not many other ways I can say it."

"Yeah," Travis said picking up his empty glass to turn upright. "And our next choice is punishable by death."

He spoke softly, leaning toward Travis. "Really, because I feel dead every day of my life and four days ago, I looked at the blank stare of the most beautiful dark-skinned girl, her brown eyes looking at me, asking why I did this to her. I'm not doing it anymore."

"That would be what? Breaking Law Number A1, we die slow?"

"Stuart," a voice called.

Stuart looked at Travis. "He thinks if he calls, I will come running."

"Will you?"

"Tonight? Aye. He needs to think he's in control tonight."

Stuart started to walk away.

"Hey," Travis called, motioning with his head. Stuart came back.

"You do know your accent is totally annoying and would be difficult to put up with for anything longer than three minutes."

Stuart faced him. "While your sarcasm and attitude are easy to deal with." He smiled.

"Stuart." Walter called.

Stuart turned away and headed toward the table where he leaned over to have Walter whisper in his ear.

Travis closed out the bill for both their drinks, then looked at the door in the mirror. The lights from outside seemed to beckon like a chance at something they never thought they would have. Blood free? Was it worth the chance? Yes, it was. He shifted his gaze in the mirror and saw Stuart standing straight, ignoring the table and watching back. Travis nodded a little and walked toward the door. He turned to see behind him.

Stuart left Bennett without a word and joined Travis standing right in front him.

Again his voice was low.

"I'm carrying everything I own on me. And I did have enough cash to make this last awhile."

Travis smiled widely. "That's funny. I seem to have done the exact same thing carrying probably close to what you are."

"Bus stop is three miles north. There is two-thirty departure."

Stuart reached into his inside jacket pocket and pulled out several pieces of paper. He handed half to Travis and put the others back in his jacket.

Travis looked at them, before sticking them in his own pocket. They were bus tickets to stops heading west, the last being Hollywood. Each ticket at night, arriving before dawn in a city where they could hole up in a hotel until the next bus left after sunset. They could hopscotch the whole way to the Pacific.

He looked around to make sure no one noticed but no one was watching them at all. Not even Walter Bennett.

"Pretty sure of yourself," Travis said.

"No," Stuart said, shaking his head. "I was sure of you."

"You know I hate your guts."

"Aye, with good reason." Stuart smiled. "I think we can work around it."

"They'll kill us if they catch us."

"So we better walk fast and not get caught."

Travis motioned to the door with his arm.

Stuart smiled and went first, pushing the door open and holding it for Travis. Travis was right behind him.

Dead Men Play the Game

CHAPTER ONE

"I feel like I have a new life and I'm going to take full advantage of it."

~William Green

Davenport, Oregon

April 4th…Decades Later…

Brunettes weren't exactly an unusual commodity. They came into Cooper's Pub all the time.

Standing behind the bar with a white rag in one hand and a damp glass in the other, Ian Stuart dried at his leisure. It was his break and he didn't feel like putting all that much attention into the regulars who knew he liked to be left alone from ten-thirty to eleven.

When the door opened about mid-way through that time frame, his gaze came up and the brunette who walked through the door had his hands freezing on his drying glass.

Women didn't shock him. He would notice when they leaned toward nice, but he only looked once and he never, ever touched while at work.

Until this brunette, with her mass of curly, waist-length hair, in her long, black leather jacket and the bluest eyes he had ever seen took one of the stools near his section and folded her arms over the counter looking patient enough to wait.

Mike, Ian's boss and fellow bartender, moved in her direction to cover Ian's break but Ian smiled at him, gave a nod of 'I got it' and shifted down the bar.

Putting down his cloth and glass, he stood in front of her, his hands planted on the counter and stared. He could not ever remember meeting a woman this breathtakingly beautiful.

She came in with a straight posture that said 'I have arrived' without giving off the arrogance that came with it. The big sunglasses she had off at the door weren't to scream attitude at eleven p.m. They were to hide the face from the public as long as she could, he would bet money on it.

Everything about her said headstrong and don't mess with me.

He had every intention of messing with her

Because he wasn't falling for the façade she gave the world. The insecurity was there, but only he saw it. Her vulnerability was subtle but alive like a current running through a body that matched the face in perfection. Even in the long black coat, she couldn't hide it. He saw pain in the eyes he didn't want there. Hurt where there should be nothing but pleasure.

He stared at her.

She stared back.

Until she finally snapped: "What?"

"Nothing," he said. "Just waiting to see if you had something fascinating to say."

She smiled at him and it had an edge to it. He thought he might have to pay for being clever.

"Oh," she said, "fascinating. That's a tough one on short notice. How about we start with a Macallan neat and then you go listen to someone else be fascinating." She dismissed him with a gaze that fell to the bar.

Smiling, he got the bottle, the glass and poured in front of her.

"Did you want that on the house or were you going to pay for it?"

"Thought I might pay. You look like your rates might be too high."

He leaned on the bar. Flirting with the patrons, also not on the list of things he did.

"I don't know. We could work something out."

She nodded her head. "Really? Like maybe you have someplace else to be?"

"You could marry me now, save time and then you get all your drinks for free."

"Sorry," she smiled sweetly. "I already promised myself to the guy parking my car. You'll have to disappear."

He shook his head. "I'm actually on break. I don't serve when I'm on break. I don't take money when I am on break. And I never, ever pick up brunettes when I'm on break."

She took a long drink. "What about blondes?"

"Nope," he grinned. "Not into blondes."

"I assume red heads and black hair is out, too?"

"Aye."

"Preference for eye color?"

"Now that you mention it…"

"Go away," she chuckled.

"I can't," he said. "You haven't given me your name yet."

"I'm not going to give you my name."

"How am I supposed to put your number in my phone if you don't give me the name to put next to it?"

"How about 'bite me'? Would that work in your phone?"

He shook his head. "Already in there. One of my roommates. He sorta looks like you, but different."

"What the hell does that mean?" she asked.

"One of those rare creatures some higher force felt the need to bestow the most incredible good looks on so the world forgets to even breathe when they walk in the room."

"You feel this way about one of your roommates? And you're drooling over me? Are we confused or just fighting it?"

4

He laughed. "He's not my type. I like them about five, what? Six? And a half. Right weight for the right build." Sighing, he leaned a little closer and sniffed. "With the touch of *Chanel #5* to tease the senses."

"What's his name?"

"Jason."

"Do you have his phone number?"

He nodded slowly. "Um huh. It's 971-325-WhenFuckingHellFreezesOver."

She laughed out loud for the first time and it was a sound that made him know he would be getting to know her better.

"Now that one I can remember without writing it down. Ask for Jason."

Ian nodded his head jerkily and pulled out his phone. "And he will say yes. You are his type."

"What type is that?"

"Female." Ian snapped a picture of her while she still smiled and put his phone away. She didn't try to hurt him or anything.

"Another man with class. I like it. And if you decide to use that photo for your private play time and I find out about it, I will shoot you."

"Now officer, really? Is that allowed?"

Her gaze snapped up and her look took on an edge.

"Bulge in the jacket on your hip and your badge is still on your belt."

She looked down at it then back at him.

"You didn't even go home to disarm before you came in."

She drank more, almost to the bottom. "I had an extremely shitty day at work lasting sixteen hours. I got off fifteen minutes before I got here where I planned on a quiet drink alone. Go figure." She smiled again.

"Do you want another?"

She shook her head.

He turned back around to the counter, got a tall, thin glass, filled it with clear bubbles, added a pineapple chunk, two cherries and an umbrella. He set it in front of her.

"That one's on the house."

A simple Sprite and she smiled. "I have been walking by this place for the last eight years and I never stopped by."

"I've worked here five. Our timing sucks, Suzy."

"What?"

"I'm guessing. Suzy?"

"Do I look like a Suzy?"

"Mildred?"

She glared at him.

"Trudy?"

She looked him up and down, taking in all his details. The long hair, the rings. She hadn't mentioned the accent and they usually mention it first.

"Hamish."

"Hamish?" he asked.

"Yeah. You're a Hamish. I'm good at this. It's part of my job and training."

"Trudy," he replied. "You suck at it."

"Naw. I nailed it. It goes with your Irish."

His gaze narrowed at her and he growled a little. One thing he hated was his Scottish confused for Irish.

Her smile told him she knew what she had done. He debated about letting her have her victory or continuing the sparring match when she stood, reached into her pocket and dropped a much larger quantity on the bar than the cost of one drink.

He picked up the money and sorted it as she turned.

"Hey," he said. He held up most of the cash that he kept between two fingers. She walked back toward him.

"I never charge my dates' full price."

"So if you get a date with someone, let her know."

He leaned across the bar, stretching, stuffing the cash into her breast pocket, accidently feeling more than he should, but not disappointed in himself for doing so.

"I just finished the first date I've had in years and it was a hell of a lot more enjoyable than the last one I had."

"I'm happy for you," she said deadpan.

"Tomorrow night? Same place? Say ten-thirty so we get my whole break?"

She tilted her head. "I had a shitty day at work. I don't do bars. And only needed to get away and think for a few minutes tonight. Chances of a repeat are slim."

He smiled. "Ten-thirty and we get the whole break. You come in late again like you did tonight and we'll get cut short. My boss is ruthless, you know."

"Good night, Hamish. Tell Jason I'll be calling."

He watched her walk away and really wanted to follow.

"Did you want to go back on the clock?" Mike asked. "Or go take a cold shower?"

"Did you see her?" Ian asked, staring at the door.

"Yeah," Mike laughed. "So did every other man in here with a pulse."

"Uh huh," Ian mumbled. "From now on, she'll only get it from me."

"Stuart, I have known you for five years. I have never seen you look twice at a patron, let alone look like *that* at a patron."

Ian looked at him. "That was not a patron. That was something extraordinary."

Mike gave him a playful shove. "You're fifteen minutes over your break and I'm ruthless, remember? Why don't you go see if someone needs something?"

Smiling, Ian pulled his phone out of his jeans back pocket and fired off a text.

Just met woman I plan on marrying.

Ian went back on the clock, turning to the man who waited, taking his order. The phone vibrated but Ian had to wait as he moved from person to person until he got everyone settled.

You have been looking since 1962. About time you got laid, asshole.

Ian forwarded the photo.

The response came back much quicker. *You are fucking kidding me? You found that in Cooper's? See if she has a sister.*

The next night Ian watched the clock wondering if she would show. Nerves weren't his style but he was on edge that he might have missed his chance.

The time on the clock passed ten-thirty and the door opened. He tried to hide the smile and watched her as she came across the room, the sound of the *Stones* blasting louder than he liked.

It was a different pair of tailored pants, a different white shirt, the same long, leather jacket with the same bulge at the side. Her hair was pulled back tonight away from her face, the make-up looking fresher than all day on the job.

She tried not to smile, but took the same stool anyway.

He continued to read the newspaper he had folded into quarters and ignored her while she stared.

"On break?"

He looked at the clock. "Aye."

"So I have to wait?"

He looked back at the clock. "Twenty-seven minutes."

"I think your service sucks."

He reached behind him, picked up the Macallan he had poured two minutes before she walked in and set it in front of her.

He peeked over the edge of the newspaper and saw her half grin and her tongue roll around in her cheek.

"Does the term 'smart ass' ring a bell?" she asked.

Dropping the newspaper in front of her so it faced her, he leaned over the bar. "I don't know Detective Barrow. Can you give me a legal definition?"

Her face screwed up and she sank in height. Her gaze came up to his.

He pointed at the photo the *Davenport Recorder* had run on the front page of the latest crime scene. Detective Barrow's photo was printed in black and white, still looking good enough to fulfill several months' worth of fantasies.

"If I am not mistaken Trudy, that looks a lot like you."

Her chin pointed down, her gaze came up to his.

"You're working the Blood Letting Case?" he asked.

The case everyone in Davenport was talking about: three murders in as many weeks.

"I'm a traffic cop," she said. "They bring me in to do crowd control while the big boys review the scene."

He leaned over the bar, pointed to about halfway down the article and read upside down aloud: *'Lead Criminal Detectives Ashley Barrow and Hunter Graham…'*

He moved back over to his side of the bar.

Her gaze snapped up to his. "Did I tell you?" she asked. "I got a promotion today. No more traffic."

"You're what? Thirty? Pretty impressive position."

"Thirty-two and thank you. Works out really nice when you're standing over the body before it's been processed. We were going to stop the personal information exchange 'bout now, right?"

"I don't know Trudy, this might be kind of interesting."

She smiled. "Men I date call me Ash. I have no idea what you should call me."

She smiled and looked in her glass. She lifted and drained it, surprising him.

"Do you know what I had to do today, Hamish?"

"If you want, you can call me Ian. I'm more likely to look up."

No one called him Ian. Stuart was what the world knew him as and Stuart was what he should be now. But here, he wanted to hear her say his given name.

She played with her glass without looking up at him. Glancing at the newspaper she pointed to a spot in the background and looked at him.

He reached over, looking close. You couldn't tell at first glance, it was so small and blurry, but it looked to him to be a gurney with a body bag on it.

She held her glass up, he looked back at the picture, then turned to get the bottle and refill.

"Thanks," she said, sounding tired. "I can't talk about the case, but I can tell you this, I had to tell that seventeen year old's mother that her daughter, missing for the last three days, is never coming home. They will be putting her dehumanized body into the ground and erecting a stone for mom to visit."

She looked right at him and drank and he didn't know what to say.

"She stared at me," Ash said, looking in her glass. "The mom. Like a truck ran her over and I would have the answers. And you know what the absolute worst part about the entire experience is and trust me, this is *my* experience. It is *my* job to tell the family and break the news and watch the fall out."

"What?" he asked softly.

She looked at him. "The tears are always silent."

She drained her glass and he thought about a third but she would be wasted.

12

"I'm not very good company," she said, looking in the empty glass. "You should find other ways to spend your breaks."

"You came here," he said. "When it got bad, you came back here."

"I'll tell you what," she said, looking at him. "You give me one more drink, blow off the rest of your shift and we'll go over to the Monte Cruz for a room and I will let you make me forget this God-damn job in any way you want."

He leaned forward on the bar so no one could hear, crossing his arms.

"Do you live alone?" he asked.

"Yes."

"Do you have family nearby?"

"No."

"Friends?"

"Hunter. But he's at home with his wife dealing with the same shit I am and we don't need to hear each other's voices anymore." She tried to smile at him. "Don't worry about it. It's all under control."

Like hell, he thought. The shifting in her seat, the down cast eyes. A proposition he was sure was out of character. She was in trouble tonight and she had come to him.

"Though I seriously have no doubt you and I will be redefining our relationship sooner than later," he said, "I'm going to have to pass."

She nodded slowly. "I apologize if I offended. I wasn't suggesting you were handy." She rubbed her eyes. "I just need to forget for a little while. Every day is fourteen hours plus of going over the same details until they blur together in full blood-red color. And I am totally out of line telling you all this and I apologize."

She stood to leave, reaching in her pocket again. He was fairly sure—with the pink on her cheeks—she wouldn't be back.

"You didn't do either," he said. "You need a friend right now. And that I can do. So aye, I can blow off the rest of my shift if you want to go somewhere and talk."

"You don't know me," she said. "You are under no obligations to fill roles you think you might hold."

He smiled, walked over to Mike.

"I'm taking off."

"With the brunette? Wow, not your style."

"It's sort of emergency and I'm all she's got."

Mike looked over his shoulder at him. "K. Be in tomorrow?"

"Aye," Ian nodded.

Mike was the easiest man on the planet to work for. So laidback he made valium look like an upper. Ian disappeared into the backroom, lifted his backpack and grabbed his leather coat.

She saw him come out of the back, his coat on and come around to the bar to her side. He reached up, took her hand and led the way, with her following.

"Where're we going?"

"I don't have a clue."

"What are we going to do when we get there?" she asked.

"We'll have to see," he said, still holding her hand.

She could feel the scotch in her head. They walked through historic downtown, the quaint area where independent businesses still opened their doors and Mom and Pop joints thrived. The buildings were old granite, two-story high. Some with plaques on the walls denoting why they were famous and what years they were built.

Ian, still holding her hand, turned left and stopped in front of the bookstore,

The Novel Shop. The lights were on and he pressed his face to the window.

"Hours ten to six," Ashley said, pointing at the sign.

A figure walked past the back counter and Ian tapped on the glass.

"What are you doing?"

He smiled at her. "Cheering you up."

The attractive redhead came forward. She smiled and unlocked the front door. "Aren't you supposed to be at work?"

Ian smiled back. "Took the night off. Maggie, this is my girlfriend, Ashley. Ashley, Maggie."

Ash extended her hand. "Why are we bothering her now?"

"Because she's got at least two more hours work and she's going to let us in."

Maggie sighed and pulled the door open, Ian kissing her cheek as he went by.

"He's my late night shopper. Never here when everyone else is but walks out with an armload."

"Amazon delivers, you know," he said.

Maggie gasped. "You're cheating on me?"

Ian turned to stare straight at Ash. "You go find two books you want me to read. I'll find two books I want you to read."

"And you would rather do this than go to the Monte Cruz and get a room for the night?"

"Sex verses a good book?" Maggie laughed. "Definitely a hard call with this one."

Ashley found a laugh that felt real.

Ian leaned over, brushing his lips lightly over hers, sending electric shock to every nerve. She was more aware of him than she had been with any other man she had met.

"We'll try that next time," he said.

He left her standing there and she began to walk the aisles. She found a couple she liked. Surprised at the book in her hand, she turned, faced it toward Maggie, and raised her eyebrows.

Maggie smiled. "That one came in by accident. I was going to return it for the exchange and decided I wanted to see what Davenport would think."

"The verdict?"

"A lot of raised eyebrows but you are the first one to pick it up."

Ash slapped it next to her first choice and headed toward the register.

Maggie laughed. "Can honestly say he probably hasn't read that one. The register is closed," Maggie said. "What he always does is I make a receipt and then he brings it by on his way to work in a few days. Does that work for you?"

Ashley nodded and handed over her selections. Maggie took them, looked at one, then the other, laughed and brought her gaze up to Ash's. "Excellent choices. He'll love them."

The receipt written, the books were in a bag.

"Is this a normal thing with him?" Ash asked Maggie.

"Books? It's his major life addiction. Bringing a girl in to get her two when he should be at work?" She smiled and shook her head. "Never before, at least not here." She raised her voice. "And if he's buying his books elsewhere, we will have words!"

"I can hear you," he said from three feet away. He hid his choices and covered Ash's eyes so she couldn't see, pulling her

17

back against him. She wiggled, his body feeling good next to hers and while he got his receipt, she thought the Monte Cruz was not a bad idea.

"Thanks Maggie," he smiled, taking Ash's hand and leading her back into the damp night. He looked up and down the street then guided her toward left. In a minute they stood in front of another bar, The Three Sisters, and he pulled the door open and led her to a booth.

"Isn't this cheating?"

"Shh," he whispered with a smile.

He sat across from her and a woman appeared at the side of the table almost immediately. He looked up at her.

"Darcia," he said.

"Are you telling me we are finally going to be able to steal you from Mike Cooper?"

"You know I have a spot for the old guy."

"Why are you here, Stuart?"

"I wanted to get away with my new girlfriend and get a couple of your Virgin Bloody Marys, though we both know I can make them better."

"Yes, we do know that. That's why we've been trying to steal you for years." The woman looked at Ash. She extended her hand.

"Darcia," she said. "The middle of the Three Sisters. If you could, would you let us know what he's like in bed? We've been trying to get him there longer than we've been trying to steal him from Mike."

Ash smiled. There was no offence in the woman's teasing. "Which one of the three has been trying?"

"We're not picky. All of us."

Ash leaned forward. "Hot," she said. "He can do things, I mean *wow*," Ash dragged out the sigh. "And stamina and he does this thing with his tongue…eww…" she pouted and pursed her lips.

"Haven't slept with him, huh?" Darcia smiled.

"Nope."

Both women laughed. Ian only smirked.

"If you two are done, I am on a date here and I would like to get on with it. The drinks?"

"Come work for us and I'll make them on the house."

"I can pay," Ian said.

Darcia sashayed away with Ash watching the nicely clad ass in the purple silk sheath. She looked at Ian. "You could sleep with that and you said no?"

"She's the ugly one. I said no to the other two, too."

"Why did she call you Stuart?"

He shrugged. "Most people do. Ian *Stuart*. I've gone by my last name since I came to America."

"Why did you ask me to call you Ian?"

He leaned forward. "Because you're special and you don't need a name everyone uses."

"Has it occurred to you, Ian Stuart, you might be reading a hell of a lot more into two nights at the bar and a few scotches than there actually is?"

He smiled and set a bag in front of her. She looked up at him, then opened it to pull out two books.

The Funny Thing Is… by Ellen DeGeneres and *The One Hundred: A Guide to the Pieces Every Stylish Woman Must Own* by Nina Garcia.

He pointed at the second book. "I figured I would start at Number One and start buying you one a week of the things you have to have."

She opened the book and looked it up. "An A Line dress. You are going to buy me an A Line dress?"

"If that is what it says."

"Wouldn't you like to check my closet to see if maybe I already own one?"

He smiled wicked. "I'm thinking if I go into your room to check your closet, I might end up checking your sheets instead."

"You have introduced me as your girlfriend twice. Don't you think since we've progressed to that level you might want to see what color they are?"

The drinks arrived, but not by Darcia. Ian smiled a thank you.

"I will," he said. "Not yet, though."

She slid his bag over to him. "You're going to read these?"

"I read cereal boxes cover to cover. I think I can handle these."

He pulled them both out and pursed his lips, nodding.

The Zombie Survival Guide: Complete Protection from the Living Dead by Max Brooks and *The Anarchists Cookbook* by William Powel.

He picked up *The Anarchists Cookbook* while she chewed on her celery stick, feeling an immense satisfaction at making him smile.

"Says right here, railroad demolition. I have been meaning to get into that, so this was a good idea. Thanks." He leaned over and batted her on the head with the book.

His phone went off in his pocket and he pulled it out to read the message.

Smiling, he slipped it back in his pocket without answering.

"Who was that?" she asked.

"That would be Travis."

"What's a Travis?"

"Nosy, busy-body."

"You keep a lot of them around?"

"He's one of a kind. Trust me."

She put her hand out. "Let me see it?"

He paused, but handed it over.

She read his message: *You're not at work. Finally getting laid?*

Bringing up the camera, she struck a seductive pose, blowing a kiss, snapped it then played with the buttons. She handed the phone back to Ian. He stopped before putting it away to read what she sent with the photo.

She knew what it said and liked the look it put on his face: *Had you been in the right place at the right time, this could have been yours.*

When the message came back in under a minute, Ian handed her the phone

Name the time, place and tell me what to bring. I'm yours. What I can do will leave Scotsman in dust.

Sorry. Scotsman wins this round.

When does next game start?

She tapped out a message

"Ian, who am I talking to?"

"Travis Ricci. Also a roommate and the closest friend I have."

Saving myself for Jason. Let him know I'm on my way.

Fucking Irishman. 34725 Pineknot. Door always open. Arrive in something barely there.

She held up the phone to show Ian. "Your best friend propositioned me, gave me the address and told me what not to wear."

Ian took the phone back while she scooted around the table to sit beside him and watched him tap out his message. She leaned her head on his shoulder and he didn't seem to mind.

Hey dick. Mine. Find your own, hope she looks half as good and maybe wears the same perfume.

Oh, the message came in. *You again. Get ass home. You forgot to do the dishes.*

I never forget to do the dishes.

Have you told her you're a neat freak?

She grabbed the phone back. *Neatness is next to Godliness. Now must object. Almost have him naked w/ plans. You are interrupting.*

I hate you both.

A second later, a photo came through.

It showed a man, his light brown eyes crossed, his dark hair messed and pulled forward, his head cocked and his tongue sticking out.

Name the time and place. Came another message.

Can see my mistake now. Will dump Scotsman. Say my place, fifteen minutes? And tell Jason to call me.

See you there.

Laughing, she handed back the phone, and went back to her seat.

Two days ago, Ian had been a stranger. Tonight, he felt like the best friend she ever had and that was a tough position to secure when you put anyone up against Hunter, her partner.

Ian sat flipping through the zombie book, managing to look sincerely interested. His jacket unzipped, he wore a blue plaid shirt untucked, and a grey T-shirt underneath. There were silver rings on three of his fingers, two on the right hand, one on the left, each with details inlaid into the metal.

He was dark when she always preferred blonds. His hair was long, when she always dated short-haired men. Left-handed when right was the norm. He had an earring in his left ear, a pale green stone stud. He was the opposite of everything she ever thought she wanted in a man until she saw him.

Men didn't come in much better packaging, but he didn't seem to realize it, making him even more appealing.

His phone vibrated again.

Ian laughed and showed it to her.

Travis says I supposed to text you?

She took the phone, scrolled through his contacts, found Jason at number four speed dial with a photo attached.

"Man...oh wow," she said staring at the incredible face, the dark hair and the greenest eyes. "What's the rest of him look like?" she asked wickedly, with a hidden smile.

"Aye," Ian said, pretending to be pissed. "I was hoping you would say something like that. It's not like he doesn't know it."

"Oh, he knows it," she said. "You can be as modest as hell and not have any hang-ups on it, but if you get what he's got, you know what is staring back every morning in the mirror."

"Experience?" he asked softly.

"Some things might look like a blessing, as I am sure you know due to your own reflection, but trust me, it's more of a curse than anything. Though fun to play up occasionally and it's nice to have someone who appreciates it, you mostly get shallow hell because of it."

Give us a sec, she texted. *Are discussing how good looking you are and what a pain in the ass it is.*

WTF Stuart?

Sorry. Not Stuart. Ashley. She attached her slutty photo and hit send.

Jason's reply came back faster than Travis's. *The Attic Room. Corner of Pineknot and Branch. Fifteen minutes. I'm buying.*

She held up the phone toward Ian, waving it a bit. "I now have dates with both your roommates." She laughed.

He grabbed the phone. Then showed her before hitting send.

Asshole. My girlfriend. Go find own.

He turned off the phone and stuffed it in his pocket pretending to be mad but his eyes gleamed and his lips tugged at the edges. "I've got news for you. You have dates with *two* of my roommates."

"How many do you have?"

"There are five of us living together."

"Cozy," she smiled.

"We like it."

She watched him, not knowing if it was the mere fact his tone dropped to serious, or the Scottish with it made it sound romantic and wanting.

"Ian," she said softly.

His gaze came up to hers.

"Roger," she said.

"Not one of my roommates. You have a date with him, too?"

"My last boyfriend. Eighteen months ago. We lasted a grand total of seven dates."

"What did Roger do?"

"We were at dinner and he wanted to bring the waitress home to up our entertainment. I walked out."

"So no threesomes?"

She laughed.

"Which actually isn't a problem as I'm a selfish son-of-a-bitch and feel a bed is full enough as it is with two."

She stared back. "I never pick men up and I have never, in my entire life, had a one night stand."

He watched her talk.

"But my house is two blocks from here, I do have my own bottle of Macallan, but I doubt there is anything to eat in the refrigerator as I have been on the job a couple of weeks and haven't seen the inside of a market to do more than buy Ben & Jerry's."

"Didn't we cover this?"

"No. We covered a quick night at the Monte Cruz. I don't ever ask men into my home. I saw Roger for weeks and I never asked him into my home."

He leaned back as he thought hard.

"Ash," he said. "I don't sleep with women from the bar. It's a policy going back more years than you can imagine."

Her gaze dropped in embarrassment at having taken a fun couple of hours and ruining them into oblivion.

"I'm sorry," she whispered. "I wasn't trying to repeat what I said earlier."

"I don't do one nights either. We do this, exclusive rights are mine for a while and it might be a damn, long while. I'm thinking you're my type and I might like to explore the possibilities with a microscope."

She looked at him.

He watched back, his chin tilted, waiting for her to say something.

"My sheets are blue, I love pillows and I have a collection of pajamas from Victoria's Secret that puts most wardrobes to shame, though not one would be considered sexy."

He leaned forward, ignored his drink and crossed his arms on the table. "How not sexy?"

Feeling suddenly shy, she looked at the table. "Flannels. With matching slippers. Some with plaid pants and colored T-shirts. Socks."

His expression mixed seriousness with a level of lust that made her nervous.

"Starting with flannels, socks and matching slippers might sound mundane to you, but I'm already four steps ahead and peeling them off and they work for me just fine."

Her chin dropped, her gaze came up.

"But Ashley, I only sleep with my girlfriend. Might sound strange, especially from a bartender who gets chances, but I have old world morals and I do not do bed hopping. I don't sleep with someone who wants to get laid to forget their shitty job choice."

"Ian, I'm a cop working the worst case in Davenport's history with a Glock on my hip and no free time to shop for food. I'm not the girl you want to make that commitment with. You've known me since last night, for God's sake."

He leaned as close as the table would allow. "Detective Barrow, we've known each other our whole damn lives. It just took us a little time to end up in the same room."

28

CHAPTER TWO

Sleeping in was supposed to follow the late night. That's what Ian said before they drifted off to sleep spooned comfortably together.

When the pounding started on the front door, she hid under the pillow.

"Do you want me to kill it?" he asked. He lay face down on the mattress, both arms under the pillow his head rested on.

"No, I'll do it," she muttered through a yawn.

Grabbing her cotton robe off the end of the bed, she pulled it on while she swung her legs over the side. Fuzzy from lack of sleep, the exhaustion rammed up against an energy that made her grateful Gr'pa Jackson had foot the bill for the years of gymnastics lessons. She smiled as she walked down the hall. She couldn't do a cartwheel anymore, but last night, she was pretty sure the money was well spent.

There was a face in the glass door, watching her get close, the goatee surrounding the smile. She yanked open the door.

"What?" she snapped at Hunter.

"I've been calling for an hour," he said, stepping into the entryway and closing the door behind them.

"It's my day off. You don't get to call me at—what the hell time is it?"

He looked at his watch. "Seven-forty-two."

30

"Seven-forty-two," she sighed. "Why are you here?" She asked the question but didn't want to hear his answer. There was no way in hell he would have gotten out of his own bed on a day off unless there was a damn good reason.

"There was another one," he said.

Hearing the words, she felt it move through her body like a sad, tired thunderbolt. "When?"

"It looks like early this morning."

"Shit," she said dragging her hand over half her face.

"I got you a Danish and a cup of coffee in the car."

She nodded. "Gimme ten."

"Yeah," he said.

She left him standing there even though she knew her house was not big enough to hold secrets.

Ian lay against the pillows, the white comforter pulled up to his waist. He wore a silver chain around his neck, a Celtic knot medallion on the end. He was as Scottish as his accent and had the body of someone who worked out at the gym a couple of hours a day. He didn't seem the type, but there was no denying those results. The thought of missing the promise of what today had in store for them made her sigh.

"What's wrong?" he asked.

She reached in her closet, grabbing the closest matching pants and jacket. Pulling out a white blouse, she reached over for her boots.

31

"I got to go to work." She grabbed a pair of fresh panties and bra from her dresser drawer.

He rubbed the sleep out of his eyes. "You have today off."

"Not anymore."

She stepped into the bathroom, but left the door open. Standing discreetly out of the line of sight, she pulled on the ensemble then turned to the mirror for a quick covering of powder and mascara. She grabbed a brush and dragged it through her hair, securing it in a loose bun with a thick clip.

"We were going to watch *The Hobbit*."

"Not today," she said. She growled as she slammed the brush onto the counter.

"Hey," she heard Hunter say. He was far closer than the entryway.

She sidestepped into her bedroom, finding Hunter standing in the door. Suit, tie, overcoat. He was the picture of perfect detective while her lack of enthusiasm mixed with her loathing of her job making her feel like a train went over her.

If that wasn't bad enough, Hunter took two steps toward the bed, extending his hand.

"Hunter Graham," he said, his smile sincere.

She was going to kill him. He had to know she would kill him as soon as she got him alone.

Shirtless and naked under the blanket, Ian leaned forward, taking the handshake. "Stuart," he said.

Hunter nodded. "First or last?"

"Oh for crying out loud," Ash snapped, stepping back into the room. She sat down on the edge of the bed to pull her boots on.

"I heard voices," Hunter said, his hands up in surrender.

"Privacy, heard of it?"

She pulled out the Glock, strapping it on. She grabbed her badge, hooking it on the leather strap.

"Last," Ian said. "Ian Stuart."

"Ah," Hunter said as if he remembered the conversation. "Nice to meet you. Are you a friend of Ash's?"

Ian laughed loud. "Aye. I think so."

"Damn," she said looking down at the phone. "It's dead."

"What?" Hunter asked.

"Would you get your Irish ass out of here?" she snapped at him.

He batted her on the head. "No words against the Irish, lass."

"The battery is dead. That's why you couldn't reach me."

"I got my phone," Hunter said. "We can use that."

Ash's gaze came up to Ian's, the laughter in his eyes. He was enjoying this.

"I'll try to get back early," she said. She sighed when he heard Hunter's footfalls heading toward the front door.

"Are you going to bring your friend?" Ian laughed.

"He's not my friend, he's my partner and due for a serious accident today."

"I heard that," came from down the hall.

"Wait in the car," she shouted.

Laughter came instead of a good-bye. The front door opened and shut.

"I'll shoot him when I can get him alone."

Ian reached for her hand, pulling it forward until he could kiss the back of the knuckles.

"Sleep here as long as you want," she said. "Shower works and there is some food in the kitchen but I'm not sure what. You're welcome to help yourself to whatever you can find."

He reached up, his fingers on the back of her neck. He pulled her toward him while he leaned forward until his lips crushed down on hers. Open and hot, he devoured her mouth while her hand rested on his naked chest, her fingers fanning out over the chain.

When she pulled back she was shaking and out of breath. She didn't pull her hand off him. "You did that on purpose."

He was staring at her mouth, a grin on his lips. "Aye. I know. Wanted to make sure you would be in tonight."

"Promises of sex?"

His smiled broadened. "My break is at ten-thirty like always."

34

The horn honked in the front yard.

He was still leaning forward, still watching her mouth. He brushed a finger along her jaw.

"I was going to sleep with you again this morning," she said. "Probably later in the day too, before you went to work."

His smile took up everything she was seeing. He brushed his lips over hers. "I know."

"That's a lot of sex," she said.

"Guess I'll hang around to collect it all," he said. "Since it's mine, you know."

She started to turn away.

"Hey," he said.

She looked back and he held the handcuffs still attached to the bed frame. "Might need these for their intended purpose?"

His guilty grin could turn a woman to wax.

She pulled out the key, got close to him and unlocked them. He nuzzled her neck, his tongue making patterns, making it hard to work.

"You smell like me," he said.

"Might be because you sweated on me all night."

He wrapped a hand around her neck, pulling her close to kiss her hard on her throat. "I marked you. Everyone will stay away now."

"I have perfume, you know."

"Oh, trust me. I know, but you will not be wearing it today."

She looked over her shoulder to the door. She knew what the day held before her and she didn't want to do it. She looked back at him. His arm braced behind his head, the chain and Celtic Knot on his chest. She reached up to finger it for a few seconds.

Blowing out a sharp breath, she took a step back. "Can you lock the door behind you?"

"I can do that."

She opened her nightstand and dropped her official cop issue cuffs next to the empty holster and looked at him.

His eyes narrowed at her.

"Stopped carrying them when I made detective." She shrugged. "I just never felt the need to get rid of them."

He laughed. "Witch."

"Yeah, because you complained last night." She gave him one final brush across the lips. "I'll see you tonight." She headed toward the door. "I hate my job."

"Right now, I hate your job, too."

Ash was pulling on her leather coat when she yanked the door shut behind. She headed down the walkway to the beige sedan Hunter already had started up. She didn't want to think about what she was going to be missing today. She also didn't want to think about what it was she would be facing.

He pulled away from the curb before she finished putting on her seat belt.

The cherry Danish waited for her, a small cup of milk in the cup holder. She glanced in the backseat. Her coffee was in the holder back there. Hunter did know how to take care of people.

"What time did you get to sleep last night?" he asked as he drove.

"I don't know," she said, taking a bite of her breakfast. "Maybe three. Somewhere around there."

He huffed and shook his head. "This is going to be a long ass day."

"Yeah." She wasn't going to regret it, though. Given the same information she had last night, she would have made the same choices she made, because they turned out to be good, good choices. She thought of Ian in bed and found a smile in her grouchiness and chewed slowly on the pastry. Reaching over, she took a drink of the milk.

They went four more blocks.

"Thanks for breakfast," she said

"You know you're not dating anyone," he said with a deadpan calm.

Blond hair only a little longer than the department liked, cool hazel eyes that seemed to sparkle all the time with mischief. They had been together for almost five years and were best friends since the shootout that initiated their first day together.

"Don't. Start," she warned.

"You actually haven't dated anyone in eighteen months."

She looked at him. "Can you not hear me?"

"Roger," he said. "Roger 'Kiss-My-Ass' Swenson."

"He wasn't one of my best ideas."

Hunter looked over at her. "And who told you that?"

"Really?" she said. "You're going to bring that up now?"

He was back to staring at the road. "Me," he said. "I told you."

"You want credit? Again?"

"We're almost there," he said, heading onto the campus.

Good she thought. She could get out of the car and put some distance between them.

"There was a naked man in your bed this morning."

Her eyes closed tight. She wasn't getting out soon enough.

"I'm pretty sure you were naked under that robe, too."

She glared at him. "I can shoot you. You do know that, right?"

"Naw," he smiled. "You would miss Janey's Steak & Guinness Pie."

"You're going to save yourself with your wife's cooking? Are you that pathetic?"

"Nope." He was still smiling, looking like he had won the battle. "Just know what cards to play."

He pulled up to a spot left free. Black and whites were already on the scene as was the CSI van. The Medical Examiners van.

The day was just starting.

Hours after Ashley left, Ian stayed curled up in her bed still smelling her perfume, one of her big pillows under his head. The room was dark enough to sleep in and he would have tried if the images coming into his mind this morning hadn't been so haunting.

Memories of people from the past. Women whose names he still remembered decades later. The drinks he had poured for them still sweet on their lips. He had kissed them, too, when he never cared what they felt. He asked them to be his lover when he knew they would never leave his bed alive.

Monsters were real and there was a time, still not far enough in his past, when he led the pack and made decisions that robbed people of their lives.

He moved into the bathroom, turning on the faucet and splashing cold water onto his face, letting it drip off in droplets he swore he could hear hit the porcelain.

He looked down, seeing Ashley's pink toothbrush in a silver holder behind the cold-water handle. He pulled open the drawer next to him and found her makeup. Basic colors, blushes, mascaras—yes, more than one. There was an assortment of eye shadows. *Why on earth would any woman need that many shades of color?* On the counter was the brush she must have used this morning.

Her hair looked nice, he thought. She managed to pull herself together in a matter of minutes and walk out the door looking more than decent. He concentrated on that image. Of her alive and happy. Of *her* voice in his ear last night. They laughed as much as they talked. They played as much as they made love, starting in the shower and moving to the bed. The compatibility exceeded what he ever thought he wanted in a lover.

He grabbed a towel and wiped down his face, careful to hang the towel back up like he found it. Getting his clothes off the back of the toilet where he left them, he turned back to the bedroom, slipped on his boxers and jeans. He finished dressing; tying the laces on his black athletic shoes then turned to carefully make the bed.

Checking out the window, he made sure the cloud cover was heavy enough to get home. The predictability of Davenport, Oregon's dreary weather made it perfect for someone like him to get around.

He wanted to run to Aspen's Market, two blocks over, and stock up her refrigerator a bit, but the sky gave him enough pause to schedule that stop for tonight, after work, after dark.

Making sure the door locked behind him, he walked back to Cooper's, heading down the damp alley to the back yard. Mike's truck was gone. Ian looked up into the sky. The sun peeked through the clouds. His jacket, gloves and shades should be enough protection even at this hour of the day.

His blue bike still stood chained to the same water pipe he always used.

In less than two minutes, he was in the seat, heading home, but not his usual route. He tacked on another five miles. He saw the homeless man in the doorway no one would miss. The woman leaning out of the second story window shouting something to someone on the street. He could get in and out of her apartment in minutes.

The feedings crossed his mind. Ways to get away with them came as easy as they had decades ago.

He peddled faster, taking little heed of street traffic and the danger cars might cause. He couldn't die in a wreck. There was no point not to push the limits, rushing through lights as they already turned, changing directions as a car veered.

Physical exertion, one of the keys to fighting cravings, along with diet and supplements, he'd discovered after decades of experimentation. He wasn't built the way he was because he enjoyed working out. He did it to make sure he didn't kill anyone.

He got to the house sweaty and out of breath and carried the bike up the front steps. Using his key, he let himself in. He set the bike in the hallway that led to the basement.

The voice came out of the dining room before Ian even got the door shut behind him.

"What the fuck was that about last night?"

Ian set his keys in the bowl on the table by the front door and pulled off his sunglasses.

"I don't think you've actually asked me that since 1976."

"I don't think you're had a date since 1976. Where were you? And where did you leave the gorgeous, blue-eyed, brunette who was *way* out of your league?"

Nebraska farm boy, raised by immigrant parents, Jason Sullivan came out of the dining room carrying a cup of coffee. Just under six feet, he wore his dark hair long and shaggy. His green eyes sparkled even when he was being an ass and in Ian's opinion, that was most of the time. Jason was as Irish as Ian was Scottish and in almost fifty years, the two had yet to come to a truce.

"Didn't come home last night, either," Jason smirked. "Red letter day in history."

"You're an asshole. You know that, right?" Ian said.

Jason drank some more and smiled.

Travis Ricci came down the stairs. Standing over six-three with eyes that leaned more towards golden than brown and the Italian good looks that landed more dates than his appointment book could handle, he was a meddler by nature. He took slow steps, one at a time, his gaze traveling between Ian and Jason.

"The brunette?" Travis asked.

"You texted me, she grabbed the phone. Should I have arm wrestled her?"

"Dating you not enough, huh?" Jason teased. "She needs us, too."

42

"Bite me, Irishman," Ian smirked. "You'll never get near her."

"Hundred bucks says I have her in my arms by the end of the month."

"Fuck your hundred bucks and think of what else you can fuck if you try to go near my girlfriend."

They moved toward the kitchen where they always congregated.

Quinn Nelson, resident medic, sat at the table, his legs stretched out on another chair, his coffee mug curled in his hand. Dark blond, brown-eyed, as good-looking as the other three. He waited for them patiently. He could do anything patiently. As long as they didn't piss him off. Pissing Quinn off could end badly.

Evan Harris, the baby of the family, poured himself a cup of the expensive German import Jason kept him in and took his seat at the table, adding the amount of cream and sugar that would be expected of a seventeen-year-old kid.

Ian stopped and looked around the room. "We're having a meeting because I had a date?"

"Though you having a date might make national news," Quinn said, "we have a more serious problem." He held up three manila folders. "I was in the morgue two nights ago and heard too much so I went back last night and sneaked these."

Ian sat down and a cup of coffee appeared in front of him. He snapped up the folders, flipping through them. They were photocopies of autopsy reports of people who had come through the doors. Ian read. Last victim was a seventeen-year-old girl, missing three days. He remembered what Ash had said last night. Having to tell a mom her daughter wasn't coming home.

Neck sliced open. Drained of blood.

Ian's gaze came up.

"The Blood Letting Case is vampires?" Ian snapped.

"When I was in the morgue, the doctors talking didn't see me because why would they? Nurses blend in, right?" Quinn said. "They've never seen anything like this, they said," Quinn reported. "Slit throats, yes. Sliced necks like this, no. There's very little blood at the scenes, while the bodies are drained. They can't figure out where the blood is going and how The Blood Letting is taking it out or why." He paused and tapped on the table, alternating thumb and pinky. "Every one of us has seen bedrooms looking like this."

"Not me," Evan said.

Turned moments before his death to save him, Evan had been protected by the other four from the violence that used to make up their existence. He had never taken a victim.

"Okay," Quinn smiled. "You're the lucky one. The rest of us…"

"Davenport," Ian said. "You're going to tell me another den of vampires has picked a random town with nothing to offer to set up shop?"

"We did," Jason said.

"We were *looking* for a random town with nothing to offer." Travis said. "Stuart's right. The chances are slim. And even if they aren't, what the hell do we do about it?"

Ian looked through the reports again, afraid to say anything.

"We don't hunt. We don't take victims. We're going to go out, find the den, take them on and waste them?" Jason asked.

Ian could feel Travis watching him, reading him like no one else on the planet could.

"What?" Travis asked.

Ian looked up at him. He closed all the folders and set them on the table in a neat stack. "I say we stay lower than usual, hope they get bored and go away."

"That's a great idea," Travis said. "Brilliant. Now what the fuck aren't you telling us?"

All eyes looked to Ian.

Sighing, he gave up. If this relationship went as far as he wanted, they would meet her sooner than later.

"The brunette?" he said.

"Do we get details?" Jason asked, perking up.

Ian glared up at him. They all kept their women stories pretty close vested. "When hell freezes over." He looked at Travis. "Her name is Ashley."

"Yeah. That came across last night," Jason said. "She did introduce herself. Polite for a pick-up."

He said it only to piss Ian off. Which it did.

"Ashley Barrow. *Detective* Ashley Barrow, lead investigator in the Blood Letting Case."

Quinn leaned forward. "Your new girlfriend is investigating a series of vampire related murders?"

Evan laughed. "Classic."

Travis batted him on the head. "Genius, she's looking for us."

Letting out a sigh, Ian put his coffee on the table. "There was another one this morning."

"What?" Jason snapped.

"How can you know that?"

"Because right now I am supposed to be at her house watching *The Hobbit* with a bowl of popcorn. Instead she got called in on her day off to head back to work to investigate the new death."

"She told you all this?"

He shook his head. "She said enough. It's the same case."

"Do you like her?"

Ian looked up at Travis. "Aye. Very much."

Travis sank down into the chair across from him. "You're dating a cop?"

"When she walked in? She could have been a stock broker and I wouldn't have cared."

"Get uninterested," Quinn said, surprising Ian. It wasn't the type of declaration Quinn would make.

Ian shrugged and shook his head. "Unless she says otherwise, it's not going to happen."

Jason stepped forward. "You think this is a good move for us?"

"Do you think I'm going to tell her? Maybe drop a few clues that lead her here?"

"The case?"

"They're looking for a serial killer."

"This *is* a serial killer. A serial killer with a different skill set," Jason said. "I don't know—maybe you remember? Used to be popular with some crowds in the early half of last century. With four of us."

"Fuck you," Ian sighed.

"You're going to have to stop seeing her," Travis said.

Ian stood up, taking his coffee mug to the sink where he dumped and rinsed, placing it in the drying rack on the counter. "You don't get to tell me who to date."

"Dump her," Jason said. "You got one good, all night stay. What more do you need?"

"You dumping Sandy because we want you to?" Ian shot at Jason.

"I broke up with Sandy two weeks ago, asshole, and she was a personal trainer—not a cop looking for a killer meeting our descriptions."

"I can handle this," Ian said. "And not one of us has ever told another who they can or can't go out with." Ian reached into the cupboard, pulling out a bowl and filling it with cereal. He got the milk out of the refrigerator, stuck a banana under his arm and grabbed a spoon. Turning he headed for the door.

"We're not done talking about this," Jason called after him.

As far as Ian was concerned, they were. He would be sitting down with Ash again, sooner than later. He would see her knowing what she was facing every day and not talk to her about it. He could keep it up, he told himself. Regardless of what these idiots said, he could be with her and never give her information that would threaten them or help her case.

He took the flights of stairs to his third floor, attic room. Ian kicked his door shut behind him, making sure the door closed tight. He walked to his desk in the corner and set down his bowl next to his computer keyboard. Peeling the banana, he sliced it on top and stood as he ate.

They wanted to harass him and tell him who he could see? Ian didn't think so. Not when no sin had been committed.

This room was his world. Sleep only covered one of the things he did here. His electric piano was under the covered window, its headphones, hanging off the edge. Beside it, two guitars stood in stands, one acoustic and one electric. The bookcases across from the queen size bed were crammed to overfull with classics and modern fiction. He had a thing for reading biographies. The whole top shelf on both cases held nothing but that. A book on Rod Serling lay diagonal on the nightstand, the bookmark three quarters through.

He had left his new books at her house. Damn, he smiled. He would have to go pick them up.

Putting his spoon in the bowl, he reached for his sketchpad on the desktop. He flipped the oversized pages one at a time paying little attention to the things he drew in the last six months. It was the last page he wanted. When he found it, he turned all the other pictures over and set the pad down flat. Nothing but her smiling face stared up at him. He stayed standing and picked his spoon up, going back to his breakfast while he stared down at Ashley in pencil.

Drawn yesterday before their second 'date,' he liked it for the most part. Saw the sparkle in the eyes he had been able to capture. But there was something off on it and he hadn't been able to figure out exactly what he did wrong. Staring at it now, he realized the eyes were too far apart, her bottom lip too thin. They weren't off by much, but it was enough to make the likeness not right. He had seen her up close and personal now and he knew he could correct the problem.

He stared down at the picture. She was stunning with the kind of face and body a man fantasized about having and it was his now. He took the last three bites of his cereal and put the banana peel into the bowl, setting the bowl on the table by the door.

His furniture sat simple in oak stain, the end tables matching. The artwork on the walls was classic art posters from the ages, with a framed *Who* concert tour poster he had actually bought when he attended the concert. His room was neat, a reflection of the tag they nailed him with. The bed made, the dark blue comforter pulled tight to the plain headboard, his two pillows looked lacking now he had seen what a pillow could do to a bed.

He smiled, thinking of her this morning. They should have been allowed a few more hours.

Leaning over he searched through the load of folded laundry that sat in the basket, waiting to be put away. He glanced at the clock. He didn't have to leave for work for another four and half hours. He could change into jeans then. Right now, he pulled out a pair of grey sweats and a long sleeved white T-shirt. He still had the road on him and wanted to get it off before he tackled the corrections in this drawing.

Carrying the clothes, he headed out, pulling the door closed behind him. The bathroom was on the second floor along with everyone else's bedrooms. He managed to avoid everyone, which was a good thing. He didn't think any conversation at this point was going to go the way anyone wanted.

The shower was hot. The soap smelled clean. He shampooed and cream rinsed then stood under the spray until anything that could and might go wrong erased from his mind. The water ran cold by the time he got out.

He dried, then dressed, and draped a towel around his neck to catch the dampness from his long hair.

When he walked back into his bedroom, his dirty clothes in hand, Travis was stretched out down the middle of the bed, the sketch page in his hand. He stacked both pillows behind his head, giving him a better view.

Ian checked his irritation and tossed the dirties into the laundry hamper.

"The door was closed for a reason, you know."

Travis held up the sketchpad. "Is this Ashley Barrow?"

Ian moved to his desk, pulling out the chair to sit down, rubbing the towel on his wet hair. "It's not right," he said. "I have to fix it."

"You always think it's not right and you have to fix it."

"No," Ian said pointing at it. "It's…" He caught himself before he explained.

Travis only smiled and stared at the drawing, his lips pursed. "She's pretty sweet. This is actually better than the photo you sent around. I can see not wanting to give this up."

Ian stood up and took the pad from Travis, flipping the cover closed.

Travis braced his hands behind his head as Ian moved to the desk to put the pad back where he had left it. He took three hardback books that had been lying nearby and put them on top, hiding the drawing from the world.

"You spent the night with her. That isn't on your usual To Do list anymore."

"Exceptions to the rules," Ian said.

"It's been a long time. She must be something special."

Ian turned to face him. "Did you want something, because I had some stuff I needed to do."

51

"You've spent eighty plus years with that five page, imaginary list in your head of what you want in a woman. You think this one is going to fill it?"

"I thought I made it clear this isn't up for discussion?"

"How long have you been seeing her?"

"I don't know, Travis. How long did you see Shelly?"

Travis sat up, swallowing hard. He didn't look Ian in the eye. "Longer than I should have."

"And would you give it up? The memories of everything you had together until it was over?"

"I think about her every day."

"It's been fifteen years."

"So maybe I know something about what I am talking about."

Ian didn't have an answer.

"There's always one choice," Travis said. Ian didn't know if it was a test or an actual suggestion.

"I won't do that to her."

"Turning her keeps her by your side forever."

"You didn't turn Shelly?"

"Shelly turned me down."

Travis shifted, sliding to the edge of the bed. He swung his legs over the side and braced a hand on either side of him on the mattress. His head hung low.

Shelly died, a fact Travis had only found out three years ago when Google had tempted him into a search. Killed in a traffic accident on her bike, she was gone from this world six months after walking away from him.

Travis stood up, walking past Ian to the desk. He lifted the three hardback books and set them to the side, picking up the sketchbook. Ian let him.

Travis flipped through the pictures until he got to Ashley.

"What's off on it?"

"The eyes are too far apart and the bottom lip is too thin."

"You going to start over?"

Ian stared at the picture and shook his head. "I can fix it."

"She is sweet," Travis said. "You guys would make a good couple."

Ian folded his arms. "Thanks."

He turned to look at Ian. "Any good last night?"

Ian laughed. "You know I'm not going to answer that."

Travis looked at the drawing again. "Yeah, she looks like it. But we're going to have to go in two years from here and set up shop in a new city."

"I know."

"You're going to have to leave her behind. She's going to get hurt. Probably hate you and then go on with her life until finally, it's 2051 and she's long dead while we are still pulling up roots every seven years."

"I would ask for your point, but I think you painted it pretty damn clear. You're not going to bring up the fact she's a cop or the murders?"

"We might have to deal with that at some point. You going to see her again?"

"Tonight."

"I could order you, you know. That does come under the job description you made me take," Travis said.

"I could tell you fuck off, too, which is what I would do if you tried."

Travis laughed. "You staying the night?"

Ian pointed at the picture. "That asks you to spend the night, you going to say no?"

Travis picked up the sketchbook and cocked his head. "Okay," he laughed. "I see your point."

CHAPTER THREE

Ian mixed two Sapphire Martini's, pouring them into the chilled glass. Adding the twist of lemon, he placed them on Rita's tray then turned to get the receipt.

Tonight was like any other night only he watched the clock, waiting for her to walk in the door. The regulars who own property in the form of bar stools came in, taking their places while Ian and Mike each took a side, making their usual and adding it to their tabs.

Ian took the next order and pushed Travis's words out of his mind. It was easier to forget what the others said, but Ian trusted Travis and it was harder not to feel some part of the words in his brain. Ian made the drinks, settling them on the waitress's tray, printing out the receipt to put under the edge of the glass.

When Ashley finally came in, his senses were tuned for it. He knew even before the door closed behind her she was in the building.

He looked up, giving her a smile, only she wasn't even looking at him. Her gaze traveled down the row of stools, her usual taken. It shouldn't be a big deal but tonight it looked as if it confused her.

He motioned to the opposite end of the bar where a person vacated a stool, the vinyl probably still warm from their ass. She nodded, making her way to it. Ian's gaze caught the clock. It was eleven-fifteen and she had been going since seven this morning.

He finished up with 'every night' Craig's beer, wondering if the man really didn't have a home to go to, then reached for Ash's glass.

He had the scotch poured at the place in front of the stool before she finished settling down.

"Hey," she smiled

He leaned onto the bar. "You look like shit."

Her lips managed to curl up at the sides. "Why, thank you. Thank you very much."

"Did you eat?"

She took a drink and he thought he probably should have asked her the dinner question before pouring the scotch.

"I had some old Chinese food that was in the refrigerator. I think there were noodles and some sort of meat in it."

"What time was that?"

She looked up at him. "I have no idea."

Ian moved to the window connecting to the kitchen putting in an order of a grilled chicken breast sandwich with fruit on the side. He came back to her.

"I missed your break," she said, sounding truly sad.

He shook his head. "I traded with Mike."

She perked up. "You did?"

He nodded. "It wasn't that hard."

"Yeah, but you did it."

"I got you a sandwich that will be up in a few minutes. Why don't you find a seat and I'll finish up back here and take my break when your food arrives."

There was a booth at the back of the room, in the dark corner. She slid in, placing her drink in front of her. But she didn't touch it. She leaned her head against the upholstered back and closed her eyes.

She was still in that position when he brought over the tray. He put down the plate, her Coke and his soda and lime. By the time the tray was on the table and he had taken the seat across from her, her eyes opened wide.

"Have you had any sleep?" He asked. The light overhead casted shadows onto her face. She looked worn out.

"I think I fell asleep in the car on the way to the morgue."

"Morgue?" he asked.

"It's a homicide investigation," she said. "Takes us all sort of places. Where are my onion rings?"

"Thought you needed fruit more."

"Onion rings taste better."

He wanted to laugh but decided against it.

"Eat your apples," he said. He picked up his soda, taking a slow drink. She picked up her fork and pushed the food around but didn't make much of an effort to enjoy it.

"Are you okay?" he asked her.

She cut off a corner of the sandwich and took a bite.

"Where you do live?" she asked as she chewed.

"A couple of miles from here."

"But you don't have a car," she said. He didn't ask her how she knew that.

"I have a bike chained out back."

She nodded, her lips pursed in what looked like approval. She took another bite of the sandwich.

"Four roommates?"

"Aye," he said. "You don't want to talk about today?"

Her gaze came up to skim his. She went back to concentrating on the grape she was trying to spear with her fork.

"Brothers or sisters?"

He took another drink of his soda. He had no problem with a round of twenty questions.

"Only child."

Another bite of the sandwich. And she hadn't touched the scotch. All this was good.

"Parents?"

"Had two."

The fork stopped and she looked up at him.

"I'm sorry," she said.

"It's been a long time."

"Still," she said.

"Are your parents alive?"

She nodded. "Sorta."

Interesting answer. "Are you close?"

"She lives in Chicago."

"Is that where you're from?"

Her gaze came up to his. "I was asking the questions."

"I don't get my turn?"

The breath came out hard, her fork and knife hitting the table. She reached for the glass of scotch and took a long, hard drink.

"Not tonight," she said.

"Okay."

"How old are you?"

"Twenty-nine last July."

But then she changed directions and he wasn't sure if he could keep up.

"I'm good at what I do," she said.

"I have no doubt."

Just like he didn't have a doubt she was totally clueless to what she was up against. This case was going to go on until it was over and it wasn't going to be her or any other law enforcer to decide when.

When she drank this time, it was only to take a sip. The glass stood half-full.

"That house you live in?" she asked.

"Aye?"

"Is it nice?"

He shrugged a shoulder. "It's big. It's got plenty of room for all of us."

"Is it like a frat house?"

He laughed and folded his arms over the edge of the table. "Not a whole lot of partying going on."

She picked up the knife and fork again and stared at her plate as she cut back into the sandwich.

"Is that where you're going tonight?"

He licked his lips. "I don't really know where I am supposed to go tonight."

She glanced up at him then back to her plate.

The silence was unnerving after the banter.

"I get off at one-thirty," he said. "By the time we get the last patron out the door and clean up and close out the register, it's usually well after two, two-thirty."

"That's late," she said.

"Aye, it is."

"I think your break is about up, too."

He looked over at the clock. She was right. He had to get back to work.

She reached in her front pocket, pulling out a single key. She placed it on the table, her finger over it sliding across to him. His eyes narrowed. His breathing became a little too hard. He pictured her curled up on one side of that great big bed, sound asleep while she waited for him to get in.

She pulled her hand back. "I can't sleep if the door is unlocked. It's a cop thing. I was thinking of the blue pair of pajamas tonight."

"How many pairs do you own?"

That almost got her to smile. "I don't even know."

"So we stay together long enough for me to see you in all of them."

Her gaze came up. "If I decide I'm having a good time, I could always buy more and not tell you."

He smiled at her, liking the idea.

Reaching for the key, he picked it up and closed his fist around it. It was warm. He picked his soda to give his hands something to do and took a drink. "I'll move my bike over to your place."

"There's a garage at the end of the drive. Combination to the lock is 11933."

"I can do that," he said.

"We've been going on fifteen hour days for the last fifteen days straight."

He didn't say anything.

"We're going to try again tomorrow for a day off. I mean shit, I have got to get some laundry done or I won't be able to go into work."

He chuckled. "Okay."

"Laundry can be done while popcorn is made and movies are playing."

"Ahh," he said, getting the connection.

She opened her purse but he put his hand out, stopping her.

"My treat," he said.

"You can't feed me every night."

"I've never done it before," he pointed out.

"Oh. That's right." She looked confused again and slid out of the booth.

She leaned over to whisper in his ear. "It's okay to wake me when you get in."

Like hell was he going to. At two-forty-five he stood over her side of the bed and watched her in the light streaming in from the bathroom. She was laying on her side, facing the outside of the bed, her knees slightly drawn up. With a mound of pillows under her head and her hands curled into soft fists in front of her, she looked too damn beautiful to shake awake.

He set the key down on the nightstand, beside her mobile phone. Checking, he made sure it was plugged in tonight. Then pulling his shirt over his head, he took off his shoes and socks and reached for the buttons on his jeans, folding all and placing them on the chair in the corner. When he stripped down to his boxers, he walked around to the opposite side of the bed, turning off the bathroom light as he went. He made sure the shades were drawn and pulled back the quilt and sheets.

She shifted the moment he lay beside her, rolling toward him. He settled back against the pillow while she rearranged herself up the length of his body, fitting him perfectly, his arm around her shoulders. He looked down and she was blinking up at him.

"Hey," he said.

"Hey," she sighed, relaxing against him, her cheek and hand on his chest.

"Go back to sleep," he whispered.

She stretched and adjusted her body. "Do you want to fool around?" she asked.

He looked down at her. "You should be asleep."

"I was waiting for you," she slurred in a whisper, settling more against him.

"I'm really tired," he lied. "How about I take a rain check for later?"

She fell asleep in his arms. She woke up with his hands on her body, pushing her pajama top over her head. His mouth crushed down on hers. Her whole body vibrated, his fingers pulling feelings from her she had never experienced.

He put his arms around her, rolling until she was on top of him where he slid his hands into her pants, pushing them off her hips. He rolled again, moving back on the bed to pull them off, dropping them on the floor.

He reached into the nightstand drawer and tore the wrapper with his teeth.

Her arms lay over her head, she watched him as he lowered himself to her. He moved slow, settling over her while she pulled in air over lungs stiff with wanting him.

His face directly in front of hers, his hair fell adorably into his eyes. With a hand braced on the mattress on either side of her, he flexed his hips and her head fell backwards, her moan slow and steady. She didn't blink. As long as he watched her, she watched him.

His movements were controlled, deep, his breathing hard, his breath on her face. Until finally, her eyes drifted shut.

"No," he said. "Watch me."

She looked back at him. So close, his five o'clock shadow highlighting his face. He leaned forward, kissing her with open lips.

"I want to see you," he said, searching her face.

She nodded her head and fought to keep her eyes open. It felt good. It felt so damn good, everything emphasized by his gaze on her.

"I want to see everything," he said.

"Okay," she said, her voice breathless.

He smiled at her. His hands moved to hold her head, brushing her hair away from her face.

"I think you're even more beautiful when I'm inside you."

She laughed a little, her head falling back, exposing her throat to him.

His face fell against it, his lips opening, sucking.

"I can't see you," she whispered.

His tongue pressed against her skin. He nipped. "I'll be right back," he said and she felt him laugh against her skin.

"Can I bite you?"

"Yes," she said. Her hands fanned over his back, moving down to hold his ass as he thrust.

His mouth opened on her neck. She felt the pressure as he bit. It felt better than she could have imagined.

His voice breathless, talking against her throat. "Can I leave a mark?"

She didn't even think. "Yes."

He clamped onto the spot on her neck, sucking hard until she felt it in every part of her body. It heightened her senses, making her feel everything else he was doing to her. She dragged her nails across his back.

He started moving faster, his breathing coming harder.

He broke off the sucking, shifting over her again. He put his hands back on her head, his fingers in her loose hair. "I want to do this together," he said. "Can we do that?"

She nodded slowly.

"Soon. I would really like to do it soon."

She raised her head off the pillow, kissing him. "I can do that."

Falling back she watched him as it came crashing toward him. She could see it on his face. The pleasure in his eyes, his mouth agape, his face tense as his whole body followed. He kept the rhythm steady, the pressure hard. She watched him as long as she could, until the feelings escalated off the charts. It hit her hard, harder than she could ever remember. Her eyes closed tight, his face buried in her neck again, his arms around her, pulling her close.

She exhaled and moved her hands slow, running them up his back, her fingers spread wide to feel him the most. Her breathing came down, returning to normal while her body still tingled.

He lowered himself onto her, his head resting on her shoulder, facing her. His eyes closed, a smile on his lips.

She pulled him to her, his head in the nook of her neck, he nipped again and she loved the feeling. Her fingers tangled in his hair. She laughed low and husky. "Good morning," she whispered.

He looked from her eyes to her lips and back again. His smile spread across his whole face. He laughed. "Good morning," he said. "I woke you up. You were supposed to sleep in this morning and I woke you up."

He looked down, staring at a place on her neck. Reaching up, he ran a finger over it.

His gaze shifted to hers.

"Proud of yourself?" she asked.

He smiled and nodded his head slow. "You don't have to work today."

"And make-up will cover it tomorrow."

He rolled away to the other side of the bed.

She turned her head to look at him.

"You want to sleep some more? I can make you breakfast." He didn't make any move to get up.

She shook her head. "I can wait."

He lay on his side, his head resting on his elbow and stared at her.

"What time did you get in?" she asked.

"After two."

"So you've had six hours sleep?"

"I don't usually get much more."

She rolled on to her side, the sheet pulled up high to cover her breasts.

Neither of them said anything for a long, long minute.

She reached up, tracing the tattoo circling his bicep. It was a piece of art, very beautiful and he wore it well.

"What's this mean?"

He looked at it and then back at her. He tapped on it. "That is a creole spell designed to be a Celtic armband just for me by a creole witch named Nanette in New Orleans."

She would have laughed except for the expression on his face. "You're serious?"

He raised his eyebrows and nodded his head. "It's to protect me from the sun."

"The sun is out to get you?"

"I've got a sun allergy. It's why I live here."

"Does it work? Having Celtic ink scares it away?"

He looked at it again. "I don't think it hurts."

"What happens if you go into the sun?"

"Direct? It can get pretty bad. Scaling. Blisters. Some bleeding if it's too long."

"Ouch," she said.

"You learn to live with it."

He kept his hands on his side of the bed. She kept hers on hers.

She rearranged the pillows under her head, stacking them high while he watched. She grabbed one and hugged it to her chest, burrowing her face until only her eyes showed. She raised her head so she could speak. "I told you I like pillows."

"I noticed," he said. His smile lighting up his face.

She reached over and fingered the earring in his ear. "I bet it's Celtic, too. Like your rings. Do you miss it?"

"Scotland?"

She nodded.

"It's been so many years since I was there it's more of a concept than a memory."

"You came over a long time ago?"

"Aye. A lot of years."

"Do you want to go back?"

"I don't know," he said. "It would be so different. I don't have any family there anymore so I would be going back to see places that I may or may not remember."

"But you're obviously proud of it."

He screwed up his face and shook his head. "Naw. I just think it looks cool."

She laughed. He wrapped an arm around her waist and pulled her close. She giggled the whole way. He kissed her on her neck.

"How did you end up behind the bar?"

He kissed her again. "I'm busy here and you're interrupting."

Still laughing, she pushed on his shoulders.

He shifted his head, relaxing. He didn't hesitate in answering. "Seemed like a good job to get into. Like the nights and works out well with the sunlight thing. Pays pretty good."

"Really?" she asked.

He nodded, not looking the least bit offended by the question. "I do pretty well, but then, I don't need much. And I like the people."

She lay there, listening to his words, hearing the accent behind them, wondering what it had been like for him to grow up so far away.

"They all have stories," he said. "Sometimes you can get them to tell you without any trouble. Sometimes there's the hard cases, like you, where you have to work at it."

"I was a hard case?"

"There are two types of women who come into a bar late at night. Those who are looking for attention and those who want to be left alone. You wanted to be left alone so I bothered you anyway."

She smiled. When he reached over to brush the hair out of her face, she smiled even more.

His eyes sparkled like they always did. "What made you become a cop?"

He could fire off questions to catch her off guard when other people she found predictable. "What?"

He didn't repeat the question.

"We were talking about you."

"Now we're talking about you. I don't know much about what you do but I do know there is an edge to you that I don't see in other people."

"What's that supposed to mean?"

"You see things I don't think you expected to see. Hear about things that shock you after everything that has come through your office. And then, you can't even talk about them to a friend so you carry it all around inside you."

He was right. It made her uneasy but he was so right.

"I have Hunter."

"I think you need more."

More sounded good. A nice weekly support group she could go to with a plate full of brownies and talk about what deviance she had seen. Hunter would sit to her right and the other cops to her left. They could compare stories and see who was worse.

His hand came up, brushing across her forehead. "You see too much."

"My dad was a cop," she said, closing her eyes.

"Was he a good one?"

"No," she said, pausing. It was too early in their relationship to bring up shit. "He drank too much and hit too often."

Ian's fingertip stilled on her skin. His gaze came up slowly to hers. "He hit you?"

"He hit pretty much anything that came within reach."

"I don't like that."

The seriousness of his tone thundered in a quiet storm.

He brushed his knuckles on her cheek where her dad had stuck as if Ian knew where the fist had landed.

Snuggling back into her pillow, she held it close.

"I figured I could become a victim or a success story and do something about assholes like him."

"Where is he? Chicago?"

She shook her head against the pillow. "About ten years ago he hit a guy in a bar. Guy hit back this time, busted a pool cue over his head. My father died instantly."

"So who's in Chicago?"

"My mom and little sister."

"Are you close?"

"Not really. Do you want to have sex again?"

She liked it when she caught him off guard. He looked flustered and embarrassed and hot all at the same time. He scooted closer to her, his arm coming out to circle her waist. He kissed on the side of her mouth. "I'm going to have to go home today."

She hated the idea but suspected it wasn't a bad one.

"Need to get a change of clothes for one."

"Naw. You miss Jason and Travis."

He laughed and rolled on his back. "I can promise you. I never miss Jason."

He felt good next to her. "I'm going to spend the day in my pajamas," she said, realizing how good that really sounded.

He rolled until he was beside her, his finger tracing the mark on her neck again. He stared at it. "Do you have a tank top that goes with those bottoms?" His gaze came up to look at her.

"Want to view your handiwork?"

His grin bordered on adolescent and she loved it.

"You can put your hair up," he said.

"I think you might be thirteen years old."

He leaned over and kissed the spot. "It tastes good right there," he said, his finger touching it.

He laughed and rolled away, reaching over to his phone, picking it up, hitting the button to fire it up. He leaned back against the pillows, the sheet to his waist, his chest with its silver chain and Celtic knot lying there for her to appreciate.

"What are you doing?"

"Weather report. I can check the Internet to see what the cloud cover will be today."

"That's pretty cool."

He fiddled with the button. "And today–we have total sunshine, high temperatures and no clouds." He looked at her. "What are the chances?"

"You made that up."

He showed her the phone and there was a bright, full-animated sun staring at her.

"What does that mean?" she asked.

"I can ride home on my bike but I will probably pay for it later."

"I could drive you," she offered.

"You're not driving me anywhere on your day off. I can handle this. I've done it before."

"How?"

"Cover up. Jacket. Hat. Gloves. It will be okay."

"Or you could stay here and I can wash your clothes with mine."

He liked the idea. Had been hoping for that idea to come up.

"We still have *The Hobbit*," she said. "Three hours of uninterrupted time sitting on the couch with a bowl of popcorn. Do you like microwave or fresh with butter?"

"Fresh with butter." He said it as if it had been a stupid question.

"I have a popcorn maker and a stick of butter."

"You want me to sit around naked while you pop popcorn and we watch hobbits run around?"

"Actually," she said. "There's only one hobbit. The rest are dwarves. And a wizard."

She was avoiding the first half of his statement.

"And believe it or not, I think I might have a pair of sweats that will fit you."

"Really? Roger's?"

"On sale when I needed to paint the inside of the house."

"You have this all planned?"

"Making it up as I go."

The afternoon went off without a hitch. The sweats she had picked up were big enough for a man but a little too small for him. The Hard Rock Chicago shirt she loaned him, though an extra-large for her, was too tight. He didn't mind either one.

Not when she sat right beside him, her knitting basket next to her, her project in her lap.

He watched her watch the movie, her fingers working while she paid attention to the screen.

"What are you making?"

"Sweater for Hunter for Christmas."

"You make sweaters? For people?" The envy inched up fast.

She looked up at him while she still worked. "Yes."

He glanced behind them on the back of the couch. He pulled the afghan down, looking at the texture and the cabling in design, the mixture of colors that matched the room.

"You made this?" he asked.

She smiled and kept working. "Do you want one?"

"Do I want one? An afghan like this? This is gorgeous."

"What color is your room?"

"Blue. And black."

She nodded her head, put Hunter's sweater away and got up off the couch, moving to the second bedroom.

He paused the movie and tried to see down the hall.

She came back a few minutes later with a different knitting bag, and settled beside him on the couch while he watched.

She pulled the afghan over both their laps. She snuggled in a little bit next to him and pulled out blue and black yarn, a set of needles and started on the first stitches while he watched.

She nodded toward the buttons. "Movie?"

"I don't suppose you would marry me, would you?" he asked.

She laughed softly. "I usually try to date a guy at least a week before agreeing to that."

"You have a yarn store in your second bedroom?"

"Well stocked closet. Collecting is a compulsion. Do not ever take me to a yarn store and let me use your credit card."

Wrapping his hand around her neck, he pulled her over and kissed her.

"You don't have to do this," he whispered in her ear.

"It is the one thing I seriously enjoy and I do run out of ideas for projects. And, if you dump me before it's done, I will just have to give it to Jason." She smiled up at him.

He leaned over to kiss her deep while reaching for the remote by feel and finding the right one with his thumb. Bilbo Baggins started moving across the screen.

When the beep for the washer or dryer sounded, they paused the movie in domestic bliss, the house smelling of fabric softener and folded the load before hitting play.

"What do you want for dinner?" she asked when the final credits rolled by.

He looked at the clock. It was almost five and he had to be at work by six.

"Aren't you out of everything?" he asked.

"Mostly. But pizza delivers. Or Chinese."

"You were supposed to get provisions today."

"I can do it later."

"In your free time, right?" he asked.

Instead of answering him, she picked up the empty bowl of popcorn and the two empty Coke cans and took them to the kitchen. He picked up his would be afghan. She already had inches done on it.

It was a cute house, he thought as he followed her. Wood floors, with plaster walls painted a pale blue. Her taste in furniture leaned toward simple and clean lines. The pillows on the dark brown couch were floral adding a flare of color. It was small, only two bedrooms.

She dropped the Coke cans into the recycling bin and put the bowl in the otherwise clean kitchen sink.

His clothes hung over the back of her dining room chair. His jeans, boxers, T-shirt and flannel. Even his socks were matched. They didn't do fabric softener at the house. Feeling the laundry he was wondering why.

"Are you coming in tonight?" he asked.

She opened the refrigerator and peered inside.

"That would require me to get out of my pajamas." There was humor in her tone.

"Not a bad idea," he said. He leaned up against the doorway, folding his arms over his chest. She had stayed in the pajama bottoms, donned the white tank top and clipped her hair up. She did everything he asked and he could see his mark. He got a smile by thinking about it.

She stood up with a bottle of high-end ginger ale.

"I actually have some work to do."

"It's your day off," he pointed out.

"Some of us don't get full days."

"You are. Today." He said as if it was a fact. "You'll be better tomorrow if you give tonight a rest. Come down at ten-thirty. I'll get the cook to make you something special."

"Don't you have to go home?"

He sighed. "Aye. I thought I should head on home tonight."

She looked at her bottle and not at him. "Will you be back?"

"I think assuming I was invited back would be a little presumptuous."

"So I should, what? Start dropping all those stitches I put in and rewind the yarn into a ball?"

She took a drink and smiled over the bottle.

"You're holding my afghan hostage?" He started to move toward her.

He liked the way she fidgeted. She shifted from one foot to the other and her face glowed. He glanced up at the clock. If he rushed, he could walk the distance to the bar in under five minutes. Five minutes to dress. That gave him plenty of time with her to do all the things he was thinking about doing. And so what if he was a few minutes late. Mike would never mind.

Bike would be here, of course, in the garage. He would just have to come back and get it.

And if he happened to get side-tracked picking it up he would have to figure out another way to get home tomorrow.

He reached, wrapping an arm around her waist, pulling her close while she giggled. He kissed his mark on her neck, positive it tasted better than anywhere. That laugh, he thought as he leaned forward. Sexy as hell.

CHAPTER FOUR

Ten-thirty-five came and Ash sat in her favorite booth with a basket of onion rings in front of her, a Coke beside it.

Ian was across from her, sipping on his soda and lime. He never drank on the job. In the weeks they had been together, she had seen him at home enjoy a bottle of wine, but when he was here, it was always soda and lime

A man walked in. She noticed him because he was so damn tall, topping six three at least. Italian good looks with his dark hair brushed away from his face, he had light skin and pretty light brown eyes that looked dark in the dimly lit room.

He walked straight up to the edge of their table.

Ian did a classic double take, his gaze fixing on the strangers'. "What are you doing here?"

"You haven't been home in a few days. Thought I would swing by and check up on you, maybe meet your new girlfriend."

Ashley saw Ian smile. He motioned with his hand between them. "Ashley Barrow. Travis Ricci."

"Ahh," she smiled. "I didn't recognize you without you sticking out your tongue." Ashley extended her hand, taking his in a firm handshake, genuinely happy to meet one of Ian's friends.

Ian motioned to the bar. "Do you want something?"

81

"Sure," he said. "A bottle of something German."

"Got it." Ian slid out of the booth and headed to the bar.

"Do you mind?" Travis said motioning to the spot vacated by Ian.

"Not at all."

He took off his leather coat and tossed it to the far side, sliding in.

"Did you ride your bike here?" she asked.

"There's this thing? Came out a few years ago? I drive one a little more current."

She smiled, looking him up and down, leaning over to look at his feet and traveling his whole body.

She looked him back in the face, smiling. "High-end Lexus or mid-range American Muscle. Neutral color. Seat all the way back, for sure. Playlist? Opera but I don't know which one."

She sat back while he laughed.

"I think that might have been a little scary," he said.

Ian set out a coaster on the table, set the bottle and glass down then motioned to Ashley to scoot over. "What's scary?"

"She nailed my car when it's parked a block from here."

"You call him Stuart," she said to Travis.

"Everyone calls him Stuart. It's his name."

"I don't."

82

Ian folded his arms on the tabletop and looked up at his friend. "She doesn't." His smile teased.

Travis Ricci ignored the glass and took a shallow drink of his beer from the bottle. "Okay," he said. "That's one Ian for you and a shitload of Stuarts for the rest of the world."

Ian reached up and took an onion ring, smiling as he ate it.

She looked at the man across from her. Thirty-five maybe. Very sure of himself. She would bet money the two of them went back far enough to make their bond unbreakable.

"So what do you do Travis? Can I call you Travis?"

He nodded. "I'm the night manager at the Bell Rouge Hotel and Spa over on Gramercy."

"Really," she said. Ian sat next to her, watching her talk. "That's got to bring you in contact with a whole bunch of interesting people."

"We get our share," Travis said.

"How many languages do you speak?"

"What?" he asked with a laugh.

She picked an onion ring and grinned as she ate it.

"Why would you ask me that?"

"She's got a Masters in Criminal Justice from Portland U with a minor in psychology and she profiles at work. Don't ask stupid questions." Ian laughed.

"I manage okay with Spanish and some French, but not fluent enough to make it really count."

"Liar," Ian laughed.

Travis glared at him and Ian ignored it.

"This guy?" Ian said. "He learned Italian just so that he could read *Dante's Inferno* in its original language."

"It was a minor setback in getting my hands on a good book."

"And German. And Russian. And that brief stint you took into Japanese. Those were all minor setbacks, too?"

Travis picked up an onion ring and threw it at Ian, making Ash laugh.

"That is pretty amazing. You're one of those people who picks up languages."

"I'm okay with it and does shit for work and I don't even get compensated."

"You take me to Europe and get me into all the museums and I will see that you are well compensated."

Travis leaned forward, his smile wide. "But we get to stay out of Scotland."

"I can work with that."

Ian's arm came around her neck and pulled her against him. "You even think about working with that and we might have words."

"Travis," she laughed hard against Ian's chest. "I think we're going to Scotland."

Ian leaned over to whisper to her. "Not what I meant and you know it." He kissed her by her ear and kept an arm on her shoulders.

Travis took two swallows of his beer and glanced at the clock. "Your break is about up, *Iaaan.*"

"I'll take more," Ian said letting her go to sit back straight. "Mike won't mind."

"Think of all those tips you will lose."

"I'll survive."

Travis looked at Ashley. "I'm thinking he doesn't want us talking alone."

"What could we possibly say that he wouldn't want us to share?" Ash smiled.

Ian pursed his lips and nodded his head.

Ian's hand came down on her knee, squeezing playfully. She giggled at the tickle and tried to move away. He wasn't letting her go anywhere.

"Can I see your gun?" Travis asked.

"No."

"Your badge?"

"No."

85

"Oh come on. It's only a badge."

"And it's not here. It's at the house."

"Which means I can see it tonight," Ian said.

She half expected him to stick his tongue out at Travis. They were close. Brother close.

"How long have you known each other?"

Travis took a drink of his beer. "Seems like almost a hundred years."

She saw Ian cock his head at him and give him a sarcastic, ha ha smile.

"Where did you meet?" she asked.

Ian's hand stilled on her knee. "San Francisco."

"I love San Francisco," she said. "Beautiful city especially down by the Fisherman's Wharf. Best food." She sighed and looked at Ian. "What were you doing there?"

"Not enjoying the food on The Fisherman's Wharf, that's for sure. I was working a dive bar in Chinatown for almost no wages and getting shit tips but talk about oddballs."

"Is that where you met?"

"No. Night class in philosophy," Travis said with a straight face.

Ian actually laughed out loud. "It was English 101 you asshole. Stop teasing her."

"Why were you taking English?"

Travis cleared his throat. "I was trying to finish my AA."

Ian leaned his shoulder against hers and turned to talk directly to her. "I wanted my AA, too."

"Did you get it?"

He shook his head. "Night classes were too hard with my work schedule. But I did meet him," he said pointing at Travis. "We got an apartment. Moved in together..."

"Picked up girls," Travis interjected.

"Picked up a few girls," Ian smiled. "That was sort of it and we've been getting apartments ever since."

"And picking up girls?" she laughed.

"Aye," Ian said, drawing out the word. "We might have picked up one or two along the way." He leaned over and kissed her on the shoulder.

"It sounds as if the two of you have been making good use of your free time."

Travis smiled. "Some of those girls were pretty damn hot."

"A man with principles and respect. I love those qualities," she laughed. "Where have you been all my life?"

Travis laughed loud.

"Don't you have someplace to be?" Ian asked him.

"Are you ever planning on heading on home?"

"Sure. Probably tomorrow. I need a change of clothes. And by the way, next time you're at the store, get some fabric softener. Stuff is amazing."

"What?" Travis laughed.

"That's F-A-B-R ..."

Another onion ring flew.

"You better get back to work," Travis said, pushing his beer away. He reached over and picked up his coat.

"Don't go because he kicked you out," Ashley said.

Travis stood up. "He couldn't kick me out if he got help and tried. I'm bigger and faster and better."

She laughed at the expression Ian gave him.

"But," he said, "I do have to go into work tonight. Like I said, I wanted to make sure Stuart here was okay and get a chance to meet you, *mia bella.*"

"You've met me," she said, smiling.

"Yes, I have. Pretty impressed, too. I'll have to pass on raving reviews to everyone else in the house. Let them know you invited me to Europe, promising sexual favors to repay the hardship."

"Would I have to offer them sexual favors?" she asked, smiling up at him.

Travis nodded at Ian. "Only if you want to see his blood pressure go up."

He reached out and took her hand, kissing the back while Ian growled. "It was a pleasure meeting you," he said.

"You, too."

Ian stood up. "I'll walk you out." Then he looked back at Ash. "You'll wait?"

She picked up an onion ring and nodded her head.

While they wandered away, she got out her phone, bringing up an Internet translator. *Mia Bella* meant *My Beautiful*.

Smiling as she got an onion ring, she was thinking she could live with that.

The two men disappeared out the door

Ian walked all the way to Travis's car before he said a word.

"What was that about?"

"She doesn't know about you."

"No, she's doesn't"

"Sparks fly off the two of you like fireworks. You really think you can keep that a secret from her? She nailed my car by *looking* at me."

"Guys car, one thing. Creatures that don't exist? Not thinking she is heading that way."

"And if she does?" Travis asked.

Ian half turned to stare at him with his hands in his pockets.

"Do you have a plan if she asks the wrong question because I just spent a grand total of twenty minutes with the two of you and I'm not seeing a light, little romance going on here."

Ian stood there silent.

"How many pages does she fill up on that list in your head?"

Ian turned to face him.

"All five," Travis said. "She fills up all five pages of everything you ever wanted in a woman. Shit, Stuart. I've watched you search for almost sixty years."

"Are you trying to make a point because I'm not seeing this conversation going very far."

"She is sweet, though," Travis smiled. "Funny and quick. With the charge coming off the two of you the sex has to be astronomical."

"You think this is about sex?"

"Hell no. I've known you too long. But I'm thinking it can't be hurting all that much."

"I got to get back."

"Your break is over. Are you going to be home tomorrow?"

"Aye, I will come home tomorrow. But I'm not promising anything past that. I like it over here."

"Waking up beside her every morning? What's not to like?"

Travis hit the car remote of his Camaro—the mid-range American muscle. Grey. About as neutral as it got. He refused to think about the *Rigoletto* in his CD player.

He stopped before getting in. "I like her," he said.

Ian smiled. "I'm glad. So do I."

"Do you know how much she would fit in at the house?"

Ian sighed. "Thought crossed my mind."

"We put a muzzle on Jason, tie him to a stake in the backyard and she would probably be pretty safe." Travis laughed.

"Irishman's a lot of things. Poacher is not one."

"Why does she call you Ian? No one else does that."

He shrugged. "It's my name?" he suggested.

"I think your mother was the last person to call you that."

Ian looked out over the parking lot. "I don't know," he said. "It sorta came out."

"You like how she says it," he said with a grin.

Ian nodded nice and slow, a smile on his lips.

"That's almost sentimental."

Ian shrugged again.

"You're a damn good artist," Travis said.

Ian laughed. "Okay."

"That drawing you did of her? No way did you do her justice. I mean like capital Wow. And you're sleeping with that?"

He smiled ear to ear as he got in the car and pulled the door shut.

CHAPTER FIVE

"I have something for you," she whispered. He opened his eyes, her whole face taking up his field of vision.

Laying on her bed, her a hell of a lot closer to naked than him, they hadn't taken too much time before they had started their night off with a bang. His breathing still hard, his body still feeling the weak, tingling that let him know it had been good, he smiled at her next to him.

"No need," he joked. "This was quite enough, thank you."

She smiled and pushed on his shoulder. He rolled away pausing to pull her skirt down and cover her discreetly. He cleaned himself up and arranged his pants, zipping them up while she leaned over to the nightstand. The drawer slid open, she reached in and the drawer slid closed. She lay down beside him, still sideways on the bed. He grabbed two pillows and put them under their heads.

"Here," she said. She held up her hand.

He reached up, taking the plain silver key from her. He felt the cool metal in his fingers. He rubbed it back and forth with his thumb, looking at it, measuring the significance.

She watched him. "Works on the back door if you want to come in that way after putting your bike away."

"You're sure about this?" he asked, watching her face.

"There's a toothbrush for you to in the bathroom. It's blue."

He stood up suddenly, but she didn't ask any questions. One look at her face told him she was as nervous to give it as he was to receive. He walked to the kitchen and his leather coat, reaching into the pocket.

She waited for him on the bed when he came back in with his key ring, winding his new toy onto it to hang next to his key to Cooper's, his key to his house.

The phone on her nightstand vibrated. She ignored it for three times, before her hand finally slammed down on it.

"Hello?" He watched her put her forearm over her eyes.

"Okay," she said.

He gazed at her, watching as everything he had ignited in her just a few minutes ago seemed to be going out. The thought of the key in his pocket made his mood a little better, but it didn't save it.

"How soon?" she asked. She nodded instead of saying good-bye.

She lay on her back, her eyes closed. Ian watched her. Waited.

She finally turned her head towards his, her eyes sad. "I have to go."

"You have the day off," he said, already knowing it wasn't going to make a difference.

"Dinner is pretty much done," she said. "You can go ahead and eat."

"What about you?"

She checked her watch. "I don't think I have time."

"How long?"

"Fifteen."

He sighed heavily and pursed his lips, giving her a nod.

She didn't make a move to get up.

He kissed her again, harder this time with more aggression. She took it and gave back as much.

She pushed on his chest and moved to her closet. He lay on the bed, waiting as she rummaged through her clothes. She came out carrying an outfit, complete with her boots. Instead of the bathroom where she had hidden the first time they did this, she dropped everything on top of the bed. She stripped down naked then walked to the dresser to get a bra and panties, pulling them both on while he braced his arms behind his head and watched.

There was a domestic bliss in the way she was so comfortable with him.

"You know where you're going?"

"Yeah," she said, pulling on her shirt.

"You know what's waiting for you?"

Her hands paused then went back to work. "Yes, I do."

"Are you going to tell me?"

She sighed but didn't look at him. "You know I can't."

"Who would know?" he pushed.

She didn't answer. She finished with the clothes, got the gun out of the nightstand, strapping it on and slipped her badge into her pocket.

He got up off the bed and went to the kitchen. Working fast, he put a plate together for her then set it in the microwave. When the timer went off he set it on the table and called her.

She peeked in. "You made me dinner?"

"Not rocket science, Ash."

She took a chair then looked up at him. "That was some of the best sex I've ever had."

That got his back to stand a little taller, the pride to set a little deeper.

"Considering some of our past sex, I'm surprised you're still breathing."

She smiled and nodded slowly.

She finished the tacos and the beans and took the plate to the sink while she drank the lemonade standing. She set everything down.

She kissed him full on the mouth.

There was a honk in the front yard. She kissed him again, grabbed her keys and headed out the front door.

Ian debated whether he should call Travis and tell him there had been another one but figured he didn't have enough information to pass along. He concentrated on cleaning the kitchen and getting dinner put away. His watch told him he had to be at work in an hour. There wasn't anywhere near an hours work to be done so he got a beer out of the refrigerator and plopped down in front of the TV to dial hop while he waited.

The night at Cooper's went slow. With the regulars telling their stories, Ian tried to stay focused but when ten-thirty came and went and there was no Ash, he lost what attention he had. At one-thirty Mike told him to get out of there, that he would clean-up.

His bike was already in Ash's garage so he went out the front door and walked the two blocks. Using his key, he let himself in to the dark house. He moved quietly.

She was in bed, lying on her side. Her pillow cuddled.

"Are you awake?" he whispered.

She took in a deep breath, released the pillow and rolled onto her back, an arm flung above her head. "Yeah."

"You didn't come in tonight. I was worried."

"I didn't want to see people."

He motioned over his shoulder with his thumb. "Do you want me to go? Let you get some sleep?"

She shook her head while she stretched. "You're not people."

"I'm not," he laughed.

"You're the reason I sleep now."

Simple words felt with the impact of a freight train. She threw back the covers of the bed exposing his side and patted the mattress.

"Come on," she said.

He stripped down, dropping everything but his boxers on the ground then went in the bathroom to use his blue toothbrush. A minute later, he crawled in beside her and pulled the quilts back up over them both, tucking her in.

She slid up beside him, cuddling against the whole length of him, her hand on his chest.

It felt perfect.

"How was it tonight?" she asked.

"Long. I didn't take my break so I could get out of there quicker."

He waited for her to talk. The dark had a way of making people open up when they usually didn't.

"I have to go to work tomorrow."

Tomorrow was Sunday. Pointing it out wasn't going to help.

"What time?" he asked.

"I can go in about nine. We had a late night and I can steal an extra hour in the morning."

He rubbed her hair under his hand, waiting for her to go on.

"I have to start sifting through the evidence. It should start to trickle in about noon. There will be reports to file and photos to look at, the morgue to visit."

"Sounds like a fun day."

She blinked at him twice, and then watched him in the dark.

He rolled so he could be closer. He put a hand to her face. "Shh. Don't think about it."

"I don't want to think about it but it's there."

He kissed her on her cheek, on her forehead. He wanted so bad to make it all go away.

"Do you want to fool around?" he asked her.

Laughing, she put her head back against the pillows. "No," she said. "Sorry."

"It's okay," he said.

"Do *you* want to fool around?"

"After getting turned down by you?" he smiled.

She laughed again and he loved the sound. It meant the worst of her storm might be over. He shifted, pinning her under him, his legs entwined with hers down the middle of their bed. He braced a hand on the mattress on either side of her. Her face right in front of his, he lowered his lips until they covered hers, her mouth warm and open and welcoming.

She pulled away and he lifted his head back while staying close enough to feel her breath.

Her arms moved to his back, her hands flattening out. She licked her lips and took a deep breath.

"I have never cared for anyone as much as I care for you," she whispered.

He pulled back further, feeling the words travel across his body. Air caught in his lungs and he had trouble exhaling.

He reached up, brushing her hair away from her face. He could see it in her eyes. She expected nothing in return. But her face held uncertainty going deep. Insecurity wasn't something he ever saw in her, but he saw it now and the question of its origin nagged at the back of his brain.

"Has anyone ever told you how incredible you are?" he asked.

The shake of her head was barely noticeable.

Leaning forward he kissed her thoroughly, showed her with his body his words were true. He pulled away to whisper in her ear. "You are all mine in every aspect of the word. Can I…" he whispered. "…make love to you?"

Needing to see her expression as well as hear her words he looked her in the face, her eyes, open and damp.

He brushed a thumb along her bottom lashes, picking up the moisture. "Hey," he whispered. "What's wrong?"

She shook her head. "I've never had anyone say anything like that to me."

He smiled and kissed her gently. "I am crazy about you in ways you can't even imagine. No woman has ever meant as much to me as you."

She reached up to play with the hair in his eyes. "Have you ever been in love?"

They hadn't been talking about love and the change of direction seemed serious. He would let her have it as long as she had that look in her eyes.

"No," he said. "I've had women I was fond of. Some whose company I enjoyed. But never in love."

"Me neither. Always seemed to date losers until of late." She smiled at him and he loved the sight.

He hadn't been sure he would be able to find it tonight and tonight, she needed it.

"You're too strong to fall for a loser."

She shrugged. "Ninety percent of strong is bullshitting people."

He shook his head. "I see a confident woman who doesn't take shit from anyone."

She smiled sadly. "That was nice. Thank you."

"You don't believe me."

"I might have a little more inside information than you. It's still nice to hear."

He blew out a breath. "Ashley," he sighed. "I'm going to have to work on changing your mind."

He settled further onto her, bringing his hands close to hold her, his face right in front of hers. "Starting right now." He leaned closer, his mouth over hers. "I'm going to kiss you. Is that alright?"

She wiggled against him. Her hands moved over his back in a sensual caress. Breathing a little harder, he moved his face lower, his tongue drawing a pattern on the special spot on her neck. He stopped to suck lightly.

"You said no tonight," he whispered against her neck. "Are you saying yes, now?"

She wrapped a hand around his head, her fingers in his hair and pulled him so that her mouth sat right beside his ear.

"Yes," she whispered, her breath causing a chill that made him shudder.

CHAPTER SIX

Tuesday night, and it was only six-thirty when Ashley pulled her car into her driveway.

She looked at her watch. She must have just missed him. Coopers had only been open a half-hour, much too early for her to go in. She would distract him from his work and she knew that wasn't fair to him, no matter how much she would enjoy it herself.

Letting herself into the house, she sat her purse and jacket onto the counter and moved to the bedroom. He had made the bed as always. Her clothes were picked up off the floor and the items on her dresser were neatly arranged. She smiled, thinking about him here all day by himself. Messes were something he couldn't stand and if one appeared, he was the man to clean it up.

She took off her badge and gun and slipped them both into the nightstand drawer

Moving to the closet, she pushed dresses across the rod, looking for the perfect one to wear tonight. Modest, with an edge of sex to it.

She found one. Gauze and full of color, it hung just to above her knees. It would hug her waist and the cleavage would be low. She laid it on the bed, got a pair of sandals to go with it, and then sat them on the floor.

She went to the kitchen to see what leftovers were in the refrigerator. Not finding anything exciting, she checked the freezer

and settled on a fettuccine TV dinner. She cut the slit on the top
and put it in the microwave.

Going to the bathroom, she scrubbed off her work make-up
and plugged in her electric curlers. Taking a brush to her hair, she
got rid of the day at work.

The microwave dinged. By the time she was done with the
almost palatable food, the curlers were ready. She set her hair and
went to work on her new make-up. She was going for hot and
smoky. Picking out a deeper shade of pink lipstick than she usually
wore she tried the look on in the mirror. She finished her hair,
applied enough hairspray to seal a leaky dam and then sprayed
herself with his *Chanel #5.*

She checked the clock. There were still two hours to kill
before she could go in.

And it had been a month, at least, since she did any online
shopping. She dropped herself behind her computer and opened
her favorite sites. Done with that in forty-five with several new
pajama sets on their way that didn't fall into the 'flannel with
matching slipper' definition, she had a feeling he might be happy.
Getting up, she moved to the TV to kill time watching while
working on his afghan.

At nine-thirty, she locked the door behind her and headed out
toward the pub.

The chill in the night air mixed with dampness. Clouds hung
in the sky, blocking out the moon. Everything seemed alive.

When she came in early, his gaze snapped up like he could
feel her in the room. He tilted his head at her and checked his
silver watch.

104

She smiled and pointed to the booth in the back.

He nodded and went back to his customers.

Watching him now was as much fun as watching him when they had first started out.

Rita approached the booth. "Hey, you're early," she said. "He doesn't get a break for another hour."

Ashley liked that the other woman put them together. It seemed to matter more when people noticed.

"I can wait," she smiled.

"Scotch?"

"No," she smiled. "Strawberry Daiquiri."

Rita laughed as she took the order. She headed over to the bar and put it in.

Ian looked past Rita to give Ash a look of mock shock, his hands coming out. He mouthed the word 'What?' and she smiled.

He laughed and went back to his work, giving all the attention to his customers. He listened when they talked and he filled their drinks when they pushed their glass forward.

What would he do, she wondered, if he didn't have to work anymore. If he found out there was more to the house and to her than he knew.

Ashley had a secret.

She didn't have to work. She kept her job because there was a time when she loved it. She didn't love it anymore. She may finally put to use the money in the bank that Gr'pa Jackson had left her. What she didn't know is how Mr. Stuart would react.

She saw him sneak peeks at her, a smile on his lips. When she caught him staring at her for longer than half a minute, he had a curious look on his face, like maybe he was enjoying what he saw.

She nursed three daiquiris to the bottom before he was able to step back and pass the customers off to Mike. He got his soda and lime and bee-lined for the table, dramatically counting the glasses in front of her that he had filled with a heavy hand on the rum.

"What's up?" he asked. He stopped to lean over and kiss her on the corner of her mouth.

"Nothing," she smiled, feeling the drinks. "There was nothing to do at the house."

He slid into the booth across from her. "Daiquiris? Really?" He laughed. "You look amazing," he said. "What's the occasion?"

The compliment and the tone traveled to her every nerve. She sat up straighter and tried to brush it off. But the truth was, the words from him were more important than anyone else.

She shrugged. "Felt like it."

He took in a deep breath and let it out slow. "You're up to something."

"Me?"

He nodded his head slow, his fingers around his glass. He looked so damn good and she didn't think it had much to do with the lighting. His T-shirt was black, very plain, the sleeves riding high enough on his arms to show off the tattoo on his bicep. His hair fell forward, a strand on his forehead. He had his three rings on, as usual, but he had donned a bracelet she didn't see very often. It was on his left wrist. Leather, with silver inlay. Everything he wore showed pride in a heritage he never discussed.

"I missed you."

He shook his head. "Nope. Not buying it." He leaned forward and crossed his arms on the table. "Spill."

"You went to the other house today?" she asked.

He drank his soda. "Aye."

"You came straight here."

"That's right. I have the backpack in the backroom."

"You didn't go to the house first."

"Why?" he laughed.

"Your bike is here."

He tilted his head at her. "Aye," he said dramatically. "My bike is here."

"It's not at the house?"

"It's not at the house," he said.

She stood up. "Show me?"

He looked at her standing beside the table. His gaze started at her sandals and traveled all the way up her legs to the dress and her cleavage. He didn't take long to do it, but he did take in the full picture.

"Show you what?" He asked looking her in the eye while he licked his lips.

"I want to see your bike."

"You've seen my bike."

"I've never seen it up close."

"Now?" he asked.

She held her hand out for him to take. He reached up and took it. She pulled him along, out the front door and down the alleyway. Mike's black Silverado sat where it always was. The backyard stood empty. They couldn't even hear the music coming from inside. Ian moved to the water pipe on the other side of the truck.

"I have no idea what you are up to, but I am dying to find out," he said.

The bike was chained right where it always was.

She moved to stand beside it. "This is it?" she asked.

He opened his arms wide. "This is it."

"It's blue."

"Aye," he said, "It's blue." She felt his gaze on her like a caress.

"Blue's my favorite color."

"What a coincidence. It's my favorite color, too," he said.

Her smile grew as she reached out to run her hand over the bike's seat.

"It's a nice one. "

"Not top of the line," he said. "Mid-range. Have to go with what I can afford."

"What's it made out of?"

"Carbon fiber. Makes it light."

"I bet you can take it apart."

"Aye"

"And put it back together."

"Aye."

"And I bet you have a whole bunch of spare parts at the house and a little tool kit you carry in case something goes wrong."

"Aye, to both."

She leaned over, looking at the gears inside. Besides the peddles and the chain she was clueless.

"Works, though."

"Aye, Ash. It works. Why are we out here?" He folded his arms against the chill. He only had on the T-shirt and it wasn't enough. The damp made goose-bumps rise on his arms.

"I wanted to see your bike. It's important to you."

"You've seen it and I'm not believing a whole hell of a lot what you are saying right now."

She bit the corner of her lip and reached up, taking him by the hand. She walked around the corner of the building to the back, facing the hill. They were out of the view of anyone who might happen into the backyard.

Turning around, she leaned flat against the brick wall and pulled him until he was pressed against her. His hands circled her waist, his gaze moved from her lips to her eyes as if he was having trouble deciding on where to settle.

Pulling up the front of her short, flowing skirt, she picked up his hand and placed it on her naked skin.

His gaze snapped up to hers, his eyes narrowing. Even as he moved his fingers over her, he stared at her confused.

"I don't think you finished getting dressed," he said.

"I think I'm dressed fine."

He leaned forward as he worked his finger into her. She gasped, holding on to his shoulders as she swayed her hips.

"You've been sitting in the bar for over an hour with no panties on? In this short dress?"

She smiled at him.

He leaned over, growling into her ear, pushing her against the wall. "Oh, that's bad. That's really bad. I seriously do not like to share."

"Who's sharing?" She bit the edge of his ear. "All this is yours."

He kissed her on her neck, sucking lightly. "I like it when it's mine."

He checked his watch. "I have to be back in eighteen minutes."

She placed a hand on the front of his jeans. Rubbing up and down. "I think you'll make it with time to spare."

He looked over his shoulders to the yard around them. Rain hung in the air. The shadows around them were long.

"Shit, Ash..." his eyes closed as she unbuckled his belt. She let it dangle and unzipped his pants, adjusting to give him enough room. Reaching in, she pulled him out, stroking him. His head fell back, a moan coming out of his lips.

"This is a terrible idea," he said.

"You have a better one?" She continued to work him while he slid a finger inside her rubbing.

His mouth crushed down on hers, opened wide. She took him in, his groan more erotic than his words.

He leaned his forehead to hers. "You are so wet," he said. His eyes closed tight, forehead pressed up against hers.

She reached in the pocket of her skirt and pulled out a foil wrapper, placing it in his hands.

"That's because I want you," she said. "I want you inside me with sixteen minutes left on your break."

He checked his watch again. "That's about right."

She moaned and stretched her back against the bricks offering up her breasts.

He took one in his hand. "Here?" he whispered. "Outside?"

"Yes. Sounds incredible just to hear you say it. Can you imagine how it's going to feel?"

He took the condom and looked at it for a long time.

"Ash," he said. "Look at me."

She opened her eyes, blinking up at him. Oh, he was so damn hot with those blue eyes staring at her. He had a five o'clock shadow on his chin, and a body that used that damn bike like fitness tool. She ran a hand over his chest, feeling the muscles underneath.

He held the wrapper between them. "Ash, I can't get you pregnant."

His words passed over her slowly, but they registered.

"Not shooting with a whole lot that you have to be worried about," he said.

And she understood. It made her sad to think about. It almost ruined the whole mood she was going for here, but she understood what he was saying. "No kids?" she asked.

He shook his head. "No kids."

"I sort of hoped we would have a couple in a few years."

"We can adopt." He shot back quick. "And I'm not worried about diseases or anything I can catch or pass to you."

She heard what he was saying. She bit her lip as it processed quickly in her brain.

He looked at his watch. "Fourteen minutes. He still held the condom between them. "If you want me to wear this, I will wear it."

Up to her, she thought. To feel him slide into her. Nothing but skin to skin. She reached up, plucking the condom from his hand and reaching around to put it into his back pocket.

He let out a breath with a smile. "Ah shit," he whispered taking her head in his hand, his fingers digging into her hair. "This is going to be good."

He reached behind her to cup an ass cheek in each hand. Rising up, he lifted her as if she didn't weigh a thing, spreading her wide until she was at the perfect height. He didn't wait, didn't give any warning before he drove into her, pressing her back into the wall, his thrusts coming fast.

She moaned, her head back against the bricks. It was only him inside her, bare, sliding back and forth so smooth it was hard to draw in air. She gasped at the perfectness of it, her fingers digging into her shoulders while her body loved him.

"Look at me," he said his face only a few inches in front of hers.

She opened her eyes, watching him watch her.

"No closing your eyes," he said. "No noise."

She nodded her head. She would follow any instructions he gave to her as long as he made her feel like this.

"You're close, aren't you?"

She nodded her head, fighting to stop the orgasm from coming too quick. But he was so damn good for her. The things he could make her feel.

"Ah shit Ash. You're like a hair trigger."

She reached up, cupping his face. "Only for you."

"Ah, Ash," he laughed low. "You're going to wait. Until I tell you to. Right?"

He pounded into her. "Yes," she said. But she suspected it might be a lie.

"Shh," he said.

She bit her lip to stop from saying anything else.

"Look at me," he said. "You are so beautiful when you climax. I want to see it all."

He closed his eyes tight, his thrusts hard but controlled. "Now," he whispered in her ear.

He brought his head up, right in front of hers. She saw it in his face, the sheer pleasure he felt. He crushed his lips onto hers in a searing kiss that matched the motions of their bodies.

Keeping her pinned on the wall, he pressed his forehead against hers, his eyes closed tight, his breath heavy.

Ashley drew in a deep breath as the tremors subsided but they weren't going away quick. "Ian?" Her voice breathless.

He put his face in front of hers.

"Can I keep you?"

He laughed a little and wrapped his arms around her, pulling her close.

"Aye," he whispered. "I think we can work something out."

She wrapped her arms all the way around his shoulders and held on tight.

He pulled his face back and took a step, letting her drop to the ground.

She reached up, tucking him back into his pants, zipping him up, buckling his belt. When she was done, he placed a hand on either side of her against the wall trapping her.

"Check the time," she said.

"Fuck the time," he said. "You're going to go inside, you're going to get all your stuff, you're going to go home. No one is allowed to talk to you while you are half-naked."

She leaned back against the wall smiling, her arms still around his neck, her fingers in his hair. "I think I like you like this. Your old school is peeking through."

He tried not to smile, but there was a lift to the edge of his lip that had her leaning forward to kiss the spot.

He leaned into her again, his mouth coming down on hers hard, his arms snaking between her and the wall, pulling her closer.

115

He broke it off to whisper in her ear. "Had no clue you were this crazy, but I like that, too."

He pulled back to stare at her. "Go home. I'll be there in a few hours. Try to behave yourself."

"Okay," she smiled. "I'll be waiting in bed naked."

He groaned and pressed her back into the wall one more time, his mouth coming down hard.

She was gone fifteen minutes and he was behind the bar, his mind so not on his work it wasn't even funny. He got Rita's latest order and went to work filling the tray. Two beers, a rum and coke, a seven and seven and scotch and soda. By the time he got the receipt printed out from the register, he knew it was totally hopeless.

Rita picked the tray and Ian moved to the other side of the bar, leaning over to speak into Mike's ear.

"It's pretty slow tonight."

Mike's gaze traveled the bar and he shrugged. "Yeah, guess it is. They're not even hitting the jute box."

"Would you mind if I took off early?"

Mike turned to look at him. "Last time you left early it involved a blue eyed brunette."

Ian tried to keep his expression bland.

"Everything okay?"

"Aye. Everything fine."

"Emergency?"

Ian shook his head. "Not exactly."

Mike looked at him, waiting for the answer.

"I need to get home and have sex with my girlfriend right away."

Mike turned back to the beer he was filling. "Yeah, that's fine. You'll be here tomorrow?"

Ian smiled. "Think I would have worked things out by then."

Mike grinned. "Night," he chuckled.

Ian hit the back room, grabbed his leather coat off the hook, grabbed his backpack and headed to the backyard to get the bike.

Having to do all of that took way longer than he wanted. Getting to the house, he put the bike by the back door; left it unchained and let himself in.

She was in the kitchen when he got there. Already changed into her pajamas, her feet bare. She had a mug in one hand and a tea bag in the other.

Her gaze jumped up, her eyes wide. She was speechless for the time it took him to get half way across the kitchen.

"Don't you have three and half hours left on your shift?" she asked. She set the mug and tea on the counter.

He moved fast. He was next to her, his arms around her, yanking her close, his mouth crushing down on hers. Her hands laid flat on his chest. He wrapped his arms around her waist, picking her up off her feet while her head fell back. He chewed on her throat like he loved to do.

"What are you doing?"

He walked her down the hall, keeping her close and keeping her feet off the ground. She giggled and squirmed the whole way until the back of her legs hit the edge of the bed. She went over, him with her, landing on top of her while she continued to laugh, her fingers hanging onto his shoulders.

"We just did this," she laughed.

His body pressed her into the mattress, his chest to hers, his legs settling between hers. He put a hand on either side of her face, pushing the loose hair away so he could see her beautiful features.

He was smiling ear to ear when he leaned over to kiss her hard. "We're going to do it again."

CHAPTER SEVEN

The doorbell chimed, but Ian, in the shower, didn't seem to notice over the water. Jumping down from the toilet where she stood on the closed lid to watch him with dignity, she closed the door behind her and headed barefoot down the polished wood floors to the front door.

She answered but wasn't quite sure what to make of the kid who stood on the other side. He was tall, slim. He might be eighteen but she doubted it. His blond hair was cut floppy and he looked like he should have a box of chocolate bars with him to raise money for band camp.

She pulled back the door and smiled at him.

"Hi," he said. "You must be Ashley."

She tilted her chin at him. He extended his hand toward her.

"I'm Evan Harris. Is Stuart here?"

"Evan," she smiled. Ashley had yet to meet all of Ian's roommates. Evan, she knew was the youngest. "You're Travis's little brother. Harris verses Ricci?" she asked.

"Same mom. Different dads." He smiled and he was so huggable it was hard to resist.

She took a step back, opening the door wide. He looked at the floor like he was waiting for something.

"Do you want to come in?"

He laughed softly. "Yeah. Thanks." He stepped into the foyer.

"Ian's in the shower," she said.

He pointed at her. "Oh, that's right. Travis told us you called him Ian. Why is that?"

She walked toward the kitchen. "Come on in," she said. He followed her and she motioned to one of the dining room seats.

Reaching into the refrigerator, she pulled out a Coke, popped the tab and handed it off.

"Thanks," he said.

"I don't know. When he introduced himself to me he said Ian."

"That's funny. I've known him a long time and I've never known him to have anyone else call him that. To us he's just Stuart."

"Interesting," she said. "How long could you possibly have known him?"

Evan nodded his head slowly. "Long time."

"Who're you talking to?" Ian stepped into the kitchen, a towel around his shoulders, rubbing his wet hair. He wore his jeans and brown and black striped, button down shirt, but his feet were bare. "What are you doing here?"

"I was sent on a mission." Evan took a drink of the Coke.

"You gave him sugar?" Ian gasped in mock horror.

"Screw you Stuart," Evan laughed. He took another drink.

"How did you know where I lived?" Ashley asked.

Evan pointed at Ian. "He left a 3 X 5 card pinned on the bulletin board in the kitchen with your name and address and phone number on it."

She looked at Ian. "Really?"

"In case of emergencies. Wasn't trying to give out state secrets."

"You need to watch him," Evan said, pointing.

"You still haven't answered the question of why you're here."

"Travis is parked up the street."

"So why isn't he here?"

"He figured you were less likely to punch me."

Ian looked at Ash, rubbing the right side of his hair. "That's true, you know."

"You punch Travis a lot?"

"He deserves it the most."

She laughed and reached for a mug and the pot of coffee. She poured Ian a cup and handed it to him. He leaned back against the counter and crossed his ankles. He blew into the coffee. "What's up?" he asked Evan.

121

"He said you were funny."

"Who? Travis?" she asked.

"Yeah. Travis actually saw you then reported back what he's found. This jackass never tells us anything."

"You're a jackass," she said looking at Ian.

"They've called me worse."

"No doubt." She poured herself a cup.

"We're having a BBQ," Evan said.

"What are you talking about? We don't have BBQ's"

"Well we are now. For my birthday. And all of us have to be there."

"Travis's orders?"

Evan nodded.

"It's your birthday?" Ash smiled.

"Did you try telling him we still don't live in a dictatorship?"

"He said that it's been too long and you still haven't brought Miss Barrow to the house to meet everyone. He said you spend more time over here than you do at home. And he said if you don't start coming home after work he's going to personally start selling off all your shit on eBay."

"Which way is he parked?"

Evan smirked and pointed over his shoulder and down the street.

122

Ian pushed off the counter and set his coffee cup down.

Ash smiled. "Instead of punching him, we could go to the BBQ and celebrate Evan's birthday."

"I've met them. You're safer if we eat here."

"Oh, come on," she laughed. "I want to meet your friends and Travis says it's been too long and you haven't brought me to the house." She smiled while he glared at her.

"I think she could handle it," Evan said.

"How old are you going to be?" she asked and saw Ian's head tilt and his eyes narrow.

"Eighteen," Evan said laughing but she didn't get the joke.

There was a knock on the front door.

"I'll get it," she said.

"No," Ian said. "Let me."

She watched from the kitchen as he pulled the door back.

"Are you going to let me in?"

Ian looked at Travis. "No."

"Don't be a dick."

"Coward. You sent Evan."

She could see Travis and he was glaring, making her smile stick.

"Please come in," Ian said, stepping back.

"Asshole." Travis said as he walked by.

He walked straight to the kitchen.

"I told them," Evan said. "And you're right. He didn't punch me."

"*Mia bella,* Sunday. About seven?" Travis asked Ashley. "I think Stuart might still have the address."

"Do you want me to bring anything?"

"No. Just you," Travis said.

"Charming," she said.

"He *oozes* charm," Ian said from behind him.

"You have Sunday off anyway, right?" Travis asked over his shoulder.

"For the last five years, aye," Ian said.

"Good. We all took the night off for the chance to get to know Ashley a little better." He backhanded Ian on the shoulder. "Can you not screw this up?"

"Better?" Evan asked. "We don't know her at all. You've never brought her back to the house. Why is that?"

She saw Ian narrow his eyes at the kid and the kid laughed again.

"It's an adult thing," Ian said. "Jobs and stuff."

"Hey, I have a job," Evan said.

"Really?" Ashley said, catching the attention of each of the men in the room. "What do you do?"

"I work at Paws."

"I've never heard of it."

"It's a vet's office. I'm the night shift."

"You like animals?" she smiled. "What do you do on the night shift?"

"Field emergencies, keep the four legged visitors happy, give the meds as they come due. It's real mayhem, you know, so we have to keep every furry critter in line." He smiled ear to ear.

"Wow," Ash said. "That sounds like a big deal."

"Yeah. We need a dog at the house, but I always get out-voted."

"They won't let you have a puppy?"

Evan shook his head. "No," he whined. "It would be amazing, too. I have the name all picked out and everything."

"And what would you call him?" she asked.

"Vladimir. I think Vladimir would be a cool name for a Bloodhound."

She saw Ian look at Travis and Travis look back.

She looked at Ian. "I think it's child abuse, but that's me."

She laughed and Evan smiled wide.

'Ian maneuvered his way around Travis and went back to his coffee mug.

"There are two more?" she asked him.

"Aye. Quinn and Jason."

"Let me guess," she said. "All as delightful?"

"Naw," Evan said. "We're the best of the bunch."

"I swear," Ian said, shaking his head. "I've been working on improving his self-esteem but he doesn't seem to grasp the concept."

"I think you'll like them," Evan said. "And you don't want them getting any more curious about you."

"Why is that?"

"Well Quinn, he'll just wait and see, but he will be watching for answers. Now if Jason gets too curious—"

"It's nothing fancy," Travis said, cutting Evan off. "Hot dogs, hamburgers. Standard summer fare. We'll probably play some video games. Backyard's got a great view of the city."

Ash eyed Evan and ignored Travis's attempt to change the subject.

"Tell me about Quinn," she said.

Evan smiled at being asked. "He's nothing but a flirt. Make you smile like you've never smiled before but it's sincere so you will enjoy it."

"And Jason, what does Jason do?"

126

Both Travis and Ian stood straight and started to say something but she put her finger up and glared at them both.

"Evan is talking," she said, the warning in her tone.

The two men looked at each other helplessly.

Evan laughed. "I'm no expert but girls usually like him best," he said. "He'll have your phone number in under two minutes and he's so smooth you won't even realize you gave it to him."

Ashley laughed. "You paint a vivid picture."

"It's because they're older," Evan said. "They get away with that kind of crap while I get to be adorable."

"I think you are pretty damn adorable," she said, nodding.

Evan smiled.

Ian looked at her. "Please don't encourage him. We have to live with him."

She was laughing and looked up between Ian and Travis. "Are there any grown-ups over there?"

"We hire babysitters periodically," Travis said, "But I take the fifth on what they do once they get there." He smiled wickedly.

Evan laughed. Then Ash saw Ian's gaze shift to the clock. "Shit, is that the time? I got to go. I'm going to be late."

Ian disappeared down the hall she assumed to finish dressing.

"Mike won't mind," Travis called after him. "Isn't that what you always say?"

"Travis," she said.

He looked at her.

"What does Jason do that you don't want me to know about?"

Evan laughed and squirmed in his seat.

"What?" Travis said.

She blinked at him.

"Tennis," Travis said. "Jason plays tennis. He plays all the time. We can't get him to stop. It's like a compulsion."

Evan smirked. "When he's not on the computer breaking into the CIA, NSA or Federal Reserve."

Travis nailed him on the back of the head but the kid had been expecting it.

"Ahh…" she laughed.

"She's going to find out on Sunday. What?" Evan said. "He's going to take one look at her and tell her his life story and won't that be fun?" Evan laughed.

"Not if we tie him up in the attic." Travis looked at her. "Jason is a hacker. A small fact we try not to tell our cop friends."

"And I was having lunch with Cyber Crimes on Tuesday. Damn."

Ian came back carrying his rings and his shoes, his socks and leather coat. He dropped the shoes on the floor beside Evan's chair, then hung his coat on the back. Slipping the rings on, he pulled out the chair beside Evan and went to work on his socks

"You didn't get any dinner," she said, knowing it might be too domestic a thing to say in front of his friends.

"I'll grab something out of the kitchen when I get a minute," Ian said.

"You sure?" she asked.

He finished tying his shoes and stood up pulling on his coat. "Aye. It will be fine. You two going to hang around for a while?" He looked between Travis and Evan.

"That would be fine. The company would be nice," Ashley said.

But Travis jerked his head toward Evan. And the kid got up. "No, we'll get out of your hair. But I look forward to Sunday."

Ian leaned over, kissing Ashley full on the mouth in plain view of both Travis and Evan. "I'll see you tonight," he said. Then he turned and walked out of the door.

Evan tapped Travis on the shoulder as Ashley watched.

"What?' Travis asked.

"You might want to start putting up those eBay listings. I don't think we have anything at the house that can compete with what he's getting here."

"She didn't call," Craig said as Ian pulled Craig's fourth beer of the night off the tap. Four was the limit for Craig.

"Maybe she'll call tomorrow," Ian said knowing it would never happen. In the five years he had worked at Cooper's, Craig told the same story every night, waiting for the same phone call from a wife who left him almost thirty years ago.

When Ian set the beer on the coaster in front of the regular, Craig had the photo out of his wallet and held it for Ian to see.

Ian smiled and took it like he did a thousand times before. The edge was still torn, the color still faded and the woman in the picture still beautiful.

Ian took the photo to stare at it a moment then handed it back.

"Nice," he told Craig. "You must either be proud as hell or just damn lucky."

Craig stared at the photo and smiled. "Think I'm a little of both."

The conversation never varied, not with Craig. Not with Jim, not with Oscar, the trucker too far gone from home. Ian poured their drinks, smiled his smile and listened to them talk with genuine interest.

Someone new at the end of the bar raised their hand and he smiled and nodded. He didn't need to check his watch to know it was late to be starting a tab, but she looked thirsty enough.

"Hey," he said over the rock-n-roll that was just loud enough. "What can I get you?"

"How about a Goodnight Kiss," she smiled.

"I can do that," ignoring the suggestion that came along with the order. She was here alone and there was at least forty-five minutes on the clock.

He doctored the sugar cube, dropped it in the champagne flute and added the rest.

Setting the drink in front of her on a coaster, he smiled nicely. "It's pretty late but did you want to start a tab?"

"Sure," she said. "I have nowhere to be."

And this time, it wasn't a story he wanted to hear, no matter how nice the perfume, or pretty the face. Even if he hadn't had the most beautiful woman waiting for him, he would have passed. He went back to his other patrons.

Goodnight Kiss raised her hand into the air and tapped on the edge of her glass. Things had slowed down this late to almost a dead stop so he couldn't put her off.

He made the drink, brought it over and set it down.

"I'm Sharron," she smiled.

"Hey, Sharron. I'm Stuart."

"I like the accent. Ireland?"

He smiled anyway. "Little further northeast."

"Bet it's still green."

"Was last time I checked," he said.

"Not much going on anymore," she said, looking around the bar.

He jerked his head a bit. "Usually slows down about now. We'll get some stragglers we'll have to show the door, but we'll survive."

"I'm staying over at the Monte Cruz."

He had his hands planted wide on the bar. Glancing around he saw no one was signaling for a refill. "I hear it's nice, but I've never stayed there myself."

She looked at her drink. "Would you like to?"

He paused before answering. "Thanks. But I'm okay. Did you want to close out the tab or did you plan on anymore?"

"One more would be good and maybe I could talk you into changing your mind?"

"I appreciate the offer, but I do have a place to stay tonight and I'm actually looking forward to it."

"Wife?"

"Not yet," he laughed.

"Girlfriend?"

He smiled. "Drop dead gorgeous, built like a pin-up, willing to try anything in bed and a conversationalist to boot. Did I mention the sense of humor?"

She laughed and it wasn't a bad sound. "I guess you have every avenue covered."

"If I don't, she will find a way to cover it. Did you want one more before last call?" She hadn't touched her second.

"Naw," she said. "I'll finish off this and go see what's on cable."

"Supposed to be a real dynamite documentary on fishing industries of Portland. If it's on, don't miss it."

"I can't tell if you're trying to be cute or I got insulted."

"If you have to ask, then I wasn't as cute as I thought."

He turned away, got her ticket and slipped it to her at the bar.

Her glass was empty. "Last chance," she smiled.

"If only I could," he sighed.

She slid off the stool and gave him a last smile before heading toward the door.

Picking up what she left, he was impressed to see she tipped well even with the turn down.

Mike locked the door and he and Ian went to work cleaning the place up enough to meet health standards. After five years of working side by side, they had it down to a science and by two fifteen, Ian was out the door with a good night to Mike and headed toward the sidewalk.

He didn't get half a block before he spotted the familiar form sitting on one of the yard walls.

"I thought you had work tonight," Ian said as he got closer.

"I took off," Travis said, handing Ian one of two Styrofoam coffee cups.

"The only time you take a night off is if she's hot."

Travis smiled at him. "It was something to start writing stories about."

"Everything you remember?"

"Yes," Travis said, looking at him. "Because going three months is a hardship for some of us. Now you…"

"Don't start," Ian warned leaning against the wall where Travis perched, his feet dangling off the ground.

"You have spent more nights alone than any of us."

"Books are good," Ian said taking a drink of the brew, enjoying the heat and steam. "Did you want to stand in the almost rain and discuss my love life?"

"Janice Hooper," Travis smiled.

"Not my best decision."

"Cheated on you with a banker and you gave up women for five years."

"Got a lot done in those five years," Ian smiled.

"Breaking the streak only when your laundry list was met after a century of waiting and it came in a package that could be in a Victoria's Secret catalog. Life is so not fair," Travis sighed.

Ian smiled, looking guilty. He glanced up at Travis.

"That woman orders a drink in my section with that face and I'm going to argue when she comes back tomorrow for a refill?" Ian asked.

Travis laughed and drank. "You get the girl of your dreams, your relationship isn't based solely on sex and we all get to sit back and watch."

"Aye," Ian said, drinking with a grin.

Travis hit him on the head and laughed.

"Is there a reason why you are sitting here freezing your ass off waiting for me?"

"Used to be if I wanted to talk to you, I would wait in the kitchen or just barge in your room unannounced."

"You were good at that."

"Now I have to be more creative."

"Well can you maybe jump to the punch line? I actually have someplace to be and it is rumored to be very warm and inviting when I get there." He smiled again.

Travis looked at him a long minute, taking his time to find the words. "Dragon's Bridge, 1958."

Ian looked at him. "You want to talk about that?"

"I got thinking about it tonight after I dropped Ruth off. Back then, you left me at the bar and walked over to the table. Walter whispered in your ear."

"Did he? I don't remember."

Travis scratched his chin.

"The Blood Letting Case," Travis said. "You are dating the lead homicide detective in a murder case involving vampires."

Ian pushed away from the wall to face Travis. "We had this discussion. I am not getting uninvolved because she is tied to this case."

"I'm not asking you, too. It's too late, anyway. You two have progressed way past that point and hit the twenty year mark."

Ian laughed. "What's that supposed to mean?"

"You're an old married man and you don't even know it."

Ian laughed.

"But isn't it weird?" Travis said.

"What?"

"Den's find each other, whether they are looking or not. They always find each other in whatever shitty town they are in. And this is Davenport, population twelve. Why haven't we seen any sign of them?"

"We don't do that," Ian said. "We live under the radar and stay clean. And if they did, what? They're killing people and we don't do that anymore."

"And if one of us gets stopped when we're out alone," Travis said, "we won't be able to defend. We lose one and you know what," he said looking at Ian and shaking his head, "there isn't one I am willing to lose."

"Oh, come on," Ian smiled, "We could give up the Irishman easy."

Travis stared off into space before turning suddenly to face Ian.

"Stuart," he said serious. "About two weeks ago I was coming home from the hotel. I was still miles away, nowhere near downtown or our house. I was out there on the streets using a route I rarely take."

"All right."

Travis looked at him, then away. He looked back. "I would bet you a hundred bucks I saw him."

"Who?"

"Walter Bennett."

"What?"

"I swear to God. He was walking up a street about an hour before dawn, he had a woman with him and a guy and they were moving along like nothing. His hair was different, of course, as was his clothes. But this guy was the spitting image of what I remember Walter looking like."

"Travis, 1958 is a long time ago. We see people all the time that look like people we think we knew."

"I know. Stuart, I know. And there is no way in hell it could be him, but I would bet money it was. I thought I would get home, forget about it, and move on. I didn't tell anyone because I didn't want to look paranoid, but I cannot shake this feeling."

Ian leaned back against the wall. His coffee almost done, he knew he had to get back to Ash soon, but this, this revelation was too huge to ignore. Travis didn't do bouts of paranoia. He was as level-headed as they came and had served as the leader since day one.

"New Orleans. Davenport Oregon." Ian shook his head. "I don't see how. Walter liked crowds, big dens, people to look up at him and make him feel like he was the leader. He wanted big cities where victims were handy and could be accumulated and disposed of without notice. He wouldn't do a small town like this." Ian looked at Travis. "He wouldn't. Davenport wouldn't serve any of his needs."

"Depends on his needs, doesn't it? And he always had one he favored."

Ian shook his head and looked to the side. "No. I don't see it."

"You knew him better than anyone."

Ian sighed and his gut wanted to crawl out of his body. "I don't know. Maybe. I was there long enough to witness, but I tried to stay clear."

"Maybe I'm wrong," Travis said.

"You have to be. It's not possible."

Travis looked at him. "Say it is possible. Would he come after you?"

Ian thought about that. "Aye. No doubt. 'No' wasn't his favorite word. And I left with you."

"You're not gay," Travis said.

"He never seemed to want to hear that in the hundred times I told him."

"I was hoping you would make me feel reassured and tell me I was imagining things."

"You are imagining things. There's no way in hell for him be here. Someone is here, someone we haven't seen, but not him."

"So why don't I feel better?"

Ian shrugged. "Too much caffeine after midnight?"

Travis laughed a little. "I am tired tonight."

"Too much Ruth," Ian smiled.

Travis smiled back. "Can never have enough Ruth." He turned and started to walk away.

"Where you going?" Ian asked.

"Home."

"On foot?"

"Car is about a half block up. Seriously, this part of town may look amazing, but shit, the parking sucks."

"Bikes," Ian smiled. "I have been telling you for years. Bikes are the only way to travel."

"You going home to get laid?"

"I'm going to Ash's."

Laughing, Travis turned and headed down the street his hands in his pockets. "That's what I said," he said over his shoulder.

Ian went in the opposite direction, moving faster than before. Not only was he late getting back, but now he had images from his past to keep him company. Walter Bennett was never a friend, no matter how many years they shared side by side. Safety was in numbers and that was the only thing that kept Ian around. To think of Bennett nearby now, that was frightening.

He pulled his leather coat tight against his neck and stuck his hands into his pockets against the damp chill.

When he got to the house, expecting the lights to be off, they were on instead and he sighed. He used his key, hung up his coat and headed down the hall to the home office, where she sat at her desk in her green and purple pajamas, her grey socks on her feet, her hair braided over one shoulder.

He leaned up against the doorjamb. "I distinctly remember putting in an order for naked and in bed when I got back."

"Did you?" she said as she stared at a photo in her hand. "Seem to recall something about that but the memory is all fuzzy and out of focus."

"I got to tell you, I had high hopes."

"Should I point out life is full of disappointments?" She leaned forward and dropped the photo on top of the others with an exhausted sigh. This case pulled her closer and closer into an abyss she couldn't escape and he didn't know how to help.

"I could be, at this moment, at the Monte Cruz having wild sex with some blonde named Sharron who I would never see again and yet, here I am, looking at you looking at dead people."

Her gaze came up. "Ahh. Were they hitting on you again?"

"She thought I was Irish."

Ashley managed a sincere smile.

He walked over to the desk and picked up the top photo, looking at it. He knew death and carnage from too many years living on the wrong side of humanity. Looking at this crime scene photo in his hand, though, he worried about her.

"How do you sleep at night?" he said.

"With a gorgeous Irishman pressed up beside me."

He dropped the edge of the photo so he could look at her with narrowed eyes.

"I'm sorry," she smiled. "Did I get the country wrong?" She raised her hand and motioned with her fingers. "Gimme that. You know you're not supposed to."

Mock glaring at her, he picked up another photo which he also knew he wasn't supposed to look at. It was a close up of a neck wound. He could see it plain as day. The cut was a technique to hide punctures and any vampire worth his salt carried a blade for this purpose. Ian wanted to tell her *what,* not *who* she was looking for, but he couldn't. He would risk not only his entire family, but a life-style they fought to achieve.

"Still nothing?" he said.

"Radcliff has come up with a theory."

"Radcliff?" He said, surprised. She never gave up details.

"Our coroner."

"What's his theory?"

"Vampires," she said.

Ian's gaze came up slow. "Vampires?"

She stood up and took the photo from him, holding it with one hand while pointing at the slice in the neck.

"Apparently you can't see it up close, but under a high powdered microscope if you look at this wound in the neck, it's actually a slice made with a blade through two puncture wounds."

She kept the photo and sat back down.

"Vampires?" he asked again.

"Radcliff thinks Davenport has been overrun by night-stalking blood-suckers."

"Does Radcliff smoke a lot of pot?"

She laughed. "Yeah. Really, because that is the theory that makes the most sense of a case that makes no sense at all. God, I am tired."

He looked at her, her elbows on the desk, her face in her hands, and reeled from hearing the mere word come out of her mouth. She had the answer now and passed it by because really, who would ever think vampires lived in Davenport, Oregon? Or, for that matter, were watching her across the desk as she dropped her hands and looked up at him, a hunch to her shoulders.

"She didn't give any specifics," he said. "But I got the idea it would have been an interesting journey into sexual gratification."

Ash smiled a little. "Your latest conquest?"

He nodded with a crooked grin. "Told her I had plans for the night, though, with a gorgeous brunette, naked in my bed willing to do anything I asked."

"That's kind of hard to compete with, and who knows, she might have more energy. Did you get her room number?"

"I thought I might give the gorgeous brunette a serious chance at winning my affections first."

"Um hum," she smiled. "You have requests that need filling? Because I know for a fact your afternoon was kind of a full calendar."

"I suffer from short term memory loss. I might have forgotten to mention it."

"Yeah," she sighed with a smile.

She was playful and fun, even at this hour when most people were attempting to get some sleep. He looked at her in the lamp light and saw the smile, the tease, but he saw the drain, too. Her eyes lacked a little of their spark, her skin a half shade away from perfection. The hours she kept these days, the things she saw on the job, were sucking away her vibrancy.

"You okay?" he asked softly.

She smiled up at him, but he saw behind it.

"Sure," she said. "I'm up for whatever you want. Got to keep the Monte Cruz babes at bay. Handcuffs are in the nightstand as usual. Vibrator is where it always is."

He grinned back at her. Stepping forward, he flicked off the desk light, reaching across the surface to pick up her hand. He held on tight as she stood and walked around the furniture. He leaned over and kissed her gently on the lips.

"I have a wild idea," he said.

"Do we need the bath paints?"

He laughed. "I think we'll be okay." He led her down the hall to her bedroom, pulled back the quilt on the pristinely made bed and motioned for her to get in. She complied and he pulled the blanket up to her shoulder then leaned over and kissed her on the forehead.

"How about we try something different?" he said, leaning over her. "Like sleep. We'll sleep tonight and see what happens in the morning."

He moved around the bed and started to strip down.

She watched him the whole way. "Ian?"

"Aye," he said reaching for his belt buckle.

"Can I tell you something?"

"Anything except your coroner's weird fascination with the supernatural."

"I hate my job."

144

He looked at her as he pulled off the jeans and left the boxers.

"I know you do, honey."

"I used to love it. Thought I made a difference, but I don't. I don't prevent crimes. I just show up after the fact to file report and do clean-up."

He went to the bathroom brushed his teeth with the blue toothbrush and came back to crawl into bed beside her. He lay on his side, his head on the pillow facing her. She watched him.

"Would you show me Scotland?"

"I would love to show you Scotland. Not this week, though. Not exactly in the budget for a while."

"Think you'll still be warming that spot when we hit the fiscal renewal period?"

He smiled in the dark. "I think I'll be warming this spot for at least that long."

"How about we quit our jobs, head to Scotland and never look back? My treat."

He smiled at her. "That would be a pretty good trick on a cop's salary."

"What if I told you I could afford it, no problem?" She blinked at him.

He reached over to play with her hair. "You are so damn beautiful."

"Yeah, but I'm thinking Miss Monte Cruz wasn't all that bad."

"Miss Monte Cruz didn't come close," he smiled.

Her eyes drifted shut.

"I always meant to go back, you know," he said.

"Where?"

"Home. I was only supposed to be in America for a few years."

She scooted over on the mattress until she was damn close but not in his arms. He draped one over her, to pull her a little more.

"Missing a boat isn't always a bad thing."

CHAPTER EIGHT

Saturday afternoon, when Ashley should be home with Ian, Captain Zane Toure leaned into the squad room, his hand still holding the doorjamb. "My office," he said. "Now."

She glanced at Hunter, who sat at his desk, then lowered her sandwich to the paper towel she had folded.

"He says now," Hunter said

Ashley growled quietly then followed him into the office. Hunter took the chair on the left. She took the chair on the right.

"Any updates?" Toure asked. Dark skinned with brown eyes emphasized by the royal blue tie he wore with his white shirt. The tie sat loosened, like Toure had been trying to escape the stress of their ongoing nightmare.

"Not since this morning," Hunter said.

"Five victims. And it's the weekend. We've got to figure this out. The FBI is coming in on Monday and we have to have something to show them."

"There's no pattern on timing. Just because it's a weekend doesn't mean there will be another one."

Toure leaned back in his chair. "It doesn't mean there won't." He leaned forward, folding his arms over his desk.

"You're both free tomorrow?"

Ashley and Hunter exchanged looks.

"That doesn't sound good, sir," Hunter said.

Toure nodded. "I don't see here we have any choice."

"That will be the fourth weekend in a row we'll have come in and accomplished nothing," Ashley said.

Hunter closed his eyes and huffed. Ash knew he was thinking about the time he was missing with Janey.

"If you think it's necessary," Hunter said.

Ash leaned back in her chair and folded her hands over her middle. She tilted her chin and thought real hard about the words that were about to come out of her mouth.

"I have plans," she said quietly.

Toure narrowed his eyes at her. "That I assume you can change."

She was shaking her head slowly. *Evan, Travis, Quinn and Jason.* "No, I am sorry, sir. I can't."

"And what is so damn important that you will walk away from an ongoing case?"

She looked Toure straight in the eye. "Ongoing case? This case is going to continue to be ongoing. Fourteen hour days, six to seven days a week is not fixing that. And me, I have a previous obligation that I have to be there for. So this once, I can't. Ask me any other time and I will see what I can do. But this weekend…I'm sorry."

Toure stared at her for a long minute. The second hand on the clock on his wall swept halfway around while the tension in the room skyrocketed.

"You can change it," Hunter said.

She shook her head again. "No. I can't. People are counting on me."

"Yes, Barrow," Toure said. "We're counting on you. Just like we have always counted on you and we'll continue to count on you."

She brought her gaze up slowly, seeing the pissed look in Toure's eyes.

She thought of more late nights than she could count. She thought of the faces of parents who would never see their kids again. There had been too many teenagers in the morgue, too many crime scenes where the blood of the victims decorated the walls. The job sucked and it was never going to change. And if you can't change the job, then it was time to look for new routes into happily ever after. She had more money in the bank than any of them could imagine. She didn't have to work. She hadn't had to work for six years.

"I'm sorry, sir. But no."

"Is this like the last time you gave me lip? A date you had waiting? Did you stay up too late again last night after taking another bartender home?"

She shook her head again and pursed her lips. "No, I'm still sleeping with the last one I found."

"You're not going to take this seriously?"

149

She stood up. "I'm not going to take this any way." She pulled off her badge, placing it on the desk in front of Toure. The gun she kept. It was hers.

Thank you, Gr'pa Jackson.

"Ash," Hunter gasped. "No."

Toure looked at the badge then brought his gaze up to Ash's. "This is not something you can second guess. I accept this and I will not give you another chance to earn it back."

She blinked hard at him. "I can live with that."

She turned and headed out the door, Hunter right on her tail.

"You can't quit."

She turned to look at him. "I'm sorry. I am so sorry. But I can't do this anymore. I don't want to do this anymore."

"Since when does what we want have to do with us actually doing the job?"

She stopped to look at him. "I would say that statement is an excellent example of what the hell I am talking about."

She turned and moved to her desk. There was nothing on it that was personal. She looked at her locker, thinking about what was in there. She pulled her purse out of the bottom drawer and pulled on her coat and she really had everything personal that she ever had in this office.

He followed her to the elevator. "If you tell me Stuart had anything to do with this, I will hunt him down and shoot him."

"My decision," she said. "Totally my decision. He doesn't even know."

"Where are you going now?" He looked panicky.

She held the elevator doors open with her hand. "I don't know. I kind of feel like I could use a new dress and a pair of shoes for the BBQ tomorrow." She stepped back and the elevator doors slid shut.

The dress was going to have to wait, though. Driving home, she pulled the car into her driveway and looked at the house in broad daylight. The shadows looked different.

Things were going to change now. She was going to have to talk to him, explain to him about Gr'pa Jackson and everything he had left. She had never told anybody, never trusted anyone enough. She knew intimate details of Ian's life but she didn't have a clue how he would respond when she told him she had money.

She got out and headed in the back door. The TV was on, a hockey game playing, but unwatched. Ian was at the dining room table, his bare feet propped on the chair next to him. The newspaper he was currently reading open and a cup of coffee beside him, his fingers in the handle. All the blinds were shut.

The breakfast dishes done. If he had had lunch, he had already cleaned it up, washed everything and put them away. He was neat in ways she had only ever dreamed about.

His gaze came up to meet hers, looking surprised. "I didn't think you would be home until after six."

She put her purse down on the counter beside her and pulled off her coat. "I took the rest of the day off."

"What's the occasion?"

She bobbed her head. "I didn't feel like working."

He blinked at her a few times looking a little confused. Then his hand came up, reaching out toward her. "Come here."

She stepped forward. He sat up, dropping his feet to the floor and closed the newspaper. He put his hand up, catching her on the back of the neck and pulled her down. He kissed her on the lips.

"I think that sounds like a really good idea."

She stood then took the chair across from him. He got up and pulled a mug out of the cupboard. "Fresh pot," he said. "You got time for that?"

She smiled "I think I can fit it in."

He poured and got the milk out of the refrigerator and added sugar. He placed the cup down in front of her.

"Want some more news?" He asked, taking back his seat. He laced his fingers back into the handle of his own cup.

She took a sip. He had nailed it perfectly. "What?"

"I've got tonight off."

"No you don't. It's Friday night and you always work Friday nights."

"I don't work *this* Friday night."

"How come?"

"Mike called. His cousin came into town from Phoenix. The two of them used to own a bar together down there in the dark ages. Now they like to get together couple of times a year and spend the night serving like the good ol' days."

"That doesn't seem fair," she said.

He smiled. "I'm good with it and in case you missed the important part, I am free for the whole night." He raised his eyebrows a couple of times. "Sounds like you might be free tonight, too."

"I need to run to the store and get some supplies, but beyond that, yeah, I guess I am."

"What do you need supplies for?"

"I want to make chocolate-chip cookies to take tomorrow night."

He smiled. "You bake?"

She smiled back. "I've been known to heat an oven."

"It's not necessary, you now. Travis said to bring yourself."

"I want to."

He nodded his head.

"Do you have to take your cell phone tonight? I mean since you are off officially?" he asked.

She shook her head slow. "No, I do not need to carry my cell phone. In fact, I would seriously prefer not to carry my cell phone. What did you have in mind?

"I didn't think you'd be home for another four hours."

"Want to fool around?"

"At three o'clock in the afternoon?"

"At three o'clock in the afternoon when I have work off and you're not going into the bar."

He leaned back in the chair, stretching out his legs. "That is true. You make a very valid point but," his voice trailed off.

"But?"

"But if we fool around now, what are we going to do when we get home tonight?"

"Where are we going?" she asked.

"I was thinking dinner at a nice place downtown and maybe a movie."

"Hmm," she sighed.

"What?"

"I wonder if there is a play going on. I bet it would be too late to get tickets."

He stood up and headed down the hallway to the second bedroom, walking around the free-floating desk to fire up her computer. He sat in the chair and started typing. She stood in the doorway and watched.

"There's a production of *No Strings Attached* playing at the Grand Central tonight at eight." He looked up at her. "Interested?"

"I love plays. I can't remember the last one I saw. What is it?"

He looked back at the screen. "It's a musical. Says it's about a struggling band. Says it's got three stars."

"What do you think?" she asked

He typed some more. "Seating available on the left side, row sixteen."

He looked up at her again.

She laughed. "Is it something you would want to do?"

He only smiled. Stretching out his leg, he pulled his wallet out of his back pocket and withdrew his Visa card.

She stepped forward. "No," she said. "I can get this."

He glanced up at her. "My treat."

"It was my idea."

He started typing. "And you're my girlfriend and I am taking you on the date you want. How often do I get to take you out?"

"Ian?"

He looked up at her.

"What do you think about money?"

He looked back at the computer screen. "Nice to have to pay bills."

"What about enough to have some fun?"

He kept on typing paying more attention to the screen than the conversation. "What? You mean like Kardashian type fun? I'll pass."

She tried to smile. "You wouldn't want a nice piece of change to play with? Maybe do something you've always wanted to do?"

He looked back at her. "I'm doing everything I want to do. Why did you bring this up?"

She lied and had never done that with him before. "On the way home. I heard on the radio about a lottery winner getting their dream vacation."

"Where did they go?"

One lie usually led to another which is why she never did it. "New Zealand. The whole Hobbit thing."

He smiled. "You'd probably like that."

"Would be fun. Want to come?" She smiled.

"How about I concentrate on tickets and then we pick out a place for dinner?"

She sighed, giving up for now. "How long is this going to take?"

"What?" he asked.

"Ordering the tickets."

"I don't know. Ten minutes max."

She stepped back into the hallway. "I'm going to go get naked and wait for you in bed."

"Five minutes max," he corrected himself.

She was in bed as promised when he arrived a few minutes later, but his mood unreadable.

She lay back against the pillows, the sheets hiding her breasts, her hair fanning out. He stood and stared at her from the footboard.

"What?" she finally smiled. "You're supposed to be over here."

He held up a small sheet of paper between two fingers and aimed it at her. "You want to tell me about this?"

She looked at it pretending to read what she already knew was there.

"What about it?"

He turned it to read. *"Dr. Richards. Tuesday. Four-thirty on the first."*

"Yes," she said. "I actually memorized it before I put it in my phone."

"What is it?" He asked.

"It's a doctor's appointment."

"Ash?" he snapped.

She sighed hard and set up, holding the sheet in place. "I've been tired. I thought I should have it checked out. It's no big deal."

"It's a big enough deal that you're seeing a doctor over it."

"I have been working a horrible case with horrible hours and a horrible schedule. I wore myself out. I thought I would check it out to see about a B shot or something."

"When was the last time you jogged?"

"I don't know. A week, maybe."

"Closer to two, I think," he said. "And your weight is down."

"Woman's weight," she mocked glared. "Brave man."

He stared at her.

She sighed. "A few pounds in the last few weeks."

"How few?"

She stalled and smiled. "Wouldn't you rather discuss it over here?"

He didn't move and she sighed.

"Five-point-six."

"That's six pounds. In two weeks?"

"No, that's five-point-six pounds."

"I'm into new math," he said. "I round up."

"Ian, please. It's flattering that you are worried. No one has ever done that before but I really think this is nothing more than me just needing a check-up and talking to someone about adding more greens to my diet."

"You're not worried?" he asked.

"Not at all," she said, "I feel tired a lot. Winded. I want to see if I can fix it."

"Do you feel sick?"

She shook her head. "I get tired easily and sometimes it's hard to breath," she smiled and pointed at the paper. "It's just precautionary."

He looked at the yellow sheet and rolled his tongue in his mouth, and she saw him thinking.

She pulled back the blankets on his side of the bed, exposing a leg high enough to tantalize and tempt without revealing.

"Come here," she said, rubbing her hand over the sheets. He put the paper on the dresser and moved around to his side of the bed.

"I think you might be trying to change the subject," he said without a smile.

She pulled the quilt up further, his lips pursing as more came into view.

He smiled only a little. Reaching for the buttons on his shirt, he pulled it off.

The play had been amazing. Well, the concept of the play had been amazing. Ashley didn't think the actual play was as good as it could get but sitting in the dark, Ian's hand in hers, the live performers, the live audience, clapping and missed lines of dialogue, it had all been as wonderful as she remembered.

She leaned back in her chair in Al Dente Italian Cuisine and watched Ian pour out the wine into her glass. They were into their second bottle of Chianti and it was going perfect with her chicken parmesan. Ian set the bottle back down on the table.

He looked sharp. His hair brushed back away from his face, his shirt a crisp white, unbuttoned low, his Celtic knot showing silver on his chest. He had on black dress pants and a pair of black leather shoes.

He had borrowed her car this afternoon, after she had gotten back from the store, to drive to the house and pick up the dress clothes. Seemed they weren't the type of thing that he kept around on a daily basis.

"Why don't you move in?"

His gaze came up to hers, a small smile on his lips. He picked up the breadbasket and folded back the napkin, finding it empty.

"And how many glasses of wine have you had?" he smiled, leaning back and picking up his glass.

"Three."

He held four fingers and silently mouthed the word. *"Four."*

She fidgeted. "You've been counting my drinks?"

"I count everyone's drinks. Occupational hazard. Let's me know when I should cut them off. And you," he pointed at her dramatically, "are about there."

160

She felt herself pout. This wasn't going as she had planned. Though thinking about it with her fuzzy brain she didn't think she had thought about it at all. The words had suddenly been there and they made sense. She picked up her glass and drained it. Picking up the bottle, she poured herself another.

"That's how we're going to play it?" He almost laughed. "What am I going to do with you when I get you home?"

"It's not home," she said. "It's my home. You're just hanging out."

His jaw twitched, his head leaning back. "I don't think it's a good idea right now."

"But you practically have already."

He took a few long breaths. "I need to keep a presence at the house."

She leaned back against the chair and narrowed her eyes at him. He picked up her water glass and sat it closer. "Drink some water."

She ignored him. "I don't get you five."

"And you're drunk. So you need to be careful about what you say for the rest of the night." He looked so damn serious.

"I'm not drunk. I'm happy."

"I like happy drunks. They're the most fun to deal with but I don't want you to have any regrets in the morning. I mean besides the massive hangover you're going to have."

She leaned forward, her elbows on the table. He reached up and picked up her wine glass moving it out of her reach. She made a noise in her throat.

He gave her a sideways glance. "Excuse me. Did you growl at me?" He laughed.

"Give it back," she said.

He mirrored her with the elbows on the table. "I will think about it. Do you want dessert?"

"Of course I want dessert."

He was whispering as he leaned closer. "I'll get the dessert menu."

"Five of you," she said before he leaned away. "Ages Evan to Travis with everything mixed in between and I can't see a single common thread among you."

He leaned back and signaled to the waiter. "Saves on rent. And it's nice to have a bunch of people all in one place."

"It's like a great big party always going on," she said. "Except I never see any of you do anything together except Travis who appears periodically. This BBQ on Sunday seems to be a big ass deal."

He shrugged. "We work. We hang out. No big mystery."

"It's like you have a secret."

His gaze snapped up to hers.

"Like there is something holding all of you together that you don't want the rest of the world to see."

He cleared his throat and took a drink of his wine. "I'm actually not there most nights," he pointed out. He looked straight at her. "I'm with you. At your place. Gave me the key and everything. Remember?"

"I don't understand."

"I want you to drop this," he said.

"Ew," she said. "That sounded grouchy."

"I like things the way they are. I want to keep them like that for a while. Even after this conversation, cuz seriously, I doubt you're going to remember much about it in the morning." He pushed on the edge of the water glass. "Drink the water. Please?"

He said it with such sincerity, she couldn't say no. Reaching up, she picked it and took a sip. The waiter appeared beside the table.

"Dessert menu?"

Ian smiled up at him. "Aye, thank you."

The waiter walked away.

"You're wrong."

His shoulders sank when he sighed. "About which part?" His gaze came up to hers.

"I'm not drunk. Takes a lot more to get me drunk."

"I've never seen you that way so I guess it could be true. Would say you are definitely feeling it, though?"

She nodded her head. "Feels pretty damn good. I mean as long as I didn't piss you off."

He watched the flame on the candle in the middle of the table. "You didn't. It's flattering you asked."

She regained her wine and knew he was right. Drunk or not, she didn't know. She did know she was going to be feeling this in the morning.

"I think I'm going to sleep in tomorrow."

He laughed. "I have no doubt that you will."

She tilted her head and smiled at him. "Thank you," she said.

"For what?"

"For tonight. For dropping everything and putting this whole thing together because I came home early."

"I got tonight off, too. Everything worked out perfect."

She had had enough to drink. The subject slipped back into her mind. "What would you do if I told you I was worth a million dollars?"

"I would say you definitely have had enough to drink."

"No, really. What would you do?"

He leaned back in his chair, his hands folded and thought about it. "I don't know. The sex is pretty damn amazing but I'm not sure it's enough to deal with that kind of a headache." His smile was charming.

"We would be over?"

"I'm not overly fond of money or those who have it so I would have to think."

"We're done because of an interest rate?"

He nodded slowly. "Sorry. I wouldn't want to, but I don't see where money and I could exist in the same universe. Why? Are you hiding a fortune from me?" He was smiling, looking adorable.

She laughed but the edge on her gut couldn't be cut by all the wine she drank. "Dad was a cop, remember? Not a lot of savings going on."

"So don't buy any lotto tickets and we'll be fine."

"Want to skip dessert?" She suggested. "Maybe swing by the store on the way home and pick up all the makings for a hot fudge sundae then sit and watch all this week's recorded Daily Shows?"

He leaned over picking up her hand. He rubbed his thumb over the back before he raised it to his mouth and kissed it. "That sounds like the perfect ending to a perfect night."

It was perfect. At least she thought it had been perfect. She remembered dinner, she remembered the store and all the toppings. There was a vague recollection of him helping her into the house and the TV going on, but after that, it was a blur.

She woke face down on the bed, flat on the mattress her hands tucked under the pillows.

He poked her on her side. "Here. Drink this."

She rose up and found him holding a glass of something God-awful.

"I'm not going to drink that." She lay back down.

"It will help."

"What is it?"

"Scottish. I've used it before."

She didn't move. "It looks bad and it smells worse."

He sat down beside her. "You don't want me to have to get violent here and mess up your pillows when I pour it down your throat."

She rolled over, flat on her back, her hands raised beside her. "You wouldn't even try."

He held the glass out to her.

"Did I ask you to move in with me last night?"

"Aye, you did."

She closed her eyes and covered them with the palm of her hand, remembering the conversation. "And you said no?"

"Aye, I did."

"So why are you here?"

"Do you want me to go?"

Her hand came down on his knee. "No, No. Of course not."

"Do you trust me?"

She sighed dramatically, letting it drag. "With my very life."

He held the glass out toward her.

"What's in it?"

He looked at it and gave it a smell. "Beetroots, grapes, plums. And you drink it with these." He put two aspirin in her hand. "And when you get up, I want you to drink three glasses of water."

"That sounds really horrible."

He picked up her hand and wrapped her fingers around the glass.

"We had beetroot in the refrigerator?" she asked.

"Aspen Market opens at six."

She looked up at him, trying to smile but the headache made it hard. "You walked over to the market for this?"

"It's two blocks, Ash."

"For me?"

He rubbed her hair and smiled at her.

"Why don't we have sex?" she asked.

"Oh," he laughed. "You would be such a good time right now." Standing up he moved away from the bed and headed into the hallway, talking over his shoulder. "Take a shower. Get going on your cookies."

"Where are you going?"

"Garage. Got to go take my bike apart."

She closed her eyes confused. "Why?

He called from the kitchen. "Because you drive a car that Matchbox could put their logo on, and the bike won't fit in whole."

"Why is the bike going in the car?"

"Tires are flat. I need to take it back to the house and fix 'em."

She puckered her lips and narrowed her eyes. "I think you're being mean!"

She heard the backdoor open. "Told you not to have the last glass of wine." His voice faded and the backdoor closed.

"Tires look fine to me," she said to the empty room.

She set his concoction on the nightstand and fell back on the mattress. Had he told her that? Not to have the last glass of wine? She didn't remember. She remembered she swore up and down she wasn't drunk but lying here feeling like she could die, she was afraid he might know the business a little better than she did.

She looked at the offending glass, and moaned. "Oh fuck," she said. Sitting up she picked it, tossed the aspirin to the back of her throat and she drank it all down.

CHAPTER NINE

He came back in covered with enough junk on his hands that he had to go directly to the sink. He scrubbed up hard, getting bike residue off his hands. The whole house smelled of chocolate chip cookies.

Ash still wore her pajamas, her hair still a mess. Looked to him as if she had crawled straight from bed but she was pulling the first batch of the cookies out of the oven and setting them onto the stove.

He came up behind her as she took off her oven mitts and pulled the hair away from the back of her neck. He kissed her on the spot he exposed. "You stink," he said.

"Won't affect the cookies."

His hands were on her waist, pulling her back into him. "Feeling better?"

"Not bad, though I don't remember you telling me not to have the last glass of wine."

"It was after the Daily Shows. One of our own bottles." He motioned to an empty Merlot by the sink.

She screwed up her face. "Oh."

He smiled. "Right before I poured you into bed and turned down your sexual offers."

She looked over her shoulder at him. "I offered?"

He nodded his head sharp. "I declined."

She pulled at her pajama bottoms. "How did I get into these?"

He walked toward the table. "That would be me. And I think I deserve hazard pay for the experience."

Two boxes sat in one of the spare place settings, neither large, but stacked and held together with black curly ribbon. The wrapping paper was white with black paw prints all over it.

"What's this?"

She looked over her shoulder. "It's for Evan."

He looked at her, looked at the box then back at her. "You got Evan a birthday present?"

"It's actually not unusual when you've been invited to the party."

"You just met him," Ian pointed out.

She just met him, and the paper had *dog* prints. Evan loved dogs. Wanted a dog. Worked with dogs, and Ash had gotten him something to do with a dog?

He turned to look at her a moment, not understanding the emotions that ran through him. She watched out for him. She watched out for his friends. That would put her where? In a class by herself?

"He's important to you," she said.

He stared at her, weighing the words, trying to file them.

He pointed at her pajamas. "Is that what you are planning on wearing tonight?" He stared at the BLT sitting at what they would probably call his seat by now.

She walked to the refrigerator and poured a glass of lemonade, setting it down near his sandwich.

"I was half way thinking of walking into town. There's a boutique there, Hidden Elegance, with this dress I've been eyeing in the window."

He looked at his watch before sitting down. "We leave in five and a half hours. Have time for a shower and all that?"

"It's only a couple of blocks. Bike in the car?"

"Garage. I'll do it after this. Thanks by the way,"

He picked up his sandwich and took a big bite. "Wow," he said as he chewed. He could get so used to this kind of life. "That's good."

She smiled and brought him a still-warm cookie to put on the plate. He glanced up at her and felt himself being reeled in.

"Are you mad about last night?" she asked.

He took another bite and shook his head. "It was a great time. Play sucked but it was still fun. Would be better if we could get more nights like that."

"So what I said…"

He put the sandwich down. "We discussed it. It's over. We can move on."

She nodded her head then picked up the spatula to start moving the cookies to the cooling rack. He hadn't even known she had cooling racks.

"You're not going to let it go, are you?" he asked.

Her gaze came up, her eyes wide. "I didn't say anything."

"But you were thinking about it."

She stood up straight and faced him and he felt a fight coming on, their first. His mood shifted from cookies to the impossible he wanted and couldn't have.

"No, Ian, that's not what I was thinking."

He snapped up from the table, the chair sliding back rough on the floor. Ash jumped back and held the spatula between them.

"And what were you thinking?"

She stared at the floor. "I was thinking it probably wasn't right of me to quit my job yesterday and then wait twenty-four hours to tell you."

Her gaze came up scared to meet his.

Totally blown away, he stared back. "What?"

"It's not the kind of relationship we have. Holding things back from each other."

That brought on a wave of guilt, spiking his irritation. It was exactly the type of relationship they had.

"But if I open one door, another is waiting and I didn't want to get into it while we had a chance at some fun last night and tonight."

"What are you talking about?"

"That's why I was home early. I turned in my badge, pissed off my Captain and really upset Hunter who blames you, but I'll take care of that."

"I don't give a fuck what Hunter thinks. You quit your job?"

The timer went off, making her jump. She pulled out the next batch while he processed her words.

"So no emotion involved," he said. "You were looking for a roommate to pay half the rent? Was I supposed to take the second bedroom? Take out the garbage on Tuesdays and the recyclables on Friday?"

She looked and he saw her pulling in her emotions, gathering strength. "Actually, the house is paid off and there is no rent so I was only looking for company and I thought we might actually share the same bed we've been sharing. If you prefer the other room, I can move my yarn and the desk."

He chuckled and stepped toward her, surprised when she stepped back.

"Your historic downtown, two-hundred-year-old rock house with its aged oak floors, beveled windows and plaster walls that has got to be valued at seven to eight hundred *thousand* is paid off? On a cop's salary?"

"Seven-hundred and eighty at last appraisal and yes."

"And you quit your job."

She put her hand up as she backed away. "Stop there, Ian. You're scaring me," she whispered.

And he could see it on her. He had seen hundreds of victims in his arms with that same pale expression and trembling lips. They had usually begged. She stood her ground and he knew cop would override vulnerable woman.

Not knowing what he truly showed to her now, he thought about the emotions running hot through him and concentrated on pulling them in.

"Why would I be doing that?"

"I don't know. There is something different. I can't explain it. Something you've never let me see. I don't like it."

"But I like you quitting your job and your house is paid for?"

She left the cookies on the counter and turned to head down the hallway. He grabbed her by her arm and pulled her to a stop. He reached up to run his hand on her hair and kissed her shoulder to calm the fear he could feel coming off her. He had never scared her before.

"Talk to me," he whispered.

"Why?" she said. "I'm getting the feeling it doesn't matter what I say. I already blew it last night and you're on the way out the door."

"You asking was complimentary. I want to say yes. You have no idea how bad I want to say yes, but I can't and I can't explain why. But your job and the house? You're leaving out ninety

174

percent of the story and right now we need a hell of a lot more than ten percent."

"I tried to tell you. A couple of times and every time I brought it up, you shot it down. Last night at dinner you said you'd leave if…I tell you now and you will pack and go."

He pushed her up against the wall and she sucked in a breath. He leaned into her, feeling her shake. "I'm not going anywhere."

She licked her lips before she bit it. "I don't want to break-up," she whispered.

"Why would you think we were breaking up?"

"You hate money. I have it. My grandfather left it to me. And he bought me the house. I could have covered the tickets last night. And dinner. I could cover the trip to Scotland I asked you about and it wouldn't even hurt a little. Last night you said you couldn't live in the same universe as money and I have it so I deduced from your statement you will not be living in the same universe as me."

A tear slipped from her eye and ran down her cheek.

"I had to keep that from you," she said. "Lie to you, because as long as I could keep it from you, you would stay."

He brushed the tear off her cheek with his thumb.

"Shit Ash, this is so not fucking fair. Hypothetical question asked in a restaurant when you were drunk? How do you even remember that?'

"Because I knew when you said it we were on a clock and when you found out we would be done."

He pushed on her shoulders a little, pushing her into the wall while he took a step back, weighing that one sentence, hearing the ring of truth to it. He couldn't think of a thing to say because she was right and he hadn't been lying. He hated money. Always had.

She smiled as the first tears were joined by more.

"Yeah," she whispered. She turned and headed into the bathroom, locking the door.

He followed, trying the knob and thought of her propensity for online shopping. High-end stores who always delivered overnight. Things he should have questioned. Purchases when they were out and always the best. She never flaunted it, but she didn't live deprived. She drove that damn Dodge Dart, for God's sake when she could probably do better.

How many pairs of Victoria's Secret pajamas did she own? He didn't even know but he was never surprised when a new pair appeared on her body.

When the door wouldn't open, he knocked. "Can we talk about this, please? The hypothetical was evaluated to reality and we need to discuss this."

The shower turned on, but the sound stayed steady. No break as if she had gotten in.

"Do you want me to cancel tonight?"

"Yes."

He heard the lie in her tone. She had been looking forward to tonight since Travis and Evan had been here. The whole house smelled of fresh baked cookies to prove the point.

"I can go, Ash. If that is what you want."

Trouble was, it wasn't want he wanted. When a hundred years of socialist thinking slammed into a little money in the bank, then ricocheted onto Marylyn Monroe's favorite perfume on a woman who Ian was convinced wore it better, his doubts started to spin out of control.

When her yes came, it came soft and full of pain. In her mind her prediction was coming true and he realized losing him might be her worst fear.

When had a woman ever offered him the whole asking nothing in return?

"Fuck it," he whispered. He grabbed the doorknob and using strength, a secret he kept from her, he twisted and broke the lock, opening the door.

Her startled gaze came up and she jumped off the closed toilet where she had been sitting.

"If you had told me that first night in Cooper's, I never would have taken you out."

She sat back down, pulled her legs to her chest and wrapped her arms around them. "I wasn't trying to—"

"I know," he cut her off. "Not first date conversation, but now we have a situation that we have to deal with."

She wouldn't look at him. "I'm sorry," she said softly. "It's my fault for keeping things from you. I won't blame you if you want to go."

He sighed hard and dragged a hand through his hair. Seeing her sad and ready to let go without a battle because she thought it was what he wanted, tore at a heart he hadn't really been sure he still possessed.

Fuck Victoria's Secret, though he would enjoy what they delivered. Fuck any bank where she kept the funds. And fuck whatever this cool, old, funky house was worth.

Priorities sometimes had to be rearranged.

"You hated your job," he said. *"I* hated your job. If you have money in the bank that means you don't have to be working those hours and seeing those things, then I would like to have a serious conversation with you."

She turned her head, keeping it on her knees as she blinked at him.

"I was skimming this girly magazine the other day. Not one of those, but like a catalog and there was this awesome tan sweater in there that I really liked. Looked complicated, but I kept the picture and now you have all this free time and I was thinking…"

She ran across the small gap and his arms came up to hold her tight. One hand fisted in her hair. He spoke directly into her ear. "We'll figure it out. Somehow we'll work it out."

"You're making out in the entry way?" Travis said as he walked in.

She laughed and stepped back, out of Ian's reach. "Any place we can," she said.

"My kind of woman," he laughed. "You ready to dump him and try something new? Everyone knows I'm a lot more fun."

In another time and place Travis' joke might have been okay. After their fight this afternoon, Ian felt its sting.

"Nope," she said, shaking her head. "I like it here."

That stung more.

Travis picked up her hand kissing the back, said. *"Mia bella."*

Ian stepped up. "Oozing charm."

Travis looked him up and down and slapped Ian's gut with the back of his hand. "What's wrong with you?"

"Nothing," Ian said.

Travis eyed him. Then he turned and put his arms around Ashley's shoulders. "Come on. We set up out back and we have people that want to hear your life story."

Travis opened the door, letting Ashley and Ian go out first.

The backyard was a thing to behold. Large, with a slanting hill, several sitting areas with huge, comfortable looking wooden chairs with tables set in several locations. An arbor stood at the top, lights glowing in the dark night, illuminating the deep color of the wood as well as the vining plants all around. There was a small pond nearby, a stream heading down to the base of the hill into a larger one. Plants edged all their sides, a four-foot Asian temple reproduction nestled by the stone edge.

Shocked by the beauty and tranquility of the atmosphere, Ash took in a breath and imagined all these plants in full bloom come summer.

"So which one of you is out here trimming the hedges?" she asked.

"The guy I pay once a month," Travis smiled.

She looked at the pond.

"Okay, the other guy I pay once a month."

Ash smiled and loved what they had built.

The spread sat in the arbor holding all their supplies. There was a chest with ice-cold beer and soft drinks, assortment of condiments in a variety of colors.

Ian dropped her hand and moved to the chest. He poked around for a few minutes before coming back over to her, holding out a Coke.

"Did you want a beer tonight?"

"No," she laughed. "No alcohol."

"That's what I thought."

Buns of both types sat on plates. Her cookies were out, a chocolate cake, and a couple of different types of salads. The BBQ was already fired up and the burgers and hot dogs cooking.

The birthday boy appeared in front of her to welcome her with a grin, but smiled wider when she handed him the boxes. Laughing, he ripped into them where he stood, laughing harder when he got to the book: *Owners, a Dogs Point of View* and a mug stating *I Don't Need Therapy. I Need a DOG* in bright red letters.

Holding the presents, one in each hand, he threw his arms around her and hugged her tight.

She hugged him back, seeing Ian and Travis both smile.

He wore a white muscle shirt on his surprisingly buff frame. On his left bicep was a tattoo of the toothy Count from Sesame Street, a 1,2,3, 4 , arched across the top. She smiled when she saw it.

"Nice ink and very appropriate, but aren't you a little young?" she asked.

He looked at it and smiled. "Hey, you like it? Pretty cool, huh? You can get a guardian to sign for anything these days." He pointed at Travis. "Do you have any?"

She shook her head. "Never took the plunge, though I did think about getting a tramp stamp once. The whole name just intrigued me. 'Tramp stamp' like I could be so wicked if I just got it."

"You wanted a tramp stamp?" Ian purred. "Hmm, that would have been nice. What kind?"

She made it up on the spot. "It was a Celtic Trinity Knot."

Ian clutched his chest and sighed dramatically. "Now you're just being cruel."

Travis laughed from ten feet away.

Evan turned to go and show his presents to the dark haired guy on the bench who sat alone a short distance away.

One of the roommates came up to her, extending his hand. "I'm Quinn," he said. He was good-looking, young with sandy blond hair cut in a conservative but long style and a light goatee beard around his mouth. His eyes were gentle brown, his smile genuine.

She shook his hand. "The flirt," she smiled.

He laughed and leaned a little forward. "Excuse me?"

"I was told you were the flirt that would make me smile, but," she added raising a finger, "it would be a sincere smile and I would enjoy it forever."

He laughed harder. "Stuart told you that?"

She shook her head. "No, the cute, little guy."

"What did he tell you about Jason?"

"Smooth. Would have my phone number in under two minutes and I wouldn't even realize I gave it to him."

Quinn laughed more. "Little rug-rat knows us pretty damn well." He looked at Evan. "I'll have to figure out a way to get even."

"You work at the hospital?" she asked."

He looked back at her and smiled. "Yeah. Can't keep me away."

182

"You enjoy it?"

"Very much. I hang out in various departments bugging people until they tell me things they didn't know they were going to share. You can see some real weird ass shit, but this is hardly flirting material. I should ask you to dance or something."

She leaned closer to him to whisper. "There's no music."

He met her halfway in the lean, hitting her with the predicted smile. "Thought I noticed something missing. How about we just make out?"

She stepped away from him, her hand covering her mouth as she laughed harder than she had all night.

Travis came up to them and they turned toward him.

"Did I miss the joke?"

"He's propositioning me."

Travis pointed at Quinn. "This one? I think you got some of us confused." He pointed to the guy sitting off by himself, his feet raised and crossed on a second chair, a beer in his hand.

"It's that one you have to watch for."

"I heard that," the other guy said, taking a drink off the bottle, his smile playful. He didn't move from his position.

"Evan," he said from his perch, "get me another beer and I might forget the rumors you're spreading. Otherwise I'll have to take drastic measures against your hard drive."

Evan grinned and got Jason the beer before Ash met the last member.

Travis batted her on the shoulder. "Not drinking?"

"Had sort of an alcohol induced wild night yesterday and I don't want to have to drink any more of that hangover shit he made me this morning."

Travis laughed and looked at Ian. "Beetroot?"

"Among other things," Ian said.

"That's my man," Travis said.

This was his family, unconventional to say the least, but hardcore loyalty seeping from the seams. She drank her Coke and smiled and watched him talk with each of them. There was affection here, maybe more than you would see with a family sharing DNA. She wasn't really sure. It wasn't the kind of home she had been raised in.

"How long have you guys been together?" she asked, directing the question to no one in particular.

Ian turned to her first, before he looked at Travis who looked back. Jason glanced at Evan. They all looked at her.

"Wasn't trying to put one out there to stump you," she said.

Ian smiled. "No, it's not that. It varies. Travis and I started out together. Quinn came to rent a room. Jason had finished his degree and the same thing. They never left and Evan? Um?" He looked at Travis.

"He had been with Mom forever. Then she remarried and that didn't work out. I took him."

Because Travis and Evan looked so much alike, she thought. Cop instinct went off screaming bullshit but the why escaped her.

"So how long?" she asked.

"Years," Ian said. "For Travis and me about ten. For the rest, it varies. Evan since he was fifteen, Quinn a while. Jason, too."

She pointed at Jason and his eyebrows went up with another smile. She spoke to Ian. "You said degree. He got his degree. He's twelve."

Everyone laughed but Jason. He gave her a sarcastic smile that was funnier than all the rest.

"Oh come on," she went on, "if he came in the bar, you'd card him. There is no way in hell he's been around years."

"He's a lot older than he looks," Travis said.

Hands came down on her shoulder from behind and she turned her head to see Quinn leaning forward to whisper in her ear. "I was going to make you up a plate. Did you want a hamburger or hot dog?"

She smiled and looked at him over her shoulder. "You know I can sense a diversion when I see one."

"Hamburger, then?" he smiled. "Everything on it? And we have potato salad, and tomato, onion and avocado salad. Travis is our master chef. Which would you like?"

"Potato and I'm not falling for it," she smiled.

He kissed her quick on the cheek but she saw his eyebrows go up and the wicked smile and eye roll as he walked by Travis and Ian.

She glared at both of them, trying to figure it out. Making up a story about this didn't make sense. They made her laugh and she liked the feeling. It brought a sense of belonging that this might be home.

The party went on, everyone laughing, having fun. Evan's birthday cake, sat demolished on the table with licked candles and dirty plates around it. The round of Happy Birthday had made him smile and blush at the same time.

Ian came up behind her, surprising her. He wrapped an arm around her neck and pulled her back until she leaned against his chest. He kissed her neck.

The quiet Jason finally walked up toward them, his hands in his baggy jeans, a bright orange T-Shirt with a denim long sleeved shirt over it. He had a leather necklace on with a silver Celtic cross hanging on his chest, a matching leather bracelet on his wrist. The real life version left his photo on Ian's phone in the dust. Early twenties and way better looking than the average movie star, he had long, dark hair cut shaggy, his smile leaned more toward the mischievous while his green eyes looked at her with a mixture of humor and danger.

"Jason," she sighed.

"Hey, gorgeous." He said it as if he had known her his whole damn life.

Ian glared at him and pulled her to the side, keeping Jason on the other side of him.

186

"Problem?" she asked.

"Stay away from him," Ian grinned.

Jason laughed. "Why is that?"

"Besides being Irish? One, you already have a nickname for her and two, if I leave you unsupervised you'll not only have her phone number in three minutes but probably a date booked, too."

Jason laughed louder. "I already have the phone number. The date should be a piece of cake."

"What?" Ian snapped with a half laugh.

"Davenport PD. Detective Barrow, genius. Not hard, though give me a minute and I'll work on getting the cell in her pocket, the home phone on the counter, her birthday to send flowers and her social just because it will really piss you off."

"Do you have any idea how much I hate your guts?" Ian laughed.

Jason tilted his head and showed his best smile. "Only matched by mine for you, sweetheart."

Ash looked between the two of them, the aggravation alongside the admiration neither would ever admit to.

She looked at Jason and smiled. "917-555-1212."

Jason took a step back and laughed at the bogus number while Ian batted her on the head.

"Did you want to write that down?"

"No," Jason said. "I think I got it. Thanks."

Ian motioned to her drink. "Do you want another Coke?"

"I'll be up all night. Do we have any other choices?"

"I'll check." He leaned over and kissed her on the cheek.

Jason still stood beside her, his hands in his pockets.

"Where'd you go to school?" she asked him.

He scratched his nose and managed to look modest. "MIT."

"Really? Not easy to get into."

He shrugged like anyone could do it. "Suppose it depends on what you bring in. I had a good GPA and a few scholarships with an essay and letters of recommendations. Standard shit."

"I'm impressed."

He smiled at her. "Don't be. Not that big of a deal."

Ian got to the ice chest and started pulling things out.

Travis joined Jason and Ash. "Did you bring your gun?"

"No."

"Your badge?"

"No."

He rolled his head to the side and whined. "Oh come on. You know you're going to show me."

She smiled up at him. "I don't think so."

"Come on. Show me."

188

She laughed. "I don't have them."

"Aren't you supposed to walk around armed and dangerous?"

"No," she said.

Ian was pulling out cans and looking at labels. "How about a Sprite?" he asked over his shoulder.

"Sounds good," she called back.

Travis drank his beer. "Go get them," he pushed.

"I turned them in," she said.

"What?" Travis asked.

"Wait a minute," Jason said. "Turning them in? Isn't that another way of saying you quit?"

"That's exactly what it means," Travis said. He looked at Ian.

"I knew," Ian said. "I found out late, but I do know and it's cool."

"You were so cool, a super woman with an 'S' on your chest," Evan said. "A homicide detective."

"No 'S', but a lot of long hours doing bad things makes your life hurt, Evan. This is a good thing."

"Can I ask how you plan on managing?" Travis asked.

"He's the meddler," Ian said. "Don't ever be surprised he asks."

"I have some savings and a plan or two in the works. I'll be okay."

189

"Shit," Quinn mumbled. "Quitting."

She smiled, "Yeah, quit I did, but that's not the biggest problem."

"What's the biggest problem?" Travis asked.

She pointed at Ian. "My partner thinks he put me up to it. He finds him and you may have a room to rent."

Standing on the back porch, Ian took a drink of his beer and stared at the city scape lit up in front of him, the sound of the stream gurgling not twenty feet away.

"Where's the guest of honor?" Travis asked.

Ian looked over his shoulder and saw his friend sitting down in one of the chairs.

You could hear the TV blaring and the laughter from inside the house. Travis was asking only to make conversation.

"Family room. She's playing Battleship with Evan. Quinn is waiting to play winner."

"Jason?"

"Sitting in the corner with his laptop probably breaking into some secret government agency who will show up on our door and arrest us all."

"Most men look up porn. We had to get stuck with a genius who gets bored easily," Travis said.

190

Ian laughed.

"So what was the fight about?"

Ian glanced back at Travis in time to see him stretch out his long legs and drink from his beer. Ian looked back to the night sky.

"What fight?"

"The one you are trying to hide from me who's known you since 1928."

"Nineteen-twenty-eight doesn't count," Ian said. "You took off. You can only start counting from 1958."

"So?" Travis asked.

"Private life. Ever hear of it?"

Travis laughed. "When was the last time you had a private life?"

The backyard lay in front of him. There was no comfort in seeing it. "I think it was the early sixties, but I wouldn't swear to it."

"So?"

"Started with her asking me to move in and then escalated a bit to some financial shit. It was pretty stupid, I guess."

"Which bothered you more?"

Ian glanced at him then away.

"The moving in or the financial shit because I know you love that."

Ian's head snapped up. "Please do not try to help."

"What?" Travis laughed. "I'll grant you've been oozing out of here, but no one has any illusions about the room upstairs now serving as a storage locker."

Ian turned slowly around and folded his arms over his chest.

"What's the problem?" Travis asked.

"Gee. Let me think. What could possibly be the problem?" He glared at Travis.

"So you think all your secrets will come out by living there?"

"I need to be here."

"No, you don't. We know where to find you."

"Can you shut up?"

"What are you worried about? That we'll forget to pick you up when it's time? In our timeline two years barely even registers. So go enjoy them in the place where you can enjoy them the most."

The silence hung around for longer than Ian would have liked but he didn't think he had the right words to break it.

Travis laughed. "Those questions we were worried she might start asking?"

"Aye?"

"She started asking them," Travis pointed out.

"I do realize," Ian said.

"They're going to escalate. Do you have a plan?"

Ian only turned his head to give Travis an irritated smile.

"She's crazy about you," Travis said.

Ian looked at the ground between them.

"So what aren't you telling me?" Travis asked.

Ian shrugged. "I don't know what to do. I feel like it's already been a lifetime with twice as much waiting ahead for us and I love every minute."

"Tell her," Travis said.

"And put every one of us in danger?"

"You think she would lead the hordes with pitchforks or torches?"

Ian smiled. "No. I think she would crawl into bed and ask me to show her what's new."

"What was her secret?"

"Money. Apparently enough where she can take some time off."

"Great," Travis laughed. "One of your favorite subjects. And you're a murdering vampire who not only hasn't taken a victim since 1958, but you led all of us out of the dark and into the Promised Land."

"Aye," Ian said. "Davenport."

Travis laughed. "This round's Promised Land. Who knows the next?"

The backdoor opened. Ian and Travis turned around at the same time. Ash stood in the doorway, the door in her hand. Her faced glowed, the smile a mile wide. The dress she bought today looked better now than it had when they first got here, the waist cinched tight. Ian took half a minute to really concentrate on her. Her hair loose, still holding its wild style. Her eyes bright, full of life and fun from her time in this house.

"Who won?" Travis asked.

"He creamed me. Kid's a master of the board game."

Ian smiled. "Quinn's playing?"

"Yeah."

Travis raised his eyebrows at Ian. "I'm going to go see what's on cable."

Ash took the step out of the house and Travis took the step in. He patted her on the shoulder as he walked by.

"You have a nice bunch of people here," she told Ian.

"Thanks."

"Tonight was fun. I'm glad they put the whole thing together."

He reached out, picking up her hand. He brought it to his mouth, kissing the knuckles. "I should have brought you over before."

"Were you hiding me or hiding them?"

"Neither," he said. "Think I wanted you all to myself."

She smiled and leaned up against him. "Not a bad answer. What about the tour?"

"Sure," he said, reaching for the doorknob.

Ian took her by the hand, walking toward the stairs. Up in his room, he closed the door behind them while she wandered in, taking in everything around her. She took in the posters on the wall first, looking at each one thoroughly before moving to the next.

He moved to his stereo, hitting play, filling the room with quiet rock from The Animals singing the House of the Rising Sun, while she walked to the electric piano. Reaching out, she ran one finger silently down the keyboard as she walked toward the guitars and then to his desk. The drawing had been left out.

She picked it up, staring at it a long time.

She turned to him. "You drew this?"

He nodded. "First night we met."

She looked back at it. "It's really good."

"Thanks."

She looked at the piano and the guitars. "I guess there is still a lot we don't know."

"Aye," he sighed.

She walked around to the bed, standing on the same side she would if they were at the house. Her side. His side. It had come so naturally it was hard to remember when it had been any different.

195

She reached over, running her hand flat against the quilt. His fingers flexed, aching to be on her now.

"Are we okay?" he asked.

She looked at him. Standing straight, she slid off her new dress, pulling it over her head while he silently watched. Braless, wearing only black lace panties, the dress hit the floor and his mouth went dry.

She pushed her fingers into the edges of the panties and slipped them down her legs, dropping them on top of the dress. Totally nude, she lifted the edge of the quilt and sheets and slipped into his bed, lying back on the pillows with both her arms raised above her head.

He managed to find his voice, though when it came out it was hoarse. "I have actually never had a woman in this room."

"Not in this bed?"

He shook his head slow.

"Do you have any idea how sexy that is?"

Aye, he thought. Right now, he actually did

She pulled the quilt higher against her breasts before sliding toward the edge. She was getting out, he realized.

"I'm sorry," she said, looking every inch as if she meant it. "I can—"

He stepped the rest of the way, until he was at the foot. There was no footboard here between them. Just him and the mattress with her skin on his sheets.

"No," he said. "No. You're fine. You're perfectly fine."

She relaxed, leaning back again. "Are you sure?"

"Positive," he smiled. He suddenly felt a whole lot better.

She turned around and stacked one pillow on top of the other before lying back down. "You don't have enough pillows here," she said.

"Easily fixed." He reached up and unbuttoned his shirt then pulled it off, then his T-shirt, dropping them both where they would fall.

"You slept here," she said, stretching out. "I like that."

"I'm glad."

"Do you want to draw me?"

He kicked off his shoes and pulled at his socks.

"Like this?" he asked, motioning to her lying out in front of him.

She nodded slowly, letting the quilt fall to show one perfect breast.

"What if someone found it?" He undid his pants, pulling them and his boxers off in one smooth move.

"You could have it framed," she said. "Hang it right over there." She pointed to a spot on the wall.

He walked around the bed to his side, and slid into the sheets beside her. Reaching for her, he pulled her close. He looked down, tracing a finger along her shoulder, feeling the skin quiver. "This is mine," he said, kissing the place he touched. "It's not getting hung on any wall for anyone else to see."

She stared at him, her arms coming around his shoulders.

"What do you think about me moving in next weekend?" he asked.

She lay back on the pillow, her arms on his shoulders and stared up at him.

She was so quiet he went on talking. "I could probably get Jason's SUV Saturday night. There's not a lot up here so it wouldn't take too many trips. Might even be able to get Evan to help me pack up everything."

"I don't understand. You said you couldn't."

He glanced down at her. "I can make it work. I *will* make it work."

She took a long time to answer, making him nervous.

"I would like that," she finally said. She moved her fingers across the skin of his back.

He looked down at her. "I'm an idiot."

"How so?"

"I already live there."

She nodded her head slow. "I kind of thought so, too. That's why it was such a shock you didn't want to be with me."

He leaned over, kissing her. "You're the only one I want to be with."

198

She grabbed him around the waist, rolling with him until he lay on his back and she was hovering over him.

He leaned away from the bed, his hand on the back of her neck, pulling her to him until his mouth crushed against hers. She had never taken him so high so fast. He picked up her hand, kissing her along the inside of her wrist, his eyes closed, her skin soft.

She sank down onto him, engulfing him in her perfect heat as she let out a low moan of pure pleasure. He slid in smooth and sexy. There was no barrier between them and she was so wet when he hadn't even touched her.

She took his arms, pinning them over his head, bent at the elbows, haloing his head. She held him there. When he tried to move, she pressed gently, keeping him in place. It was her in control now, her demanding from him.

She rose and lowered herself slowly; her eyes closed tight, her breasts above his face. He watched her while she rode him. She started out slow and steady, building as the minutes ticked by, her hips coming down harder and faster, her sounds matching the pace she kept. He thrust up into her with each movement. He couldn't get any deeper inside of her.

He tried again to pull his arms down, but she pushed harder, holding him in place.

"No," she groaned. "I want you like this," she said.

His head fell back against the bed, his mouth open. It felt too good. Too tight. He wanted to hold her, he wanted his hands on her body.

He heard the snap in his own head. The sound that meant he needed more.

He yanked his arms from under her hands, her eyes snapping open in surprise. When he flipped them over, she uttered a soft "No," but he didn't listen. She cried out when he took it up a notch. Reaching up, he held her arms like she had his, only with him, he was stronger.

He had her trapped when she didn't even know it.

His kissed down her throat while he held her still. When she tried to pull away, his grip tightened, keeping her helpless under him. His teeth grew and he didn't try to stop them. No words came to his mind as he only concentrated on her body under his and two short years. They were only going to have two short years before he had to move and leave her behind. It wasn't enough. It was nowhere near enough.

He flicked his jaw, his fang cutting her in the right spot. She gasped but he couldn't tell if it was pain or pleasure and right now, he didn't care. His mouth wide, he sucked, drops of blood falling against his tongue. It was her. Only her. Metallic and sweet and he wanted more.

The taste took his urgency and turned it to craze. It was in him now, his true nature crawling along his nerves, making him shake with want.

He opened his mouth wider with every intention of sinking his teeth deep into her throat and drinking what she had to offer.

She was his, he thought, his eyes closed tight, his mouth latched on to her neck.

"Ian," she whispered and he heard the panic. She pulled at her arms, struggling against his hands. He closed his eyes tighter and tried to pretend it was ecstasy he felt in her when he knew it was fear.

He knew how to do this, how to make it good for her. He struck when they shuddered in his arms. It always had been with every faceless woman he had ever taken. When they wouldn't feel it until it was too late. He pounded into her harder to bring her to that point, to feel her climax around him so he could swallow her blood.

She tried to pull her arms away, but he kept her helpless "Ian. Stop. Please stop."

He sucked for another few seconds. Then he let go of her arms, pulling his mouth from her neck with a growl and a gasp, the horror of what he was about to do hitting him like a two by four.

He rolled away before they were done, putting distance between them. Lying on his back, facing away, he forced himself back down. His breathing hard, concentrating on each breath, letting it out slowly. Self-loathing coated each thought at what he had almost done to her.

"Are you okay?" she whispered.

His head turned toward her, his gaze meeting hers. She didn't have a clue what had happened. What kind of violence he was capable of. She was confused and unsatisfied and there were no words he could offer her to make it better.

"Are you?" he asked.

She nodded her head. "Yeah," she said softly.

But she wasn't. He could read it in her eyes and in the way she bit on the corner of her lip.

It was too soon to reach for her, too soon to have physical contact with her. He didn't trust himself right now, couldn't guarantee her safety.

"You're awfully quiet." Her voice was soft, barely above a whisper. His gaze shifted to her neck. There was a pinprick showing red. He swallowed hard.

"I need a minute." He answered honestly, giving her no explanation.

"That's okay," she said. "I'm not going anywhere."

Only she was. He looked at her lying against the one feeble pillow he had to offer her and he knew they were done. He couldn't see her and keep her safe.

CHAPTER TEN

Ashley stood at the railing, her arms spread wide against the cool metal. It was a remarkable view. The whole town seemed to light up in front of her, the air cool against her skin still warm from his touch. Beside her, the larger pond, with orange fish coming up for a hand out. She could hear the stream behind her gurgling. She didn't know what had happened between them upstairs.

He came up behind her, holding a beer toward her. They clinked the necks together and she smiled up at him. "Cheers."

His strained smile made her edgy. She took a drink. He matched her.

"You're awfully quiet," she said.

"Not really," he said.

But it was there, between them. Something he wasn't saying. Something that had her suddenly nervous.

"What happened?" she asked.

"I don't want to talk about it."

She licked her lips, took a drink and looked out over the city. He was shutting himself down, pulling away from her.

"We're not okay," she said.

He looked away, his gaze traveling over the view.

"Yeah, that's what I thought," she said. "Upstairs?" she asked.

"I said I don't want to talk about it." His tone had her flinching.

He looked over his shoulder to the house. He looked at her then, his eyes sad, his mouth set in a straight line. "Will you be coming into Cooper's on Tuesday?"

The question took her by surprise.

"I thought. Yeah. Maybe. If you're not too busy."

"Aye," he said. "We'll be busy. It's probably best if I concentrate on work."

Her eyes narrowed. When had he not been able to take his break with her? He always had the time, no matter how busy they were he got his break.

"I can't do this," he said. He drank from the beer bottle.

"Do what?" She swallowed hard.

"This," he said. He used the beer bottle to motion between the two of them.

She lowered her beer and stared up at him, feeling his words throughout her body. Nausea started low in her gut, rising up, threatening to choke her. Of all the things she thought of at that moment, she pictured his blue toothbrush sitting next to hers in the holder in the bathroom.

"You are going to break up with me."

He opened his mouth but closed it before anything could come out. He lifted the beer and took a long drink instead.

"So, not moving in next weekend?" she asked.

"No," he said, looking at the ground. "I can't."

"Is it because of upstairs?"

"No," he said, shaking his head before taking another drink. "I don't like liars. You should have told me sooner."

She took three steps toward the house, setting her beer down on the closest table. It hurt so much inside there was not even a word to describe it.

"You said it was okay. We would work it out."

"I was wrong. The more I think about it the more I just want to get you out of my fucking sight."

Staring at him, her jaw dropping open, too shocked to respond. His entire personality seemed to have changed in minutes. The gentle, playful man she had known disappeared. A straight back, hard-faced bastard stood in his place.

He drained the bottle, then walked over and picked up her beer and started working on that one.

She turned to stare at the now pale view, feeling the words more than hearing them, thinking of him shoving her away upstairs. Heart pounding in her chest, her breathing hard as she finally felt her insides breaking.

"I don't want to see you anymore," he said.

Her eyes drifted closed. The first tear fell, but she didn't brush it away. Even from the back he would know what she was doing.

"Do not come here again. Stay the fuck out of Cooper's and I'll send someone over to pick up the shit I left at your house."

She stepped into a past she had never shared with him and found the father who thought violence would fix the problem, a mother who looked the other way and a little girl who learned early to pretend and become someone else in order to hold her head high. She brought that lesson forward, pulling on it, shoving it into her pain for the strength to get through the next few minutes. She turned to face him, cop now and not a victim.

"You're not going to do it yourself?"

"And give you a chance to sweet talk yourself into another fuck?"

He couldn't have hit her with less impact.

She looked at the beautiful yard, glowing with soft light and water, the echoes of the party in her head, his gentle hands holding her, pulling her away from Jason, talking with Travis and every single one of them.

She had belonged. For a brief glimpse of time, she had finally belonged among friends and family. His about-face left shockwaves.

"Because let's be real," he said. "Of the hundreds of chicks I have laid, not one spread as fast as you. Though to be fair, you do give the absolutely best blow jobs I have ever had."

She stood caught in an alternate reality she couldn't grasp, too shocked by his look, his words, his actions to do more than try to shuffle it all into place. Straightening her shoulders she tilted her chin, all the while the pain making her want to puke.

"Practice," she said. "I got a lot of practice when I was younger."

"I have no doubt," he said.

The verbal slap hurt more than a physical one would have.

She moved to stand in front of him.

"Can I have my keys, please?"

He looked at her for a long minute. She stood there, waiting, her hand out. He reached in his front pocket, slapping them down into her hand.

Her fingers closed over them and she waited. "Thank you," she said.

"Anytime," he snarled.

She had the perfect comeback for a situation she was losing, that used his friends in suggestive ways which would sky-rocket his fury. It would hurt him. She glanced up at him and thought of the gentle moments, the kind times he had shown her. He had been good to her while it lasted and she didn't want him to feel the pain he was inflicting.

"I can honestly say," she said softly, "I never expected it to last a lifetime, but I never thought we would end like this."

"Reality is a bitch. And so are you. Get out of my fucking house."

She nodded and turned, heading toward the gate that led to the alley, leaving anything she had brought with her tonight for them to divide.

She got three steps when the figures appeared in front of her on the walkway. Two men. One blond. One dark. One shorter than the other, both smiling at her with smiles defying reality and eyes a weird shade in the dark.

She stopped and stared at them.

"Hey Stuart," the blond said.

Taking a step away as they came forward, she went back to the safety of the yard.

Behind them, several more men came through the gate creating a barrier on the walkway. They had a look about them. A look of danger, which was hard to ignore.

Ian's hand slammed down on her shoulder, yanking her back further than she could imagine, shoving her behind him.

"Walter?" Ian gasped. His tone said shocked. "Max?"

"You will never guess who I ran into while I was in San Francisco," the dark man said. "Had all sorts of questions."

"Oh, you son-of-a-bitch," Ian said, moving backwards, forcing distance between her and them.

"That is one damn fine looking broad," Max said. "Where the hell did you pick up something with that kind of class who can give blow jobs, too?"

Ash paled. Ian took steps back, forcing her to move with him.

"Fuck," Ian muttered. "So you're new best friends. How sweet. Looks like you might have something on your mind. Want to say it and go?"

"Their faces," she whispered.

"I know, honey," he said, touching her hand as he moved backwards slowly pushing her toward the house. She looked over her shoulder. They were never going to make it.

The man out in front spoke. "Friends is a strong word. Once you get kicked in the balls by the best you had, you look at what comes next a little more leery."

Ian spoke to the crowd while moving them back. "Maybe what you had isn't what you thought because I can guarantee you never had anything that you think you did and I couldn't have made it more obvious at the time if I tried. But Max, it didn't work out but when you left, you left a friend."

"Ran out of money. He's got lots."

The man he called Walter sniffed the air.

"She's human," Walter said.

Ian backed up further. He was bigger than her, blocking her view with his wide shoulders.

"What the hell is going on?" she whispered.

"Right now," Ian said, talking slow. "There are a shitload more of them then there are of me and we're fucked unless someone inside looks out a window."

"Shit," she mumbled.

Looking down, she noticed the bulge in his back jean pocket. Hope—smiling a little, she pulled out his cell phone and speed dialed three. Speed dial three was Travis. And a second later, she heard Travis answer. She whispered soft against Ian's shirt.

"Backyard."

"What?" Travis asked.

"Now," she whispered and the phone went dead.

"Who are these people? " she asked, peering around Ian.

"Guy on the right is Walter Bennett. Asshole. Guy on the left, Max Garcia. Also an asshole. The rest, who gives a fuck? "

"Hi," the dark haired man—Max—said. He wore round tortoise shell glasses which actually would have looked good on his handsome face if she didn't hate his guts already.

"We haven't met formally, but I hear you hang out here a lot." He looked up at the house. "It was always nice here. My room was in the basement but it wasn't bad. I liked it."

"What?" Ash gasped.

"Is she on the menu?" the man to Walter's right asked. "We haven't had a bite all day and could sure use a little pick me up."

"She's mine," Ian said surprising Ash. Break-ups tended to relinquish possession. "Want to try to get near her?"

"Yeah," Walter said. "Planning on marrying her from what I understand. You finally found someone to match up to that idiotic list that kept you dateless for decades."

Human? Decades?

"What are you talking about?" Ian said.

"You remember a pretty face," Max said. "You told her you were going to marry Ashley."

"Not an idea I'm opposed to but I never said that," Ian said.

A woman walked into the backyard by the same gate, moving slow to stand by Walter, a hand on his shoulder.

"Sharron? Miss Monte Cruz?"

"Yeah," Max said. "Picked her up in Phoenix, if you can believe that. Can you imagine living down there with our skin condition?"

She purred in Ian's direction. "We could have had so much fun. Goodnight Kisses are so sweet."

"A trap, Walter?" Ian snapped. "You set a fucking trap for me?"

"Yeah, should have known better. Pick-ups never worked with you."

"What the hell was supposed to happen? Me go back to the hotel and then what?"

Walter laughed. "You never would have made it to the hotel."

The backdoor slammed back against the house. Ash looked to see Travis charge through the yard with Quinn and Evan. There was no denying the balance of power shifted.

Travis grabbed her roughly by the arm, yanking her away from Ian and tossing her at the stairs, away from the crowd. "We got this. Get in the house, Ashley. And close the door."

She started toward the stairs while keeping her gaze on the yard.

"Ah," Max sighed. "The Primary. Here to get everything under control."

"God, I hate your motherfucking guts," Walter said to Travis. "I always did, even before you stabbed me in the back a dozen times. You were always just so fucking annoying. And shit, tall. Why the hell are you so fucking tall?"

"I'm heart broken," Travis said. "I was secretly in love with you and hoping we could get something started the next time I saw you."

"Fuck you."

"Yeah," Travis said. "That's sort of what I was thinking."

"Gay jokes? All these years and you start off with gay jokes while you two have been living together for half a century?"

Travis blew him a kiss.

Evan leaned over to press his shoulder against Ash's middle, he had her lifted and pinned with strength she couldn't fight. Faster than she could blink, they were up the stairs and he tossed her into the house.

"Stay inside," Evan said before yanking the door shut behind him.

She was up and off the ground, pressing up against the glass.

"Hey, Gorgeous, what's going on?" Jason asked from behind her, sounding cheery as he entered the room. She couldn't pull herself away so he pushed, looking out the window.

"Shit," he said, reaching for the doorknob. He stopped to stare at her, his green eyes more dangerous than before. "Fuck," he snapped. He closed his eyes tight and slammed his open palm on the door.

"What the hell is going on? Who are these people?"

He looked at her, then looked out the window but didn't say anything.

"Go," she whispered.

"I can't," he snapped, then looked at her. "We don't do things like that. We don't leave women unprotected. Shit," he said again.

She pushed him over and looked at the back.

"I've never met them," he said, "but I bet I know who they are. Stuart will be their first target."

"Walter. And Max. He said the other guy was Max. They looked funny."

"Max? " Jason looked at her. "Max is back?"

She tilted her head. "Who the hell is Max? Why would anyone come after you five?"

He laughed sadly, raised his eyebrows, bobbed his head and ignored her question. He looked back outside. She could see his whole body vibrating.

"Go" she said. "If you can help, go."

His gaze snapped at her. "Not our style to leave women alone. Especially…" He cut himself off and motioned to her with both hands up and down. "Like you."

She reached for the doorknob. "Then I will do it."

He grabbed her, yanking her back. "No offence, sweetheart but those guys will eat you alive." He smiled sarcastically and nodded his head. "Literally."

She grabbed him by the denim shirt and pushed him toward the door. "Then get out there."

He shoved her up against the wall. "If I go that leaves you vulnerable. You cannot open this door. We go down, you stay inside, do not, no matter what they say, invite them in or go outside, not even to help us. No matter what they say, Ash, do you understand? Do not leave here until after sunrise and then get out of town before dark. I mean out of town and not down the block. Do you understand what I am saying?"

She was shaking her head hard. "Not a word of it."

"Fine, did you hear what I said and can you follow the instructions?" He gave her a goofy face. "I have very good penmanship. Do you want me to write them down?"

She narrowed her eyes at him.

"Gorgeous, they need me out there. I am better than most of them. I have a higher body count than any of them and I know what I'm doing. I have to get out there but I can't leave you unless I know you are safe."

"Yes," she snapped. "I understand. Stay inside. Sunrise. Leave town. Now go. Don't let them hurt him."

He nodded and moved to the wooden knife block on the counter, grabbing two in one hand then turning back. He stopped on his way to the door to push her back against the wall, pressing up against her. He leaned over, his eyes closed, his open mouth covering hers, his hand curved on her neck. Chaste but undeniably out-of-the-atmosphere hot, his lips played with hers, spiking up the hunger as her back arched and her hands clutched his shoulders. He leaned on her longer than they had. His mouth moved only enough, pulling more from her, making her sigh before he finally pulled back with a heavy breath and a wicked smile.

"Nice," he whispered.

She slugged him on his shoulder. "Why the hell did you do that?"

He smiled at her, still holding her neck, still leaning on her. "You really are gorgeous and the name fits. And either I am about to go get myself killed or I'm going to live long enough to have you tell Stuart I did it and it's going to sky-rocket his piss off mode, so either way I win because his piss mode with that accent, is funny as hell."

He blew out a hard breath and backed up. "Don't suppose I could get those phone numbers? You know, just in case I came back?"

She glared at him.

"Yeah, I'm going," he smiled. "Do not under any circumstances follow. Understood?"

She nodded and he was gone.

She ignored him and reached for the knob and opened the door and took a step out so she could keep track of the score. The dark night and low lights carried their voices like an amplifier. She could hear them all, even the ones facing the opposite way.

"Hey," Max said, moving to the side, his hands out in submission. "This is a talk between friends."

"Nine of you, four of us. That's friendly," Ian said.

"Who's counting?" Walter smiled evilly.

The men in the yard, moved, circling. Travis and Evan watched while she watched Jason join, bringing them to five.

"Quinn," he snapped and Quinn looked up.

Jason tossed him one of the two knives and Quinn caught by the handle as if he had a blade in his hand his whole damn life.

Ian faced off Walter. Travis headed in Max's direction.

The charge in the yard was off the charts. The fact her guys looked so damn relaxed while the others shifted feet and moved side to side, scared her even more.

"What do you want?" Ian asked.

"You," Walter said. "We want you to come home."

"I assume the recent color is you?"

Walter shrugged. "Got to keep amused. Blood Letting," he laughed. "Can you think of a better name?"

"You need to go," Travis said, taking a step forward.

Walter laughed, his hands in his pockets. "We like it here."

Ash tilted her chin and watched and listened.

"She doesn't know, does she?" Max asked

"What do you want?" Ian snapped.

"I answered that," Walter snapped back. "Why don't you get it? We'll forget the warrants for your deaths, forget the betrayals and we'll forget about the bodies you left. We'll even forget this asshole who orchestrated the whole thing and accept the strays you picked up on the way."

Ian looked at Travis, then looked back at Walter. "Travis didn't orchestrate anything. It was my idea. I had to talk him into it."

Walter laughed. "Right."

"Aye, right," Ian said. "See, I hated your guts about as much as you hated his, only more. I couldn't stand to be in the same room with you. And hitting on me every other day because you would not hear 'no'? I had to get away from you or lose my motherfucking mind."

Walter narrowed his eyes at Ian and smiled ugly.

"I've been watching," Walter said. "The things you have done. Behind the bar Tuesday night?"

217

Ashley gasped. Walter took a private moment between them and turned into something ugly. She closed her eyes thinking of a night suddenly cheapened by prying eyes.

"What I do with my girlfriend, is none of your business," Ian said. "She is under our protection."

"A human under a vampire's protection?" Walter laughed. "Not unless they're on the menu."

Travis looked at Ian. Ian looked back. "I think that was the sound of our cover being blown to hell." Travis said.

"Fuck," Ian sighed.

She stepped into the yard, way further than she intended. "What?" she snapped. "What did you say?"

Jason shifted fast, taking up residence directly in front of her, his back to her front. He stood between her and the yard, the knife ready. He didn't look as relaxed as he had.

"What did he say?" she snapped.

"Nothing I'm going to repeat. You going to get back in that house or did you want me to divide my attention?"

Jason started backing up until he bumped into her and she was forced to go back. He got her to the door.

"Do I get a choice in this? I can help." she asked.

"No you can't. Not with this."

"Cop, remember?"

"Don't give a shit, remember?"

He tried to push her back but she hesitated. Two guys watched and moved toward them.

"Quinn," Jason snapped.

"I got 'em. They won't get two more feet and if they don't know it, they're stupider than they look."

One of the men turned to look at Quinn. "What the fuck did you say to me?"

"You're one of us now, Ash," Jason said. "Now get in the fucking house before I die protecting you."

She stepped across the threshold and she heard him sigh. His shoulders relaxed a little more.

"Really?" Jason said to the guy moving toward him, heading for her. "Ash, do not step out of the house again. You promise me and I'll believe you."

She didn't want to but she did. "Yes."

"Hey Stuart," Jason called down the hill.

"What?" Ian said without turning around.

"Girlfriend is tucked away but there's an asshole here who wants me to get started. You have an opinion on that?"

"I'm not sure." Ian looked at Walter. "Do I have an opinion on that?"

"We were family Stuart and you walked out the door to hang with this asshole?" He pointed at Travis.

"Call your guy back or my guy starts cutting, and I'm willing to bet my two best can take out your six and since you already know my best, you know what he can do."

"Because Nelson and Sullivan are the best, right?" Walter sneered.

"Aye, they are. And your man is about to die."

"Hudson," Walter called up the hill. "Drop it for now."

"I can take him," the man in front of Jason said.

"How the hell do you know who I am?" Jason asked Walter. "You met them. You've never met Evan or me. Did Max give us up?"

Walter laughed.

Ash took a step back into the kitchen. They were going to kill each other. They were really talking about killing each other.

"You really thought you would keep it from her, Stuart?" Walter asked.

"I think we have established her position and you can back down on that," Ian said.

"Her position?" Max laughed. "I heard what you think of her position. You dumped her about one minute before we came in the gate. Want to tell Jason back there he's defending your reject?"

"Really?" Jason chuckled. "That's cool. She's pretty damn hot. When I'm done up here, I'll see if she wants to go get a cup of coffee. There's a really great place open late not too far from here."

"Yes," Travis said. "He broke up with her. Must mean we don't care. Why don't you go ahead and grab her so we can get back to the important shit in our lives."

"Really," Walter sighed. "You don't mind?"

"Naw," Travis said. "You only have to get her past those two in the back. Oh and of course, then you have to get past us three to get her out the gate. Shouldn't be a problem."

"Five to nine," Walter said.

"Yeah," Travis said. "And our worst is still damn good thanks to hours of training with Nelson and Sullivan." Travis chuckled. "So basically, your nine doesn't do all that much to our fear factor."

Walter walked away a few feet then came back to stare at Ian.

"Stuart?"

"Walter," Ian smiled back.

"You no longer have that great conversationalist waiting in your bed to do sexual favors for you. Sharron here is still in town."

Sharron gave Ian a smile and took a few steps toward him.

"I'll pass," Ian said. "My memories of the absolute best are good enough to sustain me."

"Oh come on," she purred as she moved forward to put a finger on his chest. "I can be a lot of fun."

Ash saw his hand snap up to grab the other woman. "You are about to get hurt."

"You're unarmed," she smiled.

"I will pull your fucking heart out through your throat."

"Come on," Walter said. "Why haven't you turned her? You have had a thousand opportunities. I don't even think she would fight you. Well not a lot, at least. Besides, the struggle is a turn on, remember? The perfect foreplay leading to the main event."

Travis moved past Ian.

"I like her," Travis said. "A lot. She's one of my favorite people and shit like you will not be going anywhere near her. Do you understand?"

"I don't hear so good."

"Then hear this," Travis said. "Jason...go."

Jason stood by on a hair trigger. The command came down and he moved. Two swipes of the knife with his body moving in fluid motion and the other guy hit the ground, clutching his throat.

When Jason started, Quinn went into action, moving fast and swift with deadly accuracy and a grace that shouldn't be applied to weapons. Between the two of them, in seconds, four of the other guys were gone. They were just gone. Standing and trying to defend and then a blast of grey dust she didn't understand and the bodies were *friggin'gone.*

The eyes of her men turned from their natural colors to dark in the night. Mouths which had been normal changed as teeth grew and the attacks continued.

She slammed the door, understanding the words that hadn't made sense while still denying them in her head.

Through the window, she watched. Travis grabbed a man, sinking his teeth into a neck while Jason, Quinn and Evan moved through the bodies and Ian fought Walter. They were efficient and experienced, guilt free.

When Walter screamed in pain, holding his arm at an odd angle, those who stood against ran toward the gate, Walter with the woman in tow.

Ash watched them all, her breath fogging up the window until she had to wipe it away. Still holding the doorknob in her hands, she turned it, but all of their words screamed in her head. She held it until the metal felt warm.

Her men checked each other, then turned toward the house. They looked normal, their mouths the same, their eyes no longer dark. Except the blood running down Travis's chin and onto his shirt.

Ash spun before they were halfway up the steps. She grabbed her purse as she swung past the dining room and made it to the front door.

She got it open only three inches before Ian's hand slammed onto it above her, shoving it closed. He reached around her, flicking the lock into place.

"You can't leave," he said.

She saw him in her mind. Teeth and eyes and Walter's words. She backed away from him, sliding to the side, putting as much distance between them as she could.

"You told me to go," she said.

"You can't."

"You can't stop me."

"Actually I can. And I will."

He didn't make a move toward her. "They're out there," he said.

She looked over to the door but didn't see anything through the glass window.

Swallowing hard, she looked at Ian.

He stepped back, raising his arm to motion to the kitchen. "Come back in. I'll make you a drink."

"You told me I couldn't see you here. You don't get to—"

"Please," he snapped, making her jump.

She moved slowly back into the dining room where she set her purse down and moved into the kitchen.

Jason was opening a first aid kit, Quinn waiting with a slash on his forearm. Evan sat at the table with a hole in his shoulder and stain on his muscle shirt. Travis stood at the sink, rinsing his face. He picked up a dishcloth and rubbed it over his chin, leaving it stained pink. Blood still marred his shirt. He set the towel on the counter beside two bloody kitchen knives.

Ian walked past her moving to the cupboard where he got a glass and a bottle of scotch. He poured, screwed the lid back on and held the glass up for her to take. His knuckles held red, angry abrasions.

She stared at them, but didn't move.

"So," Jason said as he was working on Quinn. "Ash, I was thinking maybe next Saturday? Pick you up about seven? Maybe some dinner and see a movie?"

"Shit, Jason," Travis snapped.

"What?" Jason laughed. "It just got announced to the world they broke-up. I want to be sure and secure my position in line, cuz I know for a fact *he's* going to be asking." He pointed at Quinn.

"Yeah," Quinn said, "but I was going to wait until we got the blood cleaned up and I got a chance to explain my preference for nighttime dating."

Ian stepped forward, picking up her hand and putting the glass in her fingers.

"Please," Travis said, "assure me you didn't have sex behind the bar with Walter watching."

Ian swung around to glare at him. "I hadn't really thought Walter was watching, but now that you mention it and after what I just heard, I'm thinking I might be wrong."

"Good job," Travis said, dragging out the words. "Man, I hope it was good."

"It was. Superb. Fantastic." Ian said. "You can't imagine how amazing it was. Now you want to shut up?"

Travis pursed his lips. "Sarcasm doesn't help."

"But being attacked in our backyard by people who shouldn't know where we live, I think that does require it."

Travis looked at her. "You broke up?"

She turned and walked away.

"Ash?" He said. "What happened?"

She spun back around and spoke to Travis, ignoring everyone else. "Yes. We broke up. Highlight of my night." She pointed toward the back door. "I mean, before the gangland war in your backyard. Thank you for a nice evening. Can I go home now?"

"Why?" Evan gasped. "You were perfect together."

"Apparently not…" she stopped, remembering his words, remembering her father's, both emotions mixing to pain.

"What?" Travis asked.

She thought about the answer, thought about what she wanted to share, realizing she didn't give a damn anymore.

"My father used to call me a slut," she said only to Travis. "When I was fifteen years old and had never kissed a boy, he would scream it at me in that voice that made you shudder when he was drunk. Tonight felt like that a lot."

Travis's eyes narrowed and his shoulders flexed. "What did he say to you? "

"Stuart?" she asked, seeing the shock of the name change on Travis's face.

She cleared her throat and stared at Travis's brown eyes, concentrating only on them. "Apparently I'm a bitch. And a cold hearted liar, but hey, I hear I give the best blow jobs ever so I guess we all have our purposes after all, right?"

She shrugged and tried to laugh, but couldn't look at any of them in the face. "I was leaving and then they were there. I couldn't get to the gate."

"If you had gotten through the gate," Jason said, "you'd be dead."

"No," Quinn countered, shifting his gaze to Jason's.

Jason's smile was sad and he nodded his head. "That's right," he said. "You're right."

Travis knocked Ian on the head. "You did that? And you did it cruelly with insult and malice?"

"Remember the personal life thing we talked about?"

"Calling one of my favorite people a slut doesn't come under personal life."

"I didn't and it does and it's none of yours."

"You better have a damn good reason that doesn't end with Jason driving over to her place on Saturday, because let's be real, you feel that way and can treat her that bad, I'd like to get my name in that line, too, to show her what romance and respect look like."

Ian turned to glare at him. "That would make her what? House entertainment?"

Ash's gaze fell to the ground.

"Classy Stuart," Travis said, "Must have been hard to get her agreeing to the separation if you talked sweet to her like that."

"I date a girl. It's over. My friends start drawing straws. You have another name for it?"

Done with Quinn's arm, Jason shoved Ian from the back, pushing him three feet. Ian spun, looking ready to escalate, but stopping.

"Yeah," Jason said. "It's called friends with taste and why don't you show some. You want to be pissed your number one showed up, than be pissed. Don't take it out on the class in the room."

"So the whole house wants to date her?" He talked about her as if she wasn't even there.

"I don't know," Travis said. "We didn't ask Evan."

Ian turned toward her.

She stared him in the eye. "It actually only counts as house entertainment if I fuck all three. If I only pick one I should be safe from being called public property. The problem is trying to narrow it down to which. All the talent looks so *yummy* with such a variety of *tastes* and *textures.* It would be kind of like walking into Baskin Robbins and not only having to decide on which flavor, but having to choose between a cup or a cone. I might have to take intimate interviews. I don't want another mistake."

She saw Jason lean over to Quinn and whisper. "I so get first dibs." He said with a smile and sparkle in his eye that didn't say sex and actually helped her feel a little better.

Ian glared at her. "Did you enjoy that?"

"Probably more then you enjoyed calling me a slut."

"Enough," he snapped. "I did not."

"Fuck you didn't," Travis snapped.

Ian looked at him with narrowed eyes, then back to her. "I apologize if I offended."

"You know what? You did. And tonight? I was supposed to have a good time with my boyfriend's family and then head on home probably to fool around." She walked toward Ian. "But no, I have a hamburger, play a couple of board games, then get dumped into painful oblivion and before I can leave, we're attacked by *nine* people suffering from anemia. I don't feel like accepting your apology. My night sucked and I actually have a feeling it's still going to get a hell of a lot worse."

"Are you done?" he asked calmly. "We can talk if you want."

"What," she looked at him, her hands out, "could I possibly have left to say to you?"

She walked away from all of them, the images of the backyard playing in her mind slamming up against a broken relationship she had thought was perfect. None of it made sense. Nothing she heard or saw. Nothing he said, all so out of character. She turned to find them all watching her. She took a drink of the scotch and shook her head, trying to ignore the splatter marks on Jason and Quinn's shirts.

"Ashley, monsters are real," Evan said from his seat.

She moved back until she was flat against the refrigerator and all of them were in sight.

"Jason, what do you do?"

229

"What?"

"What do you do? "

"Um, computers. I own a computer company. I work out of the house."

"Work out of the house and midnight gym visits," she said quietly. "Quinn, nurse with night shifts at the hospital, works out in the windowless basement. Evan nightshift at Paws, basketball pick-up games after dinner. Travis, night manager at the Bell Rouge, late night jogger. And Stuart, bartender, night shift. Bike. You all work nights. You play nights. What? You all have the same sun allergy that Stuart told me he had?"

Travis sighed and nodded. "Yeah. We all do have the same thing Stuart has."

"Monsters," she whispered. "How do you tell the monsters apart from the good guys?"

"It's pretty easy, Gorgeous," Jason said stepping toward her. "The good guys will kick your ass back into the house then stand side by side united while the other guys try to get to you and you know what? They never will. Not while one of us still stands."

She didn't think she had anything to say to that.

"And pissing him off?" he pointed at Ian. "It's been a hobby of mine since 1967, the whole Irish/Scot thing. I seriously have never gotten tired of pushing his buttons."

"Speaking of which, are you planning on continuing to call her that?"

"What do you care anymore?" Jason asked.

Ian glared at him.

"Does it bother you?"

"No," Ian said. He was so obviously lying.

Jason laughed and crossed his arms on his chest. "Yeah, I think I will."

Ian turned away. "Prick."

"1967?" she asked. "Yeah. Can I go home now?"

"They're waiting outside right now, Ash," Quinn said.

"They were after you," she replied. "All of you because you have death sentences and strays and hell, I didn't understand half of what they were talking about."

"Sweetheart," Quinn said, "I think you understood every word."

"What the hell does highest body count mean, Jason?"

"It means I've killed more people than anyone here, which means I am more ashamed of my previous life and I don't like to talk about it. Stuart doesn't talk about his beginnings back in Scotland, not even after three bottles of whiskey—only US brewed in this house—as we had to pick borders. Evan won't talk about his family in Seattle or the basketball player he was. Quinn, do not under any circumstances mention two names to him: Anna or Fred. And Travis," Jason said. "Ask him anything. He'll share it all."

"Bite me," Travis said.

Jason smiled.

Ian looked at Jason. "If we weren't fucked before we are now."

"Do you honestly think after all I said to her in the house to warn her before I went out and what she witnessed in the backyard told her anything she wasn't already thinking? We were fucked the moment Walter and Max came in the backyard."

"What did you tell her?" Travis asked.

Jason looked at him and shrugged. "I had to leave a woman behind. Law #6. We don't do that and you know that so I left strict instructions. I told her to keep the doors shut, not to invite any of them in if we lost. Stay inside till sunrise. Get out of town before dark and don't look back."

Travis was nodding. "That sums it up pretty good. We were fucked."

Ash leaned her head back against the refrigerator and closed her eyes. "Radcliff is an idiot," she said.

"Who is Radcliff?" Travis asked.

She opened her eyes to exchange stares with Ian.

Ian looked at Travis, then back at her. "He's the coroner who's been working the case. He came up with a kooky theory on the Blood Letting Murders, one our beautiful detective here dismissed as impossible."

"No way," Evan said. "He figured it out?"

She stared at Ian. "You knew."

"We figured it out after the third victim. Quinn found the reports in the morgue. There was no way I could tell you, Ash. Not and not risk exposing everything we've built."

"Five of you," she whispered, staring at Ian. "Living with a secret holding you all together none of you want the rest of the world to know."

"Bitch to be right, isn't it?" His smile was sad.

"You knew," she said. "You knew I was going to figure it out and you had to try to stop me."

He stared at her.

"What you said out back..." she whispered.

"Honey, cruel was the only thing that would work," he said softly. "I had to get you out of here before something happened. I was too late. I'm sorry."

"Ashley," Evan said quietly.

She looked at him.

"I scored twenty-six points my last game before I came to live here. There was a scout in the crowd. We had talked before. He was going to offer me a scholarship to The University of Washington with a full ride for four years."

"That's a nice school Evan...," she said. "...what year was that?"

He looked at her and smiled sadly. "1972."

Ian walked over, took her drink and handed it to Travis. He grabbed her by the shoulder, shoving her toward the door. "Let's go."

She tried to pull away from him, but his grip was too tight. "Where are we going?"

"Upstairs."

"Fuck that," she snapped.

"You know you don't swear, right?" he said pushing her toward the door.

He stopped to turn toward the rest, her face toward them all.

"You know what I'm going to do?" he asked.

They all looked from him to her and back.

"Do we get a choice at this point?" Quinn asked.

"I'm asking," he said.

Travis rubbed his eyes. "Stuart. She knows everything. All you're going to do is confirm and file it in order."

"Evan? Jason?"

They both shrugged.

"I still call dibs," Jason said.

Ian turned them, heading toward the stairs.

"No," she said, trying to wiggle free. "I'm not going anywhere with you."

She fought him the whole way and no one in the room came to her aid. He pushed her along in front of him, in total control. She had never felt this kind of strength in him.

He had her up the first flight of stairs. While she had felt she could take on any situation she ever faced, she was forced to admit she couldn't even stop her boyfriend.

Her *ex-boyfriend.*

At the top of the stairs he pushed open his door and shoved her inside. Evan was behind him, carrying her purse, glass and the bottle of scotch. "She's going to need this."

"Thanks," Ian said. He shut the door behind him and flicked the lock.

CHAPTER ELEVEN

He set her stuff and the bottle on the table by the door. He placed her glass next to it, though he really wished she would take a couple of drinks to maybe calm down her nerves.

She stood at the far end of the room, the unmade bed between them.

Pale, wide eyed. He had never seen her look at him like this, not even when he was telling her all those God awful things he never meant.

They were the hardest words he thought he would ever have to say. Looking at her back away until she was almost to the far wall, he knew they were just the beginning.

He rubbed his face with both his hands, pulling hard. "I don't have a clue where to start," he said. He dropped his hands and stared at her looking just as beautiful as always, lost in a puzzle she didn't understand.

"But I am sorry about what I said," he said.

"Am I supposed to say thank you?"

He shook his head. "No. I only want to make sure you know I didn't mean it."

"So what do we do now?"

"I don't know," he groaned. He nodded over his shoulder. "That down there, though? We vote. We don't make major decisions unless we vote and it has to be unanimous."

"Good to know," she smiled sarcastically.

"I thought maybe that was a good place to start."

"Or we could start with the dumping that makes no sense. Or the knife-fight in the backyard. Or how about you standing across from me four days ago saying you didn't have a clue what was going on in this town."

He pursed his lips and nodded. "Those are good places, too."

"There was a *knife-fight* in your *backyard*," she snapped.

"Aye," he said, "I noticed that." He looked at the door then back at her.

He stopped talking and stared at the floor.

"Are you going to talk to me? Or just stand there?"

"Can I get away with just standing here because shit, I really have no idea what to say."

She moved past him, heading toward the door and reaching for the handle. He grabbed her by both shoulders and that was a mistake. Her under his touch was not the direction they needed.

He held on, pulling her toward him, leaning his forehead against hers, his hands sliding down from her shoulders to hold her arms. He could feel her, smell her perfume, see her long lashes over her closed eyes.

"I…" he started, pausing for a breath. "I really didn't think we were going to pull that off."

"You've done that before?"

"Not the same. Never those odds, never with someone so important up for stake and all of us wanting her safe."

He leaned back to find her staring at him. "I didn't…" he tried and stopped. "What I said, those things I said. I didn't mean them. Not any of them. I had to be cruel to get you to go or else you would always want to try again."

She looked up at him.

"The break-up was real. I'm not taking that back, but what I said to get it, I didn't mean any of it." He closed his eyes. "I had to hurt you enough so you would walk away."

"Why?"

"Because I realized you going was necessary and if I tried to talk it out, you would have argued."

"You know I'm not understanding a whole hella lot of this."

"Probably not my right to even ask, but a hug would be pretty sweet right about now."

She stepped back, away from him until his hands fell off her. He bobbed his head, disappointed but not surprised. "Aye," he sighed.

She backed away from him, putting distance between them. She stared at him, waiting.

"I don't know what to tell you. You saw way more than we ever intended but we didn't expect the attack." He closed his eyes. "There was no way to pull you out before it all went down."

"And you won," she said.

He shrugged. "We were all good on our own and then we came together to make us better."

"I knew you were good at your job. Knew you were great in bed. I even knew you were a fair to excellent cook." She leaned a little forward, her voice changing. "You were killing people."

He sighed and rubbed his face again. "No, we weren't. They weren't people and to get technical, I didn't kill anyone. The guy I had, he got away and damn on that one. It was Jason and Quinn who got fatal while Travis maimed a little. But Ash, they were here to kill us. I'm not kidding. It really was them or us and we had you in the middle."

"Do I want to know why someone wants you dead?"

"Travis thought he saw Walter a few weeks back but he wasn't sure and we were convinced we had to be wrong."

"Sullivan and Nelson, the best? That's Jason and Quinn, right?"

He shrugged. "They are, Ash. I'm sorry. I've seen more knife fights than you can imagine and I would never go up against either of them."

"Because you're a knife fighter?"

Not the direction he meant to take this.

239

"Aye," he replied. "I've been in a few. None recently."

She stared at him, her expression pale and emotionless.

"Do I even know you?"

His nod was shaky. "You know the me I am now. And me now is all that matters."

"They attacked. Why?" she asked.

His hands came out from his side. "It was me they were after. It might have been Travis, but I have the longest history with Walter so he was probably after me."

She seemed to calm down a bit as she thought. "Walter's a friend of yours?"

"No," he shook his head, looking at the floor. "He was never a friend." Ian rubbed his face and walked away, thinking of a way to describe. Sighing hard he turned back to her.

"I was around Walter for about five years, pretty much because I had nowhere else to go. Walter, on the other hand…" He stopped then looked at her waiting. "Walter wanted a relationship with me that wasn't possible. What he proposed was not something I found appealing and I turned him down. He kept his distance, but never gave up hope, I guess. When I left, from what I heard, he took it bad."

"Walter is gay. He wanted you. You said no."

Ian nodded, his smile pursed. "That would be the direct way of saying it, aye. I didn't have a problem with the gay. Not even back then. It just isn't me and what he was—was unappealing on any level." He closed his eyes and shook his head.

240

"What was he?"

"Bat-shit crazy with a love of torturing people."

"Nice," she whispered.

"I met up with Travis, we got along and came up with a plan unheard of in our society. Even talking about it together was dangerous. We walked away from a bar leaving everyone behind, carrying everything on us that we wanted to keep and caught a bus. We wanted out Ash. We hated what we were and we wanted out. We never looked back."

"Travis, the primary? I thought he worked at Bell Rouge."

Ian shook his head. "A Primary is the leader of a den. Most dens follow some sort of governmental process, but we've never considered ourselves traditional so we by-passed most of it. We did make him Primary as he was the oldest." He shrugged. "In effect, Travis is in charge of the house and we all recognize it."

"Law #6?"

Ian nodded. "That's part of the governing. Law #6 is The Law of First Blood. It's got a couple of parts, but what mattered tonight is a woman must be protected. It's a very chauvinistic society. Jason, in essence, broke that when he left you in the house."

"What happens to him?"

"Um…" Ian thought. "In some dens, most actually, he would come under punishment. We don't follow strictly here so nothing will happen to him and we thank him for the knife out back."

"And if he was somewhere else?"

"If he was somewhere else, he would be tortured for three days and face expulsion from the den."

"What?" she gasped. "For leaving me in the house for twelve minutes tops when there was no danger there?"

"We have strict laws," Ian said. "Well, they do. We're sorta lax in a lot. We don't torture here or expel or give death sentences."

"Max?"

"Max was one of us. His room was in the basement off the weight room. He tried to leave the life behind, but couldn't take it. Living like we do, to get here, is not an easy process. He had repeated relapses and was asked to leave. He was our friend, though, even in the end. I can't believe he would do this. Walter, he will stab you in the back and suck you dry and make you beg but Max, he's only a screw up. Harmless."

"Why didn't you kill Walter tonight?"

"Fuck," Ian groaned, walking away to drag his fingers through his hair. He swung back around to stare at her.

"That is something you can do, isn't it?"

He nodded. "I wasn't carrying at the time. I haven't carried in decades. Shit," he said. "Quinn hasn't even carried and he is the deadliest thing you ever saw with a blade."

"The flirt?" she said. "The sweet, gentle, doe-eyed guy who put my dinner together? Deadly?"

Ian let out a slow hard breath and nodded to the side. He spoke calmly. "Aye. He is. He is the coldest, most efficient killer I know. Man, you have a fight, you want him on your side and not the other. And even he hasn't carried in decades."

"Decades," She asked. *"Decades?"* She nodded her head and pursed her lips. "So, not twenty-nine? How many candles do I put on your July cake?"

He groaned and sighed and saw no exit.

"How old are you? How old is Travis? Actually, forget you two. How about Mr. MIT with dibs, who I thought looked as if he should be carded? He looks like he graduated last year, and then, it was ahead of schedule."

Ian was giving up. "Ahead of schedule is right." Ian laughed a little and stuck his hands in his pockets. "He is an asshole of genius who drives everyone crazy. Got into college early. Got his BS early. The degree he was working on? It was his Masters, months away from completion and he had already been accepted into the PhD program. Do not," Ian laughed, "play Trivial Pursuit with him."

She glared at him, her lips tight.

"What?" he snapped. "What do you want me to tell you? The truth? I'm trying but this isn't easy."

She walked forward until she stood in front of him. "What part of tonight do you think was easy on me?"

He looked her in the eye. "Mr. MIT is eighty-nine. He was turned at twenty-three and I am not kidding, he gets carded every *single time* he goes out and it drives him nuts. It's kind of funny you picked that trait to nail him on as it annoys him the most. And aye, he and I go out of our ways to bother each other so thank you for adding to that."

He smiled sweetly.

She didn't laugh. "The rest of you?"

"Can I get out of this?"

"Do you think you can get out of this?"

He sighed hard. "I'm a hundred and sixteen. Travis is three years older than me. Quinn would be next. He hits a hundred in November and Evan, who really is the baby of the family, is only fifty-nine."

She stared at him blankly.

"We all stopped aging when this life was forced on us. What we were when it happened, that's the age you see."

She looked over her shoulder to the window that overlooked the back yard. She looked back at him. "You're kidding, right?" She drank off the glass.

"I will get you home tomorrow and you will be safe as long as you don't invite any of them into the house. They can only come at night and they won't be able to get near you if you don't invite them in the house. They have to be invited. Do you understand?"

"Vampires." She said and he didn't say a word. "That's the word you're not saying."

"Not a word any of us ever really use. We know what we are. We don't have to discuss it among ourselves."

"You have a sun allergy. Have any aversion to garlic or maybe mirrors?"

"You're not going to listen?"

"To all of you being vampires? Why would I listen to that? I don't believe in vampires," she said slowly so he heard each word.

He walked around the bed, closing the distance between them. She backed up with every step he took until there was nowhere for her to go.

"You want me to prove it? After what you saw outside? Everything you heard?"

She stared at him with wide blank eyes. "Why haven't you?"

"What?"

"Whatever Walter was talking about? The struggling?"

"I don't do that," he said. "I haven't done that in many, many years. None of us have."

He sighed hard and pulled his fingers through his hair. "Ashley, it's important you understand. We aren't like the ones who were in the yard. They will kill you or turn you or leave you in pieces. But us, the five of us, we haven't been like that in forever. Each for our own reasons walked away from a life that is impossible to walk away from. We fought for what we have and earned it and we found each other and we're blood free. We stopped being those kind of monsters and I swear to you, four out of five of us were as terrifying as what you saw tonight and worse, but we stopped. We couldn't do it anymore. What we did when we left, it broke our laws and it put death warrants on all of us but Evan, and we started living like a bunch of guys under one roof."

245

"Why Evan?"

He sighed. "He's a special case. The way he was found and turned. He was never a true vampire. Never hunted, never took blood. We protected him from all of that." Ian tried to smile. "We taught him to fight in case we faced a night like tonight, but he's not like the rest of us."

"Who have hunted and taken blood," she said softly.

He sighed again and closed his eyes, seeing his mistake too late. "Aye," he said. He looked at her. "Four of us were vampires in every sense of the word for longer even we like to think about. All of us still have nightmares of what we did."

She stared at him a long time. He could see her processing the facts. She was trying to grasp it but it was too far out there.

"Churches, crosses, mirrors?" she asked.

He shook his head. "Myths. There's no religion involved. We can go to church, pick up a cross. I use a mirror every day to shave and I carry a driver's license with my photo on it."

"That doesn't make sense."

"Really?" he snapped. "It doesn't? Throughout history, all these people who have come up with vampires and legends, how many of them do you think really found a real vampire who gave an interview about all the ways to bring us down? Garlic?" he laughed. "Really?"

She stared at him.

"Not. A. One," he said.

"Driver's license," she said. "You don't have a car."

"I drove here tonight."

"Can I see it?"

He sighed once, took a deep breath then reached in his back pocket, pulling out his wallet. He took out the license and handed it to her. She took it, holding it by the edge and staring long and hard at the photo. He wished for the slightest clue as to what this exercise was proving. He kept quiet, though, letting her process as she needed.

She nodded her head and took a step forward, handing the license back. She pointed at it. "Good picture. Not easy to get a good picture on a driver's license. Then again, looking like you…" She walked to the other side of the room.

"Ashley," he sighed. "I don't get the feeling you're fully tracking the conversation."

"Because this is a talk that should be easy to follow?" She laughed a little. She covered her face with both her hands and rubbed hard. She dropped her hands.

She nodded and screwed up her face, pursing her lips. "What is real in your world?" she asked.

"Are you listening to anything I am saying?"

"How do you do it?"

"We work our asses off to blend in."

"No, no," she said. "None of this makes any sense." She tilted her chin at him and glared. "So what makes a vampire a vampire?"

He shrugged. "I don't know. Most of the blood stuff you've heard is real, though we have learned to live without it."

"Vampires who don't drink blood."

"To take blood you have to take victims. We didn't want to do that anymore. We quit."

"Victims. You took victims."

"Can I please get out of this talk? Let's go back to the knife fight, or break-up or why I didn't tell you when I had the chance?"

"You killed people?"

He rubbed his eyes. "Aye. I did."

She sank down on the bed, a hand planted on either side of her. She shook her head and looked to be thinking hard.

"I'm strong," he said. "Stronger than a normal person."

She looked at him.

"It's for hunting. Strength makes it possible for us to take down a victim bigger than ourselves with little struggle. Most things we can do are geared with hunting in mind."

She didn't look like she believed him and right now, he couldn't blame her.

"What else?"

He tried to think. He felt like he was taking a test and the answers mattered. "Senses. We have heightened senses. Sight, sound, everything. We can see real good in the dark."

"So touch. You can feel more? Better sex?"

His laugh was uncomfortable. "I'm told. But I don't know what you are actually feeling so I can't really compare. It's pretty damn good, though, better than when I was human."

"And your ability to…um…go more than once. Not like most men."

He nodded but held back a reaction. "My metabolism is different than a human's."

She blew out a breath and stood up to walk away. She shook her head. "Do you think I am believing any of this?"

"I'm a predator, Ashley, who fights it all the time. I chose a life style contrary to my creation and it is a daily, uphill battle. I have been craving blood since 1958 but I stayed clean and I have not taken another victim."

She turned away, her head bent. "I don't believe in vampires," she whispered.

"You don't believe me?"

She looked back at him. "No, I don't."

He sighed hard. "After what you saw in the backyard? Bodies vanishing into dust. After what you heard? What Jason and Quinn said?"

"I'm not really sure what I saw. It could be something explainable. And what they said? It could be a big joke you all came up with to make the ex-look stupid."

"I have never talked about this with another person. Do you have any concept of what kind of trust that takes?"

She shook her head.

"Fine." he snapped.

He blew out another hard breath; moving fast, he grabbed her off the bed. His arms around her waist and yanked her to him when she wasn't expecting it. With his other hand on the side of her neck, he held her steady. Quicker than she could protest, he dropped his face to her neck, her hands going to his shoulders. He closed his eyes and using his long teeth, he bit down into her neck, keeping her still, pinned with his arms, her head falling back, a gasp escaping her lips.

Sucking softly, he tasted her on his tongue, more than he had before. He moaned, pulling her tight against him in pleasure. She coated sweet and he forced himself to remember this was a show for her benefit and not for him. Still, he couldn't quite get himself to stop right when he should so he held her for a moment longer while her fingers clung to his shoulders and a sigh escaped her lips.

He pulled his face back to stare into hers, both their breathing hard.

She opened her eyes. "Did you bite me in the neck?"

He smiled a little. "Aye. Enjoyed it, too."

He leaned back down, covering her mouth with his, kissing her wildly while her taste was still on his tongue.

250

She shoved on his chest and he took the momentum, stepping back. She reached up to put two fingers to her neck, looking at the red on the tips.

He wanted to finish what he had started. He blew out breaths and forced his pulse to come down.

"You said you didn't do things like this."

"I don't take victims. Believe it or not, that was a form of sex. Totally okay between lovers."

"We're not lovers."

He nodded his head sideways and blew out a breath. "Broken up or not, we will always have been lovers and I will be thinking about that for about three hundred years."

He walked over to the table and picked up her glass. He brought it to her. She took it, downing the whole thing in two swallows.

"Evan brought the bottle," he said. "You can refill as much as you like. And I can make you morning hangover shit tomorrow."

"Everything you said was true?"

He nodded. "I'm sorry. I couldn't tell you."

"How?"

He shook his head. "Vampires never discuss how they were turned. Too personal."

"Is this why you dumped me?"

He licked his lips and thought about telling her the truth then decided to go with the lie.

"It was never going to last. We move every seven years. Even if I could have kept it a secret from you, in two years I will have to move out of here and leave you behind. You can't stay twenty-nine forever living in one spot."

She looked at him. "Walter said you wanted to marry me."

He stared back. "I don't know actually where that came from. I must have said something to Miss Monte Cruz, but I don't remember."

"You weren't opposed to the idea."

He nodded. "Aye, that I remember. But it doesn't mean it was something I was planning on."

She nodded her head and handed him the glass. He refilled it and gave it back to her. She drank that one down, too. The scotch was going to leave last night's wine in the dust.

"Too bad," she said. "I was having a lot of fun."

He reached, pulling the edge of his sleeve into his hand. He blotted at the mark on her neck. "It's still seeping," he said. "It wasn't deep. Only trying to prove a point." He smiled sadly.

She reached up to touch where his hand was, looking at him.

"You can sleep up here," he said. "Don't try to leave," he said. "They will be out there waiting for you."

She nodded her head and stared into her empty glass.

She looked up at him, her eyes bloodshot, still shaking.

252

"You're a vampire," she said. "It's why you couldn't move in."

He nodded. "I need to be here at least part of the time. We count on each other."

She looked at the glass. "I saw you tonight with them, I mean before the bad stuff. You are so close to each of them." She smiled and looked at him. "Even Jason."

"We have been together a very long time."

She looked up at him, trying hard to smile and get past everything he had said. "When did you come to America? You've never told me."

His arms came out. "I'm tired of talking about me."

"When were you changed?"

"We call it turned. And it was 1926, New York. That's all I will tell you."

"What were you like human?"

"Different. You've had three scotches. You're very likely drunk by now, Ashley."

"I know, but you're the one who's been pouring."

He managed to smile. She was right. He should have stopped her. "Is me telling you anything else going to make a difference?"

She shook her head and shrugged. "I don't know. I don't know what you're going to say and I don't know where we go from here once I hear it."

"We don't go anywhere. I meant it when I said I couldn't do us anymore."

"And that's definite?"

He nodded. "It can't get any more definite."

"I don't get a say in it?"

"You can say whatever you want, but it's a relationship that will no longer have me in it so you will be talking to yourself."

"Fine. Then it won't hurt for you to tell me. When did you come to America?"

His head started to hurt.

"1922. I came through Ellis Island and got work in New York."

"Doing what?"

"Slaughter house." He looked at the ground and shrugged. "Pretty gory but the money was okay."

"And home?"

He looked at her. "Didn't you hear Jason? I don't talk about home."

"You really going to turn me down tonight?"

He looked away and rolled his eyes to the ceiling. "Fuck," he muttered. "I hate talking about home. It's everything I had ripped away from me, and the people I didn't get to say good-bye to."

"Parents?"

"My mum," he said. "My dad died when I was ten. But I was the middle of five, all of us close and I never saw them again because I was in the wrong place at the wrong time. That's how it works, you know. That's how it happened to every one of us. You think you're standing beside some normal guy and an hour later your whole life is fucked up."

He looked up at her.

"Why didn't you ever do it to me like Walter said?"

"I got lucky," he said. "I have it pretty good here and I found an unconventional family, but it's not a life I would ever force on anyone I cared about, especially you."

"You told me you were an only child."

"I tell you I have siblings and you're going to ask questions, ask to see photos." He shrugged. "Only child is low key."

"You don't know what happened to any of them?" she asked.

He shook his head. "I became a vampire and I stopped writing and then they stopped and the years passed until it was the sixties and I realized I didn't have anyone left."

She walked over. She reached up and picked up his Celtic knot on his chain in her fingers while he watched. She stared at it and rubbed it back and forth between her thumb and forefinger.

"What were their names?" she asked quietly. She stared at the knot, the edges of her eyes full.

"I don't like to think about them," he said.

Her gaze snapped up to his.

He sighed and closed his eyes. "James was first, five years older than me and named after my dad. Then there was Violet. Me. Edith was right behind me, within a year. We were tight. And then Samuel, the baby. He was six years younger than me." He looked at her.

"Your mum?"

She even said it right and that made him feel more than he should.

"Charlotte Mae Stuart. I don't know what happened to her."

"What happened to your dad?"

"My dad was James Malcolm. There was a fire at the mill. He didn't get out."

"You wear it to keep them close," she said looking at the charm in her fingers. "You never forgot them."

"It's my heritage and a good look and nothing more."

"Bullshit. You're more Scottish than anything. You show it off every day with what you wear but you never talk about it."

"Is that enough?"

"Why did you come to America? You loved it there. You loved them. Why give it all up?"

"I answered your questions. They have nothing to do with vampirism anymore."

"In a few hours the sun is going to come up and you will go to sleep right here. I will walk out the front door and never be back. I'm not going to get another chance to ask you anything else." The tears came in pairs about the time her voice cracked.

And there was nothing he could do to make this easier on her.

He swallowed hard and had to take a minute to shut down his own emotions. He wanted to step back, to put distance between them but she still held the knot and he couldn't make himself break that contact.

"I started working at the paper mill when I was fourteen. It was horrible work for shit wages. I wanted more. I worked there until I was twenty-five, when I came up with the brilliant idea to hop a steamer to New York."

He held her face again and leaned forward until his forehead was on hers. He closed his eyes tight. "I don't want to talk about them anymore. It hurts to talk about them."

"I don't want to hurt you, but I feel like I finally know you. All the time we spent together. I know your favorite wine, your favorite beer. I know how you like your eggs cooked in the morning, but it took the horror of tonight for me to finally really get to know *you* " She dropped the knot and took a step back.

"We can stop?"

"You have been very forthcoming. Thank you." She stepped away from him and wandered across the room again, this time with a small stagger in her step.

"They would have hated me," he said. "They would have hated me for what I became."

She turned toward him.

"My mum," he laughed and actually found some joy in the memory for the first time in years. "She was so beautiful. Never got old. Even with five of us under foot and her man cold in the ground, she kept the glow that made her young. I think there are some days I really still miss her."

Ashley smiled at him.

"She was Catholic and believed in heaven and hell." He laughed sadly and brushed at his own eye." We went to mass every Sunday, took communion and gave confession and there was no way in hell I would have ever been able to convince her that there was no religion involved. She would have hated me the most." Feeling an engulfing sadness he laughed again. "Worse. She would have been afraid of me."

"You were raised Catholic?"

He nodded. "There could be seven feet of snow in the middle of winter and all of us with the croup and she would line us up and march us out the door for mass."

He put his hands up and covered his face, grinding his fingers into his eye sockets. The pain didn't stop the images from crashing into his brain.

"I only saw her cry twice. In my whole life, only twice."

"When?" Ashley asked

He dropped his hands to stare at her. "The day the foreman came to tell her that dad was dead. And the day I boarded the train for Glasgow to catch the steamer. She begged me not to go." He put his hand on his forehead and closed his eyes tight. "How could I do that to her?"

Ashley looked at him and shrugged. "You wanted an adventure."

He dropped his hand and took a deep breath. "I don't want to talk anymore. We're done. No more questions."

She walked up to him, put her hand in his and kissed him on the cheek, not moving back, but whispering in his ear. "Stuart, you're a good man. Don't even go to those places that make you doubt that. Just remember the good you had with them and know you have a good heart."

She stepped back and looked down and walked away.

It took a minute after the show of sincere kindness for him to find his voice. She could still offer that to him after what he was doing to her.

"You can go home tomorrow. When the sun is up. I trusted you with this and I never trusted anyone else."

"The tattoo," she said. "You told me in the beginning it helped protect you from the sun."

He sighed. "Aye?"

"It really does work?"

"Aye. It does. We all have our own form of them. Got 'em in New Orleans from a priestess for a ton of money. There's things mixed in the ink. Blood, ash. Bunch of other stuff. Makes it so we can take some sunlight. Not a lot. But enough to get my bike home after sunrise. Enough?"

"I don't want to break up. Can I stay? Please?"

"No."

She turned away.

"Ashley. I wish it could be different."

"That's okay. I already have two dates lined up for next weekend with the possibility for a third. I'll see how that goes."

His stomach lurched at the joke. "Probably would be better if you stayed away from vampires, particularly those I can stake in their sleep."

She looked at him. "Why would you do that? It's you walking away. Three men told me tonight they would like to date me. The one I was crazy about explained I was disposable and let me go. I get to choose."

He smiled when he didn't feel it. "Choose differently."

"Do you want me to tell you which one I would pick? I can number them one, two, three for you."

His eyes narrowed at her and he realized no, he really didn't want to know which one of the three she preferred. He turned around to walk away.

"Ian," she whispered.

She said Ian, not Stuart. He looked back at her, feeling heat in his gut.

"I know about you now." Her voice rushed. "I know about all of you. Doesn't that make a difference?"

"Who the hell is ever going to believe you?"

"For us?" she said, her voice a whisper, her eyes looking hopeful.

"There is no us," he snapped, feeling the pain of his own words. "Do you understand? Finding out about me doesn't change anything. We are done and begging is very unattractive. It was fun. It was one hell of a good time, but it is over. You need to get out of here in the morning and then I don't ever want to see you again."

She didn't brush away at the tears. "You were mean before, in the backyard."

"And I mean every word right now. There is no future for us and I don't want to play anymore."

He did it for her. And she would never know. She would only remember him as the bastard who broke her heart. When she looked back on their time together it would be with nothing but pain until one day, she felt nothing for him at all.

He couldn't look at her anymore and not feel the engulfing sorrow he caused her. He turned away.

"Jason kissed me," she said quietly.

He stopped and turned back to her. She wasn't looking at him.

"What?"

"In the house, in the kitchen. During the fight, before he left to help you. He kissed me." She nodded and shrugged. "It was nice. He's a real good kisser."

Ian stared at her, speechless. That was stepping way over the line even for the Irishman. Ian looked a long second, picturing every detail. Jason's hands on her body, his lips touching hers. Those fucking, annoying green eyes staring into her baby blues. Fury almost shoved out despair.

Without another word, he turned and slammed his door on the way out. He took the steps two at a time until he got to Travis's room, the master with its own bathroom. Ian opened the door without knocking and walked straight up to the bed, ignoring Travis, who lay out in front of him a book in his lap. Ian grabbed one of Travis's pillows and he picked up the extra quilt that hung over the foot board. Without a word, Ian started out toward the door.

"Pretty brutal, don't you think?"

Ian swung back around. "What do you want me to do? Poetry maybe?"

"She didn't deserve that."

"You heard?"

"Of course I heard." He pointed at the heating grate that made everything in each of their rooms audible. Travis stood up and took the last pillow off his bed, forcing it into the grate.

Tears weren't something Ian ever dealt with. Feeling them burn behind his eyes now confused him and infuriated him.

"She's going to get killed. You know that. She stays with me and that little scene that played out in the backyard is going to get repeated only it's going to be her that gets in the middle and Evan won't be there to run her up the stairs."

"You're awfully wordy tonight. Is it helping?"

"Fuck you," Ian snapped.

"Three hours ago you're in the backyard treating her like the love of your life in front of your entire family and then you throw her away. You're in love with her. Do something about it, asshole."

"I did. I let her go."

"There will never be another Ashley. You have waited your whole life for this."

Ian headed toward the door and got as far as turning the knob in his hand and pulling back before slamming it shut again. He turned to face Travis.

"What is your suggestion?"

"Offer her a lifetime. I would lay even odds on her taking it."

He felt a tear slide down his cheek. He knew Travis saw it, too. "I can't," Ian said. "I can't do that to her."

"I would have turned Shelly if she would have said yes. I loved her so God damn much that I told her everything and begged her. Here we are fifteen years later and instead of a woman by my side, she's got a grave in LA that I can't even go and visit."

Ian closed his eyes. "I know what Shelly meant to you and to lose her like that, but this is different. Shelly said no to you," Ian said.

"That's right."

"Did you ever think to turn her against her will? To hold her down while she struggled and there was nothing left between you but fear and fury?"

Travis took a deep breath and let it out slow. "Is that what happened upstairs?"

Ian half nodded.

Travis' voice dropped. "When it was over and the fury was gone, did you explain? Did you offer her a choice?"

"I didn't know what to say."

"I think the vampires in the back offering to eat her might have been a clue that she was somewhere off the yellow brick road."

Ian shrugged, his arms coming away from his body and slapping back down.

Travis sighed. "You had already broken up with her, by the time things went down with Walter. Because of what happened between the two of you upstairs."

Ian swallowed. Another tear fell. If it had been anyone but Travis, Ian would have tried to hide. "I told her to go. I was cruel and insulting."

"You can't let it end like this. It's not fair to either of you."

Ian put his hands on his face again and squeezed his eyes until it was painful. He dropped his hands. "Did it cross your mind to cover the vent before you heard everything?"

Travis shook his head. "Figured it was information I was going to need when I tried to glue everything back together."

"Stay out of it," Ian snapped.

"Walk upstairs right now. Crawl into bed with her. Ask her to stay then casually nibble on her neck."

"No."

"Then you're an idiot who deserves to lose the best thing you've seen in over a hundred years. Shit, I'll date her in a heartbeat. And hey, if not me, sounds like Jason might be interested in more than just a sample. He's already got a head start. He had to have only had a couple of seconds. You think he went for the whole deal and tongued her or just a smooch?"

"Do you actually have any doubt I won't stake that fucking Irishman in his sleep for touching my girlfriend?"

Travis smiled at him. "*Ex*-girlfriend, which means she's available and Jason can touch what he wants, with her permission." Travis smiled wide and stared at the ceiling. "I wonder where I placed. One, two or three? You like to think you're in the number one but this is pretty stiff competition with competent flirts."

Ian's back went straighter than it ever had, his head tilting.

"Yeah," Travis said, his face smug. "That feeling in your gut right now? It's called jealousy and if you think it's bad with us just saying that wait until six months from now and there's a black Volvo you've never seen parked in her driveway overnight."

The hands went back to his face, the fingers pushing so hard into his eyes they would leave bruises. He took in a deep breath. "Is there any part of you that thinks you are helping?"

"I don't know. With her body, I assume she's great in bed, but you're the only one who knows for sure. Might get new intel here pretty quick. Jason usually waits a few dates playing the romance game before he gets personal. Quinn will take his time with seduction and persuasion, and me, well I know what I like."

Ian dropped his hands and stared at Travis, breathing hard and heavy.

"She was comparing us to ice cream," Travis said. "I wonder what her feelings are on Italian gelato."

Ian turned and headed toward the door.

"Was that enough kick to get your ass upstairs or do you want more? I can keep going."

Ian swung around, vibrating with fury. "I see three empty rooms in the house, looking for renters and me with Evan sitting down to dinner."

"Stuart, she did not freak out over us. I think she would accept it," Travis snapped. "Offer it to her. Give her the chance to decide. She might say no. Shelly said no. But Ashley, she might surprise you and say yes. And then none of this is going to matter."

Ian motioned with the pillow and the quilt. "I'm taking these."

"Sorta figured that part out myself. You going back upstairs?"

"No."

"Do you mind if I go upstairs?"

Ian's head snapped to the side, then came back around.

"Knock yourself out. Want some pointers on what she likes best?"

"You are a fucking idiot."

Ian had no comment to that. Travis was right. He was a fucking idiot and nothing was going to change that.

"So I just get to lay here with no pillows and listen to your ex cry herself to sleep?"

Ian threw the pillow at him. "I'll steal one from Quinn."

Quinn had his door open before Ian got there, the pillow held out. "Travis is right," he said. "She's amazing and one of us will gladly step up, but shit Stuart, you're all she wants. You let her go and you will always regret it."

Ian grabbed the pillow and turned toward the stairs. "We have got to get a house with worse acoustics."

Ian went to the living room and the couch. Placing the pillow on one end, he laid down, pulling the quilt over him. He let everything rush through his mind like white water until there was no answer. He held the knot on the chain in his fingers and thought about people he pretended not to think about. Ashley gave him that, he knew. A chance at good memories when there had been only a black hole. The sun peeked through the edge of the blinds but he lay still, searching for the right answer.

About an hour later, he heard his bedroom door open. He didn't move. He closed his eyes and listened to her come down one step at a time.

The front door opened. It shut. And Ian let out the breath he had been holding, wondering about her hangover. She would suffer all day and he didn't want that but there was nothing he could do.

He heard a car engine start in the distance.

It was official. Ashley Barrow was out of his life.

PART TWO

Customs of the Vampires as laid down by

Balbus, Iovita and Varius.

The Second Generation of VampiresAristocracy, Rome, A. D. 10

#3. The Creator of the Newborn is responsible for the Newborn in training, in laws and protection.

#4. It is the responsibility of the Newborn to learn the laws, the customs and the hierarchy of the den. Ignorance is an excuse not tolerated and punishment will be enforced for infractions.

#7. To protect The Society, human laws will be obeyed. Discovery by violation will lead to the destruction of The Society. Punishment will match Laws in severity for the vampire who violates.

#11. Time moves night to night, turning into years. Death wins in the end with all, time taking the memory of he who came before. No vampire shall mourn or grieve or speak again of the fallen.

CHAPTER TWELVE

"The most dangerous creation of any society is the man who has nothing to lose."

James A. Baldwin

Two a. m. and Ian stayed on his bed, his head resting back, his drawing pad on his knees. The house was dead tonight as he was the only one home. Jason had headed out to the gym an hour ago which was good as Ian still wasn't speaking to the Irish bastard.

Everyone else was at work.

It was Ian, alone with his dark thoughts and a pencil that refused to cooperate.

He kept reaching for that happy memory, the one when the two of them had been at their absolute best. But six tries in with an outline and shading started and all that came out of the pencil was the look in her eyes when she had asked to stay, that she didn't want to break-up and he had said no.

Slamming the pencil down beside him, he ripped the sheet off and crumped it into a half torn ball to toss next to the others cluttering his floor.

He closed his eyes and tried to make sense. She was safer far away than closer and this was the way it had to be.

270

Only he missed her. One day away and he couldn't imagine what a decade would feel like without hearing her voice, smelling the Chanel when it mixed with her own chemistry. The hair, bunched in his hands as he made love to her.

Fucking Irishman, he thought, his eyes squeezing closed.

The last person in this house to show her any gentle affection and it had been the Irishman. And she had enjoyed it, if Ian could read women right. Jason had kissed her and she had enjoyed it. Fuck, he thought, his thumb and finger rubbing his eyeballs hard.

His phone vibrated on his nightstand. Reaching for it, he was surprised to see her name. He read her message.

They turned me. They hurt me.

He forgot how to breathe.

He read it three more times, his brain coming into hyper-focus on the words screaming at him in his head in her voice.

Throwing his legs over the bed, he grabbed his shoes, pulled on his coat as he ran out the door. He had the bike out of the hallway, out the door and down the front stairs faster than he ever had before.

Gasping for air that didn't match his high physical fitness, he ran lights, dodged the few cars out at this hour and covered the four miles in minutes. He dropped the bike by the back door before he even finished stopping, moving to the steps and freezing.

The door set ajar and her phone sat balanced precariously on the knob. He grabbed it, checked to see the message sent from her, and then he pocketed it.

He pushed on the door slow, careful to enter the dark house without back-up, but knowing she was on the other side of the threshold moved him forward. His head came up immediately, every nerve in his body alert.

The scent of blood engulfed the house.

Fuck back-up. He didn't even close the door behind him. He raced down the hall to her bedroom, stopping stone still in the doorway. Slowly, he reached out and flicked on the switch beside the door, exposing everything in vivid color.

Ashley lay naked, face down diagonally on the mattress, her head hanging off at a bad, uncomfortable angle. One arm hung with her, the other on the other side of her, flat against the mattress.

Blood stained the soft blue sheets with dark splotches. Her pajamas, her favorite green and purple pajamas, were torn and defiled, lying on the floor. The window to the right was completely smashed out, the glass on the inside, on the floor. The blinds had been ripped out of the top, the gauze curtains waving in the night breeze.

Air stuck in his chest, the realization of what was in front of him coming slower than it should. Swallowing hard, he took the three short steps to the edge of the bed. Denying what he already knew, he reached down, picking up her wrist, placing his fingers over the spot where there should be a pulse. He concentrated, holding on longer than was necessary but there was nothing. He set her hand down gently and placed the same two fingers to her neck, slick with blood, hoping for a different answer, but no.

Grief wasn't an emotion he had ever really experienced. He felt it now, taking over all of his nerves at once. He sank down on the bed beside her, his hand brushing her hair in a gentle caress. Feeling helpless, he closed his eyes. He should have been here tonight. He could have stopped them.

Her gun lay beside the bed on the floor, beside the blood that had dripped and splattered.

He reached over, picking up the Glock, popping the magazine. Shots had been fired. She had tried to fight but she hadn't known what she was up against. He sighed and wiped his face dry. Maybe she had. Maybe he had told her everything she needed to know last night.

With shaking hands he opened the drawer to the nightstand and slipped the gun into its holster where it belonged, and slid the drawer shut. Reaching over, he rolled her and slipped his arms under her back and knees. Moving her gently, he repositioned her on the bed, pulling two big pillows under her head the way she liked and arranged her arms on either side of her body. Leaning over, he grabbed the edge of the opposite side of the quilt and pulled it over her, covering her to her breasts.

He walked down the hall to the open front door, closed it, snapping the lock.

Going to the kitchen, he got a knife out of the rack on the counter in case of company, stuck it in his back pocket, then got a pan of warm water with some dishcloths and went back to the bedroom, pulling the quilt off a portion of her, keeping her respectable. He used the dishtowel to wipe the blood from her face, from her neck.

He could see her injuries as he moved down her body. Multitude of puncture wounds on each of her wrists, one set on the inside of her left elbow. Two fingertips on her right hand had been sliced with a knife, one on the left. Her thighs had superficial cuts. Dozens of them. No feeding could have been taken there. They were for pain only.

Bruises covered her face, one eye purple and swollen. On each of her sides near her ribs were small holes like he had never seen before, where blood had seeped out and dried.

The bottoms of her feet held burns with red and dark skin and blisters. He ran his finger over the edge of her foot, careful not to hurt her when he knew she was feeling no pain. He thought long and hard on this injury, feeling the personal nature to it.

On her neck, most important, two sets of puncture wounds beside the shallow one he had left last night.

He worked down her body wiping and rinsing the cloth, changing out the water often as to not leave a residue. He rubbed at the spots in her hair.

He worked on her, front and back, erasing any sign that they had left on her. He looked closely at her arm. There was an injection wound at the junction of her right elbow. He didn't know what it was.

He took the water to the kitchen and dumped it out then went back to the bedroom. He moved slow, concentrating on what had to be done and not what had been done to her. It was the only way to keep his own fury down. Turning should be a simple process. What had been done here tonight sat in a different realm of their existence.

274

He went to her dresser and got another pair of pajamas. Pink and white, he struggled them onto her until she looked clean and fresh.

In the bloody sheets.

He lifted her, carrying her to the couch while he remade her bed and wiped stains he saw. There were splatters on the nightstand. He got those, too. The one on the wall above the headboard was harder to get off but he scrubbed it without dulling the paint. When he was done, the room looked like it always had and he had a pile of bloody sheets and clothes.

On the floor, under the edge of the bed, he found the knitting needle, bloody to the top and he starred at it, his mouth hanging open, air tight in his chest. The holes in her sides. They had stabbed her with it. Lips pressed together, jaw set tight, he hadn't even heard of anything like that at a turning. Throwing it in the garbage, its memory seared in his mind.

He picked her up, placing her in the bed, tucking her in with the pillows the way she liked. He laid her on her side, a big pillow beside her, her arms draped over it. It was her favorite position to sleep in and he wanted her to be in her favorite position.

Gathering everything bloody, he shoved them into her fireplace and set them afire. He didn't even stand back to watch the flames.

His work done, he looked around at the rooms. He couldn't see anything else he could do to make this a different time or a different place. He saw the paper bags sitting by the front door. Going over to them, he knelt down to peek inside. Clothing smelling of fabric softener, books. CD's. All the stuff he had brought into the house, packed up and ready for pick up, including his half-done afghan. *The Hobbit* DVD was on top. In the bathroom, his blue toothbrush sat in the garbage can.

Ignoring the hurt, he turned the light off and went to the kitchen where he got ice from the freezer and poured water from the tap. Her back door had a broken pane in it. Glass littered the floor. He left it there and went to the bedroom, turned off the light and sat down in the overstuffed chair in the corner.

He checked his watch, and took a drink. He wanted scotch, but alcohol wasn't going to be good for her and he wanted to be ready.

She was coming back to him.

The knock at the door came about eleven o'clock. Still sitting in the chair, still waiting, he checked his watch, looked over at her then headed down the hallway.

Hunter had his face pressed up against the glass.

Ian opened the door then stepped back out of the light.

"I should kick your ass," Hunter snapped.

"You could try."

"What are you doing here?" Hunter asked and for a minute Ian worried she may have said something about the break-up.

"I'm always here," he said smiling, standing back to let Hunter enter.

"Where's Ash?"

"In bed."

"In bed?" He looked at his watch, then looked up at Ian. "I'm blaming you, you know."

"For?"

"For her quitting."

Ian shook his head. "She didn't even tell me she had done it for two days."

"You didn't have anything to do with it?"

"Why would I want her to quit her job? She was good at it."

"Yes, she was. Damn good. Best partner I ever had. I'm thinking if she acts quickly, there might still be a chance to get Toure to reconsider."

Ian shook his head. "I don't think she wants to reconsider. I think that's why she did what she did."

Hunter put his hand on Ian's shoulder. "I bet between the two of us we could get her to change her mind."

Ian tilted his head. "I would have to think about that. I don't want her doing anything she doesn't want to do."

Hunter sighed. "Fine. You think, but think fast. Why didn't she answer her phone? I've been calling."

"She might have turned it off," Ian lied. "I didn't hear it."

"And you've been here all morning?"

"It's where I usually spend my nights."

"Can I see her?" Impatience edged Hunter's voice.

"She's pretty sick."

"Sick how? What do you mean she's sick?"

Ian shrugged. "Not sure. Came on pretty strong." He checked his watch again, wondering how long it would take for Ashley to come back.

Hunter pushed passed Ian, walking to the doorway to Ashley's room. All the blinds were drawn, making the room dark, the torn one tacked into place. Hunter reached for the light switch and Ian grabbed his hand.

"No." Ian nodded toward her on the bed. She was curled up, holding her pillow looking utterly peaceful. "She was throwing up all night. Fell asleep about an hour ago. I don't want to wake her."

Hunter looked at him. "How are you doing? Did you catch it?"

"So far I'm fine."

Hunter looked back at Ashley. "She does look comfortable." His gaze shot up to Ian's.

"What?" Ian asked.

"Is she pregnant?"

Ian actually managed to laugh. "I wish."

"You didn't knock her up? That would explain this and why she left the job."

He shook his head slowly. "We're pretty careful."

He looked between Ian and Ash. "You guys would have cute kids."

"Thanks. Do you want her to call you when she wakes up?"

Hunter shook his head. "Tell her to take a few days. You going to stay here with her?"

Ian nodded. "Won't go anywhere until she is back on her feet."

Hunter headed toward the front door, stopping before he reached for the knob. He looked at Ian. "I wasn't sure about you, Stuart. When she quit I thought of many ways of making you pay."

"But?"

"She sure has been happy since you came around."

Ian's smile might be genuine, but it hurt. "Thanks."

Hunter smiled then walked out the door. Ian stepped forward, turning the lock. He glanced at his watch. It had been about twelve hours since she was attacked. There was no predictability to how long it took. He had taken two days. Quinn, ten hours. There was no rhyme or reason to how long it could take to turn.

He went to the bedroom where she still lay stone, cold dead and picked his water glass. Going to the kitchen, he got more ice, more water and went to his seat.

Keeping the lights off in the room was important. Sensitivity would be the first thing she felt. He stayed in the big chair in the corner of the room, the glass of ice water on the small table next to it. Sitting in the dark, waiting, the ice slowly melted until it finally disappeared altogether.

He picked her phone off the table and stared at her message for the twentieth time, still trying to make sense of it. The time stamp told him when the text had been sent and she hadn't been here lying on her bed dialing him. She had been dead a while at least when the text hit his phone.

So who sent the message?

And if it was only to trap him here, why hadn't they come back? The knife he carried all night sat on the nightstand.

Who could let this happen to her, stand back and watch, and only when it was done, send for help?

And how had they gotten her phone?

He scrolled through her contacts, seeing all his friends listed with photos she had taken at the BBQ. He rested his thumb over Travis, but paused.

His gaze came up. Ash in that bed, this was Ian's story and he had to open the next chapter alone. He shut down the phone and set it face down on the table.

She stirred finally, catching his attention. He stayed in the chair, watching it happen before him.

After fifteen minutes of gentle thrashing, she finally sat bolt upright in bed, gasping in a breath. Her hair messed around her face. He could see the paleness of her skin, her lips.

280

Disorientation was common. Confusion and memory loss, too.

"Can you understand me?" he asked quietly.

Her face came up, staring at him across the room. Her fingers tangled in the sheets. She pulled them toward her but didn't answer.

"Do you know what I'm saying?"

Her chin moved a fraction.

He swallowed hard. "Do you know who I am?"

Again, a slight nod, but she didn't make any effort to go near him. He stayed in his chair, one leg crossed over the other, his hands on the arms rests.

"I broke up with you because I love you." He licked his lips and let that sit in the air for a long minute. Her eyes narrowed, her chin tilted.

"That last night, in my bedroom," he said. "I almost turned you. Before I had even told you what I was, I almost became violent and hurt you. I didn't know anyone was coming to attack that night. I wasn't cruel to protect you from them. I was trying to protect you from me."

She blinked hard and a hand shifted, moving into her lap.

"I knew then it was only a matter of time. Maybe the next time we were together or the next but it was going to happen and I would lose control and I wouldn't be able to stop myself. Letting you go was the only way I could protect you, because I love you too much to have this happen to you."

The words left his body, a deep breath following.

Her hand rose to her neck, to the spot that was supposed to be only his. She rubbed back and forth and she had to be feeling the puncture marks.

"They made the decision for us," she whispered.

"Do you know who they were?"

She shook her head. "I don't remember."

"That's normal," he said. Holding on the sides of the chair, he pushed himself up and walked the few feet to the edge of the bed. She was almost in the middle, leaving room for him to sit down beside her. She didn't move away.

"I felt myself die. Didn't I?"

"Aye," he replied.

"I'm like you?"

"I'm sorry," he whispered.

"You could have stopped it?"

"I don't know," he said. "Maybe. Kept you at the house."

"I would have been safe at the house?"

"I don't know. Maybe. Probably."

He remembered a conversation they had ages ago, before they had even been dating. She talked about telling the parents and the thing that stuck with her the most: the silent tears. He looked at her now and he understood what it was she had been trying to say that night.

He picked up the dry washcloth he had placed on the nightstand and used it to wipe first one of her cheeks then the other. It was a good effort, but more tears replaced the ones he removed.

"Did you want to be like this?"

He shook his head again, reaching up he slid his fingers into the hair by her face. "No one asked me what I wanted. It was scary and violent and I woke up like you did."

He brushed the hair out of her eyes.

Placing the wash rag in his lap, he reached for the knife. He pumped his right fist several times getting the blood to flow faster for the vein to pop. Using his left hand, he cut into his right wrist. She gasped as she watched him, pulling away.

"No," he said. He put the knife down and reached for the back of her head, pulling her closer. "You have to feed," he said.

She shook her head violently. "No. I'm not—"

"You're going to be weak and you're not going to heal. Not if you don't feed."

Her eyes closed tight, the look of horror on every feature. He lay beside her, against the pillows and reached an arm wrapping around her. She leaned back against him, cradled in the nook of his arm.

"You said you don't drink blood," she said.

"We'll get you there, but right now it's too new. We have to get you strong."

Her tears were no longer silent and each tiny sob broke his heart. He raised his arm toward her.

"Please," he said. "Let me help you."

She stared at the open cut that dripped blood down on the cloth.

"You can smell it, can't you? You want it."

She shook her head. "No. No. I don't."

"It's okay," he said.

"But you—"

"You can't hurt me. And losing a pint or two will be no big deal."

She sat up, turning toward him while he lay against the pillows bleeding. Every drop on the washcloth was a drop she needed and he had to make her understand that.

"Are you still you?" she asked.

He hadn't expected that question. "Aye. Still me. Nothing's changed."

"I was really in love with you, you know," she said. "Till death do us part kinda love. I wanted to spend the rest of my life with you."

He closed his eyes and stopped counting drips. When he opened them, he put a hand to her face, his thumb rubbing across her bottom lip. "I'm still me," he said again.

She closed her eyes and lay down beside him, cradled in the nook of his arm. Reaching up, she grabbed hold of his wrist and pulled it to her mouth.

CHAPTER THIRTEEN

Ian looked at his cell phone, checking the time. It was only three o'clock in the afternoon and he had just gotten Ashley settled and resting on their bed. She lay on her side, her knees drawn up toward her chin, her skin pale. The gauze he had wrapped around his wrist might be a sign he was trying, but it was also notice he couldn't do enough.

He pulled back the blinds, looking up in the horrifyingly bright day. He might risk it in the car, but Ash didn't have a fancy tattoo. He thought of calling for back-up but there was nothing anyone at the house could do to help.

He had to get her out of here. The house had been compromised. That gave him four hours until sunset to get her ready.

He moved to the closet pulling out her suitcases and a carry-on from the top shelf and began to grab her favorites. Anything he could think of from underthings to clothes to pajamas and slippers to the toiletries stocking her bathroom. He got her make-up, her shampoos. Anything he had ever seen her use. He got the pillows off their bed, leaving her the two she was using, and took them out to the backseat of the car. The sun hid behind the trees, putting him in the shade. He went back in for the bags of his crap.

At six-thirty he gave himself thirty minutes to get her ready and then finally woke her up.

"What?" she moaned when he shook her.

He put a hand under her shoulder, lifting her to a sitting position. "Come on. We need to get dressed."

She sat on the edge of the bed. "You are dressed," she said looking at him. "Nicely, too."

He smiled. Jeans and his plain old blue striped shirt but it made her happy. "You feeling better?"

She shook her head. "No. I think I liked the hangover better. Can you make some more of that shit?"

"I could," he said as he reached for the pants and Hard Rock T-shirt he had laid out. "Still have all the stuff in the refrigerator, but I don't think it's going to help this time."

He knelt in front of her.

She hooked her finger into his silver necklace, pulling it toward her until she had the Celtic knot in her fingers. "I like this. It's very you."

He let her play with it.

She sighed. "It's important."

He looked up at her.

"James. Violet." She spoke slow, straining like it was hard. "Edith. Samuel."

He reached up to cup her cheek in his hand. "That's pretty impressive. You were listening."

She shook her head. "I don't know who they are."

"That's okay. I do."

"What's going to happen?" she asked.

He paused long enough to rest both hands on her knees.

"We're going to get through this together and figure some sort of plan. We need to get you changed. Think you can do that?"

He reached for her hand holding the chain. "Let's go." She dropped the charm.

"Weak," she said. "Sounds like too much trouble." She tried to lie back down. "I just want to sleep."

He grabbed her by her shoulders. "Nope. Gotta sit up."

He held on, letting her find her balance until he was sure she wasn't going over. He moved a hand on her cheek. A hundred years ago, when he woke up, he drained a man without even thinking. She was running on what little he could spare.

"You want to feed again?" he asked her.

She shook her head. "No."

"Might help."

She shook her head harder.

"Bra?" he asked.

She shook her head again. He set it to the side and picked up the short-sleeved T-shirt. He stuck her arms through the holes, pulling it down over her head.

"Sweats are going to be trickier. You up for it?"

"Am I?"

He let her sit on the edge, pulling off the pajamas and pulling the pants up her legs to the tops. Helping her to lift her shapely bottom, he pulled them under, keeping her feet off the floor for as long as possible.

He moved to the suitcase, putting the pajamas inside.

"Is there anything that you want to take that you might miss for the next few weeks?"

"Gr'pa's watch," she said, surprising him. He didn't know she had treasures. He looked to see her pointing to the small top drawer on the left hand side of her dresser. A couple of seconds of digging and he found the black velvet bag and let the gold watch fall into his hand. It was smooth, plain and initialed Rolex. Gr'pa had good taste.

"Beautiful," he said.

He slipped them in the front pocket of the suitcase.

"Okay," he said, zipping up the bag. He reached for the handle and lifted.

"Didn't you break up with me?"

He was almost to the doorway. Her memory would be shoddy for a little while and he was fine with helping her get past that, too.

"Aye, I did."

"Why are you here?"

"I'm supposed to be here."

Her jaw twitched. "I don't get it."

"Trust me."

"I do," she said. "I always have."

It hurt to hear her say those words. She was only in this shape because of him.

"I'll be right back," he said. "I'm going to put this in the car."

When he got back, she was curled up under the blanket, her pillow in front of her. The sun was going down and he wanted to be out of here before it hit the horizon. It might be uncomfortable for her in the car until it was totally dark, but it wouldn't be deadly.

He went to the closet and got her a pair of slippers that he stuffed the bottoms with toilet paper for padding. She didn't seem to be showing any pain from any of the injuries, but that didn't mean it wasn't going to change when they walked out of here. He put a hand on her shoulder.

"Honey," He said shaking her.

She didn't move. She didn't open her eyes.

He reached for both her shoulders. "Come on. We're almost ready."

"Who's James?" she asked. But her gaze was distant and he wasn't sure she knew she asked.

"I knew him a long time ago. I'll tell you about him sometime."

"Samuel?" She stared at the bandages on her fingers, looking confused.

"Him, too."

She was back sitting on the edge of the bed. "Can I have a brush?"

He stood straight. "Aye. Of course." He moved to the bathroom.

"And an elastic band?"

"Got it." He brought them both to her. She went to work, brushing her hair but the strokes were short and hard.

He knelt in front of her and gently slipped on the slippers. By the time he finished, she had her hair plaited in one thick braid, pulled over her shoulder.

He smiled at her. "That looks nice."

"You said Travis had all the charm."

He smiled again and put his hands back on her knees. "Are you ready?"

"I don't even know where we're going. I don't know what we're doing."

"We're going back to the house. It's safe over there and I want to get you someplace safe."

"We don't live here anymore." She said it with such sadness.

"No. We don't." He looked at her. She looked distant. Something was way off.

"Ashley," he said. "Look at me."

It took about three seconds too long for her eyes to focus on him. They were bloodshot and damp.

"Are you tracking?" he asked her.

"I don't know." Her voice cracked and it scared him. "I don't understand what's happening. Who are these people?"

He reached for her face again, holding her with both his hands, his thumb brushing her lip. "It's just us. There's no one else here."

Her hands settled on his wrists and she brought her gaze to his.

"Deep breath." He held on to her face, as the fear traveled across his nerves. "I want you to take a deep breath. Let it out slow."

She shook her head harder and tried to pull at his forearms, yanking him away. He didn't let go.

"Detective," he snapped hard and she flinched but he got her attention.

She stared over his left shoulder to the corner. He looked over there, half expecting to find someone standing in the room.

He looked back at her and held her hands in both of his. "Ashley, look at me."

She shook her head and covered her face with both her hands. He reached up to pull them down, keeping them in his hands.

"Ashley do you know who I am?"

She shook her head harder, dislodging a tear that had been holding on in the corner of her eye. She tried to push him away. "No," she said.

"Come on. You're doing so good. Don't give out on me now. Take a deep breath and blow it out."

She closed her eyes tight and did what he said.

He moved his hand to hers in her lap, holding her fingers tight in his. "Again."

"James?" she asked. He didn't have a clue why she focused on his brother but he let her have it.

"No, I'm not James. We'll talk about James later."

God, she looked so confused and lost.

He stood up. "Okay, sit right here for a minute. Don't lie down."

"No," she snapped. She grabbed his hand before he could move and pulled him back near her.

He knelt down on one knee, holding both her hands. "I'm going to go into the other room to pick something up. Okay?"

She stared at him with no expression.

He blew out a hard breath. His patience wasn't giving out but his ideas were. He thought for a minute then looked at her.

"Can you count?"

Her head bobbed.

"One to twenty. You think you can do that?"

"Yes."

"Okay. Close your eye and start at one. By the time you get to twenty, I'll be back."

She folded her hands in her lap and closed her eyes. He stood up and rushed, hearing her slow progression the whole way.

He put her into a black hoodie and pulled the hood up over her head and yanked it down low so it covered more. He put her sunglasses on her face and her winter gloves onto her hands. When he stood back, she looked like the Unabomber, but since that was what he was going for he was good.

He put a hand under her elbow and lifted. "Come on."

"Where we going?" She asked again.

His patience didn't have an expiration date. "I'm going to take you to the car and then I'm going to drive you to the house. We're going to stay there for a little while."

"Ian," she said.

He felt some small victory. "That's right."

"But I'm the only one who calls you that."

"My mum used to call me that, too."

She stopped and picked up a foot.

"What?"

"Hurts."

He leaned over, scooping her up, getting her to the door and the driveway.

"Who's James?"

"James was my older brother. You never met him."

He had pulled her Dodge Dart forward hours ago, getting it out of the line of sight from the street. The passenger door was open and ready for him to slip her inside. He secured the seatbelt.

"Okay. You want to go now?"

She nodded.

The sun set low when he pulled the car out of the driveway. Traffic downtown was a bitch as always but he got through. She leaned toward him, away from the window, trying to get away from what little light still peppering the sky.

Parking proved worse than the traffic and he had to settle for a space halfway up the block and on the other side of the street. He put the car into park and set the brake.

"You awake?" he asked.

She nodded her head. "Yeah. Feel like shit, though."

"Probably a flu," he said. He looked at her. She seemed to buy the answer he gave.

"What's my name?" he asked her.

"Ian."

"And James?"

"James is your brother." She looked at him. "Which means Samuel is your brother, too."

"Progress," he smiled. He reached over and picked up her hand in his, giving it a squeeze.

"Why are we talking about your brothers?"

Pursing his lips he shook his head while watching her. "Not a clue."

She looked out the window into the night. "Where are we?"

"Remember my house? Where we had the BBQ? We're going to go in there and see if we can figure this out."

"And you'll be there?"

He squeezed her hand again. "I'm not going anywhere."

She turned away.

"Ashley, do you know who I am?"

She looked at him. Ian waited while she thought it out. "Yeah."

She looked away.

"You're lying, aren't you?" he asked.

She turned to face him. "I'm not sure. Is that bad?"

He let out the breath that had been stuck in his lungs while holding on to her fingers. "I think we might be able to work with it."

Her head turned back to look at him. "What's wrong with me?"

He reached up for her face, running his knuckles over her cheek. "I don't know."

She looked out the windshield. "I don't know either."

"You ready to go up to the house?"

"Who are you?" she whispered.

"You sit there and wait for me. I'm going to come around the car and get you, okay?"

She nodded.

"We're about half a block from the house and then we have the stairs out front. I can't carry you because of the neighbors. Neighbors might question. You're going to have to walk. You good with that?"

"My feet hurt."

"I know. You can lean on me and I will take the weight."

She almost made it. It was slow but she got to the top of the stairway, before she gave out. When her knees buckled, he figured they were past the neighbor viewpoint. He leaned over, scooping her up.

He hit the doorbell four times with his elbow while he pulled her tight against him.

Jason pulled opened the door. He looked at Ashley in Ian's arms.

"You broke my date," Jason said.

"Not now," Ian snapped. "Invite us in."

"You want me to what?" Jason choked, his eyes wide with shock.

"Do it," Ian snapped.

Jason stepped back, opening the door wide. "Would you like to come in?"

Ian stepped over the threshold.

Travis leaned in from the kitchen. Evan from the family room.

"What is going on?" Travis snapped.

"Evan," Ian said. "Front pocket. Left. Keys."

Evan moved quick, sticking his hand into Ian's pocket. Evan dangled them off a finger.

"Her car's down the street. Right side. I need everything out of the back seat and the trunk. Take it to my room."

Evan backhanded Jason on the chest. "Let's go."

"Why did you need inviting in?" Travis asked.

"I didn't."

Travis's gaze dropped to her.

"What's wrong with Ashley?" Quinn asked.

Ian moved toward the stairs, Quinn right behind him.

"What are we doing?" Travis called after him in a cheery voice.

"Moving in."

"You already live here. You know that, right?"

Ian got to the top floor. "Had crossed my mind."

Travis came up behind Ian as he lowered her to the bed. Ian reached up, pulling off the sunglasses and gloves. He unzipped the hoody and pulled it off as gently as he could.

"Move," Quinn said, pushing Ian aside.

"Are you going to tell me why your ex-girlfriend is passed out on your bed?" Travis asked. "Why didn't you come home last night?"

Ian ignored the extra words. "They killed her."

"You didn't do this?"

Ian stood straight and turned slowly to glare at Travis.

Travis put both his hands up, palms out. "Hey, I thought it was a good idea."

Ian pointed at her. "This was not a good idea. They came into her house last night when she was alone. There was nobody there to protect her."

"Did she say who?" Travis asked.

"Who do you think?" Ian snapped.

Travis looked confused. "She invited Walter in? No way. She would have known she was in trouble." Travis thought. "She would have called."

"She was dead when I got there."

"Turned. You know there is a difference."

Ian looked at him. "You might think you know the difference, but when you find someone who matters bloody and cold and check for a pulse, dead is just fucking dead."

"She's not dead now, Stuart," Quinn said. "She's got a wild pulse." He kept his finger over her wrist. "Fuck."

"What?"

"I've never felt anything like this. I can't even count—it's so fast. When did she wake up?" Quinn asked.

Ian checked his watch. "The first time? About seven hours ago. Around one."

Quinn looked up at him. "What do you mean first time?"

"She went back to sleep."

"She woke up and went back to sleep?" Travis asked. "Newborns don't do that."

Evan came in carrying the suitcases. He put them by the door.

Jason dumped the four pillows onto the edge of the bed then took a step back.

"You do realize that's my Saturday date, right?" he asked. "I was hoping for a little more interaction." His tone held none of his usual humor.

"The paper bags are downstairs," Evan said. "Walter turned Ashley?"

Ian shrugged his shoulders and shook his head. "I don't know who did this but it seems logical."

He pulled her phone out of his back pocket and handed it to Travis. "Check outgoing texts," Ian said. He looked to Quinn. "Can you help her?"

"Is she okay?" Evan asked. "She doesn't look okay."

"Wait a minute," Travis said, looking at the phone. "She sent you this?"

Ian shook his head. "No. She was already dead when that went out. I got the message and I was at the house in minutes."

"God," Travis snapped. "You fucking moron. Did it occur to you to call and say 'Gee, I have an issue' or were you trying to walk into a trap and get yourself killed?"

"It wasn't a trap because no one else ever showed up and no, it actually didn't dawn on me to do that until this morning when the sun was already up and you couldn't get to us. That came in," he said pointing at the phone. "Getting to her was the only thing on my mind."

"So who sent it?" Evan asked.

"Jason, can you trace it?" Travis asked.

"Yeah," Jason said. "But we already know so there is no point. It went from her phone to his. Won't tell me who hit send."

"But I don't understand," Travis said. "You've got a bandage on your wrist. You fed her. Not much, but some. She should be a little weak but fine."

"I fed her three times."

Quinn arranged her, pulling her legs straight and adjusting her shoulders so she was flat. "Did she take a lot?"

Ian shrugged. "It doesn't come measured."

"How long?" Quinn asked. "Two minutes? Five?"

"About five I guess. I wasn't timing it. I tried to get her to take more but she wasn't interested."

"Strong or weak?"

Ian thought. "Weak and hesitant. I had to force her."

"So she's low," Quinn said.

"How can you tell?" Travis asked.

"The sweating. And her breathing are pretty good clues. She's also off color by four shades. She needs blood."

"How much?" Jason asked. "How much blood?"

"I don't know," Quinn said. "More than we have between the five of us."

Ian saw Jason move to Ian's computer. Without sitting down, Jason leaned over the desk and started doing whatever it was he did on computers.

Ian had his drawing and his bike. Jason had his computers. Quinn had his medicine.

"She likes pillows," Ian said quietly.

Quinn nodded and put an extra pillow under her head. He picked up both her hands, looking at the tips of her fingers and the bandages Ian had put on. "They milked her."

"God, Quinn. They tortured her." His voice cracked.

Quinn looked at him. "What else?"

"Cuts. Over a dozen. None real deep."

"Where were they?"

"You can help her?"

"I don't know. We're working on that now."

Sighing, Ian tried not to think of Ash's modesty. "Upper and inner thighs. None below the knee."

"Were they bled?"

"I don't think so. They looked to be for show and pain. Some were deep but not stitches deep."

Quinn looked at him.

"Her sides," Ian said.

Quinn lifted her shirt and looked at the same holes Ian had found. Quinn touched two or three of them then looked at Ian.

"Knitting needle. I found it under the bed. It was bloody to the end."

"Oh, shit," Quinn said, touching them again. "Fuck," he muttered.

Ian already had one of the slippers off. He pulled on the second when everyone got close to see the burns and blisters.

"Foot roasting?" Evan gasped. "They burned her feet?"

Ian stood straight while they looked closer. "You really want to make a guess this wasn't Walter?"

Foot Roasting, a medieval torture technique, adopted by the vampire society to punish personal insults.

Ash had done nothing to anyone.

Ian had walked out on Walter in Walter's mind.

"What about sex?" Quinn asked.

"Vampires don't rape," Travis said. "Not in the playbook even for us."

"We're not talking us," Quinn said. "We're talking about a psycho who took an evening out to inflict this kind of damage on someone he didn't know."

Ian shook his head. "No, I don't think so. Not that I saw. She was nude when I found her, but I didn't see anything that made me think it."

Quinn ran a finger along one of the bruises on her face. "Whoever it was could over-power her easy. Why pound on her?" He looked sat Ian. "There is nothing to gain with that."

"What can I do?" Jason asked returning from the computer folding a piece of paper from the printer and slipping it into his back pocket.

"Go get me my bag," Quinn said.

Jason ran out of the room.

"How long did it take her to wake up?" Travis asked.

"I got to the house about one-thirty this morning and the party was already over. She woke up about one in afternoon."

"I don't understand," Travis said.

Ian turned on him. "That's what she's been saying for the last hour. She doesn't understand. She's scared. She doesn't remember."

"All of that is normal."

"No," Ian shook his head. "No, what I just watched for the last hour, that was not normal. She woke up and would be coherent one sentence than the next she was in an altitude we've never heard of. She thought there were people in the room with us. She was talking about my brother, James. Asking for him."

"Why? You don't even talk about your brother."

Ian's hands came out from his side. "I don't know. I know she knew who I was for part one but by the sequel, I could have been the man on the moon."

"You understand," Travis said, "Ash doesn't do confused and afraid. I think if you gave her the right frame of mind, she could kick all of our asses, probably at the same time."

Ian pointed at the bed, "And yet, look how she spent her evening while I pouted over here."

"They drained her to almost dry and didn't put enough back in to compensate. She's low." Quinn said.

Travis said, leaning back. "That's a lot of hours for a body to be low on blood. Serious intense confusion wouldn't be too far off."

"Evan," Quinn said, interrupting. "Go downstairs and get me a pan of cool water and stack of washcloths."

Evan ran.

"What's wrong?"

Quinn looked up at Ian. "She's got a pretty high fever. Her pupils are dilated. Her pulse is going about hundred miles an hour and I don't think she's breathing too good."

Jason came back, handing off the medical bag. Quinn unzipped it and pulled out a few instruments. He got an electric thermometer and put it in her ear.

The fear sunk deeper into Ian's gut. "What does all these mean?"

"A new vampire wakes up the first time hungry, pissed and more full of themselves than they've ever been. They don't come back in a near coma and confused." Quinn looked between Ian and

Travis. "She can't take care of herself. If we don't do something…"

"Consider her adopted into the den." Travis snapped. "Now fucking do something."

Technically a voting matter, yet no one in the room objected.

Ian stood up. "Look at this." He extended her arm, showing the mark on the inside of her elbow, the tiny bruise around it.

"What the hell is that?" Travis snapped.

Quinn looked at it, touching it. "It's injection site, straight into a vein. Whatever they gave her they wanted it to hit fast."

"How fast?"

Quinn shook his head. "Seconds, maybe. Depends on what it was. Get me that info and I can tell you more."

Quinn pulled out a stethoscope. "Roll her over."

Ian placed a hand on each of her shoulders, pulling her toward him until she rested on his knees.

Quinn lifted up her shirt and started listening to things. He kept his eyes closed, deep concentration on his features. He took several minutes, moving the stethoscope around to different positions before he pulled her shirt down.

"You can lay her back down."

"What was that?"

"Our heart rate runs in the 120 sphere. Hers, off the charts. And it's not only racing, it's pounding like a freight train. And she's breathing short. Her lungs aren't pulling air all the way in. You can barely hear it moving back and forth."

"You can hear all that?" Travis asked.

Quinn nodded. "A lot you can learn from all this stuff."

"Like how to get her to sit up and start talking?" Ian asked.

Quinn tilted his chin and shrugged. "I think it's going to take more than me for that."

Jason looked up at Ian. "I really don't like it when people fuck with our people."

Quinn put the stethoscope away.

Ian looked at Quinn. "Can you help her? Please?"

Quinn shrugged. "Stuart, I don't know exactly what's wrong."

"But you know this stuff," Ian said.

He sort of nodded and looked at her. "It's all guess work."

"So guess," Travis said.

He reached back into his bag and pulled out a plastic thing, putting it on her finger. He left it there half a minute then pulled it off to read.

"Ninety-four percent."

"Ninety-four percent what?"

"Oxygen. This will track her O2 but I can tell you off the bat it should be giving me errors as ours is too high for it to read. Ninety-four is about right for a human, dangerous low for us."

"What does that mean?" Ian asked.

"It means her O2 is off. We need to get it up." He tossed the do-dad to Jason who caught it.

"I need that to read at two-hundred to two-ten. Higher would be better. Think you can rewire it to work?"

Jason smiled. He could rewire anything to work anyway they wanted. "Don't be insulting."

"What do we do?" Travis asked.

"I can bandage and treat the rest. The feet are going to be hardest, but it's not going to help with her breathing or the fever. We need O2," Quinn said. "A couple of tanks would be good. I can get the supplies we need out of the hospital to make it work with no one seeing, but I can't carry a tank."

"We fix the oxygen we fix her?"

"I hope so. There's something going on in there that is really weird for what she went through. Turning shouldn't do this. Any chance we can find out what was injected?"

"We don't know for sure who did it, so we don't know who to ask. If it was Walter, we don't know where to find him."

"It was Walter, but hell if I know how. She wouldn't have let him in."

"The O2. Where do we get that?" Travis asked.

Quinn pursed his lips and thought. "I can call Carlos. See what he can dig up for us. For the right price he can get whatever you want however fast you need it and deliver it smiling."

"I can cover that," Jason said.

Ian looked at him. In the hierarchy of financing in the house, Jason led by miles. "Thanks," Ian said.

Jason smiled with a nod. "Got to get her ready for Saturday," he grinned.

"What will it do?" Travis asked.

"Even if she's not breathing deep, the O2 is more concentrated."

"And that's what's causing…"

Quinn nodded. "Confusion, pupils, heart racing. Could be that simple. But the wounds and what they did to her? She had to be awake for just about all of it and this wasn't a short romp through the hayfields. They were there awhile and she's going to have some damage." He looked at Ian. "The inside kind."

"I can fix that," Ian whispered.

In their old world, there existed a little technique called *suggestion*. Used for mind control in trapping and securing victims. Right here and right now, though, it could easily be used to wipe a memory.

Travis looked at him. "We don't do that anymore."

Ian glared back.

"Um…" Travis corrected. "We don't do that anymore until after we can talk to her and get some information."

Travis reached into his pocket, pulling out a Swiss Army knife. His face winced tight when he sliced his wrist open, letting the blood fall on Ian's floor and bed. He sat down next to Ashley. He pressed his wrist to her mouth but she shook her head against it before finally, reluctantly, taking it.

He looked up at Ian. "She doesn't have her teeth."

Ian shook his head slow. Newborns *always* came with their new set of fangs.

Ian turned away, facing away from all of them as thoughts slipped slowly through his body. Grief started slow and he had to forcibly shove it out of the way and tell himself hope existed.

She slowed down with Travis until she finally let go and settled back onto the pillow her eyes closed.

Travis took one of Quinn's wash rags and pressed it against his wrist.

Quinn got the pan of water and moved it closer, dipping in one of the clothes. He wrung it out and folded it, placing it over her forehead. Getting two more, he wet them, rolled them in to a ball and stuck one into each armpit. The next, he lay over her chest.

"She's going to freeze," Ian said.

Quinn shook his head. "Her fever is 106. 2, Stuart. Way above us and we run hot."

Jason reached for the knife, cutting his wrist and sitting down beside Ashley.

"We're not going to get enough blood into her like this," Travis said. "We can't spare that much."

"Think about it," Quinn said. "In humans fever is caused by infections. Bacterial, viral. Vampires don't catch germs."

"So what's causing the fever?" Ian asked.

Quinn pointed at him. "That is a very good question."

Jason finished up, grabbed the other washrag. "Evan, let's go. We'll take care of the blood."

He headed toward the door, Evan right behind him.

"Where you going?" Ian asked.

Jason looked over at him. "Pig farm is about fifty miles north. Pretty rural. Easy to get in and out of. No one will see us."

"How do you know that?" Travis asked.

Jason pointed at the computer he just used. "Internet, duh. How do I find anything?"

"You've never told us that," Travis snapped.

He only smiled and patted his back pocket. "I got the directions. Hour each way, couple of hours to do the deed. We should be back by midnight. You two secure Carlos and the oxygen. Quinn stays here with her. Does that sound like a plan that will work?"

"Jason," Ian called. "I appreciate the offer for the O2."

Jason stopped in the door and turned around to look at Ian. "No problem."

"But do consider your hot date canceled for Saturday."

"Damn," Jason grinned. "I was really looking forward to that."

"You lip-locked with my girlfriend and I have real issues with that despite the help."

Everyone's gaze snapped to Jason but he only grinned wide.

Jason laughed. "I knew she would tell you. That's a hundred bucks you owe me. In my arms, in under a month."

Ian took a step forward and Travis put a hand on his arm to control.

"It was real nice," Jason said. "But then, she wasn't your girlfriend when I did it, was she? If I had known it at the time, I might have let you four thrash it out for a few more minutes without me and done a little bit more experimenting."

"The fact we were broken up at that particular moment and you didn't actually know it means you were kissing what you thought was my current girlfriend."

"Yeah? So? It was only a little kiss. Besides, I was heading out to fight to the death and thought we might actually lose. If a chick is going to be handy and be willing, it's a nice way to check out."

"She was willing?"

"She actually didn't fight all that much, not at all as a matter of fact. She didn't even slap me." He grinned. "In fact, I think she enjoyed it as much as me and man, did I enjoy it."

"And you, of course, you gave her the choice in the whole matter."

"Naw," he smiled. "I was pretty quick and she was pretty damn shocked. Still, it was real nice."

"And you knew if I found out it would piss me off enough that you really might die outside of battle?"

"Stuart, ninety percent of the shit I do around you, I do to piss you off for the sheer pleasure I get out of pissing you off." He laughed. "Can't really explain it. It's just fun."

Jason turned and walked out the door. Evan followed.

Travis looked at Ian. "He's spent about fifty years looking for the perfect way to push the exact right button and I think he might have found it. Do remember where he's going and why he's doing it when you start to plan his murder."

CHAPTER FOURTEEN

When the doorbell rang, Travis pulled it open.

"You are fucking kidding me?" he said to the man standing on the porch.

"Can I come in?" Max asked.

"You lived here. You don't need to ask me that."

"I think under the circumstances, I should be asking for permission."

Travis stood back and waved his arm.

Max Garcia stepped into the house he used to call home.

Travis shut the door, screamed for Evan and slammed his hands down on Max's shoulders, his six-three plus spinning Max's five-ten and shoving him up against the wall, a forearm on Max's throat.

Evan appeared.

"Get Stuart. Tell him to come armed," Travis said.

"Travis, I didn't know. I swear to God I didn't have any idea what he planned. He told me different and I fucking believed him."

"So coming here is what? Repentance? You're still active."

"Yes. Not like I was. Way different than I was before, but yes."

Travis heard the footsteps on the stairs and turned to see a barefoot Ian pulling on a T-shirt over his grey sweats as he hit the entryway. He tried to shove Travis out of the way but Travis stayed forefront and pushed Ian back.

"Do you know what they did to her?" Ian yelled, trying to grab him. "Do you have any idea what they put her through?"

"I was there, man. I will never forget what they did. Can we talk? Please? I just want to talk. If you want to slice and dice after, fine, but let me help you."

Travis pulled Max off the wall and tossed him to Ian, who may have come down unarmed, but didn't waste a second in letting his lack of sleep stop his fists from explaining his fury to Max.

It was Jason and Evan who finally dragged Ian back while Quinn knelt in front of Max without checking a single wound.

"I like Ash," Quinn said. "I didn't get a whole hell of one on one time with her but we take her welfare very personal."

Max looked up at him.

"I'd say you're lucky you're not dead yet. And I would add I think the night is still very young."

"I didn't know, Quinn. I met him a couple of months ago and I didn't know. You guys know I'm a bastard but I am not setting up friends and I am not setting up some innocent beauty to go through what they put her through."

Jason handed him his glasses. "You know you have perfect vision and these are a joke, right?"

Max took them and didn't reply to the question.

"He was trying to get her to denounce Stuart," he said. "Their relationship, anything between them. He wanted her to recite this asinine poem he had written about how much she hated Stuart."

Travis saw Ian's eyes close tight.

"And she wouldn't," Max said. "They stripped her for humiliation. The other stuff…" Max had trouble breathing before snapping his gaze up to Ian's. "She never made a sound. No matter what they did. And she knew, I could tell by her face, she knew she was never walking out of there and she wasn't giving them you."

"You were in the room?"

Max shook his head. "I broke out a window."

"To watch?" Ian snapped.

"To beg them to stop."

Quinn put a hand under Max's elbow and helped him to his feet without examining him and led him to the dining room table.

Everyone filed into the dining room.

"I've been in San Francisco since I left and I wasn't kidding. I was totally broke."

Travis tilted his head at him.

"I didn't stop. I couldn't stop, but I go longer than I ever did. But this one night, I scored and I had a little money and I went to a bar and I swear to God he was just there. He talked for a good twenty before I realized who he was. And he still, fifty years later, was talking about the one that got away." Max looked up. "He talked about you, Stuart. How good it had been, the love of his life. I let him ramble and he bought me a drink and I left. And we did this again, couple of times a week for a month."

"You told him."

"No," Max said. "Not at first. It's like you said, we left friends. But I saw no sign of the man you had talked about. I knew he was hunting, but he was subtle and usually pretty alone. There wasn't a crowd. After a couple of months of it, though, he said he wished he could have one more shot at a talk and I left with that."

"But you knew what he was."

"Everyone of us has changed from where we were fifty years ago," Max snapped, "all of you—most of all. So why couldn't he?"

Travis closed his eyes and rubbed his forehead.

"One night I told him. I knew where you were and he said that was interesting and he left. I didn't see him for a couple of weeks. He started coming back in, talking nice, slowly building, until he finally offered me a price for a trip."

"How much?" Jason snapped.

Max's gaze shifted to his. "Ten grand. And I had maybe five bucks in my pocket so I said yes and he and I came here alone in his car and got a hotel on the outskirts, which was when the Blood Letting started. He and I were the first and I started to see the edge to him that you used to talk about. He wasn't kind with his victims. And he liked to bring teenage boys back to the hotel and I would disappear and so would they. That was three months ago. There are more victims than are on record they just weren't reported. Mostly homeless."

"Why didn't you visit?" Evan asked. "We were friends."

"I know. And I came by a couple of times but I didn't stop. Something was off and I was trying to figure it out. I was with him and it was starting to feel weird and I didn't think you would like it."

"Warning might have been nice."

"You could have stopped all of this, couldn't you?" Jason snapped.

"When we came here that night, it was only us, him and me. I knew he had others coming into town but I didn't know he was Primary or he had a den and I didn't know the plans. He said he wanted to talk to you. We were outside the gate listening to the break-up when he told me everyone inside dies. And then all these vampires were just there."

"You sided with him."

"I'm a fucking coward, you know that. He would have killed me if he didn't think I was with him. When we left here, we went back to the den. His arm was broken and he was pissed and everything you ever said about him was right there." Max raked his hands painfully through his hair. "He didn't want to talk to Stuart. He didn't want another chance. He wanted Stuart dead and he wanted to make sure he suffered as much as possible. He wanted Travis to watch because he blamed him for breaking them up."

319

"Them?"

Max's gaze came up to Travis's. "Walter and Stuart. In his mind there had been a relationship. The rest of you, he didn't care how you died as long as this house was left abandoned and empty with all the cars in the driveway and a mystery to go with it."

"Melodramatic bastard," Quinn said turning away.

"How does Ash fit into this?" Ian asked. "She didn't do anything and she was gone out of here."

"He watched the two of you for a long time. He knew you were lying when you broke up," Max shrugged. "He knew you would throw yourself in front of a bus to protect her."

He took a deep breath and stared at the table. "We went out that night. Walter, the girls and me and I didn't know where we were going and I didn't ask. Figured it was Blood Letting business and I was hungry so okay. I didn't know whose house it was. The three of them walked in but I had never been there and I was stuck outside, asking for them to bring me in on it. I heard the gunshots and there was this one startled yell, but then nothing. That's when I started looking in the windows and I saw them in her room, what they were doing and I was pounding and yelling and no one was showing up in that neighborhood to help. I broke out the window to try to talk to them, but they ignored me and kept going and it got worse until I couldn't watch anymore. I sank down under that window. Stuart, I would have stopped them. If I could have gotten in, I would have slit every one of their throats."

"You could have called. We could've got it."

"I am sitting in the middle of your girlfriend's murder and I'm thinking you're not going to be logical when you arrive. So I

320

chickened out." He looked off into space. "I thought they were going to kill her. But I saw them turn her and I knew there might be some hope."

Time paused until Max cleared his throat.

"I was turned in 1952 and I think this was most horrific thing I've ever witnessed." He wiped the moisture from his eyes.

"Three hours and eighteen minutes after they walked in the door, they came out the back. I was waiting and I beat the shit out of Walter. His arm was bandaged from the break so he was easy. Did not have a weapon or I would have killed him, probably the girls, too. Walter could barely stand when I was done and the girls stood and watched and laughed like it was a joke. Ashley's phone fell out of his pocket. I don't know why he had it, but I grabbed it…"

"How did you know it was hers?"

Max looked up at Jason. "Wallpaper was still set to a photo of the two of them and I didn't think it would be Walter's first choice. "He shifted his gaze to Ian and laughed a little. "God, you are one-motherfucking-great-looking-couple. Like designed for each other. It's sorta irritating," he smiled.

Ian shook his head in disbelief in response.

"Walter crawled off and I stood at that window and looked at all that beauty lying on that bed, looking so asleep." He laughed a little. "Even like that, she was still stunning and she was coming back. But so was he. He told me while I was beating him. She was going into his stable for barter until her time ran out," he said. "Then he would bleed her himself. I didn't understand what that meant but I knew she needed help fast. I sent the text, left the

321

phone and waited in the backyard out of sight until just before dawn in case Walter did decide to bring friends back to take out Stuart."

"You could have done something."

"I couldn't get in."

"Fucking *9-1-1* would have put a real damper on their night's activities."

"Oh God," Max moaned. "I never even thought of that. We don't think like that. Human help wouldn't cross our mind."

Travis cleared his throat. "That's a real fascinating story and thank you for the gory details we were imagining but not seeing."

"I couldn't stop him," Max said. "But I did what I could for her. She's not some chick. She means something here for some reason I don't know cuz I never saw it in any of you before, but she matters beyond a blow job."

Stuart backhanded Max in the face. Max's head snapped to the side.

"I'm sorry," Max said, wiping his lip. "That was out of line."

"Why the hell risk coming here tonight? You had to know we would kill you," Evan asked. "Even *I* want to kill you if they'll let me, and they never let me do shit like that."

"For Quinn," Max said.

"What?" Three voices snapped.

Moving stiff, Max reached into his jacket pocket, pulling out a small, glass medical vial, an inch and half tall with a top that took a syringe. He set it on the table.

"I don't know what this is, but I know it has to do with that 'times up' comment. And I know it's what he injected into her."

Quinn grabbed it, reading the label.

"After Walter's beating, I snuck into his den and took that. Thought you might need it. I watched. They drained her, injected, then put the blood back. I don't know if it makes a difference."

"Who?" Ian snapped.

"Girls did the work. He enjoyed his brew."

"What is it?" Travis asked.

"Multroxon. I've never heard of it," Quinn said.

Max looked around as if realizing something for the first time. "She was turned. Why isn't she here? She should be here."

"She's in a coma, Max," Ian said. "Has been since I brought her back."

"What?"

"Whatever this is," Quinn said, holding up the vial. "It changed everything about being turned."

"It wasn't the one dose. He used it on her a couple of times. He never said how much or when, only that he had been in her house and he was injecting her before Stuart got back from work."

"She never had injection marks," Ian said.

Quinn shrugged. "Between the toes, under the tongue. Hell, using her ear piercing and he would have hidden it from you. Has she been different?"

"Oh shit," Ian moaned. "She had a doctor's appointment coming up. Made it because she started feeling fatigued and short of breath."

"How long ago?"

He closed his eyes struggling on no sleep. Travis could see it. "She told me. Um…" he rubbed his eyes. "It started a couple of weeks ago, I think. She didn't give me a date."

"Den," Quinn asked. "Where is the den?"

Max looked down and appeared to be thinking.

"Do you have any doubt about what we will do to get the information out of you?" Jason asked.

Max sighed and looked up. "Outside of town. There's an old church. Deconsecrated. Used to have a nunnery and parsonage behind it."

"Lourdes?" Travis asked. "It was the Catholic church before they built the new one in town."

"There was a care-taker living in the nunnery. He's one of us now. The rooms were cleaned up a bit and that is where Walter has everyone stashed."

"How many?" Travis asked.

"He can't get a lot of people to follow him. He's too nuts even for what we do. He's tossed out the Old Laws and he's making new ones up as he goes. Who was here that night was it, except for the Newborns who couldn't take the trip. You took out five. Four Newborns from town held up and then the care taker."

"That is a lot of vampires with little activity in town," Travis said.

"Mostly Walter's been sharing what he brings home. Taking homeless and prostitutes. Teenagers who wouldn't be missed, but it's a small town and he can't do what he really likes. The Blood Letting Murders were done on purpose to get your attention, though none of us anticipated Stuart's cop."

"The Newborns should be easy to take out. The rest…"

"The girls are the worst," Max said. "I mean we are talking Manson Family mentality. They will follow him anywhere and they take pleasure in everything they do. They make him look sane. If he says cut themselves six times on the left arm they will cut seven to make sure he knows they're his."

"You can't stay here," Travis said.

"I know," Max said. "I didn't plan on it. I'm getting out of here as fast as I can. He finds out I came here and it will be me you find in dust in the backyard tomorrow."

He glanced up at Ian and then down. "Stuart, you were always good to me no matter how bad I screwed-up. I'm sorry she got dragged into this. I hope you really do know I would have stopped it if I could."

"Right now, I'm not feeling that means much but maybe someday it will."

"Good enough," Max said, getting to his feet.

He stopped to grin at Ian. "But damn, where did you find her? That body alone…" Max said, flinching when Ian raised his hand again.

"Just kidding," Max said, holding up his hands in surrender.

"We get it," Travis snapped. "She's built and we don't give a shit. We give a shit she's been asleep for two days, dropping weight like crazy, sucking oxygen faster than we can get it in the house."

"I'm sorry," Max said. "I really did like it here. I should have been standing on your side, but then, if I had, he never would have found you and I think even my fucked up subconscious will be living with that one for a long, long time."

He headed toward the door.

"Wait," Jason said, running up the stairs. He came back a few minutes later with a small cloth bag.

"It's not ten grand but it will get you out of town and maybe you can get your head together."

Max took the bag, stared at it and weighed it in his hands. "You kidding?" he said to Jason.

"I liked having you here. You were a lot of fun. But if you give me another two minutes to think about it, I might go back wanting to slit your throat."

"Got it," Max said, turning toward the door.

After the door shut, Quinn stared at Jason and Jason stared at Quinn until Travis broke the silence.

"What?"

Jason reached in his back pocket and pulled out two knives he had grabbed when he hit his safe. One wooden handled with gold trim and a fold up blade. The other a silver switchblade with a pearl handle.

"Want to take a ride?" Jason asked Quinn.

"I was waiting for you," Quinn said. He caught the switchblade.

"No," Travis said.

Jason looked at him. "You're going to stop us?"

"You two stay. Get started on figuring out what this crap is about," he motioned to the bottle. He brought his gaze toward Ian's. "We'll go."

"We're better than you," Quinn said. "You know that."

"And I know he can use a computer better than us, too, and you know what you are having him look for. There is no need to split us from what we do best."

"What about me? ' Evan asked. "I want to go."

Travis looked at him.

"No," Stuart said before Travis could.

"That is not fucking fair. You can use the help."

"And who is going to be here with her if she wakes up?"

"That's supposed to be you," Evan snapped. "So I should be going and you should be staying."

"I can use the computer in your room until you get back," Jason said. "That puts us both in the room with her."

Stuart glared at him. "Thank you."

"He has every right."

"It's not his right I'm worried about."

Three hours later, Stuart came up the stairs to his open door and found papers on the floor, Jason's feet on his desk and Quinn sitting on the edge of the bed reading printouts.

Ash still slept, her face pale.

Jason's feet hit the floor, the chair came around and he faced him.

"What?" Quinn asked.

"Place was abandoned. Judging by the bodies and decomposition it's been a couple of days at least."

"How many?"

"Three. The caretaker—we think—and two kids. A guy and a girl. Looks like a last hurrah after using them for a while. They were done pretty brutally."

"Did they, by chance, leave a note stating a forwarding address?"

Stuart, exhausted in mind and soul sank down on the bed beside her. "No we checked every building and every room twice. There was nothing."

"You think they gave up and left?"

Stuart brought his gaze up. "Aye?"

"I love it when you have that conviction in your voice and you're sure of your answer," Jason said.

"What have you found?"

"Not much yet. It's obscure, that's for sure and I'm having trouble digging it out."

"Thought you found everything."

"I didn't say I hadn't found it yet. Just that it's giving me problems."

"Do you guys mind moving downstairs. I'd like to—"

"That's cool," Quinn said getting to his feet and gathering what papers he had.

Ian curled up next to her, his head on the pillow, his body pressed to her. She ran warmer than she should. No solid food had passed her lips in days and as much blood as they were putting in, there should be some sort of output. There was nothing but her asleep in a world he couldn't reach.

He draped his arms over her, pulling her close.

"I'm coming for you. Just wait and don't give up. I'm coming."

CHAPTER FIFTEEN

Exhausted, defeated with fingers hurting from so much typing when typing is all he did for a living, Jason heard the footsteps coming up to the door and had time to shut down one screen that mattered and bring up another of Playmate July 1982 before the door opened and Travis came in.

Travis stared over Jason's shoulder.

"I see we're working real, real hard."

Jason looked at the picture and smiled. "A perfect 36/22/36."

"Do I look like I give a fuck? What the hell have you found?"

Jason turned to Quinn who read through some files on Jason's made bed in his tidy room. Quinn's knee pulled up under him, the folders balanced. The fatigue sat obvious on him. Wrinkling of the brow, the circles under the eyes. Quinn had been up since she came in the door, searching for the answer he was sure he would find.

"Quinn?" Travis snapped, Quinn's chin came up.

"What?"

"What do you have?"

"Not much yet," Quinn said.

Travis snarled at Jason. "It's been two days Mr. MIT computer genius. You do this for a fucking living. If it was porno game you would already have it. Why can't you find anything?"

"This stuff is like lost in space," Jason said. "Someone hid it deep. I've gotten a couple of files on a government program it was used in but nothing on how it works or how to fix it."

He picked up a couple of stapled papers he knew were pointless but Travis wouldn't and handed them off.

Travis looked at the sheets, flipping them. "Daybreak?" he asked.

"It was the government sponsored program that used this shit. It was for behavior modification. They used it on inmates and mental patients. We know what they did with it. We don't how it worked."

"We are running out of time. You know that."

"We're very aware," Quinn said looking at the files, dismissing Travis.

"What do I tell Stuart?"

"Tell him we almost have it and she'll be fine in a day or two." Quinn kept his chin down but his gaze up.

Travis stared at him. Then he turned and slammed the door on his way out.

Jason spun his chair to face Quinn straight on.

"How long do you think we can keep this up?"

"Until I figure it out."

"Is that before or after she dies?"

Quinn's gaze came up pissed. "You want to walk into Stuart's room, Stuart who hasn't slept in four days and tell him everyone who has taken this drug died? Be my guest."

"You think you are going to find an answer in those pages? I have printed a thousand pages and nothing so far."

"Find me the chemical make-up."

"Where? Where do I look for that?"

"I don't know," Quinn said. "Use your magic powers and make it appear. There might be something in the chemical compound that has a counter. We might be able to use that."

Jason's hand slammed down on a stack of papers by his keyboard, tossing them up to scatter.

"Her O2 is dropping every day. She doesn't have any more time and you know what? I'm not real sure under the circumstances what happens when she dies. Does she turn to dust or do we have a body we now have to deal with?"

Quinn's fury was palpable. "You think you are helping?"

"You think Stuart is going to go with the pig farm idea? Take care of the problem? Not sure he'll bring flowers. Cuz we don't have many choices."

"Chemical. Compound. Now."

"She is suffocating, Quinn and those blue eyes are not going to open again and dammit I want to try one of those hugs I don't have to steal. But she is *dying*. Right now. She might not have twenty-four hours left before it wins. And if he loses her, I bet you everything I have he's not far behind. He will *never* recover. You want to do more web searches? We have done days of web searches. It's not there. We're searching for air."

Out of sleep, his fear visible on his features, Quinn slammed the papers into his lap. "What do you suggest? We don't know fully what it is, we don't know how it kills, we don't know how to stop it. So, Mr. Genius 162 IQ, what do you want to do?"

Jason leaned back in his chair and stared at July 1982. Pretty nice, he thought as the real, useful part of his brain clicked ideas passing in rapid succession. He'd had as good as 1982. He'd had worse. Worse was generally better in what they were setting out to accomplish.

An idea slid slowly into position like a photo in a slide show, the bright white light behind illuminating and calculating what he was now focused on. He reached up and turned off the monitor because to be real, he didn't care one way or another about Miss July. He kept it around to throw off Travis when the need arrived.

He turned his chair to look at Quinn.

"What do you think of when you think of Ash?"

"What do you mean?"

He shrugged. "What comes to mind?"

"Kick ass cop. Loves Stuart. I don't know. I like her. A lot. She's funny as hell and sweeter than pretty."

"No, that's what I mean. Genetically."

"What? She's Stuart's huma…" Quinn cut himself off. The idea took hold, his head falling back. "Shit."

"Stop thinking like a doctor, asshole," Jason snapped. "Start thinking like a vampire."

CHAPTER SIXTEEN

Ian made sure she was tucked in safe, a pillow beside her if she woke up and an extra blanket on her. He didn't like to leave her. Not for a minute. He was seeing the improvements, he knew it.

Leaving the door open so he could hear, he headed down the stairs, slowed down by lack of sleep and worry and stepped into the kitchen where everyone waited.

"Is this necessary?" he asked. "I actually have someplace else to be."

"How is she?" Jason asked.

Ian looked at him. "Immobile."

"I lied," Quinn said with no fanfare. "I've been lying all week. I am sorry but I didn't see any other option."

"You what?" Ian snapped.

"Stuart, I had to—I—we—couldn't tell you how damn hopeless it was."

Ian's gaze snapped to Jason's.

"Sorry," Jason whispered.

Travis snapped. "You and Jason have been jerking off to pin-ups?"

"We had nothing to say that would help," Quinn said. "And neither one of us could walk into that room and tell you she wasn't going to make so we made shit up and we stalled until we could think of something."

Ian couldn't breathe. "*Isn't going to make it.* You said *isn't going to make it?* Her O2? You said…"

"I've been lying to you, Stuart. Her O2 never went up. It's been dropping every day. We don't have much time left."

Ian sank down in the chair and had to count breaths.

"What the fuck is going on?"

"There is a reason and a background and I can explain it to you or we move to the fast track, try our plan, hope it works and I explain later when we have time."

"Is there a halfway point?" Travis asked.

"Yes. The short version is that the center in the brain that processes oxygen has been damaged. It controls the breathing. There is most likely damage to her immune system, too, or else we wouldn't be dealing with the ongoing fever."

"What does that mean?"

"This drug was for behavior modification and I think her behavior was modified. I don't think she will function like us. I think germs and shit, will still be a problem her whole life. This drug is designed to change the way people behave. The way it was introduced, hitting her brain before the vampire blood, it was working on changing her before they were halfway done. I think it might have worked. She was turned, but what would have changed her human behavior with the drug altered her vampire, I think."

"English?" Travis snapped.

"We don't have time for this but let me try." Quinn talked with his hands. "You change the behavior of a rapist and make him nice to women. This drug acts with the therapy and prison and whatever else, and enhances what is done, making the new behavior take hold. Ash was given the drug between behaviors, human vs. vampire. I think where she would have been in pure vampire hell, she kept her human qualities. The new behavior, the vampire, was rejected by her brain for the old behavior. Her body accepted a lot of the new. Physically she'll have a lot of our traits, but I think there is some human stuff left. Does that make sense?"

"Yes and no. I don't understand why you think this? You haven't spoken to her."

"Little things. She didn't want to feed off Stuart when she woke up. Why? What Newborn doesn't crave their first taste? She was confused, imagined things. None of this says vampire except the accelerated healing on her injuries. Even the burns are already gone. And I opened the window the other day. Even in a coma, she jerked away from the sunlight. Problem was this medication was fucked up from day one. It had a major flaw that wasn't seen until it was injected into humans. It attacks the respiratory centers. Everyone in the program who took it died and the med and program were scrapped."

"Can we get back to the dying part?" Ian said. "Fuck what may or may not happen later. You are a Goddamn doctor. Do something."

"What's your plan?" Travis asked.

"The drug is still in her blood. We don't metabolize and break down things like that and she doesn't anymore either. The way it was introduced, shot in after draining, before introduction means he was going for optimum exposure. When the new blood hit, it carried it everywhere. The substance is still in there, still fucking with her. She can't heal because it's overriding the vampire."

"Why do you know this?" Travis asked.

"I read fourteen autopsy reports from people exposed to this. They all ended the same."

"How?" Stuart snapped, shooting his gaze up.

"Death due to cardiac arrest brought by pulmonary failure."

Travis put a hand on Ian's shoulder.

"Your suggestion?" Travis asked.

"I have no idea if this is going to work, but it makes sense and we don't have any other options. We have to change the blood out."

"We've got gallons of the pig blood in the refrigerator in the garage," Evan said.

"Pig blood heals us. She's not responding to it for some reason."

"So what do you think will work?"

"In a turning, vampire blood overrides human, wiping out existing diseases, replacing the bad with healthy tissue. I'm hoping it works the same way here. She needs vampire blood. More potent than what they gave and washed of what they added."

"More potent?" Travis asked.

"I'm willing to wager that Walter and whoever else was involved traded out their blood on a semi-regular basis taking victims and turnings and hell, sex. Theirs was a diluted substance. Not us. Ours is the same as it has been since 1958, 1959, 1967 and 1972. It's pure, it's concentrated and it hasn't gone anywhere. And it carries no chemicals."

"You want to give her a transfusion?"

"No," Quinn said standing eye to eye with Travis, five inches taller. "I want to give six transfusions."

"Okay, for one, there's only five of us and how the hell is that going to help?"

"It's not the how it's going to help that concerns me, it's what happens to who goes first."

"Which would be me," Ian said.

Quinn shook his head. "Sorry. No, not even on the playbill."

"What?"

"She wakes up, she needs you ready and well and your old self. She is going to have to have that. She might be dealing with a lot of shit from that night and she needs your stability. And I do not know where this plan is heading. You're sidelined. And I go last. We should be able to do this the old-fashioned way, but if she doesn't respond, we'll have to use formal transfusions. I know how to do that and I have to teach the rest of you so that there aren't any mistakes. I think by the time I go, one of you will be ready to hook me up and then the first two repeat. Who they are, I don't know."

"What happens?" Travis asked.

"Pretty simple, the first one is taking on the very drug killing her. I have no idea what that is going to do to our systems. Maybe nothing. Maybe a hell of a lot more than we are willing to sacrifice. There will probably be residual chemicals after the first. Number two will be taking those. After that, it's switching out fresh blood like opening a window to get fresh air. Each time, it's new blood bringing in new properties. It should clean everything out and maybe repair some damage."

"What happens to one and two?"

"I don't know," Quinn said. "I really don't know. Nothing? Dead? It's guess work."

"I'm confused," Evan said.

"What?" Travis asked.

"Max said that Walter said he wanted her for the stable."

"Aye."

"How does a coma fit into a stable?"

Quinn looked to Jason. "I didn't think of that."

He thought and paced twice. "Something is different about what was done to her than anyone else."

"Could be doses," Jason said.

"Does it matter?" Travis asked. "What we are going to do? Does her being different change anything?"

"No," Quinn said. "We still have the same problem and only one solution."

Travis looked at the stairs then back.

"What prep time do we need?"

"I want to do one every twelve hours for three days. To get started though, I think most of us have been there."

Quinn's gaze shifted to Evan.

"I can do it," the kid said.

"You've never even bitten before."

"So get me a God damn diagram, a piece of fruit to practice on and leave me alone. I'll do it. This is Ash and we're going to do this. She said she made brownies. I want to try them. If they are anything like her cookies, I'm keeping her."

Ian smiled. "I didn't know she made brownies."

Travis batted him. "Then let's ask her."

He turned and headed toward the stairs.

"No," Ian snapped, blocking his way.

"This is my problem. I do this. No one else."

"You think that argument has a chance in hell of standing up in this house?"

Travis pushed and Ian blocked, his hands on both handrails. He stared at his best friend.

"You got a gun aimed at her and me. You have to choose. You really going to pick me?"

"I go first."

"You don't go at all," Travis said quietly. "And you have had ten minutes sleep in a week, after nothing but hell and you are going to let go of this problem and let your family help you fix this."

Ian held.

"I will either tell them to restrain you or I will kick your ass myself which either way works cuz I always kick your ass. You fight like a girl."

"Ian," Jason said, surprising Ian. Jason never called him that. "We got this and we want to. She is part of the family and we would do it for any one of us."

"I go," Travis said staring directly at Ian. "Jason follows. Then Evan, then Quinn. Jason and I repeat with me first. Does anyone have a problem with that?"

"No." It was three voices sounding as one.

"Aye," Ian said.

"Then it's a good thing your vote was deleted in this election. Are you going to move or do I throw you?"

"She is a chick I brought home like all of us have done before," Ian said with a tear in his voice, the exhaustion breaking

343

him. "None of you should be putting yourselves in jeopardy because of it. It is *my* problem. I should do it."

Travis closed the distance, his hand coming around Ian's neck to pull him close enough to talk in his ear. "It's Ash, Stuart. We would jump off a cliff smiling if we thought it would help her. Let us," his voice shaky.

Travis let go and backed up, rocking on his heels.

The choices weren't fair. The situation wasn't fair. None of this God damn turmoil Walter had created was fair.

Ian stepped back, turning to put his back on the staircase wall, his head leaning on the dry wall, looking up.

Travis patted him on the shoulder, then stepped past heading up. Ian stood on the stairs and watched Quinn join him.

CHAPTER SEVENTEEN

She opened her eyes, blinking hard, trying to think and having trouble. Her body ached in ways she didn't really understand, the fatigue prominent.

Lying on her side, across from her she saw an electric piano and two guitars and confusion added to her taxed mind.

She felt movement behind her, a body sliding over to press up against her back, an arm draping over her to hold her close. A hand came up and pulled her hair out of the way, exposing her neck and she felt a warm kiss below her ear.

"You're moving different," he whispered in the dark. "You're awake, aren't you?"

"I'm not sure," she whispered.

"In all the time we were together," he said, "Did I ever say you were the absolutely most beautiful woman I had ever seen?"

She smiled a little and waited half a minute. "No. I think that one slipped past."

"How about in my long life, you are the only woman I ever loved?"

She chuckled. "No, I remember you calling me a bitch and telling me to get out of your house for good."

"Probably the number one most stupid thing I ever said in my life. Next time I plan on cutting a limb off to make it less painful."

Moving very slowly, jerkily she rolled over to face him on his bed.

He stayed close, a hand on her hip, but gave her a little distance.

"What time is it?" she asked, her voice hoarse.

He leaned over to pick up his cell phone. "Eight forty-two."

"Morning or night?"

He put the phone down and rolled back toward her. He was under the quilt so all she could see was he was shirtless, the chain shiny.

"Night."

"So you just got up?"

He shook his head. "I've been up for a while." He held up a book. She reached up and took it from him, looking at the title.

"Can you read this for me?" he asked.

"You want me to read this book?"

"Only the title."

She held the book toward her and ran a finger down the cover. "You read such different books on so many subjects."

"Ashley, that's not what I asked."

"I know but you read two, three books a week?" She shook her head. "You cover so many subjects." She held the book up for him to see. "Who would think to pick this up on a whim and you're over half way through."

His sigh broke the silence of the dark room. "You're not tracking."

She stared at the book. "I'm tracking fine. I just don't want to answer your question."

"Why not?"

"Because I get the feeling it's going to lead to further questions which I also don't want to answer."

He took the book from her and turned it so she could see the cover.

"What's this book called?"

Giving up now was the easier route. He wasn't going to stop.

"*George Custer: Battle at Little Big Horn.* Is it any good?"

He put the book on his nightstand and didn't answer her. He turned to her and braced himself up on his elbow.

"So I passed?"

"How do you feel?" He asked.

"Besides confused because I think your opening statements don't match your previous statements?"

"Can you trust me for a few minutes while we get through this?"

"I did trust you. That didn't end well for me."

"I know," he said, his gaze dropping. "I'm sorry. I will spend a lifetime making it up to you if you let me, but right now, physically, I need to know how you are doing."

"Lifetime?" she chuckled, feeling tightness in her chest. "Yeah…um…I'm not sure. Tired, like my body is tired. I feel like I overslept and had really strange dreams about your friends which I don't know if I want to talk about."

"What kind of dreams?"

She looked at him, blinking trying to piece the information she had together and it wasn't working. She pulled a little away from him, afraid she woke in the middle of something. "They were here. I don't know why but it feels personal. I don't remember more."

"Do you feel well enough to humor me for a while?"

"I don't know. I don't know what that means but I'm thinking I would really rather go back to sleep."

"What's your name?" he asked.

She tilted her chin at him and thought about that.

"You don't know?" he asked.

"Ashley Kristen Barrow."

He nodded his head. "Who's the president?"

"Obama."

"Who was the president when you were born?"

She struggled for a minute, her lip caught between her teeth. "Lincoln?" she asked quietly.

"No, that one was a little earlier."

"Who was president when you were born?" she asked.

He smiled. "I was born in Britain. We didn't have presidents, but Victoria was on the throne."

"Really," she smiled. "That's cool. I like that."

"Count backward from twenty four going by threes."

She glared. "I couldn't do that if I was stone cold sober and my life depended on it."

"Math," he smiled.

She narrowed her eyes at him. "This is stupid. Why are we doing this?"

"Who am I?"

She turned her head on the pillow and looked at him. "Your name is Ian David Stuart. You were born a real long time ago. You've been living a secret life and until Sunday night you were my very adored boyfriend. Why am I here?"

"Do you know where you are?"

She nodded. "I am in your bedroom, which puts me in your bed, which makes no sense since you broke up with me on Sunday night and told me you never wanted to see me again. You made yourself very clear."

"Do you know what happened after that?"

"No." She thought then looked at him. "I don't remember going home. How did I get home? I had to have gone home that night."

"Actually, you slept here."

"What? But you said—"

"I slept on the couch downstairs," he said. "Ash, how do you feel?" He asked again.

She put her palm over her eyes. "I don't know. I'm tired and I feel weird. I'm still winded like I was when I tried to run only I haven't done anything to get it." She dropped the hand and looked at him. "My turn."

"What do you want to know?" he asked her.

"Why am I here? You said to stay away and I don't think I brought myself here."

He shook his head. "I brought you."

"Doesn't explain why."

"What's the last thing you remember?"

"I get one question and you go to more." She pushed off the bed and tried to sit up but her head went dizzy. He moved quick, right beside her. She was wearing her pink pajamas. The white shirt had short sleeves.

He put a hand on her shoulder, pushing back lightly. "Come on. Lay down."

She looked over at him. She was still used to seeing him in her bed and right now she was grateful for it.

He pushed harder but still real light. "You need to stay down."

She lay back on the pillow. He sat up on the bed, crossing his legs and facing her, wearing only his boxers.

"Do you want to listen?" he asked.

She looked at him.

"You got hurt pretty bad. I found you, stayed with you and when you woke up, I brought you here. You've been sick and we've been doing what we can to get you well."

"What were you doing at my house?"

"Max told me you might need some help and I went and let myself in."

"Max," she whispered looking down then bringing her gaze to his. "Your backyard? The screw-up?"

"Aye."

"How did Max know I needed help? Help from what? You told me to stay away."

"You were in trouble, Ash. The bad kind. There was no way in hell I was not going to be there."

"James." She said.

His head snapped up. "Why do you keep saying that? You didn't know James and I only mentioned him to you once."

She put her palm back on her eyes.

"James, Violet, you, Edith, Samuel. Your mother's name was Charlotte. Your father's name was Malcolm." She dropped her hand and looked at him confused.

"My dad's name was James. James Malcolm," he said.

She blinked at him.

"I don't talk about my family," he said. "I never have."

"Why?" she asked quietly.

"My mum." His smile was tight.

She shook her head at him.

"I hurt her. I hurt her bad. She begged me not to go and I didn't listen and I went anyway promising to come home in five years and I never did it. I don't know if she ever forgave me and it hurts when I think about it."

"So why are you telling me? I'm the ex and I don't need to hear your secrets anymore."

"Is that what you want?" he asked. "To be broken up? You look kind of nice in my bed even though you're pale and sweaty and haven't had a shower for a while."

She closed her eyes. "I didn't break us up. You did and now you're saying all these things. I don't know what I am doing here. How did I get here?"

"I'm freaking you out, aren't I?"

"Confusing the hell out of me would be more like it."

He picked up her hand.

"Can you name all the people that live in this house, oldest to youngest?"

She closed her eyes again. "You told me this. Travis. You. Jason then Quinn. Evan is the baby. I don't want to answer any more questions. I don't know why you keep asking me these stupid questions."

He shook his head. "Quinn then Jason."

She got another one wrong that she should have known. That bothered her. "Can I go home?"

He shook his head entwining their fingers.

"It's very important that I help you remember how you got hurt."

She dropped his hand and shifted on the bed, pushing away from him. "You broke my heart in more pieces than we can count. I'm not comfortable with all of this."

He moved further on the bed, away from her and put both his hands up, palms toward her. "Okay," he said. "We can do this slow. Distance is alright."

"Can you get dressed?"

"Aye." He hopped off the bed and went to his dresser, opening the third drawer. He pulled out a pair of grey sweats, then got a white T-shirt from the second drawer. He pulled it on over his head and pulled his hair out the back.

"The knot," she said, pointing.

He looked down at his chest, reached in the neck, hooking the chain in his finger pulling it out so it hung on the outside of the shirt and she could see it. He walked back over to the bed. "Can I sit down?"

She nodded.

He took the edge of the bed and watched her.

"I would have gone anywhere with you," she said. "No questions asked. Not one single God damn reservation." She shook her head and moisture threatened to fall from the corner of her eyes. "I was in love with you."

He looked at her and sighed. "Past tense?"

"No," she said.

He looked at her.

"Not past tense but I am not sure that is a good thing."

He sighed again and got a little smile on his face.

"Why do I feel like I was hit by a truck? Why am I here? Who else is here? How did I end up from my house to your room with no memory? Why…"

He put his hand up. "Too many."

"I have more."

"I'm sure you do."

He motioned to the bed. "May I?"

She nodded.

He turned around, turning off the desk lamp. He walked to the door and turned off the overhead light. He came back to the bed and turned off the light on his nightstand. The room was thrown into darkness with only the glow from the computer.

He spoke as he moved. "Hunter stopped by while you were asleep. He couldn't get you to wake up though, so he left pretty worried."

"I should call him."

"He thinks you're pregnant."

She sat up suddenly, her breath catching, the dizziness hitting hard. "What?"

Ian was smiling as he came around the bed. "I tried to convince him otherwise but he didn't want to hear it."

"Why would he think I was pregnant?"

He shrugged. "You quit your job about the same time you mysteriously got ill. He put two and two together and got five. He loved the idea, too. I can't say I blame him. I thought it sounded pretty damn sweet. Wish I could make it work for us. Watching you pregnant would be amazing."

He pulled back the quilt and got into bed with her, lying down on his own pillow to face her across the bed.

"I'm not even going to touch that comment but I am going to have to call Hunter. He can't keep his mouth shut to save the world."

"That's a bad thing?"

"Yes, it's a bad thing if it's not true." She paused and thought. "It's not true, is it?"

Ian smiled sadly. "We can't have children. It's the shittiest part of this whole package."

"You want kids?" she asked him.

"I would give just about anything for the chance to have a baby with you."

"Wow," she muttered. "From blow jobs to kids. That is a fast turn-around."

"I didn't mean it. I told you. I have told you. I didn't mean anything I said that night." He stopped, tilted his head and smiled. "Actually?"

"What?"

"I did kind of mean it because it is true. I just didn't mean it in that context."

She thought, remembering. "Practice?"

"Aye," he smiled sadly. "I don't think I want to hear any more about that."

For the first time all night she finally felt as if she was one up on him and she smiled big. "Ice cream," she said.

He blinked down at her. "What?"

"Ice cream cones. I read about it in a book. You practice by getting a double dip ice cream cone then pretending it's something else. You learn to take the whole thing in your mouth at once, you play with the ice cream as it melts, licking it off. You make swirls

356

and flicks and patterns and eat the whole thing down, using your tongue."

"You are serious aren't you?"

"I ate a lot of ice cream after I read that book. All kinds of flavors."

He was smiling. "What was the best flavor for practice?"

"Vanilla. It didn't distract from what I was doing."

He looked at the door. "Travis needs to run to the store. I think I should put in an order before he goes," he smiled.

She sighed into the pillows.

He laughed and moved closer. "That is such a fucking turn-on. I will never be able to look at vanilla again and not think of you giving head to a cone." He laughed again. A beautiful sound she had missed

"But turns-ons, that's not where we're going yet, are we? We have some things to figure out first. You're not afraid of me?" he asked.

She shook her head.

"You remember about me?"

She nodded. "Not exactly easy to forget."

"You've been asleep awhile. I brought you back here on Tuesday and it's now Sunday. We have all been keeping a steady watch on you, monitoring your O2 levels."

"What?" she gasped. "I don't remember coming here Tuesday."

"That would be the essence of coma, Ash. You were asleep. We were caring for you."

"We?"

He nodded slowly. "Everyone in the house has been helping out in some capacity. Even your Irishman."

"I have an Irishman?" It was getting harder to breathe.

"I think he thinks you have an Irishman."

"What?" She closed her eyes, thinking.

Jason kissed her. She remembered. Because something was happening. What did he say when he did it? She looked up at Ian. Stuart, she thought. She started to call him Stuart that night.

"I was never interested in any other Celtic nation," she said. "I don't know what you are talking about, but I call you Stuart now, don't I?"

He grinned and shook his head slow. "You tried to. I said no."

She sat up and put her face in her hands more confused than she could handle. Her breathe came hard and they didn't seem to be working. She felt herself start to shake.

"You said I got to call you Ian because I needed a special name for you. You said that long ago. But, I'm not special anymore."

"You're in my bed after I came running within a *second* I knew there was trouble? With my family caring for you and me at your side almost the entire time. You're settling on you're not special to me? You are the only thing that is special to me."

She slid off the bed, breathing hard and walked away. He let her, which she thought was odd. Her feet didn't hurt which she thought was odder.

She closed her eyes struggling to pull an image up that would tell her what was going on.

"How could I have gotten injured enough to be in a coma for six days?" she asked, turning toward him. "And why would I ride it out here in your house instead of in a hospital?"

"Because you were safer with us," he said.

"Safer than a hospital?"

"There are no vampire restrictions on entering a hospital. We couldn't control the situation and it was very important we control the situation."

"You're not making any sense," she said, holding on to the chair. "Why aren't you at work? You should be at work."

"It's Sunday night," he said. "Cooper's is closed tonight. Ash, you can barely stand and you are having trouble breathing. Come lie down."

She sat down.

He reached up to finger her braid. "I've only left a couple of times. Otherwise I have been laying here watching you sleep. I haven't done anything else except see how George Custer managed to get lured into a trap by the Sioux in my book."

"Work?"

"Okay, besides being Sunday, I called and took two weeks off. Mike has contacts. He had no trouble getting someone to cover my shifts."

"You shouldn't have done that."

"I've been there five years and have never taken a vacation and only a couple of days off. I think I can swing this."

"You need to work. If I'm in coma I can certainly do it without being observed."

He smiled. "That was going to happen."

She reached up to pick up the Celtic knot, playing with it in her fingers. It was the closest she had gotten to him on her own. She watched him watching her.

"Where did you get it?"

"Portland in the early sixties. Was walking the streets one night when I was feeling pretty low about home and saw it in a pawn shop window. Cost me twenty dollars and fifty cents and I never regretted it."

"You never take it off."

"Twice, when the chain broke and I had to get it fixed. Why are you so fascinated with it? It's only a charm."

She shook her head. "Naw. It represents a hell of a lot more than a charm to you. I think it's probably your most treasured possession." She smiled at him. "It also looks incredible on you."

She dropped the knot and slid a little away from him on the bed.

"If I had asked you what would you have said?" he asked.

Her gaze shifted to his. "I don't know. What do you mean?"

"I could have made you like me. I almost did. Sunday night."

She leaned away from him, her sigh coming out slow. "Sunday night." She started working it out. "Up here. After the BBQ."

He nodded. "I pinned you down and I bit you and I came very close to being violent."

Her gaze snapped to his. "I remember that. You're asking if I wanted that?"

He shook his head. "No one wants what I almost did. It was unforgivable and it was instinct. I didn't mean to do it and I did stop myself. But if I had asked, we could have gotten to the same place in a very tender, very gentle process. The end result would have been the same."

"And what would that have been?"

"If you were like me, there would be nothing keeping us apart. I only broke up with you to keep you away from me." He paused and looked down. "I don't know if you remember me saying it when you woke up. I wasn't trying to protect you from them. I didn't know they were coming. I was trying to protect you from me." He raised his gaze to hers.

"Why didn't you ask?"

"Because I didn't want this for you. It's a hard life that can make you change. I changed for a lot of years. But then I got lucky and found the right people and we built something."

"And you didn't want that for me?"

"How could I know for sure you wanted this life and were willing to put up with me for a couple of centuries?"

"Ian I would have done anything to stay with you. You are an absolute idiot if you don't know that."

He moved closer and leaned toward her, his mouth covering hers. He reached up to rub his hand over her hair as he took it deep, his lips opening, his tongue finding hers. Hot and wet, it was a memory come back to reality. His hands held onto her shoulders, pulling her toward him like she meant something to him. She felt treasured and loved in that one kiss.

When he pulled back his eyes were closed. "I didn't think I was ever going to be able to do that again." He looked at her.

"I didn't think you wanted to."

He settled back, but stayed close. "I want to play a little game."

"Don't think I'm up for that," she replied.

"We'll talk about your game later because I think I'm really interested in hearing more details, but right now, I want you to lay back."

She looked at her position on the bed and thought she couldn't get any more laid back on the bed. He fluffed the pillow around her head, pulled up the quilt around her. Pulling one arm out from under the quilt and then the other, he positioned them alongside her.

"Are you having fun?"

"Humor me." He dropped down beside her. Putting a finger on her chin he pushed her face so she was staring at the ceiling. "Close your eyes."

"This is a game?"

"Take a couple of deep breaths and then tell me three things you remember about Sunday night. Things that made an impression."

"Your mum." She turned to look at him.

He pushed her chin back. "Close your eyes and don't worry about what I'm thinking. Two more things."

"The impact of understanding your relationship with every member of your family."

"Anymore?"

"It hurt. Bad. Losing you. Like I never hurt before."

She heard him breathing hard. He held on to her hand and squeezed her fingers.

"Where did you sleep?" he asked.

"Right here, but I didn't sleep much. I had two more glasses of scotch and even that didn't help."

"Were you sober when you drove home?"

"Probably not."

"We'll talk about stupid later, right now what did you do when you got there?"

"Took a shower. Slept for six hours. Packed up all your stuff."

"Ashley, what about that night? I need you to think hard."

She shifted and his hand came down on her middle, steadying her. "I stayed up late. Kept the TV on though I don't remember what was on."

"Were the lights on?"

"Yeah. Most of them, I think."

"Bedroom?"

"I was in bed. Reading. The Dan Brown you left but not making any progress. Kept reading the same sentence over and over."

Images started in her mind, fuzzy at first. She jerked her head as they started to focus.

His fingers tightened. "Ashley?"

She gasped. "I heard glass break and then the TV went off by itself."

"There was someone in the house?"

She squeezed her eyes tight. "I got up and went for the gun."

His hand brushed across her forehead.

The realization hit like a high voltage current. Her whole body jerking before it started to shake.

"Oh my God," she snapped. She jerked up in bed and shoved the quilts off her, pushing them down, her legs scrambling to get out.

"Ashley," he was following her but she was backing away. His hands were palm out toward her.

She covered her face with both hands.

"Backdoor. They came in the backdoor."

"They?"

She nodded. "Three of them. I shot them. Oh my God."

"You're okay now."

He reached for her and she jumped back. "No."

"Calm down," he said. "You're okay. It's only me here."

"Walter. It was Walter from the backyard. Sunday night."

"Walter did this to you?"

She nodded. "He wasn't alone."

"Who?"

"Miss Monte Cruz. She was there. And another woman."

"Walter and the two women? That's who were in your house?"

She dropped her hands and looked up at him. "Yes," she snapped. "Oh my God, they—" She closed her eyes tight, the wall dropping and the memories of pain and laughter hitting her mind.

She jumped out of his reach but he kept up with her.

He grabbed both her wrists, holding them gently; bringing his hands together.

"Come on," he whispered. "Breathe. It's okay. We can do this."

She backed away, pulling her arms, trying to get away but he held on.

"No," she whispered, her eyes closing tight. "Please, no...they..."

"I'm sorry," he said, pulling on her until she was pressed against his chest.

She hit him with fists on his chest again and again and he let her, his arms going around her to pull her close. When her knees started to buckle, he went with her to the floor, until they sat by the edge of the bed, her against him, him holding her tight.

"Ashley, you remember?"

She put her head on his chest. Yes, she did. In vivid clarity as if it was happening all over again. Air caught in her chest while fear bounced in her gut.

She fisted her hand one more time, giving one last hit onto his hard pec but there was nothing behind it. She closed her eyes and shut her mind down, trying to make it all not real, but it didn't matter where she tried to direct her thoughts, it came back to the same place and the reality was too shocking to accept.

Her whole existence had been erased in a session of terror. She pushed against his chest, using him for leverage to stand up. She walked away from him, putting her back to him as she tried to weigh her feelings.

She loved him. That hadn't changed.

Whether it made a difference now or not she didn't know. Life as she knew it was gone forever. She was winded from only this conversation and the exertion with him. How would she function?

She grabbed the cord on the blinds and yanked until the view was open in front of her. She un-hooked the latch and pulled the window open. Leaning out she took a deep, deep breath of the damp night. She thought about the rain. It must have rained today and she missed it.

His arms came around her from behind, her arms against her side as he pulled her close to his chest and nuzzled her neck.

"I love you, Ashley," Kissing her on the neck, he whispered. "I wasn't kidding. You are the only woman I have ever loved."

"I know," she said, tears slipping down her cheek. "You told me that Tuesday afternoon. After I woke up. It was the first thing you said to me."

"I am so sorry." He held her tighter. "It only happened because of me. They came after you because of me."

"And if they hadn't done it, I would have asked you to. I would have done anything to keep you. Even this."

He took her by the shoulders and turned her, his arms going around her, her hands flat on his chest.

"Except they hurt you. I wouldn't have hurt you."

She leaned back to look up at him. Feeling utterly defeated she leaned against the open window.

"What do you want to know?"

"You remember?"

"I don't know. Maybe."

"Do you remember after, getting ready at the house? Talking about James. Coming here?"

"I remember Monday night in vivid detail. I remember waking up with you. I remember you getting me dressed. I don't remember anything about James. That's your brother. Why did you mention him?"

"You had a very deep fascination with him for a while."

She scratched her eyebrow. "I don't remember that. And I don't know how I got here."

"Walter, Sharron and the other woman?"

She nodded.

"Did you invite them in?"

She shook her head. "No."

"Are you sure?"

"It was late after a real shitty weekend. They came in the back door, breaking the glass."

"Remember, I told you? Vampires can't enter a house without being invited."

"I do remember you saying that. But I didn't invite them."

She nodded and turned away.

"Ashley?"

She looked back at him.

"I was turned by three bastards, too, who thought making it as painful as possible would be a good time for them. They did not do to me what they did to you, but they made it bad on purpose."

She blew out a hard breath and nodded. "They were at the house for a while with knives and—"

"I was at the house a long time. I cleaned you up. I saw what they did."

She looked at him, her body shaking. She looked at the bottoms of her feet then looked at him.

"We heal accelerated. Do you remember I said that when we were up here—the two of us?"

She shook her head.

"Most of your wounds are gone. We just have a couple of problems we are dealing with. What they did to you," he paused, "some of it was very specific in vampire law. It was a message to me. They used you to punish me."

"He knew you. He said this was for you. Then he talked about Travis."

"How long were they in the house?"

"I don't know. I passed out."

"You didn't pass out, Ash. You were dead when I found you."

She rubbed her face again and walked past him, heading back toward the bed. Sitting down on the edge, she braced a hand on the mattress on either side of her. He came over and sat down beside her matching her position.

"Are you going to be okay?"

"No, not really."

"Do you think there is any chance you will be okay sometime?"

"I don't know, Ian. I was dead. That's sorta hard to wrap my head around when I'm sitting here having a conversation with you."

"I know," he said.

370

"Why did you ask me all those stupid questions?"

"Something happened to you that was different than the rest of us. We've all turned someone at some point yet we've never seen this in anyone and most of us go back almost a hundred years."

"What?"

"Our metabolism is different than a human's," he said. "Our blood is different. You hook us up to a machine in a hospital and they'll be calling the *National Star*."

"What's wrong with me?"

"We run O2 at about 200% of a human. Yours is at about 98%. Okay for a person, but you were turned. Yours should be up like us. Quinn has been almost absent on his job because he won't leave you in the house alone. He's been monitoring everything."

"And Quinn knows because…"

"Dr. Quinn Nelson, MD. Got his license in 1940 and had his own practice until 1942. He's a nurse at Davenport Medical Center because he couldn't go back to med school with his vampire restrictions. He did make it through night school to get his nursing license, but he also keeps up his studies. He's as much a doctor now as he was then. You can trust him."

"The flirt is a doctor?"

Ian nodded. "Aye. Had his own practice. Since that's been gone he does what he can at the hospitals where he's worked. Now he's got his own personal patient and you've got your own personal physician and I think he might be in heaven a little though it's killing him to see you like this."

"Why would he care? I met him once."

"Do not doubt, for a second, the loyalty of the men in this house to you and what they would do for you. They had adopted you as one of us before you even walked in the door."

She looked up at him. "I don't understand."

"Then stop trying to figure it out." He smiled.

"Okay, then what's wrong with me?"

"Low O2 can screw you up pretty good. Physically and mentally. That's why all the questions at first, a lot of which you got wrong. We have to keep you on more rest than activity for a while."

"I'm not only altered, I'm broken?"

He bobbed his head. "You need a little mending, let's say."

He sighed and put his arm around her, pulling her close to kiss the top of her head.

She leaned back and looked at him. He pulled a tight smile over his teeth and stared at her.

"Problem is, none of them can get in your house since they were never invited. In fact near as we can tell only me, Travis and Evan can get in."

"I can't do this," she said, standing up to walk away. "I can't do any more."

"That's all right. As long as we revisit it soon."

"Do I have to go home now?"

He shook his head. "Your house isn't safe and you are well protected here."

She looked at him in the dark room seeing more detail than she had ever seen without light before.

"Ian?"

He looked at her.

"You don't scare me. Your lifestyle doesn't scare me though I think it might be hard to get used to."

"Why are you telling me this?"

"I had already made up my mind before they came. I was going to wait a few days and then rent a room at Travis's hotel and call him up."

"Why would you need a hotel room with Travis? Or do I not want to know the answer to this?"

She licked her lips and held his gaze. "If you were ever going to do it, you would've done it that night up here. You kicked me out instead. I was going to ask Travis to do it."

Ian narrowed his eyes at her. "It?"

"Change. Convert. Whatever you call it. I knew you would be mad but figured we would have a couple of centuries to work on me earning back your trust and maybe in there sometime start back up where we left off."

He stared at her a long time and she could see him processing it.

"He wouldn't have done it."

"Then I had Jason and Quinn and Evan. I planned on going down the list."

"Evan doesn't know how. And I don't know whether I should be pissed or flattered. You really wanted to take this life on?" he almost snapped.

She looked down. "Yes, I was willing to take it on if it meant I could get you back."

"And if I still didn't take you back? You would have been stuck like this. Not a good plan."

"I guess I could have approached the Irishman then," she said softly.

"Go to one of my friends because you have nowhere else to go and no clue what you are doing. That sounds good. Wonder what would you have had to do for it?"

She stepped back and felt that sting again. "I wanted to be with you," she whispered.

He walked away, looking at the floor, deep in thought.

"Only this isn't what you wanted," she said, another fear sitting in her gut. "Me, with limitations, different than I was."

"It's not that. I'm just…" he pulled his fingers through his hair. His gaze came up to hers. "You offer me everything with no restrictions and all I have done since Day One is lie to you about my existence."

"I think your motives were understandable."

374

He leaned toward her. "They came after *you*. They tortured *you*. Then took away the life you knew, all because of *me* and you stand there without any bitterness and accept it and say you wanted to be with me."

"I'm sorry," she said, backing away. "I misunderstood our conversation. I'm not thinking totally clear. I thought you were saying you wanted…"

The pain hurt hard enough to stop her words. She didn't know what came next. Where she would or what she would do but she had enough background in rejection to know she would figure it out.

"Too much has happened with too many secrets," he said, "and I don't want to do that anymore. I want to work this out."

"I didn't tell you about the money because you would have left. I brought it up a couple of times and each time your response was the same. Keeping it a secret was the only way you would stay. I'm sorry."

He laughed a little. "Because money was the worst thing we could be keeping between us? It's not like I was hiding any secrets, right?"

Her breathing got heavy, her mind foggy as she strained with the stress coming at her. "I was in love with you," she said. "I would have been shocked, maybe some disbelief. But yeah, I think I would have been willing to work with you on it."

"And if you found out I had a wife?"

Nothing could have prepared her for those words.

"What?" she whispered, shocked enough to feel the air leave her lungs and the dizziness hit her head. "You're married?"

Everything she knew, erased for a man who had a wife—and her—who played the mistress. In that split second he stared at her, she realized there had never been a future for them in all the time together and she never even suspected.

"Married?" she whispered.

"Ash, it's the last secret, I promise."

"I want to go home," she said. "Right now. I don't want to do this. I don't want to be a part of this."

"You can't go home. I told you. It's not safe there."

Her gaze snapped up to him. "And here is safe? You lied to me all this time? And *I* went through *this...why me?* If you have a wife wouldn't that have had a hell of a lot more impact than the chick you were screwing?"

"Ash, she's dead. She's been dead for a long, long time. And even without that, what I felt for her doesn't hold a candle to what I feel for you. They knew where to strike and what would cause the most devastation."

"What the hell are you talking about?"

He glanced down, then back up at her. "Her name was Abigail Regina Stuart. Born in my village, Dunham, Scotland, May 25, 1897, married to me May 22, 1916."

Breath, already shallow sat in her lungs as she stared at him. "So," she finally said. "Not the only woman you've ever loved."

"I didn't say I loved her. I said she was my wife. And it didn't go like it should and I have had to live with it my whole life and it has affected every relationship I have ever had."

"You would never commit to a woman you weren't completely in love with."

"I would if I was nineteen and living at home and my mum said I had to. It was an arranged marriage. I didn't even meet Abby—Abigail—until the Friday night before the ceremony. I mean, I had seen her in the village and church, but we had never even spoken. Our mothers came up with the whole scheme and I just showed up."

Ash walked away and sat down.

"Ash I have never told a single soul about my marriage. I mean, the guys in the house know, of course, but no one I ever dated. Mike doesn't know and I've known him five years. When I took you out the first time, I had no idea it was going to be an extraordinary relationship. Looking back, I know I should have told you."

"You have so many secrets."

"I liked Abby," he said. "I really did. She was a very nice person and I remember her fondly, but we had problems that were never going to go away and there was nothing I could do to fix it, but Ash…" He took a breath. "Abigail died."

"What?" Ash whispered.

"I buried my first wife when I was twenty-one."

The emotions that replaced the shock and anger were sorrow and hurt at what he must have felt.

377

"It was about August after our first anniversary," he said turning to face her. "This young kid with the energy of a hummingbird who helped everyone in town while training to be a midwife, started to slow down with no warning. By Christmas she was coughing up blood and I was trying everything I could think of but we didn't have a lot and I couldn't afford all the doctors." He shrugged. "Then one day in May I went to work because back then organizations like the mill didn't think sick wives were a reason to take off time. I came home early and found her still in her nightdress. She was gone."

He looked down. "She was ten days shy of her twentieth birthday."

He looked at Ash, blinking his long lashes.

"I couldn't help her, Ash. I would have and I did what I could because she was a nice person, I wasn't the right man for her. She knew but she tried anyway. She really did try to make me happy as much as she could." He looked down. "I don't even have a photo of her."

The pain in his voice hurt her inside.

"I was still human then. If I hadn't been, I could have turned her and the disease would have been wiped out because that is what happens when you are turned." He looked at her. "I'm not human anymore, and what I should be able to do to you was actually the cause of your illness. I can't help you either."

She stared at him.

"And I am scared," he said. "I am watching the same thing happen to another woman I care about and I don't know how to help."

378

She looked at the floor.

"Ash. I know about losing someone close. I know what it feels like to sit back and watch them as they deteriorate in front of you. I never loved her and it still was painful to see this person waste away into nothing until there was a shadow left."

"Why are you telling me this? Do you think I need to hear this now?"

"Because in 1917, I watched a vibrant young woman, who no matter how difficult she was to live with, disappear. Can you take that and put it into the context of the last week I had with you?"

"What were your problems?"

He looked down and then back up. "Abby hated sex. The only times we managed it she cried the whole time so I just gave up. That was about three months into our relationship. I couldn't even get her into it promising it would result in kids. She wanted to deliver other peoples' babies. She didn't want to create our own."

"And yet you slept beside her on those cold Scottish nights."

"How did you know that?"

"Because I know you and no matter what problems stood between you, your devotion would have always kept her close and protected."

"Thank you," he said softly. "That was very complimentary."

"It's true. You should be aware of it."

"We're trying to help you. We know more now than we did in 1917 and now I have help that matters. They came up with an idea and you came back. I think we can take it further."

"What plan?"

"You were injected with a chemical and that's not part of the turning package. It changed things. Quinn and Jason figured out we had to get that out of you. We've been doing transfusions. We've done four, but had six planned."

"Transfusions. Blood transfusions?"

He nodded.

"Where are you getting blood?"

"From four volunteers who kicked my ass when I tried to get in line."

"What?" she whispered.

"It was their idea, Ash. They wanted to. Actually none of them ever considered not doing it once we had it figured out."

"Why not you?"

He paused, not answering.

"Ian? Why?"

"In case something went wrong and we lost one of them. They wanted to make sure I was still here for you when you woke up."

The severity of a situation she should have already understood came into blatant focus. She crossed her arms tight, feeling what they had offered her in her gut.

She looked at her arms, her veins. That wasn't her blood flowing through them anymore.

"It's not a little oxygen problem, is it? I'm never going to be the same, am I? That's why you told me about Abigail."

"No, I told you because I should have told you before."

She stared at him. "That wasn't my question."

"No honey," he said. "Quinn thinks there was permanent damage to a small speck in your brain and immune system. To what extent we don't know yet. We don't know fully how the chemical affected you."

She walked away feeling like a relationship with him was similar to being caught in a tornado. She really was damaged. 'Permanent'. That's the word he used.

He walked over and pulled her in his arms, whispering in her ear. "I didn't want this for you," he said again. He kissed her neck. "But we deal with it now or we let it go."

"You want to let it go?" she whispered.

"No. That's not what I was saying at all. You *are* the only woman I have ever loved. To see you hurt because of me, to know you will carry the scars they gave you because of me, I can't even begin to put into words what that feels like. But holding you tells me we have hope and we can do this together and we will never, in three hundred years, have to be apart for a single night."

"I want to talk to Jason," she said.

CHAPTER EIGHTEEN

"What?" he snapped.

She headed toward the door. "Will he be downstairs?"

"You have been awake for twenty minutes and the first thing you want to do is talk to Jason?"

"Downstairs?"

"Ash, you can't get downstairs without help. You've been in a coma for almost a week and visiting the Irishman isn't on the top of my To Do list."

She opened the door. He was right. It wasn't easy and she had to take each step one at a time, holding the railing the whole way, him right behind her his hands out in case she slipped.

She got to this side of the kitchen doorway.

"You took care of her when she was ill?"

"I did what I could."

"You wore a wedding band?" she asked.

He sighed. "Aye."

"Where is it now?"

"I have no idea what happened to it. I left it in our house when I came to America. Do you want to know anything else?"

She nodded her head and started to move toward the kitchen. Then stopped.

She turned back toward him and started to shake. "Did you ever try to tell me but couldn't?"

"No," he said softly. "Figured I would have to someday but I didn't have a plan. Longer it went, harder it became."

She could hear the voices in the common area and wondered if she could pull off as acting normal. She turned and headed into the kitchen.

Travis and Jason were there. Travis at the stove, Jason at the table.

Both looked up with smiles.

"Hey *mia bella*," Travis said, turning off the burner and coming over to her, his hands on her shoulders. "You are up." Travis hugged her tight. "But you should be in bed."

He looked at Ian who looked at the ground. "She wanted to talk to Jason."

Jason's head snapped up. "What?"

She walked over and sat down across from him. "Is it alright?"

"I don't know. If you plan on proposing could you do it when he's not around?"

She looked at the table. "He was married," her voice soft, she brought her gaze up to Jason's.

Jason looked at her, turned to Ian and looked back. "Did you just find that out?"

She nodded.

Jason turned in his chair. "You didn't tell her about Abigail?"

Travis batted Ian on the shoulder hard. "Jerk."

"God," Jason said. "First thing in Serious Relationship 101, you tell about spouses. You always were the biggest asshole in the house."

"No," she said. "Please don't say that to him. They told me you played with computers. I think you told me that, too."

"Play?" he laughed. "Okay."

"Can you look something up for me?"

He reached a foot to his right and pulled his lap top in front of him. "What?"

"Hardwell Bank."

"New York or local?"

"New York."

"I thought you were going to want me to do something interesting. This is their web page. And not sure what this has to do with marriage. Sign on?"

"AshKriBar."

"Do you want to put in the password?" he asked, staring at her over the screen. She had his blood in her veins. Could they get more personal?

"Jackson123," she said.

He typed for a minute, staring at the screens popping up, before his head fell back a little and his gaze came up over the screen to stare at her. "You *did* want to make this interesting."

"What?" Ian and Travis asked together.

She looked at the table.

"Hate to tell you, Ash," Jason said, "but if you have never said anything, this is a lot like omitting a first wife."

"I know."

"What?" Ian asked.

Jason looked at him and back at her. "This isn't it, is it? People with this don't just have this. They have other stuff in other places to spread a little happiness all over the world."

"There's more," she said.

Jason lowered the screen and looked out toward the covered window and looked to be thinking hard. He turned back at her. "When did you out find out he was a socialist?"

"I didn't. I didn't know that. But I found out he hated money a couple of days before we broke up."

"I'm sorry," Ian snapped. "Can I get in on this conversation?"

"No," Jason said and kept talking. "What did he tell you?"

"We had a conversation about money," she said slow because it was getting hard to talk. "He said he couldn't live around it and if I came into any he would leave me."

"You actually told her that?" Travis asked Ian.

"Out of context and what we were talking about was hypothetical. I am assuming it was not as hypothetical as I was led to believe?"

She stared at Jason. "So I made up a…little…no that's not right. Um…" she searched for the word. Panic edged her gut.

"Hey," Jason said and her gaze came up.

"I grew up with breathing problems," he said. "and I know what they can do. Your body compensates taking oxygen from the brain. It's hard to think sometimes and easy to get confused. In this house, never worry about not knowing a word, okay?"

She nodded. "Pared down? Does that work?"

"You told him enough but not everything to buy time. For what? He was going to eventually find out."

"I don't know. I didn't think that far in advance. I told him the house was paid off and I had some money in the bank. That's true."

"You don't just have money in the bank?" Ian asked.

Jason shifted in his seat to face Ian. "No one in this house annoys me more than you do."

"There's a bulletin," Travis said.

"But we just got to a place we didn't anticipate where decisions you make might upset the balance of tranquility we have. You brought home a friend who is very popular. I don't think four of us are willing to see that go away because of your hang-ups."

Ian screwed up his face and rolled his eyes. "Can you explain that statement, asshole?"

"I'm talking about what she said is the truth. You did tell her that. You did mean it. Problems might evolve out of those two facts." He reached up and grabbed the laptop to turn, her hand lunged out to stop him.

"No. He finds out, I lose everything and right now, I'm thinking I don't have a lot left."

Jason reached across to put his hand on top of hers and squeezed. "So you had me check right now, when he was here, because you *didn't* want him to know?"

"You want to get your hands off and keep them off?" Ian growled.

She looked at the table. "I don't know."

"Cuz you're not thinking straight and we do have to do this to find out what happens next."

He turned the screen so Travis and Ian could read down the columns. Jason pointed to information attached.

"Ignore this." He shifted his finger. "These are the numbers you're looking at."

"You said the house was paid for?" Jason asked as they read.

"Yes."

"What else?"

"I have some properties. Some commercial rentals in other states. I own a few businesses I run silent."

"Cash?"

She licked her lips and stared at the table.

"Ash?" Jason asked gently.

"All the banks in Davenport. Maxed."

Jason rolled his tongue. "So you are telling me that right now, this minute, taking into account daylight hours, you could walk into all the banks in Davenport and walk out with a silver briefcase with over a million dollars cash, small bills only?"

She hunched her shoulders and stared at the table.

"And I am guessing you have more in other places like 401Ks and stocks and the places we put our money to watch it grow. Fuck," Jason moaned.

He leaned back and stared at her, talking to Ian. "Mr. Stuart. It would appear your girlfriend is a millionaire many times over."

"Should I go pack?" she asked softly, tears streaking down her face.

"Only if you're switching bedrooms," Jason said.

Ian slapped him hard on the back of the head.

"Hey," Jason chucked, "I don't have money hang-ups so you decide."

Ian stood up from the computer and continued to stare at the total amount on the screen while thoughts raced along his mind like coins falling from a slot machine. Only this didn't feel like any jackpot.

She had lied to him, if only by omission. Money in the bank? And a wife in the grave? Toss in a few vampires. Christ...

"Why the hell did you even have a job?" he asked.

"I had the job before I got the money. I didn't feel like quitting to travel the world alone."

His gaze snapped up to hers. "How? How did you do this?"

"I was close to my grandfather. When he died, he left it to me. I didn't know I was in the will. I didn't find out until a few weeks after the funeral when the first lawyer called. I didn't even know he had it. I mean I knew he was well off, but ..." her gaze dropped then came up.

She looked right at Jason. "When I was eleven, I stole a cigarette from my father's pack and smoked it behind the garage because what little kid hasn't, right?"

Jason kept her stare.

She nodded and took in a deep breath. She raised her right hand in front of her, spreading her fingers and flexing them. "It looks normal, doesn't it?"

"Yeah," Jason said. "You have very pretty hands."

"When my father found out about the cigarette, he slammed this hand in the kitchen door."

Jason's smile vanished. Travis took a step toward her and Ian stared at her, speechless.

"I didn't tell Ian about any of that, either. It didn't seem to have anything to do with what was going on between us. I mean, would you leave a woman because you found out she had the childhood from hell and her father was a violent bastard?"

Jason only stared at her.

She nodded. "Broke almost every bone and every finger but my thumb. It took over a year for it to heal. I was in physical therapy for ages. He told the doctor I fell off my bike." She raised her gaze to Jason's. "I didn't have a bike."

"That's why you're ambidextrous," Ian said, his voice forced. "You told me he hit."

"He did a lot of things," she said. "It's one reason I don't see my mom and sister."

"Why?" Travis asked.

Ash looked up at him. "My father was a cop. We had nowhere to go for help. Mom knew what he was doing and let him. Never stopped him because when he had another target he left her alone. She watched out for Lindsey, though. She was a baby after

391

all. They live together in Chicago and sue me every couple of years to try and separate me from the money. But I had my Gr'pa Jackson and he and I were tight." She closed her eyes, remembering. "I spent summers at their place on the beach doing things you're supposed to do as a kid and I was never afraid. My Gr'ma, that's who taught me to knit when I was eight. Every summer we would undertake a new project and she would teach me a new technique."

Jason stared at his computer. "Ash, where is your father?"

"He died ten years ago in a bar fight. And Gr'pa Jackson joined him six years ago."

"It wasn't Gr'pa Jackson I was thinking of hunting down and murdering."

Ian knew Jason wasn't kidding because right now that old feeling crept along his own nerves. They had done it before. Doing it for this, would have been a pleasure.

"Why do they sue?" Ian asked over the lead in his throat. He pictured this beautiful woman with scars she had never explained, now with more. They would eventually all fade with age as her cells regenerated, but it would be decades.

"I received eighty-seven percent of the estate after charities. Lindsey, that's my sister, she got the rest. Mom doesn't think that was fair. They come after it pretty regularly, but I have better lawyers, more financing and Lindsey's got a screwed up history with drugs and money problems."

She stood, unsteady on her feet and three sets of hands came out to help.

She smiled a little and pointed over her shoulder. "I'm going to use the...um..."

"Okay," Travis said. "You know where it is."

She walked away slowly, through the family room, closing the bathroom door behind her.

"Shit, she looks wiped."

"She was better in our room. Sharper. I think the stairs were too much," Ian said.

"You could have carried her."

He looked down at Jason. "She wouldn't let me."

"That's not actually a bad sign," Travis said. "The tenacity is still there. What are you going to do?"

"She is fucking terrified of what happens next," Jason said looking up at Ian. "She thinks she's disposable because of zeroes."

"Fuck," Ian said pulling his finger through his hair. "She said she had money. She told me the house was paid for and she had money."

"And she still couldn't buy her way out of the attack that left her permanently altered, both mentally and physically." Travis said.

"So the question to the Scotsman is," Jason said, "do you stand by a hundred years of socialist thinking or do you reach out and take the girl?"

"When did the two of you become such best friends?" he snapped at Jason.

"I was only sitting here. Do not take your situation out on me. But if you want an answer, it might have to do with the computer I can use and not the man. Unless…"

"Unless what?"

"Maybe it has nothing to do with money. Maybe it's too much work to commit to a woman with severe health problems you will be facing like *f-o-r-e-v-e-r.*"

Ian's fury soared. "For a man who changes women like socks, I would shut the fuck up."

"Yeah, but my socks aren't made of gold and you just struck it rich. Do you have any idea what I have in the bank?"

"No," Ian snapped. "And I don't care. I never have."

"Stuart, I have several million. She leaves me in the dust," Jason said.

"Do either one of you think you are helping a bad situation?" Travis asked. He looked at his watch. "She's due for another transfusion in five and half hours. Quinn will be back and I'm up and I am thinking we aren't doing it the old fashioned way."

"Abigail was sweet," Ian said. "You know that."

"Actually I don't." Travis snapped, looking at him. "I never met her and only have your word on it and right now, I have to tell you I don't give a damn. She is a faded photo in your memory you are holding up against the vivacious woman in front of us. That is where I have to focus. The fact you withheld that info to the point of pain on a person already suffering, pisses me off."

"I hate money and everything it represents."

"Who gives a fuck?" Jason said. "Get over it, because I am still open to the date I never got. I can get tickets to the *Wax On* concert on Saturday. They're awesome."

"You fucking think of going near her and I gut you."

Jason smiled. "Yeah, because you've always scared me."

Ian glared at Travis.

"What do you want? I'm on her side. You really didn't think you needed to tell her about Abigail? Genius, in a relationship, a previous wife is top of the hit parade. And yes, she should have told you, too. You both screwed up. Let it go or call it. Don't drag it out because you will be pulling all of us in with you."

Ian rubbed his face. "This is a nightmare."

"No," Travis said. "A nightmare is craving blood and having no choice but to sneak around the city and find someone to kill. We used to live a nightmare. Now we live with surprises like 'Wow, we can afford a pool table.'"

"Do you hate the money more than you love the girl?" Jason asked. "Because for me, that wouldn't be a hard call. Not if I had those baby blues looking up at me the way she looks at you. And I can take her to any concert and move her to my room and she still would never look at me the way she looks at you."

Ian started to turn away then stopped. He looked between the two of them. "Do you know what she told me upstairs not twenty minute ago?"

Neither commented.

"She told me if it hadn't happened, if they hadn't come in that night? She had already made her mind up and she was going to wait a few days then ask you to do it," he told Travis.

"What?"

"She knew I never would, so she was going to ask you. And if you said no, she was going to work her way across the board," he said, looking at Jason, "until she got to one of us that would say yes."

Jason and Travis exchanged a glance. Jason scratched his nose.

"Would you have?" Ian asked Travis.

Travis thought, sighed and let his shoulders drop. "I wouldn't have blinked."

Ian's gaze shifted to Jason's.

"What?" Jason asked innocently.

"Would you have ignored what I was trying to do?"

"I don't have a clue what you were trying to do, but to keep her around? Are you an idiot?"

She came out regretting the mirror over the basin and thought maybe she should have asked for a shower before rummaging into her problems. It wasn't that she had enough, she had to add 'trashed' to them when her conversation partners were all drop dead gorgeous.

Her feet shuffling in socks, she had heard their voices but not their words and didn't know what had changed since she left the room.

They all stopped talking and a cup of Earl Grey with milk sat at her place. She sat down slow, feeling as if she moved through mud.

"What are my options?" she asked Travis.

"You options are—"

She pointed a finger at Ian, cutting him off. "I'm asking him."

"You're putting me in the middle, Ash. That's not fair," Travis said.

"You're—what? Primary? That was the word? You make the rulings and have the information."

"Shit," Travis mumbled. "It's why I never wanted the damn position to begin with."

"What are my options?"

He took a deep breath and blew it out. "Not many," he said. "You can stay here and try to work it out together, see if you can get past the things you haven't said. That could go a lot of ways. Or you could stay here *not* together and we put you in the room downstairs. It's small and doesn't have any windows but we could do it up cute. But that opens up a ton of problems."

"What kind of problems?"

Travis pointed at Jason. "Him, for one. He isn't kidding about dating you. We have had enough trouble with Scot/Irish war to be adding you to it."

Jason smiled at his computer.

"Is that it?"

"Or, we can train you, teach you to live like us, give you all the tools you need. You go off by yourself and find your own life. You'll be alone for good and that's a long time, but it looks like your finances can take care of you. Problem is a vampire on their own has a bigger target than one under the protection of a den. You might not be safe and it could catch up with you."

"I'm used to being alone."

"Last choice, you leave, find a den, join them. That would be the safest for you. I mean other than us, but you do have to take a Blood Oath and you would have to live as a full vampire. Being Blood Free brings a death sentence so you would be taking victims."

"Blood Oath. That's one of the Laws."

Travis nodded. "It's the First Law."

"Which none of you follow," she said.

"Which is why we all have death sentences on us and if we get caught it will go bad," Jason pointed out.

"Those are my choices."

"No," Ian said. "You forgot five."

"I didn't know we had a five," Travis said.

"I declare now, she accepts and we move past this bullshit and get on with our lives."

"Shit," Jason whispered.

Travis stared at him. "Do you actually know what you are saying?"

"You said it yourself. Old married couple."

"Think about this."

"What?" she asked. "What is he talking about?"

"I started thinking about this the minute she sat on that stool and you know it."

"Thinking it and doing are two different things, one leaves you with no other options forever."

"Please?" she whispered.

Jason closed his computer, sighed and leaned forward. He thought for a moment.

"Vampires don't have governments like other people, do you understand that? No courts or police?"

"I don't understand much of it, yet."

"It takes time to get it all down because it's all oral and a lot to learn. But we are self-governing within our dens. Tell me when you stop following."

"I got it."

"We have Laws and Customs that have been handed down for thousands of years that dictate what we can and cannot do. It's the only way to keep order with a violent society. Even assholes like Walter have to adhere to them cuz our punishments are usually fatal."

"I thought it was in dens?"

"Mostly," Travis said. "But if one den goes rogue, another can step up and take them down."

"Okay," she said. She rubbed her forehead to stop the headache.

"Us, here in the house," Jason said, "we're not quite like other dens and don't follow a lot of what they do, obviously, but we do recognize the Laws and Customs, even if we don't abide by things like Blood Oaths."

She nodded her head and stared intently.

"Our Tenth Law is called *The Law of Amis pour la vie*. Probably the most sacred law we have. I don't think any vampire ever thinks they will achieve it because vampires don't roll that way. Commitment is alien while exchanging partners is accepted."

"Okay, now I'm getting confused."

"In dens," Travis said, and she looked up at him, "vampires tend to trade around a lot. For sex or for fun. There is rarely any two that connect and want to take it further."

"All of you did this?" she asked.

They looked away from one another, avoiding it while trying not to smile.

Travis finally spoke up. "I would say Jason and I did some experimentation while the monk over here even turned down easy sex while in dens."

"Sex sucks if you don't give a damn about who it's with," Ian said.

"Of course it does," Jason smiled.

"I still don't understand what he is talking about," she said.

"To 'declare'," Jason said, "like he said is to accept *The Law of Amis pour la vie*. The man declares, the woman accepts. Has to be done like that, both parties saying those exact words. It's easy to do, out once done, there is never going back on it. No third parties can ever be involved in their relationship and you are together till death, both your deaths. If one is gone, the survivor cannot re-mate. It's huge, Ash. Real huge and the fact he even said it means something."

"Why would he do that?" she whispered, learning forward to talk to Jason.

He came forward too, holding her hands. "I'm not sure, but I'm thinking it's not because of the brownies we were promised."

Her gaze dropped.

401

"Ash," Jason said, "in my entire life I have never met a bigger pain in the ass, but if I were in your place, and he said that to me, I might consider it cuz I think you might actually like the guy."

"The money…"

"When he said those words, Ash, he was telling you the money doesn't matter to him. Not as much as you matter. So it's up to you and what Abigail means between you."

She thought for a minute, all the words going through her head. She leaned forward to whisper to Jason.

"He said she was good to him. I think that's nice. And he was sorry he didn't have a photo." She paused and thought. "I think it's important they meant something to each other, even if it wasn't happily ever after."

"Now will you marry me?" Jason smiled, still leaning forward, still holding her hands.

"I can't," she whispered. "I think I have other plans."

Ian reached over, slipping his arms under her, lifting her effortlessly.

Without a word to Jason or Travis, he headed toward the stairs.

She rested her head on his chest, her arms around him. "I've never been in love before, either."

"So we discover the answers together. How does that sound?"

"No more surprises?" she asked.

"You've had enough."

"When was the last time you slept?" She asked.

"Sunday night after you left. On the couch downstairs."

"How was that?"

"Terrible," he smiled.

She opened the door to their room and he turned so she could shut it.

"No one's ever carried me," she whispered against his chest.

"Get used to it." He set her down on her side of the bed and she wiggled under the covers. She pulled down the quilt for him and patted the mattress. "Come to bed and hold me."

He dropped the clothes to the floor and let them lie without folding any.

She rolled closer to him, like the times she had done before. He raised his arm, making room, and then pulled her close.

She settled against him, her cheek on his shoulder, her hand on his chest. Closing her eyes, the sigh was audible. This is how it was supposed to be.

"We don't have to be apart?" she asked.

"It might get annoying to you, always having me around."

She managed a smile.

"Though at this point," he said, "I must insist that you refrain from kissing any other of my roommates."

She rose up on her elbows and found him smiling.

"He. Kissed. Me."

"Aye, he explained the whole thing to me in vivid detail. And we'll go ahead and assume that you were disgusted, incensed and it will never be an issue again."

She smiled wide and nodded her head. "Yeah. Hated every second of it." She laughed. "But damn, no wonder he's got a reputation."

Ian batted her on the back of the head. "You had to neck with the Irishman."

"Neck? Yeah, that's right. Fifteen seconds of the hottest lips I've ever met while we were all under fire and *he* kissed *me.*"

He pulled her closer and kissed her on the top of the head. "Mine," he whispered against her.

"How am I going to know what to do?"

"You got me to teach you. And a house full of flat mates. Don't think they're going to give up on you now. We'll figure out what's wrong and find a way to fix it."

"Ian?"

"Aye," He rubbed his hand over her hair.

She put her chin on his chest and watched him. "Would your mother have liked me?"

"Aye, I think so. She would have invited you in and served you tea with her homemade scones and my God they were good."

Ash settled closer against him.

"I'm sorry, though," he said.

She looked up at him.

"She would never have approved of us."

She tilted her chin.

He laughed a little. "You're not Scottish and you're not Catholic and I swear to God that woman must have been buried with a sprig of heather in one hand and a rosary in the other."

"You're dating beneath you," she laughed low.

His eyes stayed closed but he smiled wide. "I should do something about that and make mum proud."

"I'm a vampire," she whispered.

He kissed her on the head again. "Can't think of a more perfect mate for me."

"Mate?" she whispered. "That's the word they used downstairs."

"Aye, it is."

He rolled so he was facing her, his eyes open, watching her watch him.

"I declare *Amis pour la vie*."

"It's forever?" she asked.

"Aye. It is. There's nothing like divorce in the tradition. We make this declaration and that will be it. Forever mine."

"And if I never get well? Is that fair to you?"

He kissed her head. "I want it. With you when I have never wanted it before."

"But I'm broken," she said. "Don't you want to wait and see if I get fixed before making that kind of commitment?"

"Ash, I want you any way I can have you as long as you're always with me. I don't think you understand that. Do you remember the night we met?"

She nodded.

"I kiddingly told you if you married me I would give you all your drinks for free?"

She nodded.

"I wasn't kidding."

He leaned closer to her, talking soft right to her.

"Ashley Kristen Barrow. I declare to you."

She leaned forward whispering in his ear, talking very soft. "Ian David Stuart...I accept."

CHAPTER NINETEEN

It should be getting easier. Not harder. As they moved away from the events that caused the damage, the damage should disappear.

Ian sat on the edge of the bed, his hand rubbing her head, her eyes closed in sleep, eighteen hours into the sedation.

"Ash," he tried, but there was no response.

Figuring it had been long enough, he grabbed his coffee cup, left the door open so he could hear and headed down for help.

"What the hell are you doing here?" Travis snapped.

Ian held up his mug. "I'm going right back. I could use some help, though. I don't know what to do."

"She out?" Quinn asked.

Ian nodded and Quinn checked his watch. "I didn't give her that much. No way in hell it should take this long."

"I don't know," Jason said. "The attacks I used to get would wipe me out for days. Why were you gone last night?" Jason asked. "You should have been here."

"I had to see Mike. She had been doing good and I knew I would be right back. I didn't expect her to wake-up."

"Why did you see Mike?" Travis asked.

Only slightly dazed at the question from lack of sleep and worry, Ian looked up at him. "I quit my job."

"What?"

"It had nothing to do with her money," he said. "I didn't even know about it when I decided last week. I need to be here and not there. Mike understood."

"Did you have a plan?" Travis asked.

"Savings. Both of us, I guess. Why? Was I in danger of getting kicked out if I didn't make my forty-five percent?"

Travis glared and handed him the coffee.

Each of them gave forty-five percent of their take home every month to finance their household. When one came up short, none of the others mentioned it.

"I gotta get up there," Quinn said.

"What are you going to do?"

"I have no clue. I don't understand why it reversed."

"More transfusions?" Evan asked. "I got blood. She can have it."

"When I was a kid," Jason said, "And remember this was way before medicine caught up with asthma, doctors would tell us it was seasonal and I would only have attacks in the spring, but come November and December with twelve feet of snow outside and I would wake up in the same God damn shape."

"What are you saying?" Quinn asked.

"In my very knowledgeable opinion of being a severe asthmatic for many years, triggers don't have to be obvious. I was in the room yesterday before Stuart left. My cologne might have been enough to set it off."

"I don't suppose you would finally dump your fucking cologne?" Travis snapped.

"Um, for Ash?"

"You were born asthmatic. Stayed that way until you were turned and the turning took care of it."

"That's right."

"She was the opposite. Her turning caused the disease. Why? That shit he gave her hit the brain, not the lungs themselves."

"What if he did something to it?" Evan asked.

"What do you mean?"

"I was the last one of us in school and when I was there, kids were doing stupid things like inhaling shit. Could she have inhaled it?"

"Max didn't say—"

"Max didn't watch the whole thing," Evan said. "He said he couldn't take it and sat under the window."

Quinn nodded. "Asthma could be created by inhaling chemicals. That is a fact."

"He turns it into a vapor or smoke. Forces her to breathe it on a rag. Why?"

Ian closed his eyes. "Same reason as before. Attack and destroy. Hurt what matters most to me."

"You think she has asthma?" Jason asked Quinn.

"Yeah, I do. What I saw last night was an asthma attack."

"I used to have attacks almost every week—it was so bad. I would turn this weird shade of scaring my family to death," Jason said. "Lips blue. All exactly like what we saw last night."

"Jason," Ian said.

Jason looked up at him.

"Last night. Thank you. I wasn't here and you…"

"I didn't mean it to look suggestive, Stuart. Nancy used to sit with me close like that so she could hold me about the middle and feel the difference as we progressed. She talked me through the worst of the attacks."

"Will you teach me?"

Jason smiled. "I'm not holding you, but yeah."

"And Nancy?"

"What about her?"

"You told Ash all about your sister. You don't tell anybody about your sister."

Jason licked his lips. "Ash needed something to focus on so I could get the breathing under control."

"The weather? Last movie you saw? No. You went with your forbidden subject and told Ash everything from the games you played to the tree you used to race up and you showed her the photo you carry in your wallet you think none of us know about."

Jason stared at the table.

"You never could have dated her, could you?" Ian asked. "She's reminded you of Nancy since she walked in the door."

Jason smiled up at him. "I don't think I would have kissed Nancy quite like that."

Ian's eyes narrowed.

"And it was nice, I will never deny that, but I knew before she came down about the money where my relationship with her was heading." He looked up at Ian. "Not a lot of women come that special. I get to have two and you can stop worrying."

Ian smiled with relief at the Irishman's withdrawal.

"Food?" Quinn asked. "She was down fourteen pounds at last count."

"Everything is ready to go for Eggs Benedict," Travis said. "Only have to poach the egg."

Eggs Benedict was her absolute favorite. They also had her favorite scones from the bakery in town, her favorite cuts of lunch meats for sandwiches and their garage freezer looked like a Ben & Jerry's store front.

"Evan, what's wrong?" Travis asked.

Evan's head snapped up from staring at the table. "Nothing."

411

"Really? You're sure."

"I don't know if it's anything and I don't want to say something if I'm just tired."

"Tell us what it is and let us decide," Travis said.

Evan worked his jaw back staring at no one, thinking deeply. He finally took a deep breath. "Day before yesterday I walked into the den. I didn't know who was home, but I know Stuart was on the treadmill downstairs."

"Okay," Travis said.

"Lights were all off and it was pretty damn dark. No music, no nothing for entertainment."

"Okay," Travis repeated.

"Ash was sitting in a hardback chair, facing the curtains. Not the view, the curtains. She looked off and it scared me. So I said hi."

"That was nice of you," Travis said.

Evan leaned forward on the chair, a pleading look to him. "She came out of her skin, Travis. She jumped up. She was shaking everywhere. You would have thought I had threatened her. It lasted about a minute and then she smiled and was herself."

"Shit," Ian sighed quietly.

Quinn looked around the room. "Anyone else?"

"She was afraid of the candle flames at dinner her first night," Jason said. "Understandably."

"I know," Travis said. "Which is why we haven't had candles on the table since."

Family dinners were a big deal in the house. Every night at five, everyone rotating chores. Always with a set table and candles in the middle.

"I touched her the other night," Ian said. "Just holding her but I brushed up against her side where the scars are. She jumped away, got real agitated and a minute later didn't know why she had moved and apologized."

Quinn sighed. "It's called Post Traumatic Stress Disorder. And it is a big deal. She's reliving what they did even if she doesn't realize it."

"Another problem," Jason sighed.

"Make sure she doesn't hear you say that, Jason," Ian said. "She is struggling with how much she's putting us out."

"She's not putting us out at all," Jason replied.

"She doesn't see it that way yet."

"We will have to deal with the PTSD after I get the breathing controlled. I can use valium or something to help with the anxiety. In the meantime I brought home a shitload of sample meds for asthma. We can get her started. Jason, I need a prescription pad in the name of Dr. Michael Reeves." He slid a piece of paper across the table to Jason. "This is his license number."

"Cool," Jason said. "Isn't Dr. Reeves going to object?"

"Probably not, since you haven't created him yet. How fast can I get that?"

413

"Day or so. Angelo is usually pretty quick with our documentation. I can get him to rush this and overnight it."

"What's the plan?" Travis asked.

Quinn blinked. "Mail order pharmacies will be nowhere near as hard to get scripts out of for her. And this will be ongoing so expect the FBI at the door."

"Again?" Jason smiled sadly.

"Wake her up. Nice and slow," Quinn said. "I borrowed some toys from the hospital that will help me figure this out so I need her up, fed and ready for some tests."

By the time he got her to respond, Travis had arrived with the tray and left. Ian pulled the table by the door over to set it on, while she blinked a few times and sat up. Ian moved to put the pillows behind her.

"I'm being a pain again, aren't I?" she asked.

The tray sat with the eggs and homemade hash browns beside them. Fresh strawberries, hulled and lightly coated with sugar were in a bowl, a glass of orange juice topped it off.

"And if I said I wasn't hungry?" she tried.

Ian picked up the fork and cut a slice. "Then I would say 'open' and I would continue to say it until we got through this whole plate."

"Can I please go back to sleep?"

"Nope."

She ignored the fork in front of her mouth.

When she opened to speak, he shoved in the first bite. With closed eyes she reluctantly chewed.

"That's really good," she said. "Travis?"

"Who else?" He had another bite full ready. She put her hands up to stop.

"What's wrong with me now?"

"Besides being difficult?" He smiled.

"Ian?"

"Honey, I don't know. But Quinn is coming up right after you finish this and we're going to see what we can figure out."

She leaned back and stared up him. "Walter was trying to kill me that night, wasn't he?"

Ian shook his head. "No. He could have and he didn't."

"But he did things to alter what should have happened."

Ian nodded.

"He hurt me enough to make sure I died and you got to watch."

"Aye," Ian said, putting the fork down. "I think that was probably his plan."

"Could you have declared with him?"

"If I had wanted to, aye. There are no hang-ups on orientation in the society."

"So that's what he wanted."

"I don't know what he wanted."

"The dreams," she asked. "The ones I had before. Those were the transfusions weren't they? You do them different than if we were in a hospital."

"If you are unresponsive the easiest way is the old fashioned way. We can actually do them pretty quick. With you awake, we go with hospital route and it takes a lot longer. Are you going to eat more?"

"I will. Give me a minute. You all do this and how does it work?"

"I don't understand the question."

"You need blood, but you are giving it to me."

"Oh, okay. Um," he thought. "Quinn can steal some from the hospital. Not a lot, but enough for a quick job. The rest of us? We use pig's blood, it's pretty close in composition and the best for us. We give you what has assimilated in us then we take the pigs. Process starts over and in a day or so the pig's in us is now vampire."

"Why not give me pig's direct?"

"For some reason, you don't respond to it. We don't know why. You are asking a lot of questions. Why?"

"Because I am tired of being the sidelined victim and I want to be the solution. So instead of Eggs Benedict, why am I not getting another transfusion? Why don't you lean over and do it now?"

He rubbed his forehead. "I don't know if it would work for one, and two, I would have to get permission."

"We declared."

"And Primary still out ranks that and in this case, I would have to ask Quinn if it was medically sound."

"And you are waiting because…"

She blinked at him.

"Why do you want to do it so bad? Having other guys chew on your neck is not my best form of entertainment."

"I feel like shit. Beyond not breathing okay, there is something else feeling weird and I think it's going to get worse. I want to do whatever the hell I have to, to fix it. So I will eat everything on that tray and I will push for extreme measures and in doing so I will tell Walter What's-His-Name to fuck off, go to hell and we win. I am not checking out on his orders to make you suffer and if you don't mind, I wouldn't mind a shitload and a fuckton and whatever other words you men use, of fucking help."

"Did you get all that?" Travis laughed.

Ian turned to see him at the door, his arms crossed, and his shoulder on the jamb.

"Aye," Ian said. "Why don't you get Quinn and whoever wants to go first and I will finish feeding the difficult wench."

To their good fortune, pig's blood actually froze pretty well in small re-sealable freezer bags. Though it was a bitch to put up one at a time in the chest freezer that sat by the Ben & Jerry's freezer, it preserved well and it was worth it to have the supply they were going to need. Jason and Evan had been generous in their collection duties and there was enough to keep them all going.

No one went to work anymore, all calling in sick and everyone did more than their share to get their sixth member up and running.

Physically she improved in strength. Mentally, they were all avoiding the challenge they knew would eventually show up.

Less than a week after she woke up, Ian felt her move and slid out of the bed. He thought she was heading to the bathroom but he knew she had been thrashing for hours, denying there was anything wrong.

He watched her go to the window and stare at the black-out shade. She reached for the cord to open and he almost warned but she realized first and stepped back, her arms crossed.

"What's wrong?" he asked.

She looked over her shoulder at him. "I'm sorry, I didn't mean to wake you. Go back to sleep."

"Okay," he said, "after you tell me what's wrong."

"Nothing. I couldn't sleep."

"Come back over here. I'll hold you and we'll work it out."

She smiled sadly. "Thanks but I can take care of this one. You go back to sleep."

He watched her walk to the bookshelf and start scanning titles, but he wasn't buying it.

He got up to move to her, his hands on her shoulders, him freezing. "My God, you're shaking like a leaf." He tried to rub her upper arms up and down, calming her.

She looked up at him. "Just a little cold."

"A little cold?" He ran his hand down to her lower back then up. "You're drenched. Honey?" He pulled her into his arms.

"It's nothing," she whispered against him.

He pulled back to hold her hands in both his. "What's wrong?"

"We have enough to worry about with me. Everyone is doing amazing things. I don't want all of you adding to that. This is my problem."

"Your problem is my problem."

She looked up at him. "I went from cop to victim. It's been a little bit of adjustment. I will work it out."

His breathing heavy, he spoke softly. "It's back, isn't it?"

She lowered her chin, closed her eyes and nodded a little. "How can you look at me with these scars and not be repulsed?"

He pulled her tight. "Because you are not your scars and they will fade with time. You've been doing this every night since you woke up?"

"Happens in the day, too. I try to ignore it but…" She looked up at him. "I can feel it sometimes. Like it's still real and still happening and I know it's in my head and I know I am safe here…but…I don't know what to do with this." She looked at Ian with scared eyes.

He stepped back a little. She might not know what to do but he did. He held her face in both his hands.

"Ash," he said softly. "I want you to look at me."

She did, licking her lips. "I'm sorry," she said. "I'm nothing but a problem. We fix one and another comes up. I don't know how you can do this with me." She laughed a little. "You're not even getting laid anymore."

"I think we will have time for that sometime later. Right now, watch my eyes and listen to what I say."

She blinked twice but nodded her head a little and she held his stare.

"Last Monday and Tuesday," he said.

"What about them?"

"That's April twenty-second and twenty-third. You don't remember what happened those days, okay?"

"I don't?"

He shook his head, keeping the stare. "You don't remember what happened, what was said, who you saw or what was done. You will never recover that memory no matter what anyone says or does, no matter how many years you live. You will never question any scars you have. They are just there. You will only remember me telling you it was all okay. Can you do that?"

She looked down, then brought her sad gaze up to his.

"They were bad," she said.

"They were very bad and you don't have them anymore, do you?"

She pulled away a little and looked to be struggling with it and then she melted at the knees. "No," she said. "I don't remember."

"You're not afraid."

"No," she whispered.

"And you are sound asleep."

He caught her when she followed the command, his arms going under her knees, carrying her back to the bed. Tucking her in secure, a pillow beside her and the quilt to her shoulders. He headed downstairs knowing she wasn't going to wake up and knocked on Travis's door.

It took a minute for it to pull back and a barely awake Travis to peer out.

"Remember those days when nothing happened and there were no emergencies and we got to sleep straight through?" Travis sighed at the nostalgia.

"I thought I should let you know that Ash won't be helping us anymore figuring out what happened that night."

"She's being difficult?"

"She has nothing to offer."

Travis leaned on the doorjamb. "And you did it because?"

"It was hurting her like it was still going on. She could feel what they did. I had to stop it."

"You know you can actually talk to me about this shit before you go and act."

"Not when she's terrified."

"Do you think we needed any more than we have?"

"I don't think there was anything else to get."

"I can reprimand you and tell you bad boy, but you will still just go do something like this again if it involves her."

"I will always do something like this if it involves her."

CHAPTER TWENTY

With the meds kicking in and her feeling human, Ash sat between Jason and Quinn on the couch, an X-Box controller in her hand for the very first time. Out of her pajamas at last, a couple of decent showers under her belt she was dressed in black yoga pants and one of Ian's plain blue T-shirts. Her thick hair hung loose and a little wild, her face scrubbed clean of make-up.

Evan sat on the loveseat, watching the match, flipping through the new *Calvin and Hobbes* book Jason had got him for his birthday, waiting his turn to play winner while Travis cleaned up and Ian sat in the back watching her.

She had a long way to go and Ian wasn't sure they would ever get as far as they hoped.

She slept long and deep hours. She had trouble in the evening getting up. She ate now, but her weight wasn't coming up. So far, she had managed the steps to the attic room up and down twice, but he was always at her elbow. He kept her under close watch, so far not missing the job at Cooper's.

Quitting had been the right decision. He would get used to her money. He finally knew it. He might even manage to get some enjoyment out of it.

He sat in the chair in the back corner of the room, his feet up on a footstool. The couch in front of him, the three backs to him as they played their video game on the big screen.

Jason and Quinn were as good as ever with her, explaining how it all worked step-by-step, showing her how to use the controller buttons. She was doing terribly on the game they picked, but she was laughing and kept trying and they didn't seem to be getting bored or frustrated. Ian couldn't decide if she was the baby sister they had both craved or maybe the new house mascot.

"Ash?" Ian asked, feeling his own smile.

"What?" she asked without turning around.

"Where's your VISA card?"

"I have no idea. You unpacked my stuff. Where's my purse?"

"Aye," he nodded as he laughed. "Duh. Bottom drawer of the nightstand, your side. I'm going to borrow it."

She laughed. "Borrow?"

"I'm going to steal it and play for a little while. What's the limit on it?"

She didn't answer even though Jason and Quinn both stopped talking to wait for it.

Ian pursed his lips and nodded, staring at the catalog. "I don't want to know the answer, do I?"

Lights exploded on the screen and she giggled in triumph. "Not really. But don't worry. I doubt you will hit it on one online order."

Ian laughed. "You're trying to annoy me, aren't you?"

"Since I think you're misbehaving, yes."

Travis leaned in the pass through, watching the exchange. He tilted his head at Ian. Ian raised the Victoria's Secret catalog he was studying and turned it to show Travis the cover. Travis laughed hard and backed into the kitchen. It was time to look into something that wasn't flannel with matching slippers and socks.

A minute later Travis came out carrying two cups of coffee, handing one to Ian.

"Finding the perks?"

"Things are looking up," Ian said, sipping.

"I can help you with that."

"I think I'm doing okay." Ian checked his watch. "Finish up," he said to the room.

"No," she said defiantly. She laughed at another explosion. Jason and Quinn really were amazing with her.

Ian mentally marked a few choices he would be ordering tomorrow and closed the catalog thinking that not one of the models had anything on what he had. Travis reached for it and Ian batted his hand.

"Hey, it's in the family room and fair game."

"And if you even attempt to use any part of your imagination I will be forced to kill you."

"I think what's in the catalog will amuse me enough." He grabbed it and folded it in half.

"Your choice," Ian said to Ash. "Stand up and walk to the stairs and I will carry you up or I will come over there, take you off the couch and carry you up."

"There's not a third?"

"Afraid not. Come on it's almost six a. m. You should have been in bed an hour ago."

"You're being difficult. What were you doing back there?"

He smiled widely. "Nothing."

One last explosion happened on the screen in brilliant color. "Cool!" She laughed. She handed off the controller to Jason.

She leaned over to kiss him on the cheek, making him smile. "That was a lot of fun, my Genius." she said.

She turned to Quinn and did the same only he kissed her back on the opposite cheek. "My Flirt."

She stood and started to head toward Ian. "Evan needs a puppy," she said as if she was mentioning the weather.

"What?" Travis laughed.

"What?" Evan snapped, sitting up straight.

She took complete control of the room.

"Jason's got his computers. Quinn's got his medical books. Ian's got his drawing and books and his bike. Travis, The Protector, has his meddling."

"I do not meddle," Travis said.

The other four began talking at once, poking fun at him.

"Excuse me," she said, interrupting them. "Everyone's got an interest and amusement and I think we should get Evan a puppy."

"This is a good idea," Evan said. "I like this idea. Can we do it?"

Travis looked over at Ian. "She's your girlfriend and she's causing anarchy."

"Seriously," she said. "Is there a valid reason why we can't have a puppy? He would be great with it."

"I keep trying to control her," Ian said, "But it's all that thinking for herself and feminism. I think she even reads books."

Travis smiled.

"Please," Evan whined, clasping his hand together in prayer. "Please, please, *please*?"

"I think we're getting a puppy," Ian said.

Evan came out of his chair, his arms straight up in the air. "Yes," he cheered.

"Are you ready to go up now or do you want to disrupt world order?"

She moved past Jason with an 'excuse me' and came out around the couch.

Evan met her halfway to Ian, his arms going all the way around her, lifting her off her feet and he laughed. "Thank you. Thank you."

She put her hands on his shoulder and giggled hard. "My Kid," she smiled.

"Drop her, puppy owner," Ian said as he stepped toward her.

Ian put his hand out and she took it, cool in his hand. Her fever was finally gone even though they never knew what caused it. He walked out of the room with her in tow and got her to the bottom of the steps.

"You know I could probably do this," she said.

He leaned over, scooping her up, her arms around his neck. "Saves time," he said. "And you smell really good like this."

She kissed his neck as she bounced her feet.

"That was pretty damn sweet to watch. Have it planned long?"

"Just sort of came out."

He got to the top floor, kicking open the door. "I think you have everyone in this house twisted right around your finger and we might all be doomed."

He set her down on the bed. "Under the covers."

She did. He reached for a pillow and placed it in her arms before tucking her in.

"Are we going to sleep together soon?"

"As a matter of fact, we are," he said. "Right now. For about eight hours straight."

He walked around the bed, turning off all the lights.

428

Standing in front of the closet he pulled off his shoes, putting them in the bottom. Socks, shirt, pants. They all came off, all filed into the dirty clothes hamper. He saw it was full and made a mental note for tomorrow to do laundry. Getting into the bed he punched the one pillow he could steal from her and lay down, facing her.

She was on her side, facing him, her pillow in her arms between them. She picked it up, moved it over her and dropped it onto the floor.

"Do you want a hand job?" she asked him.

He kept his eyes closed but couldn't stop the smile. "No, I do not."

"Blow job "

"Tempting," he said. "But I'll pass."

"You're no fun."

"Actually I'm a hell of a lot of fun."

He looked at her, finding her watching him, a smile on her face.

"Close your eyes and go to sleep," he said. "Tonight we will make some wild plans for hot sex."

"Promise?"

"I promise."

Her eyes closed. With no pillow between them though there was plenty of free space. She reached up without looking, finding his hand. Playing with his fingers for a minute, she found the perfect, most comfortable way to hold him. He watched her the whole time, feeling his own smile.

"Ian," she whispered in the dark.

"Yeah?"

"I love you."

He sucked it in like a breath, feeling the words through his whole body. Her eyes stayed closed but that didn't stop him from reaching out to her with his free hand, brushing his hand over her hair.

"I love you, too, Ash."

Six hours. That was usually his top number on sleep. He stayed very still across from her, thinking of the three little words, her hand still in his and he watched her in the dark as she drifted off.

He checked his cell phone. She had been asleep an hour and it didn't look as if she was waking up.

Closing his eyes, he allowed himself to follow her.

The next thing he knew she was pressed up against him, her hand running across his chest. He reached for his cell again, ignoring the fact she was naked. His six hours had turned into twelve and he finally had to admit it he needed the sleep.

Her hand traveled lower, across his stomach feeling better than he wanted it to.

"You do know I'm going to turn you down, right?"

She kissed his shoulder. "You said today."

430

"I said we would make plans today."

Her hand found its mark and she stroked him. He sucked in a breath and closed his eyes.

"I think I can convince you," she said.

Which was what he was afraid of. He rolled over, pinning her under him, capturing both her hands to hold over her head, trying to at least slow her down. Only she moaned and wiggled her hips, rubbing him even closer to her target.

"Stop that," he laughed. "You're on sick leave until further notice. Quinn will kill us both if he finds out."

"And how is he going to find out?"

"When you pass out and I have to go get him."

She leaned up to whisper in his ear. "I want you inside me." She dropped back down onto the pillow and blinked her big blue eyes at him. "It feels real nice when you're inside of me."

"Aye," he admitted. "Aye it does." He laughed.

She continued to wiggle and he started to give up. It wasn't even a fight he really wanted to win. She pushed his boxers off his hips, dragging them down his legs until they were off.

He moved to hold her face in both of his hands. He stared down at her, her smiling up at him and she looked so hot and it had been so long. Seeing her like this, he was a goner. There was no way he was walking away.

"Ash," he said feeling his pulse pick up. "Run your tongue over your teeth."

"What?"

"Do it and I'll kiss you."

He watched as she did, her tongue moving slowly, finding the teeth that had never been there before. She sucked in a breath in shock.

"Your eyes," he whispered.

"What?"

"Not red. It's the wrong term. Way too intense and personal to be only red." He brushed her hair back off her face so he could see her more clearly.

"What?" she whispered.

He shook his head, staring at the gorgeous color. "Dark rose and all yours. God, Ash. This is incredible. I never thought I would see you like this."

"I don't know what I did."

"You'll learn. It's coming slower to you but we're getting there."

He crushed his mouth down on hers, his tongue slipping into her mouth and he could feel them, nicking. Fangs when she never had them before. He held her face still with his hands, his head angling in the other direction. She kissed him back, her tongue sliding smooth across his. He shifted his weight, giving them what they craved, sliding into her wet heat in a smooth motion. She moaned, her head thrown back, her hands on his back, nails digging in. He loved the feel of those nails.

432

"Yes," she whispered, drawing out the word like it really meant something. Her legs wrapped around his hips opening her wide. He closed his eyes tight, listening to her moans, his hips keeping up a steady rhythm.

He held her face in his hand, moving it so her mouth rested against his throat.

"Do you feel that," he asked. "The pulse on your lips?"

"Yes."

"Bite," he whispered in her ear.

She froze under him, his hand still on her face.

"No," she said.

"Please."

Her head shook hard. "No. You need—"

"It's okay," he cut her off. "Trust me. Bite me right there."

She nipped.

"Harder," he said. He needed this. Oh God, he needed this bad.

She tried again and he felt it, the pressure, but it wasn't enough.

"Please Ashley. I want this."

When he felt the sting of breaking skin it was pure pleasure moving to every inch of his body. When she began to suck he thought he might die. He closed his eyes tight and felt her natural

433

instinct. His taste was in her now driving him harder and faster, wanting more.

He put his mouth onto that place on her neck. His spot. His teeth sank into her deep, making her let go of him and gasp. She tried to pull away, her hands on his shoulders pushing him but he held her steady with a hand on the other side of her neck, his fingers in her hair. His eyes closed, he sucked slowly, pulling feelings from her until her hands held onto his shoulders, her breathing heavy. He could taste her full in his mouth and nothing had ever tasted better.

"Oh God, that's good," she whispered and he pulled her closer.

Her face went back to his neck, sealing her lips over the place she had bitten, sucking on him until he didn't think he could stand it.

Sex had never been better. In those few minutes when she flowed onto his tongue, him buried hard inside of her, he was sure it had never been better. When she let go of his throat it was to throw her head back on the pillow. Tasting the last bit of her before sealing his lips over hers, swallowing her noises. His climax came with hers, rushing through his whole body, her sounds around him, telling him she was only his.

CHAPTER TWENTY-ONE

"You're sure you're okay?" he asked her one last time.

She lay back against her mound of pillows in her purple pajamas while he was fully dressed with jeans, a T-shirt and shoes.

"I'm fine. More than fine," she said. "And the blood?"

He shook his head. "There's no blood loss. It's an exchange. We just have to watch out for each other."

"Sounds kind of gross," she said.

"Aye," he laughed. "But I don't know many things that even come close to feeling as good."

He went over to his computer monitor and angled it so she could see it from the bed. He picked up a stack of movies and put them beside her on the quilt.

He smiled and reached up to run his finger over the mark on her neck.

"You're obsessed with those," she said, smiling a little.

He leaned a little to look at it then looked back at her. "Aye? Problem?"

"Is it personal or a vampire thing?" She laughed. "Because I'm not going through the rest of my life with a hickey."

His smile widened and he stood up. "Guess we'll discuss that at a later date."

"You are so immature."

"You okay on the stairs?"

She nodded. "Yeah. I can handle it."

"But you come right back up here and park your ass in front of *Titanic* until I get back. You have any trouble and anyone of them will carry you up. I would rather see that, than you at the bottom of the stairs."

She nodded. "Why do you have *Titanic*?" She laughed as she held up the DVD box.

He shrugged. "I don't even know and if I did know I doubt I would admit it."

"Cute." She laughed.

"Ride usually takes me a couple of hours. I'll try to cut it short and get back sooner."

"No," she said. "You're feeling it and it's been too long. Take as long as you need."

"Can I trust you?" he smiled. She had started to relax again.

She nodded and he turned, shutting the door behind him. In the kitchen Travis stood by the sink.

Jason was at the kitchen table, a bowl of chili in front of him.

"I'm going for a ride," Ian said as he got his own dinner. A quick bowl. He could be back in two hours. *Titanic*, if that's what she went with, would still be on.

"Nice hickey," Travis said.

Ian smiled. "I like it."

"Quinn sees it and he's going to kill you."

Ian smiled. "Not a bad way to go." He sighed dramatically. "So worth it."

"You're a cruel, gloating bastard, you do know that, right?" Travis said.

Ian poured himself a cup of coffee.

"She's feeling better?" Jason asked.

Ian nodded. "Aye. She seems to be starting to show improvement."

"How long you going to be gone?" Travis asked.

"Couple of hours. She's got *Titanic* to keep her busy so she'll stay out of your hair. Though she did say she might come down. If she does, can you get her back upstairs? I don't mind her taking the steps down, but I don't want her going up."

"Sure," Travis said. "I can do that."

"Thanks." Smiling, Ian headed toward the front door and his bike.

"Hey," Travis called. "Wait a minute. I got something for you."

Travis was patting down his front and back pockets. He moved to his shirt, patting the one of the upper left side. "Here it is!"

"Here what is?"

Travis handed over a tiny manila envelope about three inches long.

"What's this?"

Travis only raised his eyebrows at Ian and gave him a goofy smile.

Ian put down the water bottle, opened the envelope and let the contents drop into his hand.

Three shining, silver rings lay in his palm. One large, one small and one diamond with a square stone. He brought his gaze up to Travis. Travis didn't even have the decency to look embarrassed.

"These are wedding rings."

"Yeah, I know," Travis said. "That's what I ordered."

Ian worked his jaw back and forth. "What am I supposed to do with these?"

"I don't know," Travis said. "Marry her maybe?"

Ian's fingers closed over them.

"I think I can decide if I plan on getting married."

Travis laughed loud and hard. Jason joined in. Travis moved to the coffee pot and poured a cup. "You declared with her and

438

there is enough human left in her that we might as well do this right."

Ian didn't know if he should be grateful or really, really annoyed.

"I did some checking on the Internet," Travis said. "Tried Vegas, but that didn't look too good. The courthouse here closes before dark so we couldn't get in." He leaned back on the counter, blew into his coffee mug and looked up at Ian.

"We?" Ian asked. "I don't even get married in private?"

Travis laughed again. "Oh hell no."

"You're planning a wedding? *My* wedding?"

Travis looked up at him. "Her name will be Stuart."

Ian pursed his lips and worked that concept over in his mind.

"Mrs. Ian David Stuart."

"Or," Jason suggested. "Mrs. Ashley Barrow-Stuart. We can hyphenate the two."

Ian tilted his chin, screwed up his face and shook his head.

"No," Travis said. "He's still too much a nineteenth century chauvinist. Have to be Mrs. Ashley Stuart."

Ian pointed between them. "I'm going to hurt you. Both."

"We found a place in New Orleans," Jason said. "Looks really cool."

Ian stared at him, his jaw hanging. The rings were warming up in his hand. "We?"

"He needed a second opinion. And we all liked the New Orleans idea."

"*All?*"

Jason smiled and nodded. Travis drank his coffee.

"It's a place in the French Quarter. We could even get Ash her tattoo while we are there. Nanette is still practicing off Jackson Square and very interested in discussing what type of service you want."

"When did we decide she was getting a tattoo?"

"Has to have one. You know that. I was thinking of a Celtic Knot on her back at the base of her neck."

Ian pictured it and pictured it damn sexy. He actually liked that idea but he didn't feel like sharing that information with Travis.

Travis was still talking. "I figure you could wear a suit and tie, get Ash a pretty new dress. I'll give away the bride."

"Of course you will."

"Of course I will," Travis smiled. "She doesn't have any family she talks about, so she'll need someone to help her pick out the dress, too."

Ian was speechless. It was as infuriating as it was sweet.

Ian opened his hand and looked at the rings. They were really nice. He could picture one band sitting on her left hand.

440

Hell, he could see the other on his. He picked it up and looked at the diamond engagement ring, thinking it was gorgeous and he didn't have a clue about stones.

Travis pointed at them. "Those are white gold. I know you don't like yellow."

No, he didn't care for yellow gold. All his jewelry was silver. He didn't know Travis had ever put any thought into that. Ian slipped the rings back into the envelope and sealed it up. He stuck it into his front pocket.

"Where did you get them?"

"1-800-Celtic."

"The sizes?"

"Yours I knew and hers I got off her while she was asleep. You were in the shower."

Ian glared at him and Travis gave a smile in return.

"I'm going for my ride now. Think you two can stay away from the computer while I'm gone?"

"I haven't started planning the honeymoon yet," Travis said.

Ian blew out a breath and gave up. They had him outnumbered and there was not much he could do to fight against them. He turned and headed toward the door. Stopping, he spun around suddenly.

"Ashley Stuart works," he said over a grin. "Works real nice."

Ian had hardly been gone when Ash made her way down. She was in her pajamas, her feet still bare. Jason sat at the kitchen table, Travis across from him.

"Hey," Travis said, smiling. "Thought you were doing *Titanic*." He stood up and went to the refrigerator, pulling out a bottle that he set in the microwave. He pushed one minute.

"Really just want to get up and do something."

"Hey Gorgeous, you're feeling better?" Jason asked.

She nodded. "Why is *Titanic* even in this house? Macho men don't do *Titanic*."

Jason shrugged. "I have no idea where it came from. Ended up in Stuart's room, though." He nodded his head and smiled. "That might explain a lot."

Travis went to the microwave and pulled out the sport bottle. He handed it to her.

"What is this?"

"Blood."

She put the bottle on the table. "I'll pass."

"No," Travis laughed, picking up the bottle and handing to her. "We're supplementing your diet."

She took it. "This is human and I'm supposed to enjoy this idea?"

442

"Drink it. Then there's chili on the stove and cornbread on the counter."

"Can I just have the chili?"

"We would kill for a chance like this," Travis said.

"We have," Jason smirked.

"Ha ha," she said.

"I can go get Quinn and let him explain the whole thing to you or you could just trust me and do this to make me happy."

"Drink blood. You're happy. Makes no sense."

"Drink."

"I refuse."

"Fine, I'll pour. Jason, grab her arms." Travis reached for the bottle but Ash grabbed it up quick.

Travis smiled at her, his teeth bright.

"Watching all of you together is an extravaganza of entertainment. Okay Jason, you do computers. What is it you do with them?"

He looked up at her, blinking his green eyes. "Computer security. I opened up my own company and, when I'm not looking up your finances—by the way—you really should vary your passwords and not use the same one for everything from your banking to your Amazon account."

He smiled as her jaw dropped.

"And to answer your questions, I design software for corporations to prevent hackers from breaking in. When I'm not breaking in, of course. You really bought *One Hundred Sex Ways You Have Never Tried*, two *Green Day* albums and *Air Supply*? Who the hell listens to *Air Supply*?"

"What?" she whispered.

He smiled at her and drank his coffee. "Can I borrow that book when you're done? See what I've been missing?"

She smiled at him. "I think you are the most evil man I have ever met."

He wiggled his eyebrows. "Great kisser, though, huh?"

She pursed her lips and narrowed her eyes at him and tried to think of a way to get even.

"Jason breaks into all our accounts. We're used to it. And he not only keeps us in heavy financing as his income leaves the rest of us in the dust, but he does our illegal documentation, too, upgrading us every couple of years with a new age. Appearances never change, unless of course, we could get Stuart to get a haircut which I have never been able to do so." He laughed. "But we have to keep changing our birth years to keep with when we stopped aging."

"Ian had a driver's license that had a 1984 birthday."

"Yep" Jason said. "Broke in to the DMW and had one made for all of us. Next time we move, I will have to do the same thing with the new state."

"Aren't there protocols stopping people like you from doing exactly that?"

444

"Yeah," he laughed. "I design them. Pretty easy to get past 'em when you know what went into creating them."

"Don't ask him about Sandy," Travis said.

Jason laughed.

"Who's Sandy?"

"His last girlfriend who he dumped right about the time you were showing up on our radar."

"What was wrong with Sandy?"

"Nothing," Jason said. "She was great."

"So why did you dump her?"

"Because she was great."

"That makes sense," Ash said.

"I'm in no way looking for long term so when she says 'Let's…' I sorta don't."

Travis kept talking. "You want to know how he met Sandy?"

"Hey, that's personal," Jason said.

"He came out of the gym at three o'clock in the morning, stinking like a horse and Sandy is there with a dead battery and needs a jump."

"Okay," Ash said. "Hero to the rescue."

"Only when he popped the hood, the battery wasn't dead. The cables had been disconnected. He connected them back without a word, got her address and followed her home. No details on what happened next."

Ash laughed out loud. "There are words to describe men like you."

"Irresistible?" Jason smiled.

She looked at Travis. "And you, if you think that I think for one minute that you are not misbehaving at work, in a hotel of all places, on at least a semi-regular basis, then we don't know each other very well."

He extended his hand. "Hi, my name is Travis."

She laughed. "I am curious as to whether you make friendly with staff or just introduce yourself to guests as they are checking in."

He shook his head. "Who taught you to think so much?"

Travis stood up and poured himself another cup.

"Getting back on track and away from sex lives that don't concern you," he said. "You are going to be facing a lot of changes I don't think have been discussed."

"Would rather continue trying to figure out what you guys are doing that you don't want me to know about."

"As I was saying," Travis laughed. "No kids. No more birth control or monthly cycles. Can't catch diseases."

"He mentioned the no kids to me," she said. "I didn't know it had to do with this."

"I'm surprised he told you," Travis said.

446

"He didn't want to use condoms anymore."

"Ah ha." Travis laughed. "Have you always been so cavalier about sex?"

"I'm sorry," she said. "Did you not know I was sleeping with Ian?"

"Actually, I think I might have put that one together."

Jason laughed outright.

She finished her sports bottle. "Am I supposed to be liking this?"

"Yeah," Jason said. "Usually that's what happens."

She rinsed the bottle in the sink, watching the water turn red and circle down the drain. "I'd rather have the chili," she said. She moved over to the stove, filling a bowl.

Travis got up and poured her a glass of cranberry juice, sitting it beside her place. She came over with her bowl and sat down.

Travis and Jason were looking back and forth between the two of them.

"You don't want blood?" Travis asked, looking at her.

She stared back and took a bite. "I don't really think about it unless it's brought up."

"Ash, vampires crave blood," Jason said. "It's sorta like the whole reason we're a problem. We take it from people who don't necessarily want to give it up."

"You don't."

"No," Travis said. "We don't. But it's a daily uphill battle each of us faces. The cravings never stop."

"Except for you," Jason said, pointing at her. "You don't have cravings, do you?"

She shook her head. "What does that mean?"

"Vampires crave blood," Jason said. "You don't."

"All the stuff that's happened. Are you saying I wasn't changed or whatever?"

Travis shook his head. "No. There is no way in hell he didn't turn you. Too many things say you were. To start with there were teeth marks on Stuart's hickey an hour ago."

She looked away and felt herself blush.

"You got your fangs today." Travis said.

She looked up at him, not sure how she was supposed to answer that question.

"They should have come in right away. The minute you woke up. When Stuart gave you his arm at your house, you should have ripped at it. And mine, too." He pointed across the table. "And Jason's."

"You two?" she pointed between the two of them.

"You don't remember that because you were unconscious when we did it," Jason said.

She blinked at him.

448

"But you remember that night? Being turned?" Jason said.

She thought for a minute. "No. Actually I don't. I mean I know it happened, but I don't remember it happening. Does that make sense?"

Travis looked at Jason then back at her. "It makes perfect sense, *mia bella*."

Travis reached over for her hand, pulling it straight until the place where the injection mark had been on the inside of her elbow showed. He reached and touched it. "But you're not like us."

"I think you are making me nervous."

He reached up, closing her arm and putting a hand to the back of her head where he rubbed her hair playfully. "I'm not trying to."

The doorbell went off. Jason and Travis exchanged looks while Ash sat there thinking about everything the two of them had said.

Quinn leaned in the kitchen door.

"Ashley, your friend is here."

She looked at him. "What friend?"

"Your cop friend."

And then she remembered. Hunter. Ian had said Hunter had come by. She had never followed up on it. He was going to be pissed.

"You okay?" Travis asked.

"Oh yeah." She stood up.

"You're not exactly dressed for company."

"Trust me, Hunter has seen me in worse."

She headed toward the door, snapped her fingers and turned.

"Jason?"

He looked up at her.

"The book is at the house. I can get it for you once I can get back in there. You probably should check it out. Might be some things in there you want to give Sandy a call about to re-discuss your distribution of..." she licked her lips "...favors. Pages 23, 35 and um...69 were especially noteworthy."

Smiling, she turned and headed toward the den. She heard them behind her.

"I can't marry her?" Jason whispered.

"Sorry," Travis laughed.

CHAPTER TWENTY-TWO

Ian skidded to a halt, the bike diagonal on the road at the top of the hill. The view over-looking the city rivaled the one from their back yard, but it wasn't what had his attention.

Standing twenty feet ahead, Walter blocked the road. His black coat, copied from some bad movie somewhere, hung low to the ground. His light hair brushed back, eyes shining even from such a distance.

Ian looked around side to side, noting the vampires to his right and left, each one standing back, keeping their distance. He had no doubt they were only waiting for an order from Walter.

The odds were six to one and they weren't odds he would give himself in winning. Shit, he thought. This was the kind of bad that didn't get much worse.

"The den was cleared out," Ian said. "You left town."

"When Max went missing, I knew he was going to you. Bastard got away before I could discuss it in detail with him."

"How did you know I would be here?" Already sweaty and breathless from the hour ride he had done, his voice came out hoarse. His heartbeat picked up as the adrenalin kicked into overdrive.

"It's one of your favorite routes."

"Aye, but tonight?"

"Just had to wait. You were bound to show up again."

"Again? We've passed here before?"

"A couple of times. I didn't say anything."

Ian nodded slowly, while his hands gripped the handlebars tight. He calculated his chances of riding out of here. He thought about Ashley back home and what it would do to her if he was off by even a little while. The family would take care of her. Ian knew she would be safe as long as they were at the house with her. And Ashley being safe was the most important thing.

"I gave you a present and you haven't thanked me for it."

"Wasn't something I asked for," Ian said.

"Still, it's the thought that counts, don't you think?"

Ian shook his head. "If I had been looking for that kind of gift I could have taken care of it myself."

Walter walked to the side, stepping off the path and onto the grass. "I don't think so. It's not the type of thing you do anymore."

"Which is why I left it alone."

"But you can't leave it alone, can you? You're obsessed with her. Playing house with her in the cute little place she owns. Playing at the bar and taking her out to meet the family."

Ian narrowed his eyes at him. The vampire behind him took two steps forward. The two to the right followed suit. They were closing the distance around him.

"I don't think it's anything you would understand," Ian said. Time was counting down, the minutes turning into seconds.

452

"Do you like sleeping in her bed more than you like sleeping in yours?"

Ian gripped the handlebars tighter.

"I tried it," Walter said. "Cuddled up next to her while she slept and it was nice. I don't think I thought it was as nice as you do, but maybe I could understand if you explained it to me."

Rage raced across Ian's nerves like it was supposed to. Walter was trying to go for the emotional response. Throw Ian off guard so Walter would have the upper hand. Ian had to concentrate and pull it back in. He had to let it go no matter how much it disgusted him.

"Say anything you want, but it doesn't change things." Ian snapped.

"I mean it," Walter said, totally ignoring Ian. "She's sweet. You used to be strong, as strong as me, but not now. Not with this little piece of ass controlling you."

"You're taking a long time to get to the point."

"She is a fighter," Walter said. "Because when we had her pinned down on those pretty blue sheets, it was hard to keep her there. She fought us every step of the way." He licked his lips. "Sweet."

Ian shook his head. "Ash only remembers the two women feeding."

"Sharron and Candy. Sharron really wants to share some experiences with you. I am sure Ashley will understand the concept once we introduce her to the life. Sharron volunteered, you know, to go to the bar that night. Saw you and wanted to try, but we all know what that's like. And I don't think you thought to check the dishwasher for the wine glass before you cleared out of Ashley's house."

"She was milked."

Walter smiled. "I know. I did it."

Ian's eyes closed, but only for the few seconds he could spare to drop his guard. His fingers tightened over the grips until his joints hurt. Walter feeding off Ash was an image too horrific to think of. Holding a wine glass to her fingers until it filled, was not something he thought he could take.

"You don't appreciate what I gave you."

"Knitting needles, knives and flames? I'm supposed to appreciate that?"

Walter reached in his pocket, pulled something out and threw it at Ian. Ian caught it tight in his hand, staring at Walter before looking at the sterling silver lighter. The Stuart Crest was embossed on the side in full color showing only a little wear.

"I've been caring that piece of shit on me since 1953. Gave up smoking three decades ago, but couldn't let go of it." He shrugged and smiled. "Finally got to use it for a good purpose."

Ian turned his hand over, opening it to let the lighter drop. It hit the gravel with a crunch and he forced himself to forget about it.

"Ash was born in 1981, asshole. She didn't have anything to do with me walking out of The Dragon's Bridge."

"What's yours is hers and I'm thinking it hurts a hell of a lot more that I spent three hours with her rather than trying to get those same three with you."

"The injection?"

"What about it?"

"Why? Why not just turn her?"

Walter shrugged. "I OD'd that night."

"What?"

"Gave her ten times at least. How is that working out for you? I imagine she's pretty fucked up."

Ian couldn't think about it right now. Not with left and right getting closer.

Walter laughed. "1958. I think maybe you should have had a more open mind. I'm taking her back."

"No," Ian said. "You don't get her."

"Law of First Blood was mine. If she is still alive, I'm demanding possession. You were never meant to have her."

"You do not want to even think about the fight you will have if you go up against us."

"You have two choices," Walter said. "You can come with me now, come back to us and help us convince your friends to do the same, or I'm going to kill you myself."

Ian licked his lips and calculated all the distances around him.

"Brought an awful lot of minions with you for a job you want to do yourself."

"Want to?" He laughed. "I don't want to. I think we should share her, each taking the part we like best. I want the blood, you want copulation. That's actually something we could do simultaneously."

"You are a sick motherfucker," Ian said, yanking the fury back into place.

Walter laughed.

Without warning, Ian swung the bike around, heading down the one direction they weren't covering, the steep, edge of the ravine. Down the embankment, over the forest floor, his street wheels slipped on the moss and damp leaves, but he kept the bike upright. He heard Walter scream after him, but he didn't hear the words. In under a minute the voices faded and Ian was able to maneuver the bike back to a road.

When he was far enough away they could not possibly be near him, he skidded to a stop and reached in his fanny pack for his phone. He had to call home. He had to warn them.

The phone wasn't there.

She walked into the living room. Hunter stood looking at the artwork on the walls. For a frat house, the boys had good taste. A Dali Print, a Picasso. They leaned toward masculine, abstract which she had to admit, pretty much summed up the five of them.

Hunter was dressed down in jeans, a light black athletic jacket. White athletic shoes.

"Hey," she said.

He turned toward her, a smile on his face and she saw his Boston Celtics green, white and black T-shirt. He hailed from Bean Town and was probably as Irish as Jason.

"You're up," he smiled.

She looked up and down her body, her arms coming away from her before slapping back down. "Does appear so."

He stuck his hands into his pockets. "They told me you got it really bad."

She nodded.

"Got what?" Hunter asked.

Typical cop question. "I don't know what it was."

"No one took you to a doctor?"

She shook her head. "I didn't even think of it."

"You couldn't even wake up when I was here before."

"Nyquil. Double dose of Nyquil."

"Should you be taking Nyquil in your condition?"

She laughed and took a step forward. "I'm not pregnant, Hunter."

"Stuart loved the idea. You could tell."

"He did?"

"Yeah. And the two of you would have beautiful children. Really beautiful."

He said the words and they sounded nice, but the look in his eye held a glint like a knife's edge. He was trying to twist it.

"He would have married you. Very honorable man."

She swallowed hard. "I had a flu or something. It was no big deal."

"Too bad. It would have been fun to watch."

She tried to push down the regret he forced open without letting him know it bothered her.

"Recouping here was better for you than staying at your own place?" he asked.

"I had a lot of help. The boys took really good care of me."

"Especially your Mr. Stuart."

"Yes," she said. "Especially Ian."

"The measly bartender who isn't good enough to walk in your shadow."

"Excuse me?" she said. She had never heard Hunter say a mean word about anyone.

He looked at her, his eyes shining with a gleam that was uncharacteristic of his happy go lucky attitude. He didn't take the comment back or even try to expand on it. He let it hang in the air between them.

"You don't talk about him like that," she said. "I don't give a shit how many years we have together. You don't talk about Ian like that."

"Because he's the big important man in your life."

Quinn stepped into the room.

"Everything okay, Ashley?"

She smiled at him. "We're fine."

She looked at Hunter. He seemed taller. Harder. His personality off. "How did you know where I was?"

"Cooper's. Got your boyfriends address off his boss."

"Mike gave up Ian's place?"

"I might have mentioned a kidnapping charge if he didn't. The badge helped. And Mike remembered you. He didn't like to think that you had gone missing and his boy wonder might be involved."

"You told Mike…?"

He shrugged again like it was no big deal. "I let the asshole think what he wanted. Not my fault he came up with a bogus idea."

She twitched her head at him and tried to work it through. She had known Hunter for many years. Everything about him right now screamed wrong.

"What are your plans?" he asked sounding normal.

"I've been thinking about it," she said.

He took two steps forward but Ash didn't think anything about it. She turned around to face the other way.

"Like you really have a choice at this point?" he said. "Stay here with a bunch of toothless, bloodless bastards or try to get back the job you hated so much it drove you to drink like your daddy used to drink."

She turned slowly, coming to face him. Hunter Graham. Her best friend and back-up for five years-worth of shitty cases.

"Quinn," she called out and instantly he was in the open double doorway. He stepped into the room, always keeping his front facing Hunter.

Hunter's hands were out of his pocket, they hung by his sides. His back stood straight. She looked up at him, the fear hitting into her nerves like an electrical jolt. He wasn't there, she realized.

Quinn stepped in front of her and to her right, playing shield between them.

"The Doctor," Hunter said.

"One of my uses," Quinn said. "Play a mean game of HALO, too. Ashley, get out of the room."

"Where's your legendary switchblade?" Hunter asked Quinn. "They told me to watch out for it. Hear you were real, real spectacular with it when you still had your balls to go with your fangs."

"Actually," Quinn said calmly. "I don't need a blade to take out an asshole like you."

460

She didn't move.

"Do you know what I did last night?" Hunter asked. Even his voice was different. Deeper.

Hunter leaned toward her until only a few feet separated them.

"I killed Janey."

Ashley's gaze snapped up, locking on Hunter's eyes which had gone red. Quinn's arms came back, his hand finding her without ever taking his gaze off Hunter. He held her tight.

"Oh, it was sweet," he said taking a step toward her. "She was such a little thing and she put up such a fight. That was until I got my fingers on her throat and ripped it out. Then she couldn't scream at all and I got to take my time and lick up whatever dripped out."

"Quinn."

"Don't move," he said quietly.

"I'm supposed to take you back," Hunter said. "He said he wanted you back so that he could start teaching you personally. He figured you would come with me. But I don't like that idea."

His hand came up. His teeth long and shiny

"Who?" she asked, licking her lips. "Who told you I needed to go back?"

"Does it matter?"

She nodded her head. "Yeah. I want to know. Who could possibly boss you around when you are capable of so much more?"

461

He laughed. "Cop bullshit? Really Ash? You think that will work? We're smarter. Didn't you know that? Didn't they tell you that when they turned you? Faster, stronger. Everything is acute when it used to be bland."

She swallowed. "So you don't know?"

"It doesn't matter." He hissed at her. "You're not going back. You're staying right here. You're not pure enough to stand with the rest of us. They shot you up and destroyed everything you can be. You will never know what this feels like." He slapped his chest twice.

"Staying here isn't a bad idea. We like her company."

The voice came from the doorway. She looked over and found Travis standing in the doorway, Jason at his side.

Hunter's eyes narrowed at him. "They told me about you."

"Good things, I hope."

"Said you're an asshole who thinks he can rule the world."

"Ash," Travis said putting his hand out, palm up. "Get over here." He never took his gaze off Hunter.

Hunter watched her. Her whole body shook as a thousand happy memories of him flooded her brain.

"Ashley," Travis snapped.

She flinched, hearing Travis. She still held Quinn's hand, he was still in front of her, between her and Hunter.

She took a step.

462

Hunter charged, knocking Quinn out of the way. With a roar, he bent over at the waist tackling Ash like a linebacker around the middle, throwing her up against the wall, four feet off the ground, smashing into the shelves full of books and treasures.

Travis's hands came down on his shoulders, but it wasn't fast enough. Hunter had Ash by the throat, his natural nails digging in far enough to draw blood.

She brought her fists up high, smashing them down against Hunter's ears. He cried out in pain, falling backwards where Travis had the advantage. Travis grabbed Hunter, tossing him across the room, breaking the two framed drawings on the wall.

Hunter had his mind set on Ashley and he came after her again, even as the men stepped between them. Hunter grabbed and tossed, focusing only on Ash.

Eyes red. Fangs out. The superhuman strength ricocheted through the room like a misfired bullet, each and every time with Hunter back on his feet and heading toward Ash. She fought back with teeth and fists, proving to be every bit the cop she used to be. But she was feeble, still weak from the first attack.

Quinn picked up the wooden chair from the corner, smashing it to small pieces on Hunter's back. It only pissed Hunter off more and he swung around, grabbing a piece of the broken wood and raising his arm toward Quinn.

"No," Ash screamed. She rushed Hunter, hurling her whole body weight into his side, throwing him off balance and pushing him away from his target. The stake whizzed by Quinn's body, barely missing.

But Jason's shot was clear, his own stake in his hand. He brought it up faster than Hunter could move. Jason struck into Hunter's back, coming out his chest with a splatter of blood.

"No," Ash whispered.

Her Hunter was gone, replaced by this monster who wanted death and destruction, but watching him drop to his knees, his hand coming out to brace on the floor, she saw a glimpse of her old friend. His gaze came up to hers. His skin faded, turning white, aging like a mummy in a bad fifties movie. He collapsed on the floor and then he was gone, turning into a pile of dust.

Ash fell to her knees beside where he should have been.

"No," she said again. She reached into his jacket to his inner pocket and pulled out his wallet and his badge. Dropping the badge, she opened the wallet, sliding the photo of Hunter and Janey into her hand. They were only twenty years old at the time, both dolled up for their wedding.

Travis sank down beside her. "Are you okay?"

She shook her head. "No."

"Look at me."

She did.

He took the stuff out of her hand and reached under her back and knees lifting her and carrying her to the kitchen. He didn't seem to care that she fought to get down the whole way. He set her on the dining room table.

She tried to shake him off. Quinn shoved Travis out of the way

464

"Dammit," Quinn said. "Let me see."

She stopped fighting. And sat stone still, her eyes filling with tears.

Quinn gently rubbed a finger on the scratches on her neck.

"Why?" she asked.

Quinn stopped looking at her neck and looked at her. "You pushed him away."

Her eyes closed.

"He was your best-friend."

"No," she said. "My Hunter was gone."

Quinn put a hand to her cheek. "Thank you."

"Why would Hunter do that? We worked together. We played together."

"I don't know Ash." Travis said. He looked over his shoulder. "Jason get Stuart on the phone. Get him back here now."

"He was a vampire," she said.

"Yes," Travis said.

"None of you are like that."

"Hunter was here less than a week ago in the middle of the afternoon. He had to have been turned since then."

"By who? Why? Why him?"

She jumped down off the dining room table and pulled her fingers through her hair.

"It doesn't make sense." She walked back into the living room where the clothes were still on the floor. She took the badge and the picture and she held them close.

Jason came into the room, holding a cell phone. "I called. It's ringing upstairs in their bedroom."

Travis rolled his eyes. "Perfect Stuart. Just perfect."

Sweaty and hot, Ian dropped the bike at the bottom of the stairs and took them two at a time. He had never made that ride in so fast a time. Using his key, he let himself in. He panted in the entry way, listening for signs of life.

He heard a sound in the living room. Travis knelt on the floor of the thrashed room, picking up pieces of broken glass and putting them into a plastic bag. The books scattered on the floor amid the smashed shelves. The pictures askew on the wall and over turned plants.

"Where is she?"

Travis's eyes narrowed. "What happened to you?"

"Walter didn't leave. I ran into him along with some of his close, personal friends."

Travis sighed hard. "And how did that go?"

"Ash? Where the hell is Ashley?"

466

"Hunter stopped by."

"Hunter?"

Travis nodded.

"I know Hunter. He's funny. He likes to tease her."

"He wasn't teasing her tonight."

Ian looked over his shoulder then snapped his eyes back at Travis. The room had been through hell. Judging by the amount of footprints in the dirt from the smashed houseplants, it had a lot of helping getting there.

"He's dead," Travis said.

"Dead?"

"Jason staked him." He nodded at the broken chair. "With that."

It was suddenly hard to draw in a breath. "Hunter was a vampi—where's Ash?"

"Backyard."

"What? That's not safe and you know it."

"Quinn and Jason are with her."

Ian tore through the house, passing Evan carrying a broom.

The back door slammed against the house.

Still in the pajamas he had left her in, her feet still bare, she stood by the edge of the property staring over the view of downtown, the lights bright and pretty.

Jason sat to her right, looking relaxed in one of their chairs, his legs crossed. He held his six-inch, wooden handled knife in one hand, the point in the arm of the chair, spinning it slowly. She wasn't more than five feet from him. If anything came near her, Ian knew Jason could strike first. To the left, a little further away, Quinn sat with his back partially toward her as he watched the gates. He was hunched over a bit, his elbows on his knees, the pearl-handled switchblade he had carried for half a century in both hands. Both their gazes came up when Ian stepped out.

He walked straight to her, grabbing her by the shoulders, spinning her to him, pulling her close. She melted into him, her hands clutching at items that pressed against his chest.

"I'm so sorry. I should have been here."

"It was—" her voice trailed off. "He was violent and enraged. He killed Janey, for God's sake. He loved Janey more than anything."

Ian pulled back, holding her by the shoulders. "Are you okay?"

"I checked her out," Quinn said. "There's going to be some pretty impressive bruises, but the scratches are superficial. He couldn't get a grip and trust me, he was trying."

"What?" Ian asked. He lifted her chin to see the marks left by the nails.

Jason cleared his throat. "He tried to kill her, Stuart. Outright and it took three of us, plus her, to stop him. Whatever they used on her turning, they amped him up the opposite."

Ian pulled her back to him, holding her close. He looked between his friends. "Thank you."

"She's ours," Jason said softly, his voice deeper than normal. "No one touches her."

She stepped back, holding her hands out, showing Ian what she held. He reached up and took the badge. She handed him the photo. Hunter and his bride with a future. Ian looked up at Ash. "I'm sorry," he said again.

"They changed him because they wanted me."

Ian nodded. "I saw Walter. He's still here. He told me he was coming for you tonight and he must have sent Hunter to do the work." Ian slipped the photo and badge into his own back pocket and reached for her again. She could look at them later when it didn't hurt so much.

She nodded and a tear fell down her cheek. "He was my best friend. I got him killed."

Ian saw Jason's eyes close.

"You did good, Jason," Ian said, Ash pressed against his chest.

Jason looked at him, his head tilted. "I'm sorry," he said. "There wasn't any other choice."

"I know," Ian said. "You did good."

Jason nodded slowly but Ian was pretty sure this was a guilt Jason would carry for a while. Killing and Jason weren't strangers. If Quinn was the best anyone had seen with a blade, Jason was second, but it had been a lot of years since he took victims. This had been the close friend of a woman Jason held dear. Hunter's death would haunt Ash. And because of that, it would haunt Jason.

CHAPTER TWENTY-THREE

"I'm going to put her to bed."

Ash was on her second scotch. The tears had stopped but that didn't mean she felt any less sick.

"Um," she said, looking at Ian. "No offence, dear, but screw you."

"Ash, be reasonable."

"He was my best friend," she said. "He came here on orders to take me back. Where? I haven't been anywhere."

Ian looked to Travis. "Are you going to help me here?"

"You think I can do anything that will make her listen?"

"You could try."

Travis rolled his tongue in his cheek then took a drink of his scotch and spoke in a monotone. "Ash, we kind of think you're still not feeling good, and maybe you should rest while we talk about your problem and compare notes of what happened tonight."

She stared at him before looking back to Ian.

Travis looked to Ian. "I tried."

"Thank you. Thank you for that."

Travis took another drink. "How did you get past them?" he asked Ian.

"I had wheels and they didn't."

"Good riding."

Ian didn't respond.

She faced away from all of them, taking a drink. "I can't go to sleep," she said. "I can't get his face out of my mind. I sat across from him two weeks ago and he was funny and he laughed and he was concerned I was rushing too fast with my Scotsman. He wanted me to slow things down." She looked up. "He wanted a chance to get to know Ian on his own. So he would know it was okay. He was going to ask you out for a drink or something."

Ian stepped closer to her. "We're going to figure this out."

She nodded her head.

"Ash," Quinn said. "Is there anything you can think of, anything at all from that night that might help? A word? A phrase? Something he did or said?"

Ian looked at Travis who looked back.

"No," she said. "I don't remember."

Quinn dragged his hands through his hair and walked away.

"He was there for hours. You don't remember anything?" Jason asked.

She looked at Ian who looked at Travis.

Travis cleared his throat. "It may have been...um...*suggested*...at some point that that memory no longer be available."

472

Quinn looked at Jason. Jason looked back. They both turned to stare at Ian.

"You're kidding?" Jason asked.

Ian looked back at him.

"You didn't think that might be a bad idea until we were through this nightmare?"

"Jason, she was literally reliving it and hiding it from us. What we saw? It's what she couldn't contain. There was more and it was hurting her."

"What?" she asked.

Jason looked at her then back at him. "And you didn't tell her you did it."

"I would have. You know that. I was not trying to be underhanded. I was afraid if I ever told her they had existed, it would trigger it all over and next time I couldn't get them out."

Quinn looked at her. "It was that bad?"

"Aye," Ian said. "We were only seeing the tip."

"No one ever tells me anything," she muttered sitting down. "My life, and I have no idea what is happening in it half the time."

Travis closed his eyes and knelt down in front of her, his hands on her knees.

"It's a vampire trick," he said. "Used for trapping a victim. Like a mind control where we get you to do what we want. It's called 'suggestion'. We all can do it, probably you, too, if one of us showed you. Right now, it was used to erase all your memories

473

of what they did to you. Stuart is right. I saw it, too. You were in a lot of pain, mentally and physically. One of us was going to have to deal with it and take the memories away and Stuart stepped up as mate. He came to me right after he did it and let me know."

"You knew?" Jason snapped.

Travis stood up. "Yes, I knew. It had to be done. No information was worth the cost of what it was doing to her."

"Can we retrieve anything?"

"You want to?" Ian snapped. "Because you know to do that would flood her with every single detail and it would be like reliving it all over again, Mr. Super Hero."

"Fuck you," Jason sighed before walking away.

"I remembered?" she said. "I knew what happened?"

Ian leaned on to her, pulling her close. "Aye, you did. And I took it all and I am not going to second guess myself on the decision."

"Does that mean you have it now?"

He shook his head. "Doesn't work like that, honey. They're just ideas, I guess, and I pulled them out and they disappear."

"Where are they?"

Quinn came forward to kneel down in front of her. "How's your breathing?"

She shrugged.

"Trouble?"

"I guess because I don't understand how this works."

He put his hands on her knees. "It's not important how it works. We move on."

She looked at Ian. "Every time I have a bad memory, are you going to do this to me?"

"Yeah," Jason sneered. "Every time she has a bad memory, are you going to do this to her?"

"Irishman, do not even think of over stepping your ground with accusations. I will take you out," Ian said.

Jason stepped closer. "Really? Because while you were off getting a little exercise, I was killing your girlfriend's best-friend. I think tonight our perspectives might be different but if you want to step outside, I'm game for that, too."

Ashley stood, stepping between them her hand on each of their chests.

"Scotland and Ireland will withdraw their armies. This is neither the time nor the place, I am *never* the excuse and if either of you have a problem with that, then *I* will step outside with you. We will come to a place in the next minute that helps what happened and not bring it into our house because you are both assholes."

It was Jason who broke the stare and looked at her. "Did you say *our* house?"

She looked up at those green eyes, seeing a sparkle.

"I apologize if I over stepped my boundary. Heat of the moment. Now, withdraw."

He smiled, both his hands up in surrender and backed away. "I don't have any problem with the statement," he said. "Though it might be interesting to see if you could kick both our asses at once."

She took a step toward him and Quinn put his hand on her shoulder. "You're off fitness programs until I clear you so you will not be engaging in any fist fights." He looked at Jason. "She was a cop, you idiot. The body might be weak, but the knowledge is there. I will put down wagers she will lay you on your ass."

She looked at Quinn who stood closest.

"What does he look like?" She asked. "Walter?"

Jason laughed. "Not something you might need to know, right?"

"Shut up," Ian said. "Why?"

"He had to get in. How?" she asked.

"We don't know."

She waved her hands at him. Ian looked to Travis and Quinn.

"About six-feet," Quinn said. "Maybe a little more."

"Light hair."

"Brown eyes," Ian added. "He's pretty plain looking, I think. Nothing really stands out. He's there and you know it."

"That's because he's usually trying to kill you," Travis said.

She stared at the floor, thinking hard.

Travis went over to the drawer and pulled out a pad and purple pen. "Stuart," he said, holding them up.

Ian grabbed them and leaned over the dining room table.

"Does it matter how he got in at this point?" Evan asked.

"Probably not," Travis said, "but it would answer one of the questions."

The room went quiet.

Two minutes later, Ian stood straight and handed her the quick, line drawing.

She held it and stared, her shoulders sagging.

She laughed a little.

"We're finding humor in our current situation?" Travis asked.

She looked up from the drawing. "Your current situation is almost completely my fault. Somehow I find my safe haven a little tarnished knowing I dragged you into this."

"You dragged *us* in?" Ian snapped. "You do realize you have a doctor standing four feet from you at this minute because of what was done to *you* because of us. *Me*."

"Which would be my fault, too." She held up the drawing, facing it toward them. "I know how he got in."

"How?"

"I invited him," she smiled.

Travis came closer. "That Monday night?"

She shook her head. "No. It was about a month ago."

"Make sense, woman," Jason snapped.

"My dishwasher broke. Ian had to work. I called a repair man, made an appointment, only they came right over." She closed her eyes, laughed and smiled, feeling all sorts of stupid. "It was right after dark. It was this guy only, he had a mustache and I invited him in, he fixed the dishwasher and left."

"You never told me," Ian said.

"It was a dishwasher. Why would I? Living alone and taking care of my own crap actually came under the heading of what I used to do."

"You do know I could have looked at it," Ian said.

"Yeah. Probably. But why? Something breaks, I get it fixed. I don't worry about evil vampires tricking their way into my house."

Ian groaned and walked away. "A month ago?" he asked.

"Yeah, about."

"He has been coming and going for weeks."

"Max's injections," Quinn said. "That's how Walter did it. Got in the house when she was alone, a little 'suggestion', she's out and he can do what he wants. She wakes up when you come in and doesn't know he was even there."

"I think I might be sick," Ian said.

"What's 'make a den?'" she asked softly.

478

"Den's only a group that sticks together," Evan said. "The laws are in effect, but it's a safety thing so you aren't alone."

"No," she said standing up. "What is required of the actual den? The building where they hide?"

Quinn shrugged. "Dark. Four walls, a ceiling and ways to block the sun."

"There might be facilities or not. Kitchen is not required," Jason added. "They're not exactly cooking their meals."

"What about rooms?" Ash asked.

"What are you thinking?" Ian asked.

"I'm thinking we're all idiots."

"Okay," Travis said, walking away. "I can live with that assumption. Primary would want his own space. If they have the other positions filled, they might want some, too. Everyone else, whatever is available."

"Positions?" she asked.

"Primary is top. There are a couple of others below that before you get to the passives who are just basically members."

"A floor? A couch?"

"Aye," Ian said. "Newborns could be on a floor. Passives, too. I've seen dens where they crowded a dozen or more into one room."

"Nine," Ash said. "You said they had nine."

"Yeah," Travis said. "Max said Walter and four others, two of them the girls, plus the four Newborn."

She laughed again and dragged her hand through her hair.

"Does that laugh send chills up anyone else's spine?" Jason asked.

"And if you five knew where they were, what would you do?"

They all exchanged glances.

"Doesn't killing them go against your laws?" she asked.

"Aye, Fourth Law of Slaying. Vampires can't kill vampires."

"No," Quinn said. "Law of Slaying is no murder. Killing for defense because we are under attack is justifiable."

"He's right." Travis said.

"And how dangerous is that?" She asked. "Five to nine."

"You saw us take them the other night and we won," Evan said.

"It's dangerous and I could lose one of you," she said.

"Depends on a lot of factors," Travis said. "Depends on how good they are, how many Newborns and who stays here with you. Have to have a good knife back here in case it's a trap and they are really trying for here."

Travis stared at her and she blinked back.

"Where the fuck are they and how do you know?"

She had never heard that tone come out of him.

"Can't we move? Go someplace else?" she asked.

"They will always be after us, Gorgeous, and I don't think we can get all of us out of here even packing light without one of them able to track. We're good, but not that good."

She walked away, thinking hard, weighing option.

"Where?" Travis snapped. She spun to stare at him.

They were all looking at her.

"Cop 101?" she suggested.

"I don't think any of us are in the mood, Ash," Ian said.

"Take our first conversation, inject it into our second, and consider 1,234 square feet of prime, historic, real estate only four miles from here."

"What?" Travis snapped.

"Oh crap," Ian said, looking to Travis. "Walter can get into her house."

Travis chuckled.

"He went in and invited them all. They have been there since they left the church."

The room went quiet.

Until Ash finally broke it.

"Please don't go. I can't lose anyone else."

Travis stared at her as seconds ticked into a minute.

"Stuart stays," he said. "You're good on your own, and the four of us should be able to take out nine easy."

She closed her eyes. "The tats. You can get up earlier than they can. Out the door before them. By how much?"

"Depends on sunrise and how that goes and the cloud cover," Quinn said.

"Maybe half-hour."

Her head came up and she stared at them. "Burn it down."

"What?"

"Go out before they are up. Block the doors and burn the house to the ground."

They all stared at her like she lost her mind.

"Ash, that's your house," Ian said.

She swung to face him. "Really? Because I'm thinking it's four walls with a roof overhead held up against five men I adore. I'm willing to lose one of those things. I am not willing to lose the other. I just gave you permission to incinerate a piece of expensive real-estate that is actually insured for a small fortune. I'm sorry," she said, leaning toward him. "Do I get insurance on any of you if you come back dead?"

Almost all of them stared at the floor until Jason brought his gaze up to stare at her. "I don't know," he said. "I think we were all just given a hell of compliment."

"I think the point was made," Travis said softly. "And quite eloquently."

"So get off your asses and come up with a plan to make this work." She looked at the clock then back to them. "Sunrise is what? About six? It's four p. m. That gives us about fourteen hours to learn how to make a bomb."

Ash heard Travis leaned over to whisper to Ian. "I'm still Primary, right?"

CHAPTER TWENTY-FOUR

Her men had a lot of years behind them doing things Ash figured she really didn't want to know about. They had learned many things in a variety of areas—she learned—from martial arts to guns to archery to more knives. Defense had been part of the reason.

Boredom had been a bigger one. All those years trying to keep amused kept them busy.

Turned out Jason not only had *The Anarchist Cookbook* on his shelves, but a variety of other titles giving him instructions on how to build a device that would spark the gas line connection where it attached to the house.

A little scrounging for make shift parts in the garage with Quinn and in no time they had it built. Evan's obsession with working on his 1970 Dodge Challenger, lay a variety of choices in front of Jason and Quinn.

While they worked on their project, Evan turned their case of Bacardi 151 into Molotov Cocktails. When he finished with them, he moved onto a case of scotch. If anyone had a chance to leave the house while it was in flames, her boys would be ready.

"You know we can't get in to remove anything you want, right?"

"Everything I really need is in Cardmen bank in old town in a large safe deposit box. And I don't even need that. What I need is right here and I'm going to keep it."

He leaned over and kissed her. "We're going to have to start over on your pajama collection."

Four hours later, a plan in place, Ash wrapped her fingers around the glass and took another drink of the remaining scotch. She had no idea how much she had had tonight.

Travis sat across from her and one over, his own glass in his hand.

Ian was besides her, leaning toward her, his shoulder up against hers.

The exhaustion was palpable.

"Why is there so much alcohol in this house?"

"Takes more to get us drunk so we have to stock more," Travis said,

Ian looked at her. "Mike gave me his discount and let me buy it by the case from our distributors."

"Handy perk," she said.

All of them sounded wiped out. Even her own voice to her ears was off. So she let Ian fill up her glass again

She looked at Ian. "How did you get turned?"

"Same way as everyone. Violently and against my will."

"Can you tell me more?"

She saw him look at Travis. Travis raised his eyebrows then saluted with his glass.

Ian stared at her. He sighed. "1926. New York. I had only been in the country a couple of years."

"What happened?"

"I was shooting pool one night at Roosevelt's Pub. Three guys joined me. Thomas, Joseph and George."

"You remember their names."

"You never forget the details," Travis said. He thought and smiled. "Unless someone makes you."

Ian went on talking. "We shot for a couple of hours. I didn't have a lot of money. I was only working at the slaughter house so winning big that night was pretty important."

"What happened?" she asked.

"We left. They suggested a short cut down an alley. Next thing I knew I was pinned up against the bricks. George on one side, Thomas on the other and Joseph at my throat."

She closed her eyes, seeing it, feeling it.

"They switched off. I don't know for how long. I passed out. Woke up two days later in a stable stinking of manure near a horse. They had even cleaned me out, taking all my winnings."

"You were alone?"

He nodded. "Had to figure the whole thing out myself."

"How did you do that?"

"Rather quickly. There was on old man who came in carrying a shovel. I guess he was there to clean up." Ian paused, swallowing hard. "I killed him. I didn't even know what I was doing or why but I drained him. Over the next couple of months I wandered the streets at night, found others like me. We joined into a gang of sorts. It was the start of a pretty horrific period of my life."

"So everyone comes scary."

He bumped her with his shoulder. "'cept you."

She looked across the table. Travis was watching her.

"You going to tell me?" she asked.

"You know there's not a single more personal question you could possibly ask me."

"I know."

"Why do you want to know? It's not important."

"I just do."

Travis looked at Ian. Ian stared back. "What do you think?"

Ian shrugged. "It's up to you."

Travis took another drink, draining the glass. He refilled.

Travis sat in his chair, leaning forward, his elbows on the table and looked at her. "1928," he said. "San Francisco. I was followed home to my shitty, second floor apartment."

"Okay," she said.

"Knock at the door at 3 a. m. and like an idiot, I opened it."

She was watching him.

"Asshole asks if he can come in and get a light for his cigarette."

"Three a…and you let a stranger in?"

"It was 1928. You didn't think of things like bogey men."

"So you let him in and he attacked you."

"No, I let him in, I lit the fucking cigarette, he finished it and *then* he attacked me."

She looked from Ian to Travis, seeing no expression on either of their faces.

Travis watched her. Ian stared at the table.

"That's bad, but it could have been worse. Why didn't you want me to know this?"

Travis pointed at Ian. "Because he was the asshole."

She turned to stare at Ian. With pursed lips, he was looking at his glass like it was the most fascinating thing in the world.

"You turned *Travis*?"

He looked at her and shrugged. "I was hungry."

She closed her eyes, processing the information. She opened her eyes to look at him. "You turned your best-friend. Into a vampire. Because you were hungry?" Her voice went up at the end, adding a tone that echoed through the whole room.

"Wow," Ian said talking to Travis. "She makes it sound real stupid when she says it like that."

"Actually I've always thought it was pretty God damn stupid," Travis said.

"Oh, you got over it."

"Did you stay with him?" she asked.

"Aye, I did. And he took fifteen hours to wake-up and then I taught him everything I could."

"Which wasn't a hell of a lot."

Ian sat up. "We were together about a year and half. Hanging together, hunting together, but never sharing. He made me laugh."

"You pissed me off."

Ian pointed at Travis. "You didn't speak to me for thirty years."

"I don't think I really had a whole hell of a lot I wanted to say to you."

Ashley laughed. She couldn't help it. They were like an old married couple sometimes.

"We shared a room," Ian said. "In San Fran. Two single beds in a dump, he took his, I took mine and I went to sleep every morning laughing at whatever he was talking about next. He never shut up and he always interfered in everything."

"Really? Shocker." She laughed.

"One night, he didn't come home."

Ignoring the shocker comment, Travis started to talk. "Until 1958 and he walks into this bar I'm sitting in with my den in New

Orleans. Still remembered him, of course, so I might have tricked him to a walk into the back alley where I beat the shit out of him." He smiled. "That was kind of fun."

"Funny," Ian said. "Don't remember enjoying that."

Travis smiled. "I decided I felt a lot better and we started talking a bit until we realized we didn't want to do it anymore."

"We got up, walked out of the bar together, got on a bus without looking back and headed west."

"You guys take this real serious."

The both looked at her.

"Taking care of each other. I don't think I've ever seen anything like it."

"It's probably because you've never run into a den of vampires before."

She shook her head. "You two don't do what you do because you're vampires. You do it because you care about your family and about each other. Both of you would do anything you had to protect every aspect of what you have. It's pretty human of you."

Travis looked at Ian. Ian looked back. "I like her," Travis said. "She's smart."

Ian turned his head to face her "So do I. Which is why I'm taking her to bed right now."

She looked at Ian. "You smoked?"

He nodded. "It was a good way to get morons to open their doors in the middle of the night."

490

Travis sighed. "I would hit you except you're too far away and I'm too damn tired to move."

"How does it work?" she asked. "The changes and deciding to be different? All of you did it."

"What we were doing, it wasn't easy, it broke the laws of our society and targeted us. Walter found who Stuart left with and he was furious and demanded not only our blood but death."

She looked at Travis. "He hates you, too."

Travis laughed. "Oh, hell yeah. He thought Stuart left to be with me, when Stuart claimed to Walter to be straight."

"So he wants you back," she said to Ian.

Ian shook his head. "No, he wants me dead."

"What kind of changes did you have to do?"

"Primarily? Diet. We used to survive on blood. We had to try to mimic that with high protein, undercooked meats as we adapted. Real food tasted like shit and we had to train our bodies to accept it."

"We spent quite a few years pretty sick," Ian said. "Getting going was hard. Finding work that we could make it to was harder. But we did it. Keeping busy. Making sure we had as little down time as possible, which gave our minds time to shift."

"No bikes?" she asked.

Ian laughed. "Oh hell no, but we made sure to get in some physical activity to build us up and revert to normal chemicals in our body. We were mimicking human behavior trying to make it take with us."

"First year was hell," Travis said, "but then we met Quinn and he had already been doing it for about three months, but he was cheating. He had gone into Chinatown and found a real, live Ancient older than any of us. Quinn told him what he was and what he wanted and the old man came up with a potion that helped the process and reduced the cravings. We were downing it like Gatorade."

"Ancient called it our 'Ace in the Hole,'" Ian said.

"And none of you gave up?"

"There were a couple of others we picked up on the way," Ian said. "Max was one. Then Carl. Juan."

"Hannah," Travis said.

"Hannah," Ian nodded. "She was cool. Same program doing the same things we did, but it didn't take and she left. Max is the only one who came back."

"Hannah was sweet," Travis smiled sadly. "We liked her. She really tried. Had the right convictions, the cravings were too much for her."

"What makes a vampire decide one day to give up the life they have been living for so many decades?"

"We each had our own reasons. Something that made us wake up one evening and realize we still have a conscience. For me," Ian said, "there was no one event. I just sort of glided to the concept. For him," he said, pointing at Travis, "he had an awakening one night after a Christmas Eve service."

492

"You go to church?" she asked. "I thought everyone was atheist."

"I am," Travis said. "But I like to go and see the colors and scents and the ceremony. This one night turned out to be important."

"And then there is me," she said. "Turned by a villain, adopted by hopeless romantics, sick in ways that alter my existence—with more money than we will ever need."

"I don't know," Ian said. "I think you have a few more uses than all that."

"And I don't want to hear what they are," Travis laughed.

Ian smiled. "She makes a London Broil with a Baked Potato and Roasted Asparagus on the side to die for."

Travis sat up straighter. "I could hear more about that."

"And this mushroom/garlic sour cream to go on the potatoes. I don't know how she does it or what's in it, but you will take hostages to get your hands on it."

"What do I get for dessert?"

Ian smiled at her. She was watching him and trying not to laugh. "She's pretty basic on dessert, but more than willing to share. Ben and Jerry's Mint Chocolate Cookie. Makes for amazing kissing."

Travis laughed. "You had to ruin it for me."

She kissed Ian's hand. "I'm tired," she said.

"Can we go to bed?" Ian asked.

She nodded her head. He stood up and she went with him, his hand still in hers. "Want me to carry you?" he asked.

She chuckled. "No, I can make it."

Travis smiled. He was so tired he had almost sunk all the way to the table.

"You going to be able to make it upstairs?" She asked.

He screwed up his face but didn't move. "I'm still in charge, right?"

"Night, Travis."

He saluted them with his glass before lifting it to his lips. She saw him down all that was left.

Ian leaned over, lifting her anyway, carrying her toward the stairs.

He carried her to the room. She turned the handle so he could push the door open with his foot. He dropped her on the bed, watching her bounce a little and wishing he could crawl right in there beside her.

"The ride home was pretty intense. I need a shower."

She got up on her knees and leaned forward, sniffing his chest. "Yeah," she smiled.

He reached up, batting her on the end of the nose with his finger. "You want to take one with me?"

494

"No. I'm too tired, but I'll take you up on that tomorrow."

He reached over and kissed her lightly. "I get to wash your hair?"

"You may wash my hair, you very strange man."

He laughed out loud and turned to the desk, emptying his pockets, before reaching for the buttons on his pants.

"What's that?" she asked.

He looked down at the envelope. Tonight had sucked. Every aspect of the night had been a nightmare to live and listen to. He looked at the envelope and saw in it a small slice of salvation.

"Check it out," he said.

She walked over to him while eyeing him. Her movements were stiff, unsure. Picking it up, she opened it, the three rings falling into her hand. She pursed her lips and stared at them.

The expression of exhaustion and grief seemed to melt away. She looked up at him. "Something you forgot to tell me?"

He looked at her, his mouth opening and closing. This wasn't the way he had wanted to discuss it with her, but the door was open. A couple of well-placed words and he might be able to give her at least one good night's rest. He tried again. "Travis got bored this last week. He started planning our wedding. Jason helped."

Her head tilted. "I didn't know we were having a wedding."

"All four of them are in on it."

She closed her eyes tight. "That's truly intrusive and very embarrassing."

He smiled at her. "Believe it or not, they mean well and at some point they will do it again. That's just the way it is living in our circumstances."

She stood with her hand out, and opened her eyes, the rings shining in the lamp light. She looked at them closely. "They're beautiful," she said, poking at them. "Travis bought these?"

Ian nodded.

"Where did he get them?"

Ian stood close watching the expressions on her face. Surprise. Awe. Maybe some anticipation.

"Internet," he said. "Specialty site he won't reveal."

"They're Celtic, right?"

He nodded his head slowly.

"Do you know what they mean?"

"Sure." He reached, picking up her band and looking close. He pointed at the markings. "It's a double strand knot. See the two strands intertwined? They don't stop. They continue into itself, never ending. See," turning it so all the sides were visible. "It's the symbol of eternal love."

He held it toward her. She took it and spun it around, looking at it from all directions. Putting it back in her hand. She picked up the engagement ring and showed it to him.

"Can't help you there. I know nothing about diamonds, though I know he wouldn't have ordered it off the Internet unless he thoroughly checked out the seller and had it verified."

She looked up at him, her head tilted, her chin out.

He smiled. "I'm not opposed to the idea."

"Not being opposed to an idea is not the same as liking an idea."

"He picked out a place in New Orleans, in the French Quarter."

She smiled. "I've never been to New Orleans."

And that sounded like a yes to him.

"We lived there in the late fifties. Pretty cool place though it's probably changed. We've talked about heading back. We have a friend there. I think I mentioned her. Nanette? With the tattoos? She would probably like to do the ceremony if that is okay with you."

She held her hand up, the rings in her palm. "Ahead of yourself?"

He reached, putting a hand behind her, circling her waist. He pulled her until she was pressed up against him. Her hand closed around the rings and rested against his chest.

"You could talk me into it," he said, leaning over to kiss her.

She leaned away from him. "I have to talk you into it?"

He was smiling when his mouth finally settled over hers. "Or we could just do it."

"Get married?"

He nodded and put his forehead to hers.

She leaned her head back, smiling, her hands on his chest, the rings still held tight. "Is that an official proposal?"

He kissed her neck, his hands spreading across her back. "You get my name, Mrs. Stuart."

She giggled and pushed on his chest.

"It's up to you," he smiled. "If this is something you want."

"Your name? You're asking me if I want your *name*?"

"What do you think of white?" He asked. "I don't like off-white. I like white with maybe really sexy, risqué underthings that no one but me knows about."

She laughed. "You've actually taken the time to think about that?"

He smiled and nodded. "My ride tonight before the trouble started. Had a good hour to think of nothing but. I mean, come on, someone puts that idea in your head and it's not going to become obsessive?"

He saw her connecting the dots. "It was Travis's idea and he told you right before your ride."

She sat down, cross-legged on the bed. "I think the whole thing is…" she looked up at him. "Shockingly unexpected. I never considered you would ask and I'm thinking now, you never intended to."

He shrugged. "Never thought we needed to. Mated for life actually trumps marriage, but marriage sounds cool, too. He said it and I got to thinking about it, man, I can't tell you how much I love the idea." His smiled. "To call you my *wife*."

She looked up at him. "The idea of a wedding or a marriage? There is a difference."

"On the ride I figured I like white," he said. "And lace. Lace is good. And a veil. Have to have a veil." He closed his eyes and purred a little. "I could get into this. Just waiting at the top of an aisle with you walking down only for me." He blew out a breath. "Sexy."

"White. Sexy? Right." She laughed again. "You do know what century you're in?"

He smiled. "Pretty much the same one I've always been in. Did I mention the underwear? Think I would like to pick that out."

"I don't think Travis will let you do that."

"I don't think Travis will be assisting you in doing that," he smiled.

He flopped down on the bed beside her, lying on his side, braced up on his elbow.

She leaned over, kissing him until he was moaning, his hand coming up to hold her cheek.

He looked at her, his mouth open, his breathing hard. "I don't think I got an answer."

She kissed him, stood up and walked to the desk. Turning, she put the rings back in the envelope.

"Go take your shower," she said.

"Are we good? Did we settle this?"

She looked at him smiling. "Yes. We settled it." She set the envelope on his desk, on top of his sketchpad.

"We're getting married?" he asked.

She looked over her shoulder at him and nodded her head nice and slow.

He wasn't sure the butterflies in his gut were normal, but he knew this might be the best decision he ever made.

He walked over to the desk, picking up the envelope. Opening it, he dropped the rings into his hand, keeping one and sliding the bands back in. He set the envelop back down.

He turned around to her, watching her face. She tried to hide the smile. The edge of her lips went up, her eyes looking bright. There was color in her cheeks that hadn't been there for a couple of days.

He stepped close and paused, waiting for her to fidget and on cue she shifted from foot to foot while she watched his hands, making him smile.

"I am not getting on one knee."

Her head fell back and she laughed.

He picked up her left hand and with a deep breath, he slid the ring onto her third finger then took a long extra minute to stare at it, his thumb touching it. The fit was perfect.

"Damn," he said. "That looks incredible on you."

She pulled her hand back, holding it up, her fingers spread wide to stare.

"Oh shit," she smiled. She put her other hand to her tummy and took a deep breath.

"You okay?" he asked.

She threw her arms around his neck, pulling him down, her mouth on his. He pushed forward until she was leaning back against the desk, his arms around her, his lips on hers. Some things made a simple kiss better, hotter, when you weren't even trying. Holding a woman in your arms knowing you were on countdown to her being your wife—that was one of those things.

He smiled and leaned over to kiss her one more time on her neck, taking his time sucking. "I love the taste of your neck."

"Shower," she said.

"Come with me."

"I really am not up for it tonight. But tomorrow I will let you soap me up anyway you want."

He perked up. "That doesn't sound bad. I might even be able to wait."

He moaned and backed up, holding the hand that had the shiny. "Take me ten minutes."

She took three steps back and sat down on the edge of the bed, her hand out in front of her, staring at the ring.

He smiled at her then closed the door behind him.

Quinn stood outside the bathroom, leaning on the wall, his hands in his pockets, his head lowered. Ian came down the stairs, slowing down as he got there.

"What?" he asked.

Quinn looked up at him, his expression off.

"What's wrong?" Ian asked.

"Figured you'd be down for a shower after the ride."

"Aye."

"She stepped between me and Hunter."

"What are you talking about?"

"In the fight. In the living room. Hunter got a stake and had me dead to target. She stepped between us, saving me and opening Jason for the kill shot."

His head leaned back. "No one told me."

"We didn't get into details."

"You were with her when Hunter got here?"

Quinn nodded. "Mostly. He seemed off so I stayed on the stairs to listen. Hunter was her best friend. I didn't know how to deal with that."

"That wasn't Hunter anymore. You know that."

"I don't think that was it," Quinn said. "I think if it had been the same Hunter she always knew, she would have made the same choice."

Ian nodded. "I don't think she would have killed him, but she would have sided with us if forced to choose."

"What do I do? She killed her best friend for me."

Ian rubbed his face and tried to think of an answer that would give Quinn a good night's sleep.

"She's never had a family before."

"Except Hunter," Quinn said. "They were damn close. Tonight, she might as well have put the stake through him herself," Quinn said.

"I think for anyone of us, she would have. She adopted us and made us realize there was a big hole in our lives. We needed her."

"He would have killed me."

"And you would have let him to save her."

"Yeah," Quinn said.

Ian moved toward the bathroom. "Quinn, go to bed. It's late and you shouldn't think about this anymore."

"But what she did."

"She would do again. She will mourn the loss of her old friend and be thankful for the survival of her new."

"You're sure?"

Ian smiled. "Actually I don't think she's thinking of any of them right now as she just got engaged."

Quinn perked up. "What? You did it?"

"You knew, too."

"Helped pick out the rings. We're going to New Orleans? When?"

"You're her doctor."

His shoulder sank. "Oh, yeah. I can give her a check-up tomorrow and see how things are. I think she should be fine to travel in a month or two."

"That long?" Ian sighed.

"You're getting married," Quinn grinned.

"Already took a mate."

"Yeah, but that's only a declaration to each other. This is different. We never go anywhere and now we get to go to New Orleans. And she's going to have a dress. All of us will have to have new, coordinating suits. There's going to be music and vows and we'll have to have a cake and a big dinner afterwards. We have to plan this."

"You know, you guys are getting into this wedding idea to strange proportions."

"You're going to need a best man. Travis, right?"

Ian shook his head. "Travis is giving the bride away. I was thinking of you."

"What? Really? Oh, cool. Yeah, that's cool. I can do that. I want to do that. I get to hold the rings and everything?"

Ian laughed. He stepped through the bathroom door. "Quinn go to bed. We've been engaged twenty minutes. I think we will have time to iron out the details."

CHAPTER TWENTY-FIVE

Ian had just finished buttoning up his shirt when the hard pounding came at his door. He looked over to Ash sleeping on her side. She stirred and readjusted herself on the pillow but didn't wake.

He grabbed the doorknob and pulled it back. "Stop," he whispered. "She's asleep."

Evan looked panicked. "You got to come now."

"What?"

"Just come."

Ian looked at her. As long as she stayed asleep it was fine. Ian leaned into his closet, grabbed his black shoes and pulled a pair of socks out of the drawer. He picked up the check he had written this morning, folded it and slipped it into his shirt pocket. He closed the door quietly behind him and followed Evan barefoot.

They got all the way to the kitchen. Travis and Jason were staring into the backyard. Quinn poured a cup of coffee and handed it to Ian. Evan stood right beside Ian.

"Can I get my shoes on?"

Travis pointed out the back window. "Our plans have changed."

With coffee in one hand and shoes in the other, Ian stepped up to the window to see what the hell was going on.

Walter sat in one of their deck chairs, his back to the house, facing the view of the city.

"Oh fuck," he sighed. He reached up and put his shoes on the counter while he tried to get his lungs to start. His gaze shifted to the stairs.

"He's been there twenty minutes," Travis said.

"And you just now thought to come and get me?"

"I was hoping he would just go away. Where's Ash?"

"Still asleep. Thought I would leave her that way."

"Until she wakes up and finds him here," Jason said, pointing out the window.

Ian shook his head. "No, she's out pretty good. We were up for hours last night talking about the wedding."

"You think so?" Jason smiled sarcastically.

Ian looked at him, seeing Jason look behind Ian.

"Crap," Ian muttered. He turned.

She had pulled on a pair of black yoga pants, a large blue sweater that hung to her hips and grey wool socks.

"Hi honey," he smiled. "Why don't you go sleep in and we'll come get you for dinner."

She glared at him and moved to the window.

"Humph," she mumbled.

He looked at Travis.

Travis smiled back. "Talking about the wedding?" he asked happily.

Ian reached in his pocket and pulled out the check, handing it to him. "For the household."

Travis took it, unfolded it to read the numbers and nodded his head.

"That cover the rings?" Ian asked.

"Yeah. Easily. You empty your personal account?"

"She's not paying for her own wedding rings."

"God, anyone who met you wouldn't need to know any details of your life to know what century you were born in. Did you want to discuss a dowry? Maybe a couple of pigs and a chicken?"

"You know I am standing right here and can hear you," she said.

"Aye," Ian said. "About that. Jason, utility drawer, duct tape."

"Were you going to hold her down or did you want me to," Jason asked. "She can't breathe but I'm thinking she's wiry."

Travis motioned out the window with his hand. "And he's not going anywhere."

Ian looked at the clock on the stove. "Sun's up in about an hour. He can't wait forever."

"So you think if we ignore him he will go away?" Evan asked.

"Aye, he will," Ian nodded. "But he'll be back and he will be pissed. He does not like being kept waiting."

"So, what do we do? It's one of him and all of us with a small arsenal waiting to hit her house."

Ian stared out into the backward, thinking of a hundred memories Walter's mere presence brought up, none of them good. "We were thinking of having Jason and Evan doing the readings during the ceremony." He said casually.

One 'yes' sounded fast.

The second 'yes' sounded younger and more excitable.

Ian smiled while he hated the man out back. Players for the wedding were all set. Now he had to get rid of the roadblock between them.

"You want to know what I think?" Travis asked.

Ian shook his head. "Not really. I don't think it's going to make me happy."

"He's after her. Not us. Keeping us alive so we get to see it, that's the goal."

Ian looked at him. "He doesn't like women."

"No, but he loved you and making your girl into the very thing you fought to escape, now that gives him a purpose."

"So nothing has changed. We need to kill him," Ash said.

"Ash, we take down a Primary and the den will come after us."

"Their whole den is coming after us anyway. What's the difference? Quinn said it last night. It's justifiable as we're under attack."

"White," Ian said. "I like white."

Travis laughed. "You really think white is appropriate with your sleeping arrangements?"

Ian looked at him and smiled. "Aye. I like the symbolism. And I like old fashioned. And I think the concept of a veil to lift is out of the world on old school romance."

Ian reached for his shoes. Sitting on the dining room chair, he pulled them on.

"What are you going to do?" she asked.

He ignored her.

He finished and stood, taking a deep breath.

"What the fuck do you think you are doing?" she asked.

He tapped her nose. "That's the last fuck that comes out of your mouth. Understand?"

"What do you want us to do?" Quinn asked.

"Protect her, whatever it takes. Including tying down and locking up if you have to."

"You are not going to—"

She was cut off when Jason wrapped his hand around her head, covering her mouth and yanking her to his chest, keeping her struggling body trapped with his strength.

"We can do that," Jason smiled. He winced when she elbowed him, but didn't let go.

"Are you okay with this?" Travis asked. "You're walking into a trap."

"We have to face him sometime."

"And he set up all the rules, rules we don't know."

Ian picked up his coffee mug and looked at the door.

"Do we have a plan?" Travis asked.

Ian pursed his lips at Travis and rolled his eyes. He reached for the handle of the back door. Ash was screaming against the hand, struggling to get away.

Quinn's hand came down on Stuart's shoulder. He picked up Stuart's free hand and slapped the pearl-handled switchblade into it.

"You're left-handed, so hard in at the right ear, pull all the way back and across. You have to hit the spine or he recovers enough to come after you."

"You're giving me knife fighting lessons?"

Quinn smiled. "Didn't you know? It's never been me. It's this damn blade. Thinks on its own."

"Thanks," Ian smiled. He shoved the knife in his front pocket and switched his coffee to his right hand, freeing his left.

Ian blew out a breath, and then opened the door stepping out into the evening, his coffee cup still in his hand.

Jason watched Stuart walk down the stairs in the dark. Jason released Ash when Ian was far enough away and she couldn't get to him. She swung around, nailing him across the face with a slap that echoed off the walls.

"You son-of-a-bitch."

He worked his jaw then looked back at her. "Oh, come on," he laughed. "A slap is girly. You can do better."

She lunged at him, but Quinn grabbed her by both elbows, pulling her back against his chest, whispering in her ear.

"The fight is not in here. Let it go."

She panted another half a minute before yanking away and taking a step back.

Jason looked to Quinn who stared back with pursed lips.

Reaching in his back pocket as Quinn reached in his front, Jason pulled out his wooden and gold handled knife. Quinn got a blade out of the kitchen rack.

"Travis," Jason said. "You heard what he said. Tie down or lock up if you have to. And watch her. That is a pretty good right she has."

511

"Wait," Travis snapped.

They stopped to turn.

"What?"

"You really think he is alone?"

"You know he's not," Travis said.

"So we'll clear the field and you kill the son-of-a-bitch when he makes his move on Stuart."

"And me?" Ash asked.

Jason turned away, laughed then looked back at her. "You even try to step outside this time and I will kick your fucking ass when I get done. Do we understand each other?"

 She flinched at his tone. "Yes."

"Promise?"

"No."

His head snapped toward Quinn. "Fuck."

"She didn't lie to you…"

He turned around, walking right up to her. "You leave this house while we are gone and it could come down bad on us. You'll be out there, we'll have to watch out for you. Our attention divided. You willing to risk that?"

"I think you can handle yourself okay."

Jason looked up at Travis. "You will control the situation in here."

512

"You mean her?" He pointed and laughed. "Yeah. I'll control her."

"Jason," Quinn said. "Let's go."

He turned to go when she grabbed him by the shirt with both hands and pulled him to her. She stood on her toes and placed a soft kiss on his cheek then dropped down.

"Sorry. It's the best I can offer now. Engaged, you know."

"You get killed in this attack," he said, "and I will find you and kill you myself. Even if I have to go to hell and back." He patted her cheek and turned, heading out the door.

"Somehow," Quinn said in the dining room, "it hardly seems fair you keep getting the kisses while the rest of us do without."

"Bite me," Jason said. "You know we're probably going to get killed doing this?"

"Yeah. Die young, leave a good-looking corpse," Quinn smiled. "Remember that quote?"

"There were nine of them."

"So we take as many as we can and give them a chance to bring it all down when Walter is a pile of dust. Stuart and Ash live happily ever after."

"I think that sounds like a really good plan."

Jason opened the door and Evan appeared beside them.

They both looked over their shoulder.

"No," Jason said.

"It was your idea to go to the church."

"Yeah. So? You stay here. Tie her down with duct tape if nothing else works."

"When are you going to treat me like an adult and let me start doing the crap you do?"

"When you get laid," Jason laughed.

"You taught me how to do this."

"Then stay in here."

"I am coming with you to help."

Jason moved toward him. "You're going to get in the kitchen and when Ash makes for the door, which she is going to do, you are going to help Travis shove her in the pantry and bolt it shut."

"Jason I can do this."

"Evan, I have no doubt you can. But we need to put the best people for the job in the place where they work best. You are better in here and we are better outside. Do you understand?"

"You're cutting me off."

Jason reached up, wrapped his hand around Evan's neck and pulled him forward to whisper in his ear. "I would never cut you off because you're too damn good. I just need you someplace other than where you want to be."

Through the side door, into the garage, Jason and Quinn went alone and came out in the alley already knowing they were hunting a group hunting them.

Quinn moved off toward the left.

"Hey," Jason said quietly.

Quinn turned.

"We finish up here, want to grab a beer downtown?"

Quinn pursed his lips over a smile. "Yeah. That sounds good. Highest body count buys, but if you get Walter, you get to sleep with all Three Sisters."

Jason laughed. "Yes. Because getting any of the sisters into bed is hard." Jason saluted him with his knife and turned to the right.

CHAPTER TWENTY-SIX

Walking slow, his gaze rotating left to right, Ian moved down the stairs to the patio. He checked the roofline behind him, saw Travis in the window with Ash.

"It's a beautiful view," Walter said. "I can understand why you choose it."

Ian took a sip of the coffee tasting nothing. His gaze kept sweeping the yard. "Thanks," he said. "Travis designed the yard with some help. We've enjoyed it here."

"I came alone," Walter said. "If that's what you're worried about."

"And I would believe you because…?"

"I've never lied to you."

"But you did try to kill me last night which cuts into your credibility." He took another drink of the coffee.

"That?" Walter laughed. "You think I'm stupid enough not to notice the route on the left?"

"Easy to say now."

Walter motioned to the cup. "That looks good."

"Aye," Ian said. "It is."

"You're not going to invite me in?"

"No," Ian said. "I don't think I am."

Walter motioned to the chair next to him.

Ian shook his head. "I'll stand."

"What's the problem, Stuart? This could be a good thing."

"You have perpetrated how many attacks on my family and think you might still have a chance in hell at seduction?"

Walter looked up at him. "Where's our girl?"

"You, I don't know. Me, I have a girlfriend asleep upstairs."

"Go get her. I'll play nice."

"Last time you played with her you left holes in her sides ten inches deep."

"Yeah, that was me. Would like to say it was the girls, but I just told you I never lied to you." He smiled at him.

"What do you want?"

Walter uncrossed his legs then crossed them in the other direction.

"We had a lot of fun."

Fury began its journey. "And this is supposed to change my sexual orientation? Make me open my eyes and realize what I missed and go running to you?"

"Why not?"

"You know, in all honesty, I could care less about who you want to fuck, male or female. It doesn't matter to me. The fact you stalked me is annoying, but seriously none of that was what stopped me."

"What stopped you?"

"Most of us kill to survive. You're a murdering psychopath who thinks torture and death are a great way to have fun. My fiancée is a living example of that."

Walter's gaze came up. "Your what?"

"We got engaged last night. And thanks to you, it's something I can do. Just like declaring to her last week. Neither of those things could have happened unless she was turned and I *never* would have turned her."

Walter stared out into space for a second then looked up at him. "You declared to her?"

"She is my mate now and she soon will be my wife. So fuck you for how you did it, but thank you, too, because you gave me everything I ever wanted."

Walter sat silent for a long minute, staring into the night. When he finally made a sound it was to laugh. "I enjoyed it, you know," Walter smiled.

Ian glared at him.

"Her against us. The more she fought, the hotter it was. I loved it. More than I usually do." He looked up. "I think the burning was my favorite. Had the smell to go with her reactions."

Ian contained himself.

518

"How do you manage, it though? The two? One night with him, the next with her?"

Ian stared at him. "I'm not even going to bother answering that."

Being the best wasn't something Jason wore like an armband of recognition. It was something he had always done. Best grades. Best school projects. Best college. He undertook something and the grey matter he had been awarded gave him the ability to become the best at what he did.

Even defense. Because when it came down to it, there were probably more brain cells involved than mere agility and grace.

Though those, he had those too, because hell, he was a lucky son-of-a-bitch.

When the hands came down on his left arm in the dark, pinning him, he thought maybe being the best might not be enough this time. When the second set of hands came out on the right, one hand wrapping around his chin to pull his face back, exposing his throat, he was trapped. He closed his eyes and didn't even bother to swear.

He had taken out two and he had done it to protect her. Dying for Ash—he couldn't think of a better reason to go.

He felt the knife hand rise, he knew it was coming, but instead of the pain and darkness, because who the hell knew where vampires went when they died, there was a groan and the hand holding his face went lax. Jason reacted instead of thinking, striking back like a rattler, nailing the vampire to his left in a quick stroke before spinning onto the other side.

But the other was already gone, his body in the process of transforming. Jason saw the dust hit the ground and Evan standing with a bloody blade held tight in a pale hand.

"You son-of-a-bitch," Jason ground out, grabbing Evan by the face with a shaking hand to pull him close enough to lean on. "I told you to stay inside."

"You're welcome," Evan said on a soft chuckle.

"Yeah," Jason returned the laugh. "Maybe you have learned something."

"Did you want to finish or piss your pants?"

Jason put his hand on Evan's back and propelled him forward, heading further down the alley and around the house.

"I remember that day, Stuart."

"Which one. You seemed to have been invading a lot."

"The day I fixed her dishwasher. You want to know what she was wearing?"

Ian shook his head and stared at the ground. "No."

"Black dress pants. Boots. White undershirt. Burgundy over shirt. Long sleeves." He reached up and fiddled his fingers in front of him, chest high. "And a necklace. Black. Some sort of amulet. I actually thought you might have given it to her. It looked very Celtic."

Ian knew Walter did it on purpose. He was going for a reaction.

"I was there for forty-five minutes. Dishwasher only took ten. She was on the phone the whole time. I think she was talking to Hunter, about the case and about you. From the bits I picked up, I think that's what was going on. And I was just waiting there. Wondering when she would notice that I wasn't working all too hard in the kitchen. She got off the phone, wrote me a check and I left."

He reached into his back pocket, pulling out a wallet. Opening it, he withdrew a piece of paper which he handed to Ian. It was a check for seventy dollars made to D&B Appliance with Ash's signature on the bottom. Ian reached up, rubbing his hand over his chin, the nausea rising in his gut. He set the check down on the nearby table and drained the coffee mug.

"You could have killed her," Ian said in a controlled voice. "There was nothing stopping you."

"I thought about it. She was so preoccupied. But the timing didn't feel right. I knew I was waiting for something better."

"First Blood was mine," Ian said. "You have no standing here. And we're mated so the only thing that happens next is, I pick how you die."

Walter stood up to face him. "You really think that's the way it's going to go?"

"You attacked and brutalized the woman I mated. By our Laws, that gives me every right at retribution. How I choose to do it, also my right."

"You, who haven't taken a life since the fifties against me, who took ten this week. Fuck your laws. I decided I didn't like them and would make my own."

"Why did you come alone?" Ian asked him.

Walter laughed. "You believed me?"

Ian's head fell back. "No, but I also knew it didn't matter."

Ian turned to see the gates on either side of the yard.

Only, no one else came through to attack. Walter looked puzzled as his gaze moved from gate to gate.

Then Quinn came in one.

Jason in the other, with Evan beside him.

"Four," Quinn said.

"Four," Jason added.

"Two," came from Evan.

"What? No," Walter panted.

"Women?" Ian asked

Quinn raised his hand. "Bitch scratched me. Sorta pissed me off."

"And that doesn't add up to nine. Shit," he muttered.

She came across the kitchen still in the yoga pants, sweater and socks, no shoes. Travis stayed in front of the door.

"Hi," he smiled.

"Move."

"When hell freezes over."

She looked at the clock then back at him. "I think it just did. And your best friend is out alone facing his worst enemy and you are babysitting. That's kind of sad," she said.

"Guilt doesn't work on me."

"Then I guess this is where you are going to make a real serious decision in your life and it could affect the rest of what's left of it," she said.

"I let you out that door, he will kill me."

"So decide."

He tilted his head at her.

"Which one are you more afraid of?"

"Walter? Bastard doesn't scare me."

"I wasn't referring to Walter, you nimrod."

"Excuse me," he laughed.

"You are either more afraid of Stuart. Or you are more afraid of me. One will forgive. The other will make the rest of your life a living hell from every direction you can possibly imagine for as long as we are under the same roof. I can give you a few seconds to decide which is which and then I am walking out that door."

"Nimrod? Did you call me a nimrod?"

"I am getting ready to call you a lot worse even though Ian says I can't use that word anymore."

"And you are really good at doing what Ian says," he chuckled.

"Move," she snapped.

"Ash, you cannot defeat him."

"No, but I can stand as a major distraction. He's come after me before. He will again. And if the right men can figure out how to play it to their advantage, we walk away the winners. Any volunteers?"

"He will fucking kill me if I put you in the line of fire."

"Close your eyes," she smiled.

"What?"

"Close your eyes," she said again.

He knew he shouldn't but he did and two seconds later the back door opened and shut and he waited, his eyes closed tight, wondering how bad Stuart was going to hurt him.

He turned around and followed her.

CHAPTER TWENTY-SEVEN

She came down the stairs illuminated by the garden.

"I'm going to kill you," Ian said to Travis, right on her tail.

"She snuck past me," Travis said.

"Aye," Ian smirked. He tossed his empty coffee mug to the ground.

"You don't look like I remember," she said as she moved down the stairs.

"You were a little incoherent the last time we met. I don't think you liked being pinned down."

"Proud of that?" she asked Walter.

"Ash," Ian snapped. She brought her gaze to his. He stood ten feet away looking more tired than she had hoped. "Behave."

"She's a handful," Walter said. "It will take discipline to get her in line."

"Good luck with that," Ian said. He looked at her. "If I told you to get back up the stairs and get in the house you would seriously ignore me, wouldn't you?"

"She's not going anywhere," Walter said. "She is fine right where she is."

Ian looked at him and then dismissed him.

Walter sneered. "You used to eat bitches like her and toss them in the bay."

Ian looked at her standing so close. She was watching him.

"Wish I could say he was lying but I seriously was not a nice guy."

"You've been reformed," she smiled, staring at him. "Mated," she said. "That's the right term?"

"*Amis pour la vie.* No one can touch it."

Walter's eyes narrowed, his anger level seemed to go up. The control he tried to hold was rapidly disappearing.

"I created her. That trumps your possession."

"Actually, it doesn't and you're old enough to know that," Ian said.

"I rewrote the laws. The one you want doesn't exist anymore."

"Three thousand years of tradition and you decided."

Walter looked at her then backed at Ian. "We pinned, we drank. It was no trouble. She's not tough. She begged us to stop. She cried like a baby when I sliced her with the blade to milk her into her own crystal wine glass. It always tastes better out of crystal, doesn't it?"

"Three to one," Ian repeated.

"We hurt her," Walter said facing Ian. "We made it as bad as we could."

"Not an easy process to go through," Ian said. "We all endured it when it happened to us."

"Even Travis?" Walter snapped.

Ian's face screwed up and he shook his head a little. "Told her last night."

"How about the others?"

"Do you actually think you're going to make her hate me? You tell her these stories about my past and you don't think I have already visited them with her? Your whole logic is flawed. It always was. You never thought anything out that was worth doing and you're not going to win here."

Ashley asked. "Why Hunter?"

Walter turned to face her, laughing. "Your partner? Too bad he had to die. Did you stake him yourself or get one of your babysitters?"

"He was my best friend."

"Yeah," Walter said. "I saw you together a few times at crime scenes. It looked like you really got along. We turned him at his house and made his bitch watch. We tied her down then waited for him. He woke up pissed and hungry and he didn't pause. It was the meth. We shot him up with meth. Makes them go nuts and turns them into killing machines."

"Why?" she snapped.

He shrugged like it was no big deal. "Since you took my family I think it was only fair I got to take yours."

"Your family?" Ian practically choked. "We were never family. We were never going to be family."

Walter's gaze came up. "You shouldn't have left me in New Orleans."

Ash looked at him.

"Sharron had instructions. Your house should be in flames by now. I have taken everything you ever had from you and I will keep on going until your entire life is in..." he laughed a little, "...ash."

Travis turned toward the guys at the gates. "Go, now."

The other three disappeared.

When Travis turned back, Walter had a knife ready. With vampire strength and speed, he threw it, imbedding it to the hilt high in Travis's gut.

Travis gasped, dropping to his knees.

Ian spun to him, his hand on his shoulder.

Walter spoke.

"A chiall mo chridhe."

Ian, looked up, saw her moving and dove. But it was too late. She walked into Walter's arms. He grabbed her, spinning her, pulling her close, a deadly sharp knife to her throat.

And she didn't even notice.

"Fuck." Travis said on a hard breath.

Ian looked at her trapped and vacant.

"You programmed her," Ian said, hating Walter with every nerve he had.

"Handy, huh?" Walter laughed. "It's called planning ahead."

"I took every memory she had of that night."

"Which is why it was a good thing I did it the first night I was in her house."

"What?" Travis asked.

"*A chiall mo chridhe*," Ian said, "It's Gaelic for *My dearest dear*." He spoke to Walter as he came up off the ground. "You had it the first night you were here. You could have used it on her then."

"No advantage. As you can see, now I will be walking out of here."

Ian shook his head. "No."

The knife flicked enough to catch and bleed.

Ash went straight coming out of the trance. She pulled at the arm holding her, struggled for only a few seconds until she realized it was helpless.

"Crap," she said. "I did something stupid, didn't I?"

Walter leaned near the cut while Ian vibrated with helpless fury. He couldn't get her away from him. Not with that blade in place.

Walter sniffed. "It's better than chocolate, isn't it? You want to lick it up."

"Fine," Ian said. "You win. What do you want? You want me to go with you? Try something new?"

Walter laughed. "Sorry. You missed out on that chance."

"So, what?"

Walter pulled her tighter, her chin back, the knife digging in to make it impossible for her to act.

"How about we try something new," Walter said. "You pick."

"Pick what?"

"You only get to keep one. Him or her. You get to decide but one of them is ending here and you get to watch."

He looked down at Travis who stared back.

"Gun pointed at both of us," Travis said. "Which one do you choose?" He pushed up off the ground, the stain on his shirt bright even in the dark. "It would be me," he said coming forward.

"That's good for me," Walter said. "Something I will really enjoy. You walk over here. Give me no trouble while I do what I want and then I will let her go. Well, I'll let her go at some point, after I get the hell out of here. And probably in one piece, unless I get hungry."

"That sounds like a really fair deal," Travis said. He took the first step, when Ian put his hand up, pushing Travis back.

"Not yet," Ian said.

530

"She only has so much blood and I will spill it." Walter said.

"I know you will," Ian snapped. He tried to think.

Travis leaned over, holding his side before going to his knees.

"Did I mention we have a time frame?" Walter asked. "We're not going to debate this."

He cut her a little more and though she flinched, she didn't make a sound. Her neck shone wet in the dim light.

"Is there any way in hell for me to convince you Travis was nothing ever other than a friend?"

"I don't give a fuck," Walter said. Another flick. Blood seeping down her neck to the top of the sweater.

"Never fucked Stuart," Travis said calmly from the kneeling position.

"What?" Walter snapped.

"You're asking. I'm answering. Never fucked Stuart. Ash, that's a whole different story."

"What?" Ian snapped, looking down at him.

Travis's face sweaty, the pain evident, he shrugged and smiled. "Have you actually looked at what you brought in our front door?"

Walter laughed and Ian saw the knife pull away. Only a fraction but it was away.

"Travis, shut up," she whispered.

"You are fucking kidding me?" Ian snapped.

Travis looked at Walter. "Just curious what gave it away. I thought we were both very good at hiding it."

"Shut up!" she snapped and Walter cut her again. This time she gasped.

A dark figure came out of the brush in the back, low to the ground, blending in. Ian saw it coming closer. He suspected Travis had seen it first. Otherwise he wouldn't be confessing to bullshit.

Travis kept on talking. "You knew you were going to have to choose, Ash."

"Best friend, right?" Ian laughed.

"Well maybe if you hadn't taken a bite out of me in 1928 none of this would have become an issue."

Ian swung to look at Ash. "You fucking whore."

Walter laughed, his whole body taking on the humor of the new information. "You put a ring on her finger? A cheating slut who doesn't deserve to be one of us? What's the punishment for adultery once you're mated? I think involves nails and a very on fire building. I can do that. Be fun to watch."

"What, Stuart?" Travis said. "You look shocked. Four of us and her looking like that? You think I'm the only one?"

Walter laughed louder.

The shadow leapt up behind Walter, a blade in each hand flashing in the dim light as he pounced, slamming them into

Walter's back. Walter arched, screaming in pain and his knife dropped from his hand.

Ian jumped at the same instant, clicking Quinn's blade open and grabbing Walter by the neck when Walter sank to his knees, Ian's fingers digging in and holding him up.

Travis grunted and grabbed her, pulling her back and away and into his arms, wrapped safe, the knife in his stomach close to her. They fell to the ground, him taking the force, gasping at the impact.

Breathless, Max, stood up behind Walter, blood on his hands.

Ian yanked Walter forward. "Pick? You want me to pick? Why the fuck couldn't you realize in 1953 I hated your guts?"

"Stuart," Walter whimpered.

"We know where you are hiding, but I think that's moot. I think you're all dead already."

Walter grabbed on to Ian's wrist, breathing deep. "It's gone. The house is gone. Sharron dead. They're all dead."

Ian shoved the blade hard into Walter's gut to the hilt, feeling the blood on his fingers, seeing the spittle drip out of Walter's mouth.

"You want me to choose, you son-of-a-bitch? Guess what, this is my choice." He stabbed him again.

Walter gasped. "You don't torture."

"I never tortured. I killed but I made it easy for them. Now I've seen a woman who matters and the aftermath of what you did. I'll be staring at the scars for decades."

"I do good work, don't I?" Walter laughed.

Ian stabbed again, twisting the blade slow.

"I'm not going to beg," Walter hissed.

"I didn't think you would. Any den who got their hands on you would do it only worse. I don't care if you suffer in sunlight with exposure. I just don't ever want to see you again."

Ian brought the bloody blade to Walter's neck.

"She won't let you," Walter laughed. "She is a cop. Cops don't kill. Not even for revenge."

Ian yanked him all the way forward. "She's not a cop, asshole. She's a vampire."

Coming up from the right, he dug deep and slashed the blade from ear to ear, opening Walter's neck in a flood of blood covering his hand. The light in the eyes went out almost at once. Three seconds later, the flesh under Ian's hands quivered and fizzled until it burst into a flash of dust covering Ian's clothes.

Sixty years of dread and apprehension vanished as the dust rode the light breeze to scatter. There wouldn't be any tender clean-up. If anything, Travis would get the hose tomorrow.

A sense of relief flooded Ian's whole body, gratitude so close on its tail it was impossible to distinguish. He stood there, his eyes closed tight, blood on him, the dust. Ash moved closer until her hand was on his shoulder.

"You're not sleeping with Travis, right?" Ian asked.

She laughed and put her head on his shoulder. "Actually I am," she said. "We've been meaning to tell you."

He chuckled, pulling her close, his arms around her, his face in the nook of her neck pulled close, smearing her with the grime on his front.

"Bitch," he laughed against her.

"It's the height thing getting to me. I may have to give it up."

"Hello," Travis said from the ground where he bled. "A little help." Ian stepped back, out of breath after really little exertion. He put a hand on her neck trying to stop her bleeding.

Max handed him a white handkerchief, though where the hell he had it, Ian didn't know. It was the kind of proper thing Max would do.

Ian looked to the man in glasses who pulled Travis to his feet. Max leaned over to look at the knife then up at Travis. "In or out?"

"In," Travis groaned. "Quinn gets mad when we make them bleed more."

Max nodded and stepped back and stood there patiently, his hands folded in front of him, a smile on his face, his tortoise shell glasses in place. He extended his hand to her.

"Hi," he smiled. "I never actually got to meet you that night I was threatening to kill you. I'm Max."

She smiled as he turned her hand over to kiss the back, stopping with an "Ahh…so what I heard is true. You did it. Or are going to do it. That is really amazing news."

He looked genuinely happy.

"I thought you left town with Jason's ten grand," Ian said.

Max shrugged. "It was more like six-five." He smiled. "And I thought I might be able to help out here. I've been holed up in the church."

"We checked the church," Travis said.

"Knew you would so I stayed out of sight."

"Why?" Ian laughed.

Max looked away then back. "I'm a screw-up. We both know that. But the truth is, I should have been standing beside you the first round and not across. He never would have found you if I hadn't led him here. Sticking around was the least I could do."

Ash looked at Ian who looked back.

"You didn't actually have a plan, did you?" Max said. "You figured you would kill him somehow and it would work out."

"Aye," Ian smiled nodding his head. "That was pretty much it."

Max laughed and bowed a little. "I wish you both luck. As I have previously stated, you are one-motherfucking-good-looking-couple who appear to be designed for one another. Sounds as if that goes a hell of a lot deeper than the physical."

He turned to leave.

"Where you going?" Travis called.

Max looked at him. "Wherever six thousand five hundred will take me."

"Do you need more?" Ash asked.

Max turned back and came toward them. "I'm sorry. What?"

Ian smiled and looked at her then up to Max. "Did I tell you my fiancée is loaded? Tell her what you need and she will get it. In the meantime…"

"In the meantime?" Max asked.

Ian looked to Travis. Travis nodded.

"There's no one living in your room. Why don't you stay? Give it a try again? Maybe this time it would work."

"I've tried it twice. Failed both times."

"You didn't fail. Just wasn't the right time for you. Not uncommon with addicts."

"Addicts?" Max laughed. "Is that what we are?"

"Bed's made. I think there might be a few things stored, but easily moved," Ian said.

"You know I will probably hit on your fiancée."

"You would have to get in line behind Jason," Ian smiled.

"That damn Irishman," Max laughed. "Never gets enough on his own."

Ian extended his hand and Max took the handshake.

They came in the back door—Jason, Quinn and Evan—looking like the word 'exhausted' come to life. Dirty, sagging, swaying on their feet.

Ian sat in clean clothes at the table, his feet tucked under with a cup of coffee from the pot she just made. Max across from him, looking nervous.

Travis leaned back in a chair, his legs stretched out. His hand held a bloody towel to his side, the end of the knife sticking out. His skin was pale, sweaty, his breathing hard against what had to be immense pain. He stayed stoic, the leader. Two empty re-sealable bags from the freezer sat in front of him with two puncture marks in the plastic.

"Took you long enough," Travis moaned.

"Oh, shit," Quinn muttered, looking at Travis. "I'm tired. I'll do it later."

"Get your ass over here and get this thing out of me."

Quinn puffed out a breath of air, his cheeks big and moved slower than normal.

"What happened?" Travis asked as Quinn knelt down and pulled back the towel.

"She was right ahead of us," Jason said. "Got there before, but just. Evan was the only one who could go in after her and we didn't let him. Place went up like a match. They must have had it ready. I'm sorry Ash."

538

Ash stood at the oven, peeking to look at the cookies she had baked from the dough she made and froze days ago. Her clothes were changed to a clean pair of pajamas—yellow and green this time—her slippers on her feet, Ian had doctored and bandaged her neck.

"It was my idea to burn it down," she said.

"It was your idea to burn it down when it was our idea."

"I would say the house had an expiration date on it because it was going one way or another today."

"Walter?" Evan asked.

Ian took a sip of the coffee. "Back walkway needs hosing down if anyone is in the mood."

"Supposed to rain tonight," Jason said. "That's clean enough for me." He pointed at Max. "I thought I financed his trip out of here."

Ian took a sip of the coffee. "I'm pretty sure he's planning on keeping the financing, but he's staying awhile to see if he can work things out."

"Again?"

"He fucks up two minutes from now," Travis said, "and he knows how it will end. Quinn has his hands full these days taking care of our new asset."

"I got some time," Quinn said. "Don't worry."

"Thanks," Max smiled.

She pulled the cookie sheet out and set it on a folded towel. Picking up the spatula to take the first batch off she put on a rack.

She turned around to look at Travis. "Ask them."

"*Mia bella*, I am not asking any of them that question."

She folded her arms and leaned on the counter. "You have to ask them."

"You know, I have never been challenged as Primary until you arrived and they tend to listen to you more than me anyway so I don't see the point."

"What's going on?" Jason asked wearily.

"The first night Walter was here," Ian said, "I took Ash upstairs and we talked."

"Yeah?"

"I told her we never do anything without voting."

They all looked at her and chuckled. "And she thinks she wasn't voted in?" Evan said. "Does she have any idea how we spent our night?"

"Which has everything to do with *his* problem," she said, pointing at Ian, "and not me. I was brought in the door and deposited on a bed as a side show."

Jason moaned. "I'm going to strangle her," He moved forward and Evan grabbed him, laughing as he pulled Jason back.

"Did you hear us vote him in?" Quinn asked, pointing at Max.

"He's already been voted in."

"And he got kicked out. Sort of a repeat performance."

She turned around to look at Travis.

"I don't suppose you noticed the two carat rock on your finger?"

"Once again," she said. "That's him. No one else signed up for it."

Travis laughed louder then groaned. "I bought the damn thing you idiot, with their help."

"I think she's good for mere amusement purposes," Quinn said. "She looks damn funny right now." He stood up in front of Travis. "I can take care of this better upstairs." He looked at her. "And I want to see what is under that bandage."

She turned around to dump the freshly made coffee into the sink to start a new batch of Jason's blend.

"So what is the real issue?" Travis asked.

"One agreed. Four got dragged along without choice. Another showed up."

"Now can I strangle her?" Jason asked leaning forward.

The smell of expensive coffee and cookies mingled, hinting to Ian of a nice night after a terrible evening.

"So," Travis said. "My job here, because I am the one in charge, is to figure out a solution. Because, as you're saying, we don't make decisions without checking in."

She stared back.

"Have you thought maybe there might be a few other issues you should be worrying about? Because how worried are you really about something like everyone agreeing and voting a subject in?"

She licked her lips and narrowed her eyes at him.

"Privacy," he said. "Maybe privacy is something you might want to rethink. Because when you live with all these people, you might *think* you're alone in the den three days ago but it might just be a case of you not knowing anyone was in the living room reading when you made *that* phone call."

She stood up straight, her eyes getting wide.

Travis smiled triumphantly.

"Don't," she said.

"What call?" Ian chuckled.

Travis laughed harder. "Really? You can actually transfer *that much* on PayPal and get what you want *delivered*?"

Jason had his phone out and was tapping. He had already broken into all of Ash's accounts. This one was easy.

"How long were you listening," she asked.

"*Mia bella*," he smiled. "From the time you dialed to the minute you hung up, and if you think you really can get all of us out of the house on a Saturday night, you're crazier than I thought."

"What phone call?" Ian asked louder.

Jason laughed at the screen. "You are fucking kidding me?" He laughed harder. "You paid over *three thousand*? This goes for like seven or eight hundred. Tops."

Her voice dropped to a humble whisper. "There was a delivery issue with nights."

"And the fact it's being driven here from Portland," Travis said. "Have you ever heard of negotiating? Because I listened and you suck."

Quinn grabbed the phone, read and laughed out loud. "Oh yeah," he said. "We need to vote quick."

"Who's the call to?" Ian laughed.

Travis smiled at her.

"Don't. Please. It's a surprise."

"It certainly is but mostly…*Evan*."

"What?" Evan asked.

Jason put the phone in front of Evan's face, pointing at the place for him to read.

"*Youngblood Breeders*?" Evan's head snapped up, looking at Ash. "You sent three thousand dollars to a *puppy breeder*?" He went from shocked to ecstatic. "A dog?" Evan squealed. "You got us a dog?"

"She got *you* a dog," Travis said. "Without a vote I might add."

Ash's gaze dropped to the ground, looking guilty. Ian smiled and watched her squirm. "He's a Bloodhound and will be ten

543

weeks old when he's delivered on the seventeenth and they say house broken. His papers read *Vladimir von Draculesti*."

Evan's arms went straight up in the air, his whoops making everyone reach for their ears.

Ian got up and pulled her into his arms. "Guess voting isn't the issue so what the hell is?"

She sighed. "One of you enlisted. Four of you got drafted. The other just showed up."

He laughed and kissed her. "I get to keep you. I don't give a shit about the rest of it."

"I vote we keep the sneaky wench around," Jason laughed. He walked over, pulling her out of Ian's arms and into his, kissing her forehead.

"Hey," Ian laughed. "Are you ever going to keep your hands off?"

"No," Jason smiled. "Not planning on it."

"I vote if she is well enough to be making sneaky phone calls, we should start talking about re-division of chores."

She stepped away from Jason and went back to Ian wrapping her arms around his waist, her head on his chest.

"Two weeks of cooking duties." Travis smiled at his idea while he held onto the knife he really needed to get out.

Jason glanced at him sideways. "We actually don't know if she can cook."

"Heard rumors of this London Broil she does. Supposed to make you weep."

"Good place to start," Jason said. "If not, I can find some other uses for her."

Ian back handed him on the shoulder. Hard. "That is my *wife* you are talking about."

"Not yet," Jason smiled. "I still got time."

Evan danced around them all. "A puppy," he smiled. He laughed. "We're getting a puppy."

EPILOGUE: A NEW SQUARE ONE

"Every new beginning comes from some other beginning's end."

~Seneca

With things quiet these days, it was nice to sit at the computer and cruise e-mail and not think about much at all.

Only thing was, with no job and few people she really associated with, most of the e-mails were specials coming from her favorite stores offering free full size products with a purchase of seventy-five dollars or more. .

She jumped to the sites to look around. She could always use a few more eye shadows going into the summer. And hey, she might look into one of those bottle tans now that she and the sun were strangers.

She heard Ian come in the door behind her after his shower. She turned, surprised to find him in a full dark suit, the jacket unbuttoned. He had on a pressed white shirt and black tie, his hair brushed behind his ears and tamed. He had Gr'pa Jackson's gold watch attached at the pocket, the chain hanging low.

"Are we going out?"

He kind of bobbed his head. "We have plans for the night."

"We do?"

546

He nodded. "Travis had it catered and hired someone in to cook and another to serve and clean."

"So this is a big deal?"

Ian walked to the closet, facing his side and pulled back his clothes and took out a beautiful black dress. From the top shelf he retrieved a pair of shoes, laying them both out on the bed, then went back for a white gift bag setting it on the desk beside her.

"You bought me the A Line dress?" she smiled, thinking back to their first date and the book he bought with the promise to buy the items listed one at a time.

"It is an A Line. I did make sure of that, but Travis did most of the picking. I did get the shoes."

Blacked high heeled sandals with a multitude of straps across the top, ending at an open toe. She was glad her pedicure was up to date.

"What is going on?"

"I'm going to wait for you downstairs. I assume you have underthings that work with this dress?"

"I have under things that work with this dress, yes."

"Please get ready and I will be waiting. More subdued than hot, and I will explain everything when I see you down there."

"You're acting very strange."

She reached into the bag and pulled out the first of three blue boxes.

He was at the door before she caught him.

"Ian?"

He turned to look at her.

"This is a Tiffany's box. You can't get a box from Tiffany's unless you buy something from Tiffany's."

He smiled. "I believe that is correct."

She pulled the top off, her jaw dropping. Inside sat a choker made of perfectly matched pearls. Between each pearl sat three clear stones, glistering and catching what little light there was.

Her gaze came up to his.

"Ian…this is not costume and these aren't crystals."

"I'm pretty sure he put in an order for the big guns."

"He?"

"Only one other person in the house besides you could afford that."

"Jason's bought these? Ian, these are thousands of dollars."

He nodded his head slow. "Several times over, actually."

She ripped into the other two boxes. One held a matching bracelet. The other, the matching earrings.

"Oh my God," she said, losing her breath.

"You don't like them?"

"My God they're gorgeous but no. No. No. I can't…he can't…"

"He can," Ian said.

"And this doesn't bother you?"

He shook his head. "Jason spoke to me before he did it. He wanted to and he wanted it for tonight."

"Ian, I can't accept these."

"Ash," he said calmly, "You're going to accept them. And you are going to wear them tonight and let him see you love them. Because I can tell you do."

"How much?" she asked a little breathless.

Ian looked away, looked back and smiled. "He can afford it. He does real well in a lot of places, especially his job and he can afford it without hurting."

"I spent $250.00 on a pair of earrings once and I regretted it like hell. Never even wore the things."

He came back close, leaned over to kiss her on the neck. "You'll wear these."

Her gaze dropped to the gorgeous ensemble in front of her, her voice caught in her throat.

"Please get dressed," he said. "Subdued rather than hot. Wear the pretties and be down as soon as you can. I will wait as long as you need and dinner is at our pleasure so we are not on any time frame."

Her heels clicked on the tile floor, telling him she was close. She walked in the room looking more beautiful than ever. The dress, its wide shoulder caps modest, dove into a deep V between her breasts, offset by the smallest chiffon, making it proper, her cleavage covered. The two layers of black moved together as she came toward him in the sandals he had picked out.

The jewelry she wore were small pieces of art shown off in glitter and shine decorating her ears, her throat and her wrist.

This was the woman he had been lucky enough to find, a brunette who walked into Cooper's then came back a second night. She belonged to him, body and soul and him to her. He had waited a hundred years to feel the kind of love and he would treasure it for the centuries to come.

He reached out and took her hand, smiling as he brought it to his lips to kiss.

She had pulled her hair back, gathering it at her neck, letting small tendrils hang free and curl around her face. She had managed subdued and hot, and it would still work for tonight.

"You want to tell me what's going on?"

He kissed her hand again. "I'm not really sure how to because I'm not really sure how you'll react."

"What?" she whispered.

He looked out the window. All the lights were on outside, the streams running to and from the ponds. Everything had been laid out meticulously with loving care. A small table had been set up with dozens of candles giving off a glow. She couldn't see it from here he knew, but in the ground to right, under the rose bushes that would bloom in a few months, sat a hole dug out deep by Evan.

Travis, Jason, Quinn, Evan and now Max, waited.

"The other night…" he said.

"Which one? We had a couple."

"The night you were attacked here with Quinn and Travis and Jason."

She looked at him, her smile fading.

"Travis was very careful in the clean-up. He made sure nothing was lost and everything important was kept together."

She looked out the window and a minute passed before looking up at Ian. "He saved Hunter?"

Ian nodded. "Travis was meticulous with the cremains. He put him in a container and he's had him in his room. Quinn took care of the clothes. He burned them all, kept all of that and added it. Hunter's badge is still upstairs, as is a copy of the photo. His wallet, with the original so he can have a part of Janey with him. We added a photo of you, too."

She looked out the window then back at him.

"Jason's bought a very nice walnut urn and had a gold plate made for the top with Hunter's name and dates."

She looked up at him.

"His full name and birthday were on his license. The day of passing, we used what we think was the day they went to his house

551

and not the one here. We're going to erase that memory. He deserves it and so do you."

She stared out to the back yard.

"Jason also got a garden stone, a Celtic cross with a poem engraved on a boulder. We will all know he's there. No one else will suspect."

"This is Hunter's funeral," she whispered.

"No one knows what happened to him but us. We can give this to him. We want to give this to him." He pointed at the window, "the four of them have been planning this almost from the moment it happened. I was with you so I actually didn't hear about it until three days ago when Jason wanted to show me the jewelry he was looking at online."

She looked at him. "I thought there was a vampire law against this."

"There's a *custom* about death and erasing with no memory, but he was never one of them, not really. He was your Hunter and he needs to rest and you need to help us put him there so that you can have closure, too."

Without a word she turned and walked out the front door and down the steps toward them, all in matching black suits, white shirts and black ties.

Jason, with his jacket open and tie loose.

Evan with his open too, his tie askew like he wasn't sure how it worked.

Quinn stood straight, his hands clasped in front of him, his jacket buttoned, his presentation immaculate.

Travis had a white orchid with simple purple accents and a touch of greenery on his lapel.

Max stood back as if he didn't quite fit in.

Travis walked over to Evan, batted him on the jacket, then straightened the tie himself.

Jason had his done and was as pristine as Quinn before she made it to them.

They took positions around a small table that held the box with two white tapered candles on either side.

Jason reached over and placed a finger on the simple sound system set up. *The Beatles* began to sing *In My Life… "…but of all these friends and lovers…there is no one compares with you…"*.

Travis stepped forward to Ash, handing her a single, long-stem rose. He kissed her on the cheek.

"I am very sorry for your loss and know nothing we do here tonight will heal the wound, but maybe it will begin the process. And where I have to be devastated at what occurred, I have to also tell you that I am forever grateful for all the horror and sadness we faced because without them, you might not ever have come to us. And I am eternally grateful for you in our lives."

He gave her a book of matches.

"Could you please light the candles to get us started?"

She handed the rose to Ian and stepped forward.

Travis spoke for a moment to everyone present, recognizing he had not known Hunter personally.

Ian handed back the rose to Ash and spoke next, explaining he had met Hunter on several occasions.

"I am lying there, naked in the bed under the quilt, awake two minutes after our first night and Hunter walks right in like we are at a dinner party while Ash is in the bathroom getting ready. He shakes my hand and introduces himself. No Detective, though. It was straight Hunter Graham. Ash was ready to kill him and I was laughing my ass off. He was a funny guy."

Everyone laughed at the image, including Ash.

"He was a handful at times and probably as ready to shoot you that day as say hello. He was very protective."

Ian picked her hand and squeezed it.

Jason stepped forward next, pulling a 3X5 card from his pocket.

When I must leave you

for a little while,

Please do not grieve

and shed wild tears

and hug your sorrow

to you through the years…

Jason finished the poem and Quinn pulled out his card.

When I come to the end of the road

and the sun has set for me,

I want no rites in a gloom-filled room.

Why cry for a soul set free?

Miss me a little, but not too long

and not with your head bowed low…

Ian saw the tears on her cheek. He felt them on his own. Where she grieved, she would not grieve alone.

"Ash," Travis asked. "Do you want to say something?"

"No," she said, shaking her head. "I don't think so. He knew me. He knew what I thought and felt about him. We never had to worry about those kinds of things whether we were on the job or at his house. Janey made the best Steak and Guinness pie and would make it anytime I came over and all of us would drink red wine and eat and laugh our asses off. Hunter was one of the funniest men I ever met and he knew…" she laughed "…he *knew* how to push my buttons and get the most reactive response." She smiled sadly. "He was a good friend who I know would have been on the other side of the table if things had gone differently."

Travis nodded at Evan.

Evan leaned behind the table and picked up six roses, handing one to each of the six men. Then he picked up the box and placed it very gently into the hole.

One by one each of the men stepped up to the grave, paused in thought, then tossed his flower on top. Ash was last and she stood there a long time, Ian with his hands on her shoulders. He would wait as long as she needed.

When at last her rose went into the grave, she stepped back leaning against him. He held her close and Evan got the small shovel that had been out of sight and filled it in while they all watched in silence.

When he was done, Jason and Quinn set the garden marker in place, making sure it was secure and straight then stood back.

They all stared at their new garden decoration.

Ash stood there, reading the poem on the stone. *"May the road rise up to meet you, may the wind be always at your back..."*

Travis, with his hands folded over his middle, spoke. "Dinner is scheduled to be served at two o'clock. Please be in the dining room at that time. Until then, Irish whiskey will be served in the living room to get us started."

The table setting was formal, the linen and china pristine. The low set roses with their extra greenery gave a hint of Hunter's Ireland as well as a scent that engulfed the entire room. Standing at her place left of Ian and right of Travis, she watched as he lifted his glass.

Travis spoke clearly. "I would like to propose a toast to begin this solemn night of celebration." He paused while everyone picked up their untouched wine glasses, glowing red with cab.

"Here is to the tears of affection.

May they crystalize as they fall,

And become pearls, that in the years

We'll wear in memory of those whom we have loved."

Ash's gaze caught Jason's across from her. He watched her, smiling and she knew, though she would thank him, it would never be needed. His appreciation for what she did showed in his eyes and she could see this very set of jewelry with a wedding dress he would no doubt love.

She smiled, her fingers playing with the choker, his grin widening.

Looking around the table as the food was served to them by the outsiders, she knew she would have a role with each of them. Especially the Scotsman to her left, who held her hand and kissed her knuckles as the courses proceeded.

They laughed, shared, grew closer when closer seemed impossible.

"Ah," Jason pointed at Quinn at the opposite head of the table. "What was her name, what was her name?"

"Oh," Quinn said, straining. "Carry. No…Caroline."

557

"No," Jason laughed. "Carol Anne."

"Yes!" Quinn laughed again, snapping his fingers at Jason.

"Carol Anne," Travis explained to Ash "is the only girl these two ever got interested in at the same time."

"When was this?" Ash asked.

"What was it?" Quinn asked Jason. "Seventy-four?"

"I remember the stupidity," Evan interjected, "God, you guys were fucking idiots, thinking you were out sneaking each other."

"While all the time," Quinn said, "She knew exactly what she was doing and played it."

"You were sleeping with the same girl at the same time?"

"Well," Quinn laughed. "Not the *exact* same time."

"That's disgusting," Ash laughed

"Yeah," Jason took a drink of his scotch. "It was horrible. Don't know how I survived."

Smiling, she threw a piece of bread at him.

Ian stretched closer to her. "See, guys, you need to settle down, find a nice girl to have and to hold." He reached over, wrapping his arm over Ash's shoulder, kissing it then pulling her close.

They both burst out laughing.

"Only if having is three months," Jason said.

"And holding is less," Quinn laughed back.

She looked at Ian. "I don't think they get it."

Ian looked back. "Want to make a wager they cave?"

"You haven't paid me for the last one," Jason said. "Hundred bucks, in arms."

"I am not paying you for kissing my wife."

The finger went up. "Not yet. I keep telling you, not yet," Jason said.

"Wait a minute," Max said, leaning forward on the table. "Are you saying if we pay a hundred bucks we get to kiss her?" He reached in his pocket, pulling out his wallet.

Before he could get a bill out, Ian threw a rolled up napkin nailing Max in the face.

"Put it away," he laughed. "It's the Irish trying to take over again."

"Ash?" Evan said.

"Yeah, honey?"

"Tell us a Hunter story."

She smiled and pursed her lips, taking a sip of her Irish Coffee. "A Hunter story?" She thought. "Okay, I have one."

They all focused on her.

"Our partnership did not start out amicable. He was a little put off by a woman and one that...um..."

"Victoria's Secret model?" Jason offered.

"Yes," she said. "He was pretty blunt about it. He told me outright if he wanted someone like me he would go to the liquor store and buy a magazine."

She took a deep breath.

"We were out on assignment right away and we had to go into town, Sunny West for a reported drug operation."

"Sunny West," Ian smiled. "Nice. You know you can get shot in that neighborhood?"

She licked her lips and chuckled. "Yeah, I sorta do know that. We got there and he made some comment about stay out of his way and we got out of the car. And they opened fire on us at once. We got behind the car for cover and without a word to each other started firing back."

Ian leaned forward. "Excuse me?"

"Wait a minute," Quinn said. "I remember this. We had just got here. That was you?"

She raised her eyebrows and nodded. "We got all four of them, for which we were temporarily suspended while the investigation took place. I had emptied all my clips and so had he. He had even gotten to the shotgun in the car. It was empty. Black and whites arrived by now. Apparently, he told me, I had smeared my mascara, the bastard," she smiled, "but he got up to look at the other side of the car and it was riddled with a hundred holes and he started laughing."

Ian stared at her, not looking as if he enjoyed the story.

"We stood up and there wasn't a hell of a lot we could do so we opened our shirts and counted holes in our vests."
560

"What?" Ian said.

"How many?" Evan asked.

"He had six. I had four." She pointed in a diagonal pattern down her chest.

"Hunter told me it was about God damn time they sent him someone who could shoot better than they looked. We ended up in a bar that night. We took a taxi to his house where Janey was waiting. He was hours late even though he had checked in with her and that's where it all started. She had a Steak and Guinness Pie in the oven, pretty dry by now and we got a couple of more bottles of wine, I stayed in their guest room and we blew off work the next day while Janey nursed our hangovers."

"Did you say four?" Ian asked.

The table laughed. She leaned over to kiss him on the cheek.

He leaned back in his chair, shaking his head. "God I knew I hated your job, I just didn't realize how much."

"Excuse me," Ash said, picking up her glass of Irish Coffee. "I would like to make a toast if that's okay."

"That is okay," Travis said.

They all picked up their glasses.

"First, I would like to toast to Hunter. It is not a matter of how a man dies because that is really a blink of time. What matters is how he lives and Hunter lived life with laughter and love and friendship and I will always be grateful for the time he and I had together."

They all agreed, clinked their glasses each to each and sipped.

"Finally, I would like to toast to our home. I came from a shitty family, moved on through school, through university where I knew tons of people and went onto the academy. I had to fight harder as woman in both getting my job and keeping it and in all this I must have known a thousand people. I can honestly say tonight, in these circumstances, I have finally come home to where I belong and I live in a house of people who have more humanity, more charity, and more affection than any person I have ever known."

Ian smiled, leaned over and kissed her.

"Not so fast," Travis said, smiling.

Ashley looked at him.

He leaned over to the side bar, and pulled out a folder, holding it up for her to see.

"What's that?"

"New Orleans," he smiled. "It's booked. July 13th. Plane tickets are bought, hotels are reserved and you and I have an appointment on Tuesday at The Dress Closet Bridal Boutique in New Town at six-thirty."

"What?" she laughed.

"If you're going to be one of the family," he said, "then we're putting the other half of that ring on your finger."

She leaned over toward Ian, who met her halfway.

"*We're* putting on? Does he realize *they're* not actually part of getting married?"

Ian kissed her. "Honey, get used to it. In this house, they're part of every bit there it is."

ABOUT THE AUTHOR

Award-winning author, Jacqui Jacoby lives and writes in the beauty of Northern Arizona. Currently adjusting to being an empty nester with her first grandchild to draw her pictures, Jacqui is a self-defense hobbyist. Having studied martial arts for numerous years she retired in 2006 from the sport, yet still brings strength she learned from the discipline to her heroines. She is a working writer, whose career includes writing books, teaching online and live workshops and penning short nonfiction.

Follow her at:

www.JacquiJacoby.com

ALSO BY JACQUI JACOBY

With a Vengeance

COMING SOON

Magic Man

Dead Men Seal the Deal

Dead Men Feel the Heat

Dead Men Heal Slowly

MAGIC MAN

Available September 1, 2015

Enjoy the following excerpt from **MAGIC MAN**

He searched the recesses of his memory and came up empty. He had never heard the name before, never seen that face. "Why do you think I would know you?"

Her hand dropped away and she stared at him. It was in her eyes. She was scared. Of him. Of whatever she had to tell him.

"Why?" he snapped.

Her voice was almost inaudible, her gaze fixed on the donuts. "We lived together for eight years."

Peter heard her. He couldn't believe she had said what she said, but he heard her just fine. Now he just had to figure out how to get the hell out of here without crushing that last bit of hope in her eyes.

"*O-k-a-y,*" he said, planting both his hands on the edge of the table and standing up.

"No," she cried, moving faster than he had seen her move. She was in front of him, her hands on his forearms.

"Please. I'm not crazy. I swear to God I'm not crazy. We lived together. For eight years."

He broke her grip and took a step back, choking out a laugh. "I think I might remember that."

"Your house. In La Canada. We bought it together. When I got transferred to Seattle eight months ago, I signed it over to you."

Peter's gaze snapped to hers as personal data became a chip in the pot.

"How the hell do you know where I live?"

"Because I lived there, too. Please," she begged. "*Please* remember."

"You know, I know what I said before, but I think we might need to talk to somebody. A specialist."

She shook her head. "I'm not crazy."

He reached up and cupped her cheek and she looked up at him. "I think we may have been wrong," he said.

She shook her head again. This time hard. Jerky.

"You need help," he said.

She took two steps back, pushing her fingers through her hair in desperation. "I know I need help. But not that kind. I'm not crazy. I'm lost and I'm alone and there is no one who will listen. Ah shit, Peter, you don't even believe me."

He looked at her face, now almost pure white, tears on her cheeks. He felt something for her—something he couldn't put his finger on. It wasn't a memory, though. That much he was sure. Peter kept his voice soft. "What you're saying. It's not possible."

"I know it. Don't you think I know it? But it's happening. God, Peter, it's happening and I don't know what to do."

"I'll get you help—" he reached for her, but she darted out of his reach, toward the back of the room by the coffee pot.

"I know you have a birthmark on your left hip," she whispered. "I know your mom died when you were four. Shit, Peter, you take your coffee with milk in the morning. You like your eggs scrambled and hate them fried. Doesn't that mean something?"

He nodded. "Yeah. It means you might be dangerous, too."

She knew about his birthmark? His mom?

The sound she made sounded something like despair and she turned away from him, her face lowered.

The door behind him opened and Peter turned, his jaw dropping.

"Dad?"

Kenneth Mackenzie stood in the doorway, the knob still in his hand.

Peter stared at him. "What the hell are you doing here?"

"I thought I might be needed," Kenneth said in his calm voice, the touch of Scotland still lining the edges.

Peter shook his head in disbelief. What he didn't need now was his eccentric father walking in on the show. "Not now, Dad."

Peter looked back at the woman in the far corner, she hadn't turned toward them. He didn't have time for her. He didn't have time for his father. Wasn't there a serial killer he was supposed to be catching instead of dealing with this shit?

Kenneth stepped into the room, closing the door behind him.

"Alexandra?" he said.

The woman spun so fast, Peter was shocked she didn't tumble over. Peter saw her eyes go wide, her mouth hanging open as the words formed almost silently on her lips.

"You know me?" she whispered.

How the hell had his Dad done that?

Kenneth ignored his only son and walked over to her, talking as he went. "Of course I know you."

He spread his arms when he reached her. She didn't even hesitate to step into them and fall against the old man's chest. Peter just stood back and watched her crumble. When her knees gave away and the sobs racked her body, Kenneth went with her to the floor, holding her tight, rocking her as the pride completely evaporated. Peter stared blankly at them both.